The Sorrow of Sisters

The Sorrow of Sisters

Wendy K Harris

W F HOWES LTD

This large print edition published in 2007 by
W F Howes Ltd
Unit 4, Rearsby Business Park, Gaddesby Lane,
Rearsby, Leicester LE7 4YH

1 3 5 7 9 10 8 6 4 2

First published in the United Kingdom in 2006
by Transita

A CIP catalogue record for this book is available
from the British Library

ISBN 978 1 40740 137 9

Typeset by Palimpsest Book Production Limited,
Grangemouth, Stirlingshire
Printed and bound in Great Britain
by Antony Rowe Ltd, Chippenham, Wilts.

For
my husband Terry
for sharing the island with me
and
my daughter Susan
for unflagging encouragement and eagle-eyes.

ABOUT THE AUTHOR

Wendy K Harris was born in Surrey in an air raid shelter during a doodlebug attack. The youngest of four sisters, attending a girls' grammar school, she needed to write in order to get a word in edge-ways. The writing of short stories and poetry was interwoven with working as a nurse, homoeopath, counsellor, interfaith minister and sharing the upbringing of five children.

A rattling old Herefordshire rectory and aching back precipitated a change of life and she moved with her husband and a laptop into a caravan and trundled around Wales and England, finally becoming ensnared by The Undercliff of the Isle of Wight, entranced by its history of smuggling, shipwrecking and landslips. Here she was inspired by tumbling cliffs and precarious cottages to write *The Sorrow Of Sisters* which has also been trans-lated into German and Dutch. She is now working on a second Undercliff novel, *Blue Slipper Bay*.

A NOTE TO THE READER

If you should visit the Isle of Wight,
you can find many of the places mentioned
in this story. But some of them belong in the
realms of the imagination, or may have been
washed away by the sea.

WKH
Isle of Wight 2006

CHAPTER 1

My father. Eighty-five years old and still pretending. He sat at his roll-top desk, faking importance, trying to convey that I was disturbing him at some weighty task, just as he'd always done. Sometimes I wondered if he'd prefer me to call him Doctor rather than Dad. Poor old man. He looked frail. The skin drooping under his eyes and beneath his chin had a waxy pallor as if bits of him had already died.

'Dad –'

He flapped a knobbed hand to shoo me away as if I was still a small girl. But I wasn't going to be dismissed, not at my age. I spoke quietly but I could feel the anger spitting through my teeth.

'Dad, I can't believe you simply forgot about her.'

He glanced towards me, somewhere around my middle, blinking rapidly to protect his eyes from the glare of my scarlet fleece with its skating penguins. His chest wheezed under his stained, black waistcoat and he winced. I remembered his cracked rib. He'd tripped over his brass fender last week getting up to examine a patient. Another pretence of his was that he hadn't retired. Some of his old cronies still hobbled into his dismal consulting room to have their abdomens auscultated and their prostates probed. I took a deep, calming breath.

'Did you and Mother deliberately not tell me about her for some reason?'

He still wouldn't look at me – just poked at the solicitor's letter I'd placed on his desk, wanting me to retrieve it. I fought down my impatience and sat in silence, knowing it would unnerve him. Confused, he put on his glasses and peered around the cream and brown room, studying the raw anatomical models of lungs, perusing the sagging shelves crammed with dusty research, as if the answer might lurk there, contained within his life's work. It did seem to focus him, help him get his thoughts together. He tapped the letter a few times, his hand like a crusty toad.

'Really, Jane,' he rasped, 'the truth is, I haven't thought about her for years – long before your mother died.'

He turned away from me in his swivel chair as if that was that. I could smell the old leather as it creaked. Everything about my father seemed to smell and creak these days. He picked up his fountain pen. The nib looked dry and rusty. Perhaps he thought I'd go if he wrote me a prescription. I sat.

'In fact, I assumed – your mother and I both assumed – that she'd died. Lill . . . Lillian was ill when we left the island.'

He faltered over her name, lips trembling. And then a tremor seemed to pass right through his body as if an icy hand had grasped the back of his neck. I put my hand on the arm of his chair and swivelled him back towards me. I should leave him alone, let his blood pressure settle. But I couldn't.

'Dad, I don't understand. Are you saying that Mother had a sick sister, ten years younger, that she just left behind and presumed died? But why? She told me she was an only child.'

He fumbled in his waistcoat pocket for his fob-watch as if he had an appointment.

'I don't remember her telling you that.'

'Okay. Maybe I dreamt it. But even if I made it up, why was Lillian never mentioned?'

'I can't think. I expect they disagreed over some triviality and decided to cut each other off.'

'Triviality! We're talking a whole lifetime here – her little sister, her only relative. How could she?' Even as I said it I could imagine my mother doing just that. Victoria had been an apt name for her – rigid as a corset.

He gave a dry cough. 'Things happen in families – time goes by, people forget.'

Exasperated, I ran my hands through my hair. 'But Dad, Lillian was my only aunt and I knew nothing about her and now it's too late.' I felt a pulse of heat gather in my belly and rise up through my chest and face making my head zing. Perhaps I should get him to prescribe me some HRT – except that he'd probably never heard of it.

'Jane, don't get so agitated. You always were melo-dramatic. All those damn silly books you write.'

3

But I felt agitated. I felt cheated, and full of the impotent rage that I remembered from childhood that knows it's never going to get anywhere because the forces it is up against are impenetrable. And now he was insulting me. Silly books! My writing was my talent, my livelihood. He'd never even read one of my novels as far as I knew. If he had, he'd never thought to comment. I'd even dedicated one of them to him and given him signed copies of the rest.

I snatched the letter from his desk, startling him so that he jolted his sore rib. In that moment I recognised a feeling of satisfaction that I could inflict pain on him. Sometimes I wanted to hurt him so much. Oh, God, what a cow I was being. He was just a brittle old man, victim of his own generation. Contrition set in as usual. I reached towards him; he flinched away.

'Oh, Dad. I'm sorry. I keep forgetting your poor old ribs. I didn't mean to get angry.' I always ended up being the one to apologise. Why couldn't he ever reach out and comfort me? 'Perhaps you should go and lie down.'

'I'm going to, if you'll let me be.' He tugged off his glasses and rubbed his eyes as if trying to erase me from his vision. He gestured for his stick and heaved himself painfully from his chair. I longed to help him but knew I would only be rebuffed again. 'Perhaps you would be gracious enough to make me a cup of tea,' he said. I leapt up to open the door for him, trying to make amends.

As he shuffled past me he paused. 'You wouldn't have liked her – your mother's sister – strange, mad thing she was.' He looked at me at last, rheumy-eyed, and words tumbled out before he could stop them. 'Don't go over to the island, Jane. Nothing of interest there. Wraith Cottage is just a hovel. Let the solicitor sort it out. There might be a few pounds in it for you. Not worth wasting your time.'

For a few rare moments I held his eyes and then I felt a sinking down of myself inside as if I was being diminished and I had to look away. I could smell the hill fog seeping into the hallway under the front door. His stick rattled on the floorboards as he waited impatiently for me to come out of his study and close the door so that he could lock it behind me.

Emmeline stood at the edge of the cliff, looking out to sea. She had come out to watch the full moon but heavy clouds were blanketing most of its shine. She must remember not to venture too far. A chunk of land had fallen recently, taking a bite out of the overgrown end of the vegetable garden.

She peered down to the beach below. She felt momentarily giddy and steadied herself with her stick. Silver streaks of moonlight flickered on the shore mingling with the sweep of the beam from St Catherine's lighthouse. She imagined she could see Lilly running barefoot along the edge of the

5

waves, her blonde hair streaming out behind her in the wind, sand sticking to her brown legs and arms, laughing, she was always laughing.

Emmeline smiled. Lilly trailed sand everywhere, sprinkling the carpeted corridors of Wraith Cove Hotel and the velvet upholstery of the chairs. Nobody minded. The guests patted her head, her father swept her up and sat her on the marble-topped bar. Even Henry would lift her onto his shoulders and carry her down to the beach, jogging her up and down until she squealed. It was the only time Emmeline could remember seeing him smile – really smile, his whole face alight with pleasure. Victoria didn't smile though. She watched with her mournful brown eyes, waiting to catch Lilly and torture her with brushes and combs, and squeeze her wriggling feet into patent leather shoes.

Emmeline sighed deeply and closed her eyes. 'Help me, Lilly,' she called, feeling her words whipped away across the dark sea. She stood, sensing Lilly in the buffeting wind, hearing her in the tinkling shells which hung on strings from the driftwood sculptures that filled the garden of Wraith Cottage. She could see her in the shreds of mist that spiralled over the sea. Wraiths, Lilly called them, the souls of the drowned playing in the moonlight. 'You must help me remember everything, Lilly.'

'But, you know everything, Emm.' Lilly's voice was clear in Emmeline's head.

'I know what happened. But I want to know everything – all the pain you kept from me.'

'I didn't keep anything from you.'

'You protected me, Lilly – to prevent me from killing him. You closed part of yourself away.'

'I was protecting myself too, Emm. I was protecting myself from feeling your pain as well as my own.'

'We should have talked before – I didn't know you were going to leave me.'

'I couldn't help it. My heart was stretched too thin to go on. But I won't leave you. I will stay until you're ready to come with me.'

'The truth has to be told first, then I will come.' Emmeline opened her eyes. The wind had blown a clearing through the clouds and the moon was beaming a silver pathway from the horizon, across the sea and sand and cliffs. She was standing in a pool of light.

'Poor Henry, sounds like you gave the old chap a hard time,' Chas said, examining his teeth in the dressing-table mirror.

'No, Chas. A hard time would've been my hands round his baggy old throat.'

Chas closed his mouth and clacked his teeth together to test their strength. He was always tinkering with bits of himself, checking them out for durability and signs of wear. I often thought he'd make a good car mechanic. He straightened up, turned sideways, breathed in and inspected his reflected paunch. After a few seconds he released his breath and allowed everything to sag comfortably.

'This has really got to you, Janey, hasn't it? She was only an old aunt. I expect we've all got one of those lurking somewhere. Why are you so upset?'

'Oh, I don't know.' I slung my book at the bedside table and slumped down in the bed. 'It's just the usual feeling of not being considered. Apart from Dad, she was my one and only blood relative. I feel that's important. I know she only left me her cottage by default – there was nobody else – but I would like to have met her. When Dad dies that's it. I'm the end of the line.'

Chas buttoned his pyjama jacket and tucked it in. He climbed into bed, his bulk making me bounce up and down. 'You've got me,' he said, hoisting an arm round my shoulders.

I felt the comfort his big warm body gave me. I leaned against him, smelling Imperial Leather. Thank God, yes, I had him. But sometimes I felt the lack of family like an unknown void. I wondered how it would feel to be without my father, even though he enraged me and eluded my love. And Chas, who I adored and depended on too much – suppose he died suddenly. What would it feel like to walk the world with no ties, no roots? Would my close friends ever mean as much? Their families must always come first for them. Who would I leave the meaning of my life to? I suspected only one's own children could be that involved.

Chas seemed more able to accept our child-lessness than I. He came with a copious lineage, annually expanding with nephews and nieces. His relatives were larger than average humans with big mouths and ears and eyes like Red Riding Hood's grandmother. Chas was always trying to escape from being gobbled up. His family was as rotund as mine was spare. He appreciated our pared down life, just the two of us, me wrestling with words, him with numbers. He kissed the side of my head.

'It's the sort of thing that happens to nobody you ever know, isn't it? Letter out of the blue, old Auntie Lill dies on New Year's Day and leaves you her worldly goods. Could be a plot for one of your novels.'

'It certainly could not. I'd never write about anything so hackneyed.' Cheek! First my father and now my husband trivialising my writing. Did everyone poke fun of my books behind my back? 'In case you hadn't noticed, I take my craft extremely seriously. Anyway, there are no worldly goods.'

'An old cottage – that's worldly goods.'

'Dad says it's a hovel and not worth anything.'

'All property is worth something, even demolition value.'

I could tell he'd been giving this some thought. Chas divided life into three columns – debits, credits and a neat balance. Well, I suppose you would if you spent all day doing that. Just like I couldn't let go of a sentence without finding le mot juste. 'Yes, but this is on the edge of a cliff crumbling into the sea. Not even the land is worth anything, no insurance obviously.'

'Superb sea-view . . . holiday let?'

I laughed at his optimism. He had a way of diffusing my gloom. We were a bit like Winnie-the-Pooh and Eeyore. Except when it involved money and then we reversed positions. Chas fretted about our finances just like I lathered over familial angst. Ample bosoms cushioned his childhood but cash was stretched thin, whereas my cushion was financially plump but enclosed in a mausoleum. Chas yawned and checked the alarm clock.

'We could go and see it,' he said.

'Dad said to let the solicitor sort it. He said it's not worth the trip.'

'It might be fun. I haven't been to the Isle of Wight since I was in the cubs.'

'I haven't been there since I was born. And then I was whisked away before I had a chance to gulp the air in case I contracted TB. It all seems a bit paranoid when I think about it.' I imagined being sealed in an oxygen chamber and rushed amidst flashing blue lights to the waiting ferry.

'Well, it's Henry's obsession. He worked with it every day – saw what it did to people. And, I remember your mother had a weak chest. I expect he was only trying to protect you. He does love you in his funny old antediluvian way.'

'Big word – for an accountant.'

'Impressed? I've been saving it up. I read it in the *Financial Times*.'

'Perhaps we could have a long weekend on the Isle of Wight. It would do us good to have a winter break.'

Chas grunted, removed his arm and shunted down the bed. 'Have to think about it, busy time at work. Ready for lights out?'

I snuggled, drowsy against Chas as his breathing hovered between bearable and unbearable decibels. I had a picture of a small band of goblins excavating deep down inside his throat detonating tiny rumbling explosives.

I wondered if Dad was asleep in his dank home with its outdated heating system. The grey stone house was called Winter Wood, backed up against the Malvern Hills, shadowed and sombre. Was he lying awake under his stiff blankets, listening to the spatter of rain, the moan of the bitter wind, thinking about Mother or me? More likely he'd be pondering the rise in incidence of tuberculosis in dense immigration areas. Even though he'd worked in general practice for years his heart remained faithful to malfunctioning chests. He still wrote papers and sent them off to God knows where.

But I couldn't imagine my father away from his papers and the spores and must of his precious consulting room. Even Mrs Watkins, his multipurpose slave, wasn't allowed in there to dust. She was always trying to inveigle me, hoping I would chivvy him to tidy his room, as if he were an adolescent. He'd probably die slumped at his desk with his cracked stethoscope round his neck, his hand on his empty appointment book.

But Chas was right – he probably did love me in the archives of his mind. I wondered if he would have been different if my mother had lived longer. It must be nearly thirty years ago that she died, when I was nineteen. Would he have mellowed? Would they have spent a happy retirement together strolling hand in hand on the hills? Somehow I didn't think so – she was an absent woman, her life spent drawing tight botanical pictures. She catalogued her drawings using a pen as fine as a needle and then filed them in tissue-leafed albums and put them away.

If I was quiet I made her jump when she saw me but if I tried to be noisy to remind her of my existence, she seemed equally disturbed. It was as if she existed with a degree of tension that couldn't abide any fluctuation. She was as obsessed by leaves as my father was with lungs. As I grew bigger and louder and more colourful, she appeared to grow smaller and faded as if I was draining the life out of her. Her heavy brown hair in its fat chignon thinned into a peppery fold. Her drawings grew fainter too; trailing like spiders' journeys. Every time I came home on school holidays she seemed to have diminished. Her breath came in little gasps and she twitched if anyone spoke as if she were constantly being caught out. I felt I had to tone myself down, wear paler clothes, speak softly, in case she crumbled to dust like one of her brittle plants and wafted away, leaving a faint fragrance of violets to remind me that I'd had a mother.

Thank heavens they'd sent me away to boarding school. Most people's idea of purgatory was my paradise; a place where I could play out my fantasies, join the drama group, write technicolour stories, show off. I pushed my behaviour to the edge but stayed just on the right side of trouble. I was popular, the funny girl, a ringleader. I tried to avoid spending holidays at Winter Wood, jumping at invitations to my friends' homes, going abroad with them. My parents never objected to my absence.

When I was very young – like other out-of-context kids – I used to imagine I was adopted. I felt too full of possibilities to belong in that museum of a house. I used to stare at myself in the mirror, refusing to see that I'd inherited my mother's chestnut hair and brown eyes and my father's narrow nose. Inside, I was golden and ice-blue and I could fly to the aurora borealis. But the reality of my birth certificate ended that fantasy: there wasn't a set of miraculous parents searching the planet for me. Even as I grew older my restless imagination refused to be quashed. Perhaps it was a reaction to my monochrome home and the fact that I would rather read than eat. But it seemed to me that everyone contained a latent adventure that only needed a nudge to activate the most curious sequence of events.

I disentangled myself from the duvet and moved away from Chas who was emitting enough heat to keep the neighbourhood frost-free. I'd noticed recently that if I overheated I would wake sweating and gasping as if I was being strangled. I felt the relief of cooling down and drifted off to sleep wondering about Wraith Cottage and what Aunt Lillian had done to deserve her family's ostracism.

CHAPTER 2

Emmeline sat at the kitchen table in Wraith Cottage, her elbows resting in the familiar grooves of the worn wood. She was staring, gritty-eyed, at an open book. On the inside of the glossy cover was a picture of Jane, looking just like Victoria with her heavy chestnut hair and deep brown eyes. At least she didn't look like Henry. Was he dead yet? Lilly had said he was still alive – that she could feel it. But Lilly had been dead nearly five months. Anything could have happened in that time. Emmeline didn't feel anything when she thought about Henry – except hatred.

She put her aching head in her hands, feeling the few wisps of what remained of her soft curls. She knew that if she combed them they would come out leaving her completely bald. She closed her sore eyes and listened to the waves crashing against the cliff and the wind hurling sandy rain at the windows. Small branches were snapping off the trees and rattling onto the tin roof of the outhouse.

'Hold on,' she said to the cottage, feeling the slam of the gale. 'Hold on,' she said to her body,

15

feeling the bite of pain. For a moment she smelt the sweetness of roses. Gentle hands placed themselves on top of hers as she grasped her head. 'Lilly?' she whispered. She felt a kiss brush her scalp and opened her eyes. Marguerite stood beside her, pale-faced with concern.

'Will Jane come?' Emmeline whispered. 'Will I have time?'

Marguerite closed her eyes for a while and then opened them, wide and watery blue. Her mouth moved in a small smile. Emmeline got up and shuffled to the kitchen sink. She shook tablets from a bottle and gulped them down with water. She turned to Marguerite, her face trembling. 'I must sleep now,' she said.

I couldn't write. It was as if Aunt Lillian's death had put my life on hold. After Chas left for his office each morning, I went upstairs to my study and waited while my computer growled and tweeted itself through its booting up frenzy. Then I called up my Winnie-the-Pooh screen-saver to hide the blank stare of the virtual page.

What I was doing instead of writing was foraging through my old journals. I had stacks of them dating from when I first learned to write. I started from the beginning, deciphering my faded childish scrawl. Events and outings, school friends and adolescent highs and woes poured from the pages, crowding the room with past lives like resurrection day. But nowhere could I find a reference to Aunt Lillian, or any other relative. There was no mention of the Isle of Wight, my parents' past or my grandparents. My life history, spread out before me, was more about my friends' families. Where were my roots? I was amazed that I'd never thought about this before.

So immersed was I in all this introspection that I didn't become aware of the hours slipping by until I heard the rumble and click of the garage doors when Chas arrived home. I switched off the computer, half expecting Microsoft to flash me a reprimand about wasting good cyber energy.

'I think I've got writer's block,' I lied to Chas, over pasta and pesto.

'So, what are we going to do about it?' he said, fork raised.

'We? I'm not a bit of plumbing. You can't phone Dyno-Rod to come and unblock me.' We were irritable with each other. Chas was worried about his struggling financial investment department. I could feel him observing me from behind as I banged about the kitchen, making coffee. Was he measuring me up, wondering what size rod I might need? I yanked my shirt down at the back.

'What do you want to do then?' he said, choosing his words with care.

'I think I need a break. A change of place might help me get going. I'd like to go to the Isle of Wight to investigate Wraith Cottage.'

'On your own? But I want to see it with you.'

'Well, you can't get away from the office and I need to go now. I could talk to the solicitor, find

17

out what's going on. If the cottage can be sold it will give the bank balance a good boost.'

Chas leaned back in his chair thinking. With his collar open, tie askew, tipsy expression on his face – he only needed a Frank Sinatra hat and a cigarette hanging out the side of his mouth to look like a piano player in a jazz club.

'There's bound to be plenty of holiday lets on the island. It'll soon be June.' I was suddenly feeling excited. 'I might even be able to stay in the cottage if it's habitable.'

'I don't suppose it will be. Anyway, I don't want you falling off a cliff.'

I smiled. 'I wonder if it's got an Aga. All those books I've written in which they feature – perhaps that's what I need to fire me up. But then, I wouldn't know how to deal with one.'

Chas was grinning now. 'Borrow a dog. Dogs know all about Agas, they belong together. You can't have one without the other. In fact you get one free with them these days.'

'What, a dog with an Aga or an Aga with a dog?' I put my hands on his shoulders and kissed the back of his head, noticing how his greying hair was stretched rather thinly over his scalp just there. We could never stay angry with each other for long. 'So, what do you think? Shall I go?'

'Why not?' His face brightened, 'I could wangle it as a business expense for you – research for your book.'

★   ★   ★

Emmeline couldn't sleep. As the storm subsided so did her pain and she lay drifting in a silent sea of images that loomed into her mind as if her life had been shaken up in a bag and emptied out in a heap.

She was a child again, with gangly arms and legs, crouched on the wet sand with Lilly, making sand-castles. Lilly's fine hair was ruffled by the breeze. Henry stood looking down on them, brandishing his fishing net, issuing instructions. A few yards away Victoria worked at her painting, sitting on a folding stool so she wouldn't get her lace dress sandy.

Then Lilly was running up the beach, laughing. It was dark now and they were grown up.

'Do you remember, Lilly?' Emmeline whispered in the darkness. 'Do you remember our New Year's Eve party on the beach with Woody and Neptune?' She lifted a drug-heavy arm across the bedspread, reaching for Lilly's hand, finding only the flatness of the empty bed. But Lilly was there, she could sense her presence, and hadn't Lilly promised that she would always be there until Emm let go?

'Don't look back, Emm. It's all over.' She heard Lilly's voice inside her head.

'No, Lilly. We have to remember. I won't rest until I make him pay.'

'How can he pay?'

'With his confession to those that deserve to know. I want to witness that. That's how he will pay.'

'Let go, Emm. Let go and come with me.'

'I can't, not yet. Who will care for Marguerite? We have to remember everything. We need to bring it all into the present, otherwise it cannot be healed. And I will never rest. You must keep calling for Jane to come.'

'Hush now, go to sleep. I will watch over you.'

Emmeline breathed deeply, but as her body let go, she felt her mind take hold again, restless with her unresolved life.

'Remember, Lilly, New Year's Eve,' she whispered. 'We were so happy . . .'

'But you have such a good memory, Emm.'

'Not any more. The drugs have clouded my mind.'

'You can read my journals.'

'No. I need to hear your voice.'

'But, I can't tell it to you, Emm.'

'Why not?'

'Because I will feel your pain and I won't relive it as it was.'

'But it is time for me to know.'

'Then I will have to detach from you and you can listen or not as you choose. I will go and sit on my stone and tell the sea.'

'That sounds so cold, Lilly.'

'But it's the only way I can do it freely.'

Emmeline felt Lillian's presence grow less tangible. She could hear the low moan of the sea, settling itself in the aftermath of the storm. Voices came to her on the wind, laughter, the crackle of fire . . .

'Tell the truth, Lilly,' she called . . .

★　　★　　★

I can hear Neptune calling me as I stagger up the beach to my stone.

'Lillian! Come on weakling, you can manage one more dance.'

I'm so out of breath, my head is ringing – but maybe that's the gin. Emm runs up behind me and grabs me round the waist so that we both nearly fall.

'Lilly, don't be a spoilsport,' she says. 'We can't dance without you. And then we'll have a rest, I promise. Anyway, it'll soon be midnight.'

I look at her eager face in the firelight. Everything about her shines – her eyes, her cheeks, the light curls that are escaping from under the blue bobble hat I'd knitted her for Christmas. Even the misty puffs of her breath sparkle. I would plunge into the freezing sea if she asked me to. I giggle and grasp her mittened hand and we stumble back down to the flat sand. Neptune is sitting on a rock, smoking, playing his concertina, while Woody winds up the gramophone.

'This is the last one,' I gasp, 'otherwise I'll be sick.'

We prance to the Scottish reels, clumsy in our boots and winter woollies, using driftwood for crossed swords, until all four of us are near collapse with laughter. Then we crawl up the beach to our fire and coats and blankets. We sit watching the moonlight shimmering on the sea, me on my big flat stone, too tired to speak. Emm picks at the remains of the food, humming to herself.

'Okay now, Lilly?'

I nod and snuggle deeper into my dad's heavy camel hair coat, pleased that I'd kept it after he died a year ago. Victoria had insisted it should go to the WRVS, offended by my suggestion that Henry might like it. Later, when she'd gone back to the physician's house, I scavenged it from the WRVS bundle and lugged it from the hotel down to Wraith Cottage. It is far too big for me but perfect for sitting on a cold beach at midnight. I sniff a lapel. It smells of him, a mixture of Havanas and old malts and the staleness that clothes acquire when there's no longer a wife to organise dry cleaning.

Dear old Dad – Old Father William, his regulars nicknamed him. I could see him now, lurching around the bar and lounge of his beloved hotel; slapping shoulders, flattering the ladies. His voice had grown hoarse and his nose purple and pitted over the years. I was glad he'd died so suddenly, right there, in the centre of his domain – mid puff, mid gulp – struck like a harpooned whale. I hadn't wanted my dad to degenerate into an embarrassment, oblivious to ridicule.

I pull the thick greasy collar up behind my head to cushion my neck against the icy boulder. Victoria might have had the coat cleaned if she hadn't transferred her allegiance to Henry's attire. She does the sort of things that wives – and I suppose mothers – do. I don't remember our mother. I'd killed her when I was born. With her dying gasps she'd pushed me out of her body, bursting her tubercular lungs. That is Victoria's version, anyway, implying I was

22

a nuisance right from the start. Emm told Victoria she had no right to make me feel guilty, I hadn't asked to be born. Men couldn't keep their fly buttons done up – that was where the real blame lay. Victoria blushed and tip-tapped away on her high-heeled court shoes. Emm put her arm around me and said Victoria was jealous. She wanted to be the only child, then I arrived, looking just like her mother that I'd unwittingly killed off.

Poor Victoria – ten years old with a bereft father, an unwanted infant sister and her own grief to deal with. No wonder she thought I was a nuisance. I'm surprised she didn't tip me off the cliff in my pram. But why she should be jealous of me is a mystery. She is the clever one and what an artist! She paints huge pictures of the southern shore of the island. Lashing storms rage over her canvas, jagged rocks thunder down cliffs, trees poise perilously. And also, she has a beautiful curving body and long glossy brown hair. I am just straight, skinny and pale.

I nestle further into Dad's overcoat and watch the fire spit and shift, spark and settle, like an irritable dragon trying to doze off. The dank, salty smell of seaweed mingles with the woodsmoke. My stomach feels stretched with sea-sweet lobster, seared potatoes and swigs of gin. I'd helped myself to a bottle of Gordon's for Emm and me, as well as Martell and Johnnie Walker for Woody and Neptune. It felt illicit to take drink which my father had always kept locked up, but Emm reasoned it was mine now. Mine, and Victoria's, of course; I must remember to tell Victoria.

I watch the others dragging driftwood, thinking I've never felt happier. It must be the freedom. This is the first time I've celebrated New Year with my friends instead of helping Emm and Dad organise festivities for The Old Faithfuls – the folk who return to Wraith Cove Hotel year after year ignoring the postwar slump, growing seediness, encroaching damp and creaking beds. And I don't feel guilty either. The fire in the hotel's kitchen before Christmas had been due to my father's disrespect for maintenance and there is no money to carry out the work necessary in order to reopen. Emm, as manageress, sorted out the Christmas and New Year bookings, refunding deposits, cancelling orders, writing letters of apology, compensating staff.

We spent most of Christmas salvaging kitchen equipment and clearing up with Woody and Neptune's help. The fire brigade made us turn off the electricity. Victoria and Henry took all the perishable food, as they owned a refrigerator. They also took the Christmas tree – Victoria said it would go well in her drawing room. I just had time to steal the glass angel from the top – my childhood favourite. They were welcome to the tree – Emm and I always decorate one in the garden with fat and seed balls for the birds. There was plenty of food left too. Victoria doesn't know all the store-rooms like we do. It had been fun having the hotel to ourselves. We lit a fire in the lounge, sprawled on the sofas and went back to Wraith Cottage when dusk fell, to eat Christmas dinner. I have no idea what to do about the hotel and at this moment I don't care.

I watch Emm's silhouette against the glow of the fire as she sits down and inspects the lobsters. Emm is permanently hungry, always picking things clean. And yet she remains so skinny. Her long arms and legs with their knobbly elbows and knees are constantly on the move. With her soft brown hair and her round blue eyes she reminds me of a cross between a fawn and a mountain goat. She has big feet too, that know their way around the rocks and cliffs as if they have a mind of their own. My body fills up with a warm flood of joy just observing her. As usual, she senses my gaze. We've been able to do this ever since we were little girls – pick up each other's thoughts and feelings. She grins and holds out a lobster claw.

'Want any more, Lilly? I'll pick out some nice bits for you.'

'No thanks, Emm. I'm full up.' I wish I could say yes – just to have Emm feed me, to feel her gentle fingers on my mouth.

Woody and Neptune are down at the water's edge pulling their boat further in. I can see their dark shapes bending and swaying, their oilskins glistening in the lantern light. The sea sloshes and sucks at their boots. Their little terrier, Booty, is daring the waves to catch his paws, crouching, tail up, letting out excited yelps of warning. The two men talk together, their heads close – Neptune's close-cropped, Woody's wild and unkempt. I smile to myself, wondering how I was ever troubled by thoughts that Neptune was sweet on Emm.

I remember the time, about ten years ago, when he rowed proudly round to Wraith Cove from Puck's Bay in his first boat. He'd saved hard for it and repaired it himself, painted it white and inscribed Neptune in careful blue letters on the side. He was trying to appear nonchalant, imploring us with his deep-set eyes to like it. He offered to take Emm out for a row and I'd been convinced he had his heart set on her. We'd called him Neptune from then on; a name that stuck and he appeared to like. And then Woody had arrived and we understood how things were between the two of them.

We all love the sea and the wild rocky shore; we have such fun together. The four of us felt invincible until the war came and took Woody away from us and sent him back broken. But he is mending; this beautiful place and our love are healing him. We are lucky, Emm and I – it is like having two brothers. And I'm glad for Emm; it makes up for her own brother, Henry, being rather unkind to her. I reach out and touch her arm and receive a flash of white grin, a glint of blue eyes.

Woody and Neptune are dragging half a tree up the beach. They stash it at the foot of the cliff near our cave where the incoming tide won't reach it, unless there is an exceptional storm. The four of us always pile the sea's bounty there – mindful of war debris – ready to be sorted for usefulness. I pick through it for interesting shapes to decorate Wraith Cottage, Emm and the others for things to be utilised. The men have practically rebuilt their dilapidated fishermen's, cottage in Puck's Bay with materials gifted by the oceans. Those two know the sea, descended as they are from a distinguished line of smuggling families.

They join us in the horseshoe of boulders, warming their hands at the fire. Booty starts a methodical clear up of the remains of the food. Emm hands round the brandy.

'Can't be far off midnight,' Neptune says, taking a swig, shuddering as it goes down.

'Half-past-eleven,' says Emm, peering at her watch. 'I wonder what nineteen-fifty-three will bring? Resolutions, anyone?'

'Oh, let's not think about the future,' I say, not wanting the night to end. 'I just want to enjoy this.'

Woody gets out his baccy tin and offers shaggy rollups. A match flares orange and the singe of tobacco adds to the smoky air. I always worry that he will set his beard on fire. Neptune picks up his concertina and begins playing softly. I can see the wraiths begin to rise and drift over the sea, illumined by the moon. They always respond to music. Victoria laughed at me when I told her the ghosts of the drowned play at night – Silly Lilly, she calls me. But Emm never laughs, just stares at the waves, trying to see what I see.

Every few seconds a beam sweeps the beach from St Catherine's. I love the lighthouse – it seems such a symbol of human goodness – this act of safe guidance. I gaze up at the indigo sky with its brilliant stars, wondering how lost sailors could navigate by them. How must it feel to be adrift on the vast, dark sea? I can hear Neptune's boat gently knocking against the rocks – a bigger boat now with an outboard motor. But still, such a tiny vessel.

'I think this must be the best way to see in the New Year,' Neptune says, puffing rings of blue smoke. 'We should do this every year. No matter where we all are, we should make a date to come back here.'

'Sounds like an Enid Blyton pact,' laughs Emm. 'The Famous Four at Wraith Cove.'

Woody gives his slow smile. 'As long as we don't have to be heroic and rescue anybody from a villain.'

'But we'll always be here,' I blurt out. 'Why should we go anywhere else?' I feel tears spring to my eyes just at the thought.

Emm puts her arm through mine. 'Of course we will, little Water Lilly.'

We listen to Neptune playing his sea songs. Booty settles at his feet, his head on his paws.

'What are Henry and Victoria doing tonight?' asks Neptune.

'They're at a party in Ventnor. The posh crowd. Victoria bought a new taffeta gown. But I'd rather be down here.' I pull Dad's coat tighter, wishing Emm was cuddled against me; there is enough room inside for two. It is getting very cold. I can see little bursts of moisture in the air as we speak.

'Do you miss Old Father William and the hotel?' asks Woody.

'No. Well, I miss Dad, but it's nice not to be rushing about trying to keep the old place going, isn't it, Emm?'

Woody gets up and begins thrashing his arms across his body to keep warm. 'Oh, yes. I'd forgotten about your job, Emmeline. I suppose that's gone too, and what about your room?'

She glances at me and squeezes my arm. 'Lilly and I are going to have to think about all that. But first I'm moving into Wraith Cottage and we're going to live together. People can think what they like.'

'Well, that calls for a toast,' says Woody, searching through the bottles. 'I'm glad for you both.'

'Me, too,' says Neptune. 'But don't be surprised if you get a bit of stick from the local yobs. They've got nothing better to do. When Woody moved into Puck's Cottage with me, they came round every night for a while, jeering outside. Didn't they, Wood?'

'We just ignored it – best policy,' Woody says, filling glasses. 'They soon got fed up. But if you have any trouble let us know.'

'Thank you, both,' I say, raising my glass. I don't feel the least bit afraid with these two around the next bay. And who could possibly want to harm Emm and me?

'Will you have to sell the hotel, Lillian, if there's no money to do it up?' Woody asks.

'Henry wants me to – me and Victoria, that is.'

'What's it got to do with him?' Emm's voice is sharp.

'Well, he is Victoria's husband –'

'And she's welcome to him, arrogant –'

'Emm! He's your brother, don't forget.' I sometimes forget this myself; they are always so formal and irritable with each other.

'I don't care, Lilly. He lords it over everyone as if it was his right.'

'He's just trying to look after us. He says he understands how to do these things, he knows the right people.'

'Bloody nerve that man's got,' Emm mutters. 'You and Victoria are grown-ups.'

'He thinks women –'

'I know what he thinks about women! He thinks we should all get married and knuckle down to looking after husbands like stupid Victoria. I used to think she had some spirit but she's given up.'

'Oh, Emm!'

'She has, Lilly. She gave up her job at the gallery. She doesn't even paint any more.'

'She's very busy.'

'Busy! Doing what? Starching his collars? Polishing his stethoscope?'

'She's the wife of a successful doctor. That's what she wants.' I look around the circle of faces, all suppressing grins. 'Well, isn't it?'

30

Emm bursts out laughing and makes a grab for me. 'You have no idea sometimes, Lilly. If you always look for the best in people you might sometimes overlook the worst.' She strokes my hair. 'Little innocent,' she whispers.

'But you won't sell Wraith Cottage will you?' Woody sounds concerned. I remember how he used to come there when he came back from the war, injured and appalled and grieving for humanity. He would wander around the garden and cliffs, or sit in a chair at a window staring out to sea, not moving or speaking for hours. I could still feel his deep anguish if I let my soul touch his. I try to enfold his mind with love until I feel him let go.

'No, never.' I lean forward to touch him. 'We'll find a way to keep it.'

I wish I had my notebook with me. I want to write down my feelings about the lighthouse and the goodness of humanity. I want to write about the dark agonies inside Woody. I've had this urge to write things down since I was small; can even remember the first time it happened. Victoria was combing my long fine hair and tugging the tangles so that my eyes filled with tears. But the tears didn't belong to my pain, they belonged to Victoria's. I felt desperation in her, a primitive need to sink into her lost infancy, for someone to relieve her of the burden of me. She yearned to be cradled in strong arms, to be held to a breast that wasn't made of tissue paper. She wanted me

31

to stop following her around, to cease needing her and loving her. And all she could do with her rage and frustration was yank my hair.

When she'd finished plaiting and pulling, I rushed away to find paper and pencil. Words dropped onto the page, my eyes and head stopped stinging and I felt better. I hadn't questioned this, it just felt natural, to be done at times of intense beauty and pain. Years later, I told Emm and showed her my notebooks. She read and read and told me I could be a great writer like Virginia Woolf, expressing innermost feelings that everyone could recognise. But I have no desire to write stories or make anything up. I want to write down great gulps of feeling that arrive in my mind and demand release.

Sometimes I am surprised at what I've written, words I never thought I knew, as if I have a wiser, older self inside me. Or else it is the books. We read all sorts of books out loud to each other, Emm and I, in bed, lying on the beach, cosy around the fire in Wraith Cottage. We are collecting quite a library.

Distant bells from the villages dotted along the coast begin to chime and a fairy-lit cruiser out in the Channel lets off a flurry of fireworks. We clamber upright to toast the New Year. I am engulfed in a tangle of creaking clothes, warm breath and chilly noses, tobacco and alcohol, and the quick slosh of Booty's tongue on my hand, as we kiss and hug. We make the fire safe and push the boat out for the men to sail back round the rocky headland to Puck's Bay. We watch them and Booty climb aboard and putter off, their lanterns flashing on the water.

Emm and I make our way up the cliff steps, holding tight to each other and the rope rail, giggling from the gin, seeing the glow of Wraith Cottage through the dark line of winter trees. . . .

Lillian's voice started to fade from Emmeline's mind. Exhausted at last, sated with happy memories, she slept.

CHAPTER 3

It was the first day of June when I escaped. I was glad to get away – not from Birdsong, my light-filled home, the antithesis of Winter Wood, but from the interrogation by Chas, my friends, my editor, about the progress of my book. I found it a strain to lie, even though making up stories was my life's work. For the first time in my life I needed distance from everyone I was involved with. It had started at the beginning of the year with the solicitor's letter and I felt like a derailed train. I needed something to put me back on track. My friends had come up with all sorts of mid-life crisis theories and menopause remedies but the only thing I wanted to do was to find my birthplace.

I drove through the dappled New Forest, feeling indulgent towards ambling ponies and road-hogging sheep and even a couple of dusty pigs snouting along the white line. By the time I reached Lymington I felt lighter, as if I'd shed a few pounds of deceit.

I arrived at the terminal just in time for my red mini to be swallowed by the blue jaws of the Wightlink ferry. I went up on deck to watch boats puttering and sails whipping, enjoying the harbour language, the cries of the gulls and the warm, salty breeze as we slid out to open sea – if you can call the Solent open sea. I wasn't a great enthusiast of the English seaside, preferring more reliable sun, more consistent sand. But I was sailing towards the island where I was born and I felt a stirring of anticipation. I loved islands anyway. I found standing on a small mound of land encircled by sea very reassuring. Chas always liked to point out that Britain was a small island, but I meant tiny enough to be able to stand on its highest point and see all around it – every curve and inlet, every hill and valley.

I could see the Isle of Wight arriving – the Needles jabbing up out of the sea, chunks of chalk cliff, ruffles of dark trees, mysterious monuments and communication paraphernalia piercing the skyline.

'I was born there,' I burst forth to the woman leaning on the rail beside me.

'Lucky you,' she said. I scrutinised her face for traces of sarcasm but couldn't detect any.

I hadn't told my father about this journey, not wanting his censure. I said I was going to London for a few days to do with my work. He gave me his cynical look – novel writing didn't constitute work in his life view. Winter Wood was seven miles from Birdsong. I went to see him most days. Chas was going to call in on him while I was away. Sometimes I thought he got on with Dad better than I. But then he was used to his own multitude of relatives, letting their lives run through his without wetting his conscience.

Nearing Yarmouth I could see flags fluttering, masses of masts and hoards of holiday folk. 'Is it always this lively?' I asked the same woman.

'It's the Old Gaffers' Festival,' she said.

I saw a marching band of soldiers on the quay in crimson and white period costume, rat-tatting their drums like a welcoming party. 'Are they the Old Gaffers?' I asked.

She laughed. 'No, the Old Gaffers are boats. Look over there.' She pointed to a swathe of coloured sails – rusty reds, evening blues and weathered whites. 'They'll be sailing later – that's a sight to see.' She turned to look at me. 'I thought you said you were born here.'

I grinned. 'Born and banished.'

As I drove off the boat I had to thread my way through the careless crowd, street entertainers and barefoot kids in bathing costumes, dripping ice cream. Carousels and bumper cars whizzed and blared and greedy gulls clamoured around the produce stalls. The air was permeated with smells of sticky toffee and sizzling pork. And everything rode on a cacophony of music, sun-blessed and cheerful. I wanted to stop and join in but I was in the stream of traffic rolling off the ferry and decided getting in the right lane was my best option.

I headed south through farms and villages with picturesque churches and thatched cottages not unlike where I lived in Herefordshire, but miniaturised. I had the impression of stepping back in time. The roads were narrow; hedgerows and banks encroaching, the fading froth of cow-parsley being upstaged by pink campion and starry daisies. I slowed down, reminding myself there was no hurry. I stopped in a lay-by to check my map. Chas had laughed at me planning my route, assuring me I couldn't get lost on a tiny island twenty-three miles across by thirteen down. I could only go round in ever-decreasing circles. But I was a hopeless driver; anything that I spied could set me off on a story-line and take me off course. Today, however, my imagination stayed dormant and I didn't find myself on a detour.

The southern coast road was long and straight with the English Channel on my right and farmland rising to the downs on my left. I spotted walkers on the coastal path across flowery meadows, above the glittering sea. The land was sparsely inhabited for several miles apart from a couple of chalet parks, which looked like disused barracks. And then the sea cliffs reared high, thrusting layers of rock towards the sea while the gorsy hills on my left soared and I saw National Trust signs for St Catherine's Oratory. I must be getting near. The road ran downhill to Niton where people were shopping and sitting under bright parasols outside the village pub. The sea shone ahead of me now like a guiding beacon and then, rounding a bend, I saw Undercliff Drive.

This was where my cottage was – somewhere

along here in The Undercliff. One of my internal organs appeared to execute a perfect somersault. I wondered if my genes were resonating to some primordial recognition of my birthplace. But I couldn't go exploring just yet. I had to see the solicitor and collect the keys tomorrow. The road was dense with green shade, the immense layered cliff brooding on my left and grey stone walls bordering the road interspersed with crumbling gateposts and driveways to invisible properties. Ivy crept and tumbled over everything as if lending support. I wondered how Dad would react if he knew I was here.

I arrived at St Lawrence, the village before Ventnor, and found Undercliff House where I'd booked an apartment. It was patched Victorian gothic, mellow bricks draped with kindly wisteria. The drive was bordered with fuchsia hedges dripping ruby ballerinas. I pushed open the heavy, maroon door and found a note on the chiffonier informing me I was in flat number five. The hallway was wide with a sliding threadbare carpet and potted ferns and smelled of wax polish and curry.

I found five, unlocked, at the top of the house. There was a yellow Formica fifties kitchen smelling of mould and a large room with a floral double bed and a cracked black leather sofa. The bathroom was expressionless but had a decent shower. There was a pile of abandoned paperbacks, tourist brochures and house rules. Strangely, I liked it – mainly because of the bay window and the view. It overlooked a large garden with a bowling-green lawn edged with hairy tree ferns, Torbay palms and New Zealand flax. On the grass stood two white plastic tables with chairs and striped green umbrellas, and then nothing but sea, sparkling in the afternoon sun. I could see bright sails dotting the dark blue and wondered if they were Old Gaffers showing off.

I went downstairs to the car, sniffing deeply at the cut grass and spicy breeze, collected my case, laptop and cool-bag of delicatessen goodies and stacked the food in the rumbling fridge. I positioned my laptop on the table in the bay window, changed my mind and stuck it in a cupboard, not wanting to threaten my hibernating muse with premature arousal.

It was only four o'clock. Nothing to do except please myself, guilt-free for a few days. I changed into my Hawaiian shorts and top, clipped up my hair, put on my sunglasses and headed for Ventnor. The road widened and the houses and hotels adopted a Mediterranean look with pastel paint, verandas and palm trees. Flowers cascaded, acid lemon and fizzy pink, and I noticed Ventnor Botanic Gardens which I must find time to visit before I left. I drove down a hairpin road to the esplanade up which weary parents were dragging tired kids and hauling plastic bags of beach clobber. Everything seemed to be tumbling down terraces, teetering towards the sea.

I parked in the road and walked above the curved

beach that looked clean and uncrowded. The sand was dark gold interspersed with a fine shingle. Children were paddling and a few brave souls swimming. Groups of people did obligatory holiday things behind striped windbreaks – sandcastles, sandwiches, snoozing and snogging. I indulged in a wicked cream tea, sitting outside a homely café, shamelessly piling jam and cream until the scones groaned.

It was strange to think I was born here, that my father worked in the local hospital. I could find out which one. And where was the physician's house, where I was born? I'd never given it any thought because I'd left so immediately. Why had I never wanted to do this before? I hadn't needed to, I supposed. I was absorbed in my present life, Chas and Birdsong and my writing. I'd had no interest in the past and my parents had fostered none in me. Perhaps I would never have wondered, if Aunt Lillian hadn't left me her cottage.

I was born here – the phrase kept repeating itself in my mind. I felt friendly towards it, an old-fashioned town, a hotchpotch of preserved Victorian grandeur, some renovation needed – demolition even. There was a hut on the beach selling today's catch of crabs and lobsters, a digger further along heaving boulders for a small harbour. It had none of the chic of the Mediterranean resorts which I favoured, but there was something comforting about it, like putting on saggy tracksuit bottoms and slippers after a day spent in a tight skirt and high heels. Buildings had slumped and settled into their place, relaxing, waiting for the sea to decide on the next move like a game of chess. I didn't want to change anything. Even the garish orange and yellow villa seemed to blend. How sad that I'd never been here before. It might have been nice to grow up at the seaside. But then my life would have taken a different course.

I walked up the zig-zag slope down which water streamed and geraniums trailed. I wandered around the town looking at the shops – a mix of Boots and boutiques, Somerfields and souvenirs, antiques and assorted junk. I discovered a small museum with old photos on display of some of the mansions of the grand days, when royalty favoured the island and Ventnor was a prestigious seaside resort that rich Victorians used to frequent for the climate. I got chatting to an elderly man also peering. I asked him if he knew Wraith Cove and he told me he used to walk there from Ventnor when he was young but now the cliffs had fallen and the coastal path above was closed. He didn't think that anyone still lived there, it was too dangerous.

I drove back to my apartment and heated some gourmet chicken and rice. I didn't watch the news, not wanting to disturb my holiday mood with the middle-east dilemma, the new rogue virus. I phoned Chas. He had called in to see Dad, who hadn't remembered that I was going away. I opened the window and watched swallows and martins skimming the air for flies and found myself absorbed by the music of the sea – a complex sound, like wind rustling dry grasses over a monastic chant. The refrain kept running through my mind – I was born here . . . this is my birthplace.

I woke during the night from a frightening dream. I shot up in the strange bed, fumbling for the lamp, heart thumping. I got up and checked the door which I'd left unlocked. I heard faint footsteps and the distant clank of water pipes and one brief cry of a child. I poured a glass of water and sat at the table looking out over the lawn and the sea. Someone had closed the umbrellas. The moon was flashing glimpses of silver between fast-moving clouds, like a secret transmission.

What had I been dreaming? It was fading fast. I wasn't one for remembering dreams, trying to find significance in them. But this one was still lurking around the edges of my mind. It had begun with the familiar feeling of choking. That was it – as if I was under water wearing diving apparatus. Someone was wrenching the tube away from me, cutting off my air supply. I could see the surface of the water above me, the light glinting through with a reddish glow. A hand was reaching down searching for me. It grabbed my hair and yanked me upwards. I gasped for breath and tasted blood. That's when I woke.

Strange I should dream that. I'd never been deep sea diving in my life. I was a paddler. Chas was always trying to persuade me to snorkel – just to see the neon-bright fish, curious about legs. But I couldn't bring myself to submerge. Perhaps the dream was the result of so much sea in one day and being overheated. I drank another glass of water and lay down on top of the duvet, cooling off as I drifted back to sleep.

Emmeline felt better. Marguerite had sat with her all morning recharging her energy system. She felt as if every cell in her body had been cleansed of the chemotherapy and revitalised.

'Are you going out in the boat with Neptune today?' she asked Marguerite.

Marguerite nodded, throwing her arms wide to indicate the open door and windows, the sunshine pouring in.

'Then I will sit outside in the sun and read.'

But after Neptune had sailed away with Marguerite, Emmeline clambered down to the beach, surprised at how much strength had returned to her emaciated body. She made her way to Lilly's stone and pulled a handful of rose petals out of her trouser pocket and sprinkled them over it. Then she sat down, cross-legged, smiling at her own image, thinking that if anybody sailed past they would imagine they'd seen a leprechaun.

She relished the feel of the warm sun through her shirt. She breathed deeply, inhaling the smells of salty seaweed and rose petals. The sea was lazy, swishing on the sand. She closed her eyes and saw

Lilly at the water's edge, her flowered skirt tucked up in her knicker-legs as she paddled, singing to herself. It was hard to keep her away from the sea, even on the roughest days.

'Lilly,' Emmeline called. But she wouldn't look round, as if she knew what Emm was going to ask of her. 'Lilly!'

'I don't want to remember any more,' Lilly replied.

'But we have to. We must finish what we started. I need to hear it from you so that I can remember the absolute truth. I have to tell Jane when she comes. She deserves to know.'

Lillian turned and walked towards Emmeline.

'Are you sure, Emm? Does she really need to know all the details or just the facts?'

'No, I'm not sure. But I have to hear it, so that it's alive in me, so that I can feel its intensity. Do you understand? Otherwise how will I be able to confront Henry?'

Lilly nodded, her eyes downcast.

Emmeline sat, scarcely breathing, feeling Lilly's energy so close to her. The smell of roses intensified. She reached out her hand, feeling for Lilly, but the stone was flat and warm beside her. She sighed. 'Remember that night for me, my darling,' she whispered. 'Go back to New Year's Eve.'

'I will have to return to the sea, otherwise I won't be able to bear it.'

'Then take my love with you.'

'No. I can't do that.'

Emmeline felt as if something inside her skull was spiralling into darkness as she heard the sound of Lilly's voice, invoking the past . . .

I wake feeling that something about the cottage has changed. I lie still, listening. Emm slumbers beside me, her breath slow, sighing. The fire glows in the hearth, reflecting in my glass angel on the shelf above the door and the tinsel looped with the holly and ivy along the mantelshelf. We sometimes sleep downstairs on bitter nights like tonight, cranking out the bed-settee, piling it with blankets and eiderdowns. It is magical, lying in the herb-scented firelight loving each other, watching the shadows of my driftwood sculptures playing on the walls and ceiling. We whisper far into the night, listening to the rush of the wind and the plunge and hiss of the sea.

What is different? I raise my head. Drifter is purring on our feet; I can see her black back gleaming. She hasn't heard anything. Perhaps I've been dreaming. But my heart is beating faster than normal and that isn't right. There! A faint thudding. Not the familiar night-nestling of the cottage, wind gusting, boughs scraping. Drifter's ears twitch – she senses it now. I wonder whether to wake Emm. No, it must be a badger or fox scavenging, or that bit of corrugated iron on the outhouse roof that is working loose. But it's my heart that troubles me. Noises, even a new one, should feel right. This doesn't. And then I hear the door latch clink.

45

I reach for Emm's arm but her breathing has already changed.

The door bursts open so forcefully that it swings right back against the wall, knocking a pile of books and shells from a shelf. Emm and I both shoot up in bed, grabbing for each other. Drifter flies off the bed and flattens herself on the hearthrug, the hair on her back spiky. The cottage fills with a bellow of icy wind and a deep shadow lurches and fumbles around the wall for the light switch. The room blazes yellow, blinding me. I put my hand to my eyes, blinking desperately to clear my vision. I screech and feel Emm's arm pressing against my chest as if she is trying to protect me.

'Henry!' I hear her cry. 'What the hell are you doing here?'

I can smell him before I see him – a thick stench of tobacco and whisky and stale vomit. As my eyes focus I can see him swaying at the end of our bed. He is wearing his black evening suit; his starched white collar is open and his bow tie dangling. He seems enormous in our little cottage. His large head with its dark oiled hair would touch the beams if he could stand up straight. His face looks purplish-red, suffused with the cold and alcohol. His eyes are bloodshot, bulging, as he leers down at us.

'What am I doing here?' he slurs. 'More to the point, what the devil are you doing here?'

Emm pulls a blanket up to her shoulders and mine. 'Get out, Henry. You're drunk!'

He stands staring at her, rocking backwards and

46

forwards. 'Why aren't you at the hotel?' He raises an arm, jabbing his forefinger at Emm. 'What are you doing in Lillian's bed?'

'Go home now, Henry. Get out and close the door.'

Emm's voice is firm but I can feel her body shaking like mine under the covers. Henry turns and looks at the door and for one hopeful moment I think he is going to do as she commands. Instead, he slams it shut, causing the fire to flare in the hearth. In two strides he crosses the room and rips the blanket from Emm's grasp. He pitches towards us, snorting with disgust.

'Where're your clothes, you filthy bitches?' He is half-lying across the bed now, pinning our legs, holding onto the covers. I hear myself whimpering with fear. Emm is struggling to get free from under him. He thrusts out a hand and shoves her roughly back against the pillows. She grabs his wrist and bites down fiercely on his fingers. He roars and lunges at her hair, yanking her out of the bed. I scream. Emm punches out at him, arms flailing, her slight, naked body, for all its wiry strength, no match for his bulk. The back of his hand strikes her across the face with a mighty swipe and she falls backwards, hitting her head on the iron door latch. She slides to the floor, her wild eyes searching for me, her stunned mouth trying to form my name as she loses consciousness.

I think I am screaming, but no sound comes from my open mouth. My arms are sticking straight out in front of me, fingers splayed. Henry stands, staring down at Emm. How dare he look at her private parts when she is unable to cover herself. I have to defend her from his prying eyes. I lower my arms and slip silently from the bed. I bend down to retrieve my dressing gown from the floor but my head reels and I knock against a chair. He turns his head slowly towards me, scanning my naked, shaking body. I try to cover myself with my arms and hands, hardly able to stand. 'Let me go to her, Henry, please,' I stammer.

'Lillian,' he mumbles, 'little Lillian.' He stands panting, staring at me with his glistening eyes. I take a tentative step, hoping he might move but he holds up a hand. I flinch. 'You don't need her,' he says, 'she's unnatural.' He belches and wipes a hand over his mouth. 'Our mother's to blame you know . . . hated men . . . always marching off on some women's protest . . . that's where Emmeline got all this from. Did you know that, Lillian? My own mother made my sister hate me.' His eyes glaze over. 'Father didn't care. Damn good doctor though . . . I've tried to be like him – God knows I've tried.' He shakes his head as if trying to remember where he is, then points at Emm. 'She's led you astray, that's what she's done.'

'No, that's not true.' I try to see beyond him to where Emm lies. I can feel her life energy; thank God she is still alive.

'Come here to me, Lillian. You don't need to pretend. You must know how I feel about you.' He reaches out a hand and tries to touch my hair. I jerk back and that angers him. He gasps air in, his face looks bloated. 'Teasing me, are you, little bitch? You've always done that, haven't you?'

'No! I have never –'

'So, you think you can get love from a woman, do you?'

'Emmeline and I – we love each other.'

'That's because she's infected you with her lies. You don't know any better.'

I realise that, whatever I say, he isn't going to believe me and I will only enrage him more. I feel lost and weak without Emm's strength. All I can think of is trying to get him out as quickly as possible so that I can help her. He reaches out his hand again and begins stroking my hair, pulling it forward so that it hangs down over my breasts.

'Your hair's like silk.'

I will myself not to flinch away, not to anger him further. His head knocks against the bunch of mistletoe hanging from a beam.

'Ah, expecting to be kissed, are you?'

He grabs my hair in two handfuls and pulls me to him, jamming his wet, disgusting mouth on mine. I feel his teeth scraping my lips, his tongue trying to force a way in. My stomach heaves; he staggers and lets go of me.

'Happy New Year, Lillian,' he mumbles, grinning.

I try desperately to focus him on something else. 'Where's Victoria?' I stammer. 'Is she outside waiting for you?'

'Victoria?' He freezes for a moment and I think I might have succeeded. 'Sent her home in a taxi.' He tries to grab me to him again. I put a hand on his chest.

'Won't she be worried about you?'

He looks puzzled. 'Worried?' He lets out a snort of laughter, showering me with foetid breath. 'She'll be in bed with her legs locked together. She's frigid, your sister. Did she tell you that? Do you talk about me?' I shake my head so hard, I feel dizzy. 'Look at you, your little breasts, you're just a girl, you need filling out, woman's curves. You need to feel the love of a man. What could a woman possibly do for you?' He puts a hand on my cheek, raises my face. I start to cry with fear. 'There, there. You'll feel better soon.'

I wonder if he is treating me like one of his patients. Perhaps I could play into his doctor role. I wipe my eyes with my hands and he pulls his handkerchief from his breast pocket and gives it to me. It smells disgusting but I blow my nose and hand it back to him. 'Thank you, Henry,' I say, 'I do feel better now. But I'm so cold. I need to put my clothes on.' He stands watching me, transfixed. 'And,' I venture, 'we need to look after Emmeline, too. She's hurt.'

He seems to jolt back to life. 'I won't hurt you, Lillian.' He catches hold of my arms roughly. 'Look at me! Why do you never look at me like you look at my bloody sister? She's not even pretty. Not like you.' He runs a hand down my throat. 'You're trembling, like a little bird – you like this, don't you? You're responsive – not like Victoria. You're soft and alive – you want me, I know you do. And I've always wanted you.'

'No, Henry. Don't touch me. Please don't touch me.'

He grasps me firmly and pushes me down on the bed. He struggles out of his jacket and yanks at his cummerbund until the hooks give. He attempts to undo his shirt and trousers sending buttons flying across the cottage as they are wrenched off. Every time I try to struggle up he throws me back with one thrust of his hand. He towers above me, swaying, his remaining clothing gaping. His face has grown pallid and I pray he might pass out. It seems like there are two of him – a great expanse of animal flesh, inflamed and swollen, patched with coarse dark hair and then this other ashen-faced Henry at the edge, watching cold-eyed, remorseless and so loathsome. How could he mistake this for love?

Sobs rack my chest and bile rises in my throat so that I think I might choke. At this moment I would be glad to suffocate if it wasn't for my poor Emm, lying there, cold and injured. He collapses down beside me, moving his hands over my body. I try with all my might to repulse him with my fear and disgust, but he is oblivious to my distress. His face looms over me like a stone gargoyle. He sniffs the air around my head, his nostrils flaring. His voice sinks to a throaty whisper.

51

'You smell of roses, Lillian. You're so delicate, like some of my patients. They lie there looking at me, their big eyes so trusting when I touch them. They sigh when I put my hands on them as if I'm . . . as if . . .' His hands stop and his eyelids droop. I have another brief hope of reprieve – maybe he will fall asleep. But then his eyes snap open, and his voice rises. 'You would never laugh at me, Lillian, would you? My mother used to laugh at me and Father. She used to call us her soppy boys.'

His clammy hands continue exploring my body. I know then I have to escape if I am going to survive this. I imagine an iron blade like a guillotine, slicing down between us, cutting my mind off completely from him and I go in search of Emm. Her mind is unresponsive, enshrouded in a foggy substance. I try to penetrate the mist but I can find no way in. I stay with her, trying to encircle her with golden light. I can hear my body on the bed, weeping quietly, Henry's voice murmuring.

'You're wet my darling, like a woman should be. I suppose that bitch has been fiddling with you. But a woman doesn't count. You're like a virgin to me.' My sobbing continues; there is nothing else that my body can do. 'There, there, little Lillian – you'll enjoy this – you need to know what a man feels like. Then you won't want to mess around with girls any more – you'll be a real woman.'

At that moment Emm lets me in – my mind sinks gratefully into hers and it seems we comfort each other's souls while my body is mauled on the bed and hers battles with bleeding and bruising. I feel that we are floating in some life-giving fluid that is sustaining us and that nothing can pollute.

I have no idea how much time passes, but eventually I become aware of my body again, lying twisted on the bed, aching, cold, exhausted. Henry is stirring, groaning, and trying to heave himself off me. I feel him leave my body and he half-falls onto the floor, scraping my legs with his shoes, searching for his discarded clothes. He stumbles down to the kitchen end and I hear him vomit into the sink and relieve himself in a bucket. I know I mustn't move a muscle until he is gone. I can just see Emm's bloodied face near the door. I will her not to move, not to speak.

At last, Henry finishes fumbling with himself and I can sense him looking down at me. My eyes open involuntarily and look straight at him. His eyes flick away. He turns and bends over Emm. He feels her pulse, pulls her away from the door. He hesitates, and then gives her limp body a quick shove with his foot, like a child's petulant kick. 'You are not my sister,' he croaks. 'I have no sister.' He lifts the latch and clears his throat. He speaks with his back to me, loud and stern.

'You asked for it. If I hear that either of you have spread any gossip I can have you both certified and, believe me, I would do just that.'

I feel his words reverberate throughout my body as if I were swallowing shards of ice. He opens the door. I smell fresh air – sharp with salt and frost.

He leaves without looking back. The door swings shut. I watch the latch drop. There is a strange and absolute silence and then my glass angel topples forward off the shelf above the door and seems to float in the air for a timeless moment before splintering on the flagstones . . .

Emmeline found herself sprawled on Lilly's stone, sobbing, wet rose petals stuck to her cheeks. Insistent hands were trying to raise her up.

'Come on old girl,' Neptune was saying. 'You shouldn't be down here, you're not strong enough yet.'

Marguerite was kneeling beside her, wiping her tears, picking off the petals. Emmeline stood up shakily.

'I'm all right. Don't fuss. Just something I needed to do, that's all.' She stomped off across the beach to the cliff steps. Her feet seemed able to deal with the rocks. She felt strong and clear in her purpose.

CHAPTER 4

I woke late, not that it mattered. I cooked myself scrambled eggs and made coffee and sat by the open window. The dream still niggled at the periphery of my mind like the silver dazzles that herald a headache. Two little copper-haired girls in yellow dresses were holding hands and running around the lawn giggling, until the smaller one tripped and started to yell. Mum rushed out to comfort and cuddle and rub knees. She sat at one of the plastic tables, rocking the casualty, her arm around the older one who was leaning against her. I felt the familiar pang of childlessness. Would I ever stop feeling that ache? Would I ever stop wondering what a baby made by Chas and me would look like? I sighed, poured more coffee and turned my mind to plans for the day.

One of my coping strategies was thinking of what I might do that couldn't be done with children in tow. There were some advantages, but sometimes I found it hard to think of any. I washed up, sang Summer Holiday in the shower and was delighted by my first sighting of a red squirrel through the bathroom window, twitching

55

its tufty ears, obviously impressed by my singing. Wild animals and birds could always lift my mood – my substitute kids.

I found the solicitor's office too early and sat and waited, listening to the drone of business machines, keyboards tapping, glad my fingers weren't doing the typing. I hadn't written a word for months now and still felt no inclination to. Nobody knew it was that bad. I bluffed my way through the questions, even kidding myself that I was making progress when I tidied my notebooks. I could admit it now, without feeling anxious, because I was away from home and didn't have to pretend to anyone.

Bill Allain called me into his room. He looked about my age but sea-weathered. I imagined him grappling with thrashing mainsails in force ten gales, shouting instructions to tough little Ellen MacArthur type kids. Paintings of boats splashed around his walls. I wondered how he could work without feeling seasick. He leaned back in his chair.

'So, what do you think of our island?' he asked.

'Good. It seems to have a bit of everything – except cold mountains, which I don't like anyway.' I smiled. 'I was born here,' I boasted.

He leaned forward. 'Ah! No wonder you like it. You're a true islander then. You'll never cast it off, you know, if it's in your blood.' His gaze skimmed the watery turbulence of his pictures. 'I was born here too. I escaped once to go to university. But I had to come back.'

'Was that good or bad?'

He grinned. 'I wouldn't live anywhere else. Mind you, this bit of the island is the best. It still has its wild coastline and peace and quiet – most of the time anyway. Talking about coastlines, this place you've inherited from your aunt at Wraith Cove, the plans to stabilise that area are all in place now and the work should start soon. It's been held up for years by different conservation organisations. A mixed blessing depending on which side of the fence you're on – endangered species or endangered property. I'm not sure where your land and cottage figures, whether or not it's too late, but go and speak to the people at the Coastal Visitors' Centre and they'll show you the paperwork. It's possible that the land could be worth something – maybe for access.'

He wrote down directions and told me where to find the estate agent to collect the key. As I was leaving it occurred to me to ask him if he'd heard of my father and which hospital he might have worked at.

'I know the name, Doctor Henry Rampling; he probably worked at the Royal National – the chest hospital – here in Ventnor. My father would have known him. They'd have mixed in the same circles, I expect.' He got up and opened the door. 'Come and see these.' He led me back to the waiting room and pointed to framed photographs of the Royal National Hospital being constructed and visited by various dignitaries. 'Your father's probably in some of these.'

I peered at the fuzzy black and white faces – they all looked alike to me. It seemed strange looking into a past I didn't know. 'I suppose you wouldn't happen to know where the physician's house is, where my parents lived?'

He shook his head. 'Look, why don't you go and see my father? He's ancient but compos mentis. He loves talking about the past.' He wrote more instructions for me. 'Call in again and let me know what you discover.'

I crossed the road and walked down to the estate agents. The manager told me she'd sent one of the men to have a look at Lillian's cottage. She gave me a map marked with a red dotted line to show me how to find it.

'You'll need some wellingtons or walking boots,' she said. 'It really is inaccessible. Gareth had to fight his way through the undergrowth. He said there wasn't much there, just a shack really, so don't be disappointed. He found this under a pot.' She handed me a large iron key. 'But the door was open anyway. He said there isn't much inside either. It didn't look like your relative was living there. Perhaps she was staying somewhere else?'

I shrugged. 'It was the only address the solicitor had, Wraith Cottage.'

'Well, anyway, Gareth locked it up afterwards. I think he was glad to get back, he found it a bit spooky. Are you sure you don't want one of us to go with you?'

'No, really. But thanks.'

'And do take care, it's very near the edge of the unstable cliff. Call back and let me know if you want us to take it any further. You may need to speak to the coastal management team and get a structural engineer's report – we can help with all that.'

I drove back along Undercliff Drive and a few miles out of Ventnor I found the place where a new swathe of tarmac had been laid down. The collapsed road was fenced off. I pulled in and parked. I put on my walking boots and, armed with map and rusty key, set off, intrepid. The old road was impassable. I squeezed behind the fence to look. Great chunks of concrete had snapped off and dropped down the banks. The ivy was already claiming them. I clambered over a rickety farm gate and crossed a neglected field. A narrow track led out the other side which seemed the only way to go. It soon became dense and I had to watch the nettles and hold back brambles. I must have gone wrong – there couldn't be a cottage down here. I saw the tumbled remains of a building poking out of the grass. Ivy clambered over everything, snagging at my ankles as I passed, as if it wanted to climb up me too.

I stopped for a while to cool down. I stripped down to my tee shirt, tied my sweatshirt round my waist and sat down on a stump. Silence. The breeze had dropped. I looked up; the trees met each other over my head, tall and spindly. They leaned at crazy angles and I felt dizzy as if I was sitting on a sliding piece of land that might give a sudden jolt and send trees crashing down on me. I could hear a creeping sound as if everything was slowly moving like a glacier. The rustling got louder, my heart started to thump. Out from the undergrowth appeared a black cat. I laughed with relief. The cat sidled up to me and rubbed against my legs, purring. Obviously not a feral cat. I bent to stroke it, glad of the company. The cat soon got bored and turned and ran off. I assumed it was going home so decided to follow it, like Alice in Wonderland.

I came to another gate – more a hole in a fence really. There were signs here that the vegetation had been hacked back. I guessed it was Gareth, the estate agent, and mentally thanked him. The cleared area was in front of a big shed with a corrugated iron roof. Lord, was this it? To think that I'd wondered if I might have been able to stay here. I'd tried not to have any expectations but I felt a great pang of disappointment. I raised the key to put it in the lock but the cat reappeared, brushed past me and nudged the door open. I thought the estate agent said it'd been locked up.

I followed the cat into the gloom feeling apprehensive. There might be a psychopath hiding out here for all I knew. My eyes adjusted to the dim light. There were wooden crates and plastic containers stacked on shelves, a sink and iron pump, buckets and antiquated garden tools. An old tin bath with a hole in the bottom was hanging up. Against one wall was a wooden workbench. No signs of recent habitation, no half-eaten meal or overturned chair. The estate agent was right – it was an old shack. Aunt Lillian couldn't possibly have lived in this. My fastidious mother's sister? Perhaps she used to come here to be near the sea – a sort of beach hut – and lived in a neat rented flat in Ventnor. My father wouldn't have known. I smiled to myself – he hadn't exaggerated when he'd called it a hovel.

I could hear the swish of the sea; it must be very close. I went back outside. This must be the right place, there was no other path. The cat had disappeared. Perhaps it had been wild after all. The undergrowth smelled dank here where the sun couldn't penetrate. I started to pick my way through the trees and bracken. I'd only gone a few feet and realised I was at the edge of the land. I froze. I was being very stupid. I could fall here and nobody would find me for ages.

I looked down the rocky slope of cliff. I could see a patch of yellow sand sprinkled with boulders. It looked sunny and inviting. I knew I shouldn't risk it but this adventure had caught hold of me. I started to inch my way down. Dislodged stones began to clatter. Sea thrift grew in pale pink tufts and grassy knolls had buttercups and daisies nodding on them. Suspicious gulls swooped above me. 'Stupid, stupid,' I was saying, but kept going. A few feet from the bottom my boots slid out from under me and I slithered the rest of the way down thankful for my denims, trying not to think how I was going to get back up.

I looked around the tiny horseshoe bay – this must be Wraith Cove if I'd got it right. The tide seemed to be going out – there were rock pools and flotsam and jetsam thrown up by the sea – a rusty oil drum, tangles of turquoise rope, a lobster pot, plastic bottles. Between the rocks was pale yellow sand, sprinkled with fine shingle and shells and patches of pink seaweed like pickled cabbage, smelling pungent and salty. The boulders were smooth, like basking seals draped with green silken hair. The sort of beach for pottering around, exploring. There would be plenty of time before the tide turned. I sat on a rock, rolled up my jeans, stripped off my boots and socks and put my hot feet in the sea. I dangled them until the cold shock felt bearable and then wandered along the lacy edge of the waves.

This was one of my favourite pastimes – being in that meeting place of water and land. The horizon was hazy, a lone cormorant diving for lunch. To my right I could just see the white turret of a light-house further along the coast. The beam flashed as it revolved, despite the sunlight. I looked back up at the cliff and could see how it was falling away: even as I gazed little drifts of sand made their way down. I spotted an edge of stone and what looked like corrugated iron – must be the roof of Wraith Cottage – my cottage. I smiled; wondering if this was a practical joke on Lillian's part, perhaps to get back at her estranged family.

Then, out of the corner of my eye I saw something

move further along the beach amongst the rocks. I stopped. There! Something round, bobbing – a seal? How amazing that would be. I crept slowly towards it trying not to make a splash or knock pebbles. There, it moved again – my God, it looked like a human head – nearly bald. My heart thumped. Hell! Please don't let it be a dead body floating in a rock pool. I crept closer and lost sight of it. Then, nearer, I peered over a large boulder. A face gazed back at me. We both yelped in astonishment. In front of me was a small, ancient human. Wizened, yellowish brown. Bald, except for a few wispy hairs plastered like damp straw across the speckled scalp. Two enormous eyes, bulbous and blue as midsummer stared at me. A threadbare towel was wrapped around his or her waist. Gollum! I thought. It's Gollum. Time froze while we stared like two petrified meercats.

'Sorry,' I said, lamely, unfreezing myself. The little person shook itself and I noticed two small pouches trembling on the rib cage. It was female.

'Victoria?' she said, her voice high, tremulous. 'You look like . . .' She stuck her fists in her eyes and rubbed them hard, and then looked me up and down blinking. 'Are you Virginia, then? I thought . . .' Her voice faded away.

'I'm Jane,' I said clearly, trying to reassure her. She looked puzzled. 'Jane.' I repeated, before she could try out any more names on me. I'd be Veronica next or Violet. I smiled. 'I'm sorry to have startled you.'

She pulled herself upright, as if recovering her dignity. 'How did you manage to get down here?' she demanded, her voice louder, steadier.

I pointed to the place where I'd scrambled down.

'Goodness, you'll never get back up there. You'll set the cliff moving.'

'Oh, dear,' I said. 'Is there another way up?'

'Yes, but don't go showing anyone. Don't want intruders down here.' She inspected me again. 'Well, Virginia. I'm Emmeline. I expect you'd like a drink.'

I decided to let the Virginia go. What did it matter? She turned and started to track through the rocks like she knew every one of them. I could hardly keep up with her. Her skinny arms and legs bent outwards at elbows and knees and her large feet flapped like leather on the stones. What on earth was this poor old soul doing down here? I wondered what she had to offer by way of a drink. I was parched. Another foolish act of mine – coming on this excursion without water.

'Where do you live, Emily?' I asked, breathless.

She stopped and glared at me. 'It's Emmeline,' she said. 'I'm named for Mrs Pankhurst.' Her voice rang clear now. She waved towards the cliff. 'And I live here.'

She turned and clambered towards an opening in the cliff face. It was a cave screened with a trellis made of driftwood and rope and matted with ivy and what looked like honeysuckle. No, an elderly woman couldn't live in a cave in this climate. She propped back the trellis and inside there was a length of foam, a sleeping bag, a pile of books and a lantern. She reached in for a bottle.

'Elderflower?' she asked. 'It's last year's but very good.' She handed me the bottle. I gave the top a surreptitious wipe on my tee shirt and hoped I wasn't about to be poisoned. I took a tentative sip. It tasted cold and delicious. I couldn't resist another swig. I handed it back to her.

'We haven't slept out all night this year yet,' she said. 'But we do most summers. It's wonderful, under the stars and moon with the sea singing and the wraiths dancing. You must try it, Virginia.' Her voice faded again. 'Lilly loved it so much.' She stepped onto a large flat stone and stood staring down at it. A few pink petals fluttered around her feet. I wondered where they'd blown from. 'This is Lilly's stone. She'd come and sit here for hours, enchanted by the sea.'

It took a few seconds, which seemed like minutes, for what she'd said to sink in.

'Lilly?' I said. 'Lillian? You knew Lillian?' She nodded. 'She was my aunt.' She nodded again and sipped at the elderflower looking out to sea. I couldn't believe it. I swallowed hard. 'But that's wonderful – Emmeline – were you friends?'

'Yes, indeed.' She spoke so quietly I could hardly hear her.

I was getting excited now, my words tumbling out. 'Wait a minute. You . . . you called me Victoria, just now. Did you know her too – my mother?'

65

'You look so much like her. For a moment I thought . . .'

She turned away from me and seemed to droop. I could see every vertebra of her curved spine. I felt a great wave of tenderness well up in me, ending up as tears in my eyes. What was this frail woman doing here alone? I didn't know what to say to her. I could see she was trying to compose herself, making little straightening movements with her shoulders. I waited for a while. She coughed and looked out to sea again.

'Emmeline? I really don't want to upset you. But, I wonder if I might talk to you about Lillian, some time. You see, she was my only relative and I'd love to find out more about her – and my mother as a girl.'

'I know that, Virginia. I have things to tell you and show you. But not today. I have to go somewhere.'

'Emmeline,' I said carefully. 'My name is Jane. I'm Lillian's niece.'

She looked at me, her eyes like blue marbles. I noticed how yellowed the whites were.

'Jane,' she said, as if impressing it on her memory. 'Of course. Come back tomorrow, Jane. Go and get your boots and I'll show you an easier way. But you must promise not to tell anyone.'

'I promise. You have my word.' I went as fast as I could to retrieve my boots, wondering how on earth Emmeline had managed it so nimbly barefoot. When I got back she was busy sealing up her cave. Driftwood was piled up against the cliff. I noticed a circle of stones on the beach nearby, containing ash and some iron cooking pots. Perhaps she really did live out here. Still clad only in her towel, she led me further along the beach to another track, her big feet splayed out like flippers. I smiled; she actually did look like Gollum. This path up the cliff was easier and firmer. Boulders had been placed strategically to give footholds. At the top, breathless and sweating again, I looked down at the cove. The cliffs had collapsed at both ends making it impassable from the shore. I could see that it would be difficult to land a boat here too, the receding tide was revealing more and more rocks. Emmeline was looking at me as if she could read my thoughts.

'This used to be quite a popular place, but nobody comes here now.' She grinned, showing gaps in her teeth. 'Apart from Neptune, of course, and sometimes young couples moor out at sea and swim in to make love. But they never trouble us – too wrapped up in themselves.'

I suspected she was a touch senile with all this Neptune and Virginia stuff, and I wondered who the *us* was, but didn't like to ask. I felt I'd traumatised her enough for one day. But there was one thing I had to find out. 'Emmeline, where do you live when you're not in your cave?'

She waved a skinny arm towards the undergrowth. 'I'll show you tomorrow,' she said. 'Come at the same time and I'll meet you here. Now,' she pointed towards yet another rusty gate. 'Go through there, across the field – it's a bit over-grown – and you'll come to the wall of a garden. There's an old hotel in there, half-demolished. Cut through the grounds and you'll find yourself back on the road that's collapsed. Go to your left and it will take you back to where you've parked your car.' She turned then and padded away into the bushes. I followed her instructions, wondering how she knew where I'd left my car. I suppose she just assumed I would have one and that was really the only place to park.

I found my way through the old garden, which was a tangle of rampant rhododendrons and wild roses, honeysuckle and hydrangeas – the smell was intoxicating. It must have been a wonderful garden to have by the sea. The hotel was half-gone, its sign almost obscured by the words, Danger! Keep Out! I could just make out the faded lettering – Wraith Cove Hotel. I wondered to whom it belonged. I collapsed into my hot mini, starting to ache and sting all over.

Later, bathed and refreshed with lotion dabbed on my scratches, bruises, bites and sunburn, I set off to visit Bill Allain Senior – the solicitor's father. I'd phoned him earlier and he invited me round for an evening drink. He lived in a flat with an almost circular turret, which overlooked Ventnor Bay. He had a telescope set up in the window and paintings of boats around the walls, like his son. I politely sipped sherry, which seemed to be the only drink on offer, while he told me about his past as a solicitor and sailing fanatic. I was beginning to think he'd forgotten I was there to ask him about my father. His eyes were glazed and hazy with memories and sherry. After the first hour I began to feel drowsy and I decided to interrupt at the next opportunity. He got up to refill our glasses.

'Your son says you probably knew my father – Doctor Henry Rampling?'

'Oh, yes, indeed, my dear. And his father before him. Both doctors at the chest hospital here. Henry Senior was a renowned physician and your father was set to follow in his footsteps.'

Another revelation – there was an older generation of Ramplings with connections here. I'd never met any of my grandparents. They'd all died before I was born. At last, I was getting somewhere. 'What do you remember about them?'

'Not much about your grandfather except that he was dedicated to his profession, practically lived in the hospital. And your father, well, he attended council meetings, fund raising, official things like that. He, too, was a very busy man, always working.' He smiled. 'He didn't sail or get involved in the social group. I have to confess, in my world work came second to sailing.'

I quickly intercepted before he returned to his pet subject. 'Do you remember my mother, Victoria?'

'Victoria, why, yes. She was a very beautiful young lady. Always immaculate – smart suits, hair done

69

up as if she had it dressed every day. Her family owned one of the grand hotels along here some- where. I recall she was expecting a child. You look a lot like her you know.' His eyes swept over me. 'Same build and colouring.'

This took me by surprise. I must look so different to my mother with my casually bobbed hair and flowing magenta dress. And, a grand hotel! I'd never heard about that before.

'I remember we used to joke that Henry Rampling kept his lovely wife locked up in case she ran off with one of the junior doctors. Yes, a stern chap was Henry. The nurses at the hospital were terri- fied of him. I do remember that he detested his own mother – she was involved with those women who were always campaigning for something. I believe she got herself arrested a couple of times. He took offence if we ribbed him about her.' He paused to sip his sherry, his eyes turning to his pictures. I headed him off with another question.

'Do you know where they lived when they were here?'

'It would have been a physician's house in the hospital grounds. Beautiful there, overlooking the sea.'

'Oh, you knew it! The Physician's House.' I really did have a birthplace. 'I was born there.'

'Were you, indeed? Well, the senior doctors had very nice houses. The hospital was mainly for consumptives – a sanatorium really. It was famous; people came from everywhere. Ventnor itself was

70

a health resort. It was very grand in its day. Best climate in England. So, you were born there? I thought your parents had left before then.'

'No, I'm a true islander, as your son told me this morning,' I said, proudly. 'So, what is the chest hospital used for now?'

He laughed. 'Goodness me. It was demolished in the nineteen-sixties. It was falling down, rotting. It's where the Botanic Gardens are now.'

Disappointment struck again, like seeing Aunt Lillian's hovel. I'd imagined wandering around the old buildings, picturing my father and grand-father striding up and down polished wards, nurses wearing white caps and aprons scurrying around in their wake, like little sailboats.

'We were surprised when your father left. But tuberculosis was almost eradicated by then. It was generally thought that he had to go the mainland to fulfil his ambitions. After all he was only a young man – not forty, I should think. Never heard much about him after that.'

I was hoping he wouldn't ask me what had happened to Dad. I wanted to leave him with a picture of young ambitious Doctor Henry Rampling Junior, off to conquer the mainland with beautiful wife and new-born daughter. I didn't want to disillusion him with a story of dull general practice and futile research. I started to make small signs of departing.

'Well, my dear,' he said, stroking his telescope. 'I don't know if I've been much help to you?'

'It's been fascinating,' I said, getting up.

'Brings back memories,' he chuckled. 'Didn't he have a sister? I seem to remember something about a sister. I believe there was a bit of gossip about her you know. Can't remember what it was.'

'No, he didn't have a sister. Are you thinking of Lillian – his sister-in-law, Victoria's sister?'

'Maybe I am. I have half an idea that she was a bit wild. Although wild in those days was nothing to today's standards.' He got up to escort me out. 'Do come back again. I have lots of photograph albums.'

CHAPTER 5

Emmeline had been taken by surprise. She hadn't expected Jane to arrive like that, half-tumbling down the cliff. She'd felt confused, unsure whether she was fully awake or addled by her medication. She'd made a fool of herself. Fancy calling the poor woman Victoria and then Virginia. And her appearance! Jane must have thought she was some sort of sea-goblin, dressed only in a towel, with no hair to speak of. Emmeline had planned to wear clean clothes and a sunhat to meet her. But, she realised now, that was stupid. How could she have known when Jane might turn up? The solicitor wouldn't send a letter to a supposedly empty cottage to inform nobody. But what if Jane had knocked on the door of Wraith Cottage with no warning. It was only luck that she had found her way to the outhouse and come down that end of the cliff. Never mind, she had the situation under control now. She would show Wraith Cottage to Jane tomorrow, while Marguerite and Neptune were fishing and then tell her things gradually, being careful not to let slip anything that she'd got lined up for Henry to confess.

Marguerite was looking at her with questioning eyes. Emmeline wasn't in the habit of keeping anything from her or Neptune. But she didn't feel ready to say anything to them yet. She needed to be sure that what she was planning wasn't going to harm them in any way. Her fear was that Jane might have some of her father in her. She might not believe anything Emmeline had to say and then what would happen to them? But it was a risk she must take. She had to get to know Jane a bit more. She'd liked her so far – once she'd got over the shock of her resemblance to Victoria. She had seemed sensitive, intelligent and genuinely interested in hearing about the past.

Emmeline tried to stand up straighter, her spine felt increasingly curved these days. But she was determined not to die until this was finished.

I slept badly; itchy with insect bites and sunburn and thoughts that wouldn't lie down. I replayed the surreal meeting with odd little Emmeline at Wraith Cove, wondering what she had to tell me and if she would even be there tomorrow. I kept imagining my father and grandfather bellowing at cowering nurses. Dad had never shouted at me. His voice had an irritable edge but he seemed to struggle for words. And had he really hated his banner-toting mother? Perhaps she'd turned him into a misogynist. That would explain his dismissive behaviour towards females. But then again, perhaps old Mr Allain was confusing him with someone else. I seemed to have spent the day being given snippets of information by vague people that might not actually be true at all. But at least Emmeline had known Lillian, and my mother – that could be interesting.

I got up to watch the dawn over the sea from my window, sipping tea. I'd had a repeat of the previous night's bad dream. Once again I was choking beneath the surface. One hand was reaching down for me, pulling me up by my hair, and another was holding me back from below. I knew I was going to have to split apart in the middle and the pain would be unbearable. I'd never dreamt like this before. I was tempted to ring Chas, but it was too early. Anyway, I couldn't get a signal on my mobile here and I didn't want to phone from the hallway and wake the other residents.

I mooched about until mid-morning. I explored the garden and chatted with the two little sisters who were called Erin and Rhian. They held hands, jiggling with excitement, telling me they were going to Black Gang Chine to slide down the Overflow and the Plughole. Erin said I could go with them. She leant against me, patting my arm with her small soft hand. Her hair smelled of warm oranges. I watched as their mother strapped them into her car looking harassed. They waved goodbye to me, then turned to each other, their bright faces animated as they chattered.

I sat at the garden table and contented myself with watching a pair of great tits flying endlessly backwards and forwards feeding their shrilling young. Rearing the next generation certainly took energy. Would I have been a patient mother, willing to spend hours immersed in a child's world? With my role models I'd probably have packed them off to boarding school and told them not to bother me with their damn silly nonsense.

A sea mist was drifting in, obliterating the view. It swirled through the treetops, hushing the waves, subduing the birds. My moods certainly were swinging. Just as well my friends weren't here, they'd be quoting from the menopause manual. I went inside and put on an apricot shirt over my pink tee shirt to boost my morale. Was I subconsciously trying to look less like my faded mother after the reminders that I looked like her? I brushed my hair down – she always wore hers up – and put on my gold hoop earrings. I set off for Wraith Cove hoping I could remember the way Emmeline had shown me.

I parked in the same place near the fallen road and soon found the part-demolished hotel in the neglected garden. The scents seemed stronger in the dense, moist air. The long grass clung to me as I ploughed my way through. Buttercup petals stuck to my boots and jeans. I could hear the scuttle of rabbits in the undergrowth and a jay squawked a warning. I grew hot and sticky, not wanting to take off my shirt because of the brambles. I wondered if I'd taken the wrong track – it seemed much further than yesterday. I noticed a strange reluctance in me to meet Emmeline again, wondering whether I'd built this whole thing up and it would turn out there was nothing to discover. Wraith Cottage was simply a hovel, Lillian a reclusive spinster who left it to me because there was no one else, Emmeline a scatty old neighbour who knew her and my mother a long time ago.

I stopped for a moment to have a drink of water – at least I'd come prepared today. When I set off again I realised the broken gate was just ahead. Emmeline was waiting for me. At least I thought it was her. She had clothes on today, and a floppy hat. She raised a hand in greeting and I felt a sense of anticipation. I caught up with her.

'Come along,' she said.

This woman didn't waste any time on small talk. Off she went, just like yesterday, flap, flap. Except this time she had shoes on – large slip-on things like canvas deck shoes. She wore short cotton trousers and a baggy tee-shirt with a faded picture of something on it. She looked more human dressed, more substantial. I started to recognise the place where we'd arrived at the top of the cliff yesterday. She stopped. I joined her and we gazed out to sea.

'It looks a bit different today,' I said.

She nodded. 'It can change in a moment, that's the splendour of it.'

What an impressive thing to say, I thought. And the way she said it, with such conviction, as if she was truly proud of the weather. I liked her voice, it had a ring to it and a touch of refinement.

'Now,' she said. 'Follow me and take care. We're very close to the edge.'

I felt a moment's disquiet. I didn't know this woman at all. She might be crazy, push me over the cliff. I smiled at myself – was my wild imagination coming back? I followed her, watching my feet.

'You never know when some of this overhang will give way,' she said, pointing at the tussocky ground we were walking on.

Dear God, I thought, let me survive this and I'll write my novel in twenty-four hours and be kind to Dad for ever. She stopped and I stood trying to will myself to weigh less, while she fiddled with some branches. It was all right for her, skinny old thing. Perhaps nothing as heavy as me had been along here for years. The branches seemed to form some sort of barrier or gate. She hoisted it back while I stopped breathing, and then she gestured for me to go through. At least I could take a few steps inland now. I wiped a hand across my sweaty face and looked around.

Emmeline was watching me. I stood in a garden unlike any I'd ever seen. The beds were a jumble of flowers and vegetables intersected with winding paths laid with pebbles and edged with larger stones. Strange sculptures emerged from them made from driftwood. They looked like mythological creatures with antlers and horns. Ivy and roses and honeysuckle grew up rope trellis. There were oil drums and plastic containers full of geraniums, pink petunias and a riot of orange nasturtiums. Strings of shells hung from branches, and planks of wood on lobster pots made a table and benches. Hawthorn trees supported a swathe of fishing net forming a clematis canopy. There was a stone horse trough with water lilies and a flash of goldfish. I gazed around me, trying to take it all in, and it wasn't until my eyes had gone full circle that I realised there was a building ahead, through a driftwood arch. As I peered, the mist seemed to part above me and sunlight reached down.

I walked toward the low building. It had a part-thatched roof running almost to the ground on the landward side. On the front, facing the sea, there was a wooden porch and several small lattice windows. I looked at Emmeline; she nodded her head urging me on.

'Oh, my God,' was all I could say. Over the oak door Wraith Cottage was engraved in the wood. I had a strange moment of déjà vu – I didn't recognise anything but I felt something deeply familiar. My knees went weak. Emmeline's hand touched my arm. She pushed the door open then gave me a nudge.

I walked into the cottage. The doorway was low, the floor covered in uneven stone flags. The interior smelled of sooty wood fires and lavender. Driftwood hung from blackened beams and decorated the brick inglenook. Shells were piled along ledges, heaped in the hearth and dangling on strings from the ceiling along with bunches of herbs and dried flowers. The furniture was shabby – a brown sofa and droopy armchairs around the fireplace and a long split wooden table further down the room. A black cat was snoozing on one of the chairs – I supposed it was my friend from yesterday. On the table stood a catering sized baked bean tin filled with scarlet poppies, their black centres like mascaraed eyes. At the far end I could see a china sink and a black range. The walls were lined with shelves sagging with stacked books. Books were piled on the table and beside the chairs. Was Aunt Lillian some sort of collector?

I looked at Emmeline in astonishment. She took my arm and led me to the kitchen end. She pulled back a grey army blanket to reveal a door. It was secured with a length of wood dropped into two brackets. I helped her lift it out and she turned the handle. I found myself in a dark room. I half expected Aunt Lillian to be lying there in her coffin, or a camera crew to pop out and say it was all a set up. I looked around, adjusting to the gloom, and realised I was in the shack that I'd found my way to yesterday – the back end of the cottage – the bit I'd thought was it. I started to laugh. Emmeline looked at me anxiously.

'This is Wraith Cottage,' she said. 'Yours.'

I walked back into the main room. 'Lillian lived here all those years?' I asked, gazing around.

Emmeline regarded me with her prominent blue eyes. She swept back a red wool blanket hanging by the fireplace. There was a tiny stone stairway. I could just manage to climb up without bending down. On the landing was a small bed covered with a sheet, and one door, which stood open. This was a bedroom with a double bed covered with a rainbow of knitted shawls. Heavy-headed pink roses billowed from a white china jug on the chest of drawers, filling the air with sweetness. Piled books teetered. I wondered if Lillian had died in this room.

I walked over to the open window. The pink roses clambered up the cottage walls as if eager to come inside. The room overlooked the cove. I could see the lighthouse beam flashing. The weather had cleared, the sea a darkly glinting blue. A boat skimmed across, leaving a wake like heaped snow. It dawned on me then about the poppies and roses, the open windows, the neat beds. Emmeline had wanted to air the place, make it nice for me to see. That's why she hadn't brought me here yesterday. She stood in the doorway watching me, her face forlorn. Maybe she and Lillian had been good friends.

'Let's go downstairs,' I said. 'Perhaps there's somewhere we can make a drink and you could tell me about Lillian.'

Emmeline seemed to know where everything was. The power was switched on and there was an electric kettle. She had even thought to bring some milk with her. The black cat stretched and jumped off the armchair and came to rub around her legs.

'Lillian's cat?' I asked.

She put a saucer of milk down on the floor. 'Her

name's Surfer. She liked to chase the waves when she was a kitten.' She made tea in two badly-made pottery mugs. We sat at the table.

'This is so kind of you, Emmeline,' I said. 'Have you been keeping an eye on the place since Lillian died?' She nodded, her eyes huge over the mug. She seemed to have retreated into silence. I sipped my tea. 'You knew Lillian well, obviously.' She nodded again, seeming nervous. She picked up a pair of round metal spectacles held together with wire. She put them on and glanced briefly at the cover of a New Scientist journal lying on the table. Was Aunt Lillian interested in science? Emmeline took off her glasses again. 'You don't have to talk about her if you'd rather not,' I said. 'Perhaps another time.'

We sat and sipped. I noticed she was drinking camomile tea. The dusty daisy smell hung between us, reminding me of summer lanes and sunburnt feet. She put her mug down and licked her lips. I saw she had a scar on her top lip as if she'd split it badly at some time. This, with her missing teeth and her hat with the brim turned up, made her look less like Gollum and more like a little pirate. She cleared her throat as if she was putting her voice back in order.

'Virginia – I mean, Jane. There's something I must tell you.'

'Go ahead,' I said, intrigued.

'I live here – in Wraith Cottage. I've lived here for fifty years.'

Well, well. So that's it, I thought. She's Lillian's lodger and she thinks I'm going to turn her out. Poor old soul. She must be feeling really threatened by me. I smiled at her. 'Well, Emmeline, that's okay. I'm sure we can come to some arrangement. I don't intend living here, I –'

'No, you don't understand.' She pulled off her sun hat, making her few wisps of hair fly upwards. 'I want to tell you the truth.' Her gnarled hands were shaking. 'Lilly and I, we lived together.' She glared at me, as if she thought I was going to protest. 'We lived together as partners, lovers. We loved each other.' She was almost shouting, her mouth trembling, her great blue eyes brimming with tears.

Suddenly everything dropped into place. So this was the big family secret, the skeleton in the cupboard. The reason why my mother never spoke to her little sister. Yes, I could understand how prude Victoria couldn't have coped with having a lesbian sibling; especially carrying on a relationship in the same small town. Supposing her friends and neighbours found out and there was Henry's reputation at the hospital. No wonder they fled the island and left her to it, disowned her. So this was the Lillian who caused a bit of gossip in the sailing club.

I wanted to laugh but I was too aware of Emmeline's distress. I didn't want to make light of it – this was far too important for her.

'I do understand, Emmeline,' I said. 'I suppose

it was a bit shocking in those days. Did you feel you had to hide away?'

'We were never ashamed of our love, even though it shocked others.' She sounded indignant. I seemed to have said the wrong thing. 'We preferred to live as we did for many reasons.'

'Emmeline, please tell me more about Lillian,' I said gently.

'She was beautiful – I don't mean just physically – she was a gentle, loving soul. She was what is known as a sensitive – she could pick up other people's thoughts and, well, other things. It suited her, living here in these wild surroundings.'

We sat for a while in silence. I reached out and touched her hand. 'I'm glad, Emmeline, I really am. And I've no intention of taking your home away from you. You can live here for the rest of your life,' I grinned, 'or for as long as it clings to the cliff.'

'That won't be long,' she smiled, her lips still quivering.

I didn't know whether she meant her or the cottage. Questions started to pour out of me. 'But why didn't Lillian leave Wraith Cottage to you? She never knew me, and I didn't know she existed until I received the solicitor's letter. Why didn't she make contact with me before?'

'If Henry had died first maybe . . . it was difficult for her . . . she didn't want him turning you against her too.'

'Oh, Emmeline, I'm a big girl now – broad-minded – I might have been able to mediate.'

'Well, Lilly had her reasons. I won't be around for long, and she didn't want the cottage to go back to Henry. It was half Victoria's in the first place you see. But she put it in Lilly's name.'

'Why?'

'To get rid of it really, and to ease her conscience.'

'So, did you and Lillian know each other when you were very young?'

'Yes, we were always close.'

'She sounds very different from my mother. Did you know her well too?'

'Victoria. Yes. She was ill for a while when she was very young – a touch of TB from her mother. She recovered well, but her chest was weak. She was a serious girl but she loved painting, huge tempestuous landscapes. She had talent. But then Henry seemed to kill all that in her.'

I would have to think about all this later – tempestuous paintings – that wasn't the mother I knew. My father seemed to have a lot to answer for.

Suddenly she got up and jammed her hat on. 'I have to go,' she said, as if she'd remembered something important. 'Will you come again tomorrow? I have much more to tell you. Can you find your own way back?'

I said I could and she fled out of the door. Where on earth did she have to go so urgently? Just as I felt she was opening up and I was hungry for more. I sat for a while, slightly dazed, trying to absorb

85

Wraith Cottage – my cottage. I wanted to nose around, look into every corner, every cupboard, but I felt it would be an intrusion knowing that it was Emmeline's home.

As I was leaving I cast my eyes over the books – what a collection. Religion and the paranormal, science and homoeopathy, herbalism, wildlife, sealife, atlases, encyclopaedias, novels. It was like a library. I could imagine the two of them – Lillian and Emmeline – snuggled up in Wraith Cottage, reading and talking and whatever else they did together. I couldn't wait to tell Chas – the family secret had come to light – nothing but two old dykes living together, harmless, quite sweet really.

And then I noticed something familiar – a row of my novels – every one of them as far as I could tell. I picked out one of my early ones, published under my maiden name of Rampling. It was well thumbed, had obviously been read. Cheeky old things – they'd been keeping an eye on me for years.

CHAPTER 6

Emmeline was feeling energised. She knew she was being fuelled by anger and grief and hope. But she hadn't experienced so much energy for a long time and the more she felt it the more she was convinced that she was doing the right thing for everybody. She was aware that Neptune and Marguerite knew that something was going on. She had never been able to keep anything hidden from them – especially Marguerite, who seemed to know everything well in advance of her anyway. But they weren't questioning her. They knew she would tell them when she was ready.

She just needed one more session with Jane. The meeting with her that morning had gone well. Jane seemed entranced with Wraith Cottage and full of questions. But Emmeline had found herself struggling to keep down her grief as Jane talked about her Aunt Lillian. And then she hadn't found it easy to tell Jane that she was living in the cottage and had been Lillian's partner. She was frightened that Jane might get angry and tell her she would have to leave. It had all taken far longer than she thought and then she'd heard Loot barking; Neptune and

Marguerite were back, and she had to rush out and head them off.

But Jane was coming back tomorrow. She wanted to tell her enough to convince her to bring Henry over to the island and then she would have him.

She felt restless. Marguerite was having an afternoon nap. Neptune had gone home to Puck's Bay to repair his fishing nets. She wandered outside. The air was sweet with honeysuckle. On an impulse she went through the garden gate and picked her way across the meadow to the tumbledown wall that marked the boundary of the old hotel grounds. She hadn't walked this far in ages. She urged herself on to the steps of the terrace and sat down, panting. Her heart was pounding. She was being foolish, she didn't want to die yet, not now she had got this far. Her head was spinning. She leaned against the terrace wall, waiting for her breathing to slow, her heart to calm.

It used to be so different here, the roses pruned, the beds full of flowers, the lawns mown. She could hear the thwack of tennis balls on racquets. The four of them used to play together sometimes. She and Lilly were always upsetting Victoria and Henry by forgetting the rules. They would much rather have been running on the beach barefoot, collecting treasure, sorting out the cave. Those youthful days – at the time they had seemed endless but they had come to an abrupt end.

Emmeline felt anger flood her chest adding to

the labouring of her heart. She mustn't get complacent now. She had to keep those past memories vivid and clear.

'Lilly,' she called out loud. 'You must help me. You have to go on.'

'Be calm, Emm. Look at the sea. Calm yourself and I will continue.'

Emmeline looked out across the slope of the grounds to the glittering sea. It was indeed calm. She closed her eyes, listening deeply within her mind for the thread of Lilly's story . . .

My legs buckle as I get off the bed and I fall down. I crawl to the door, needles of glass piercing my hands and knees. The bolt is immovable – I can't remember having used it before. I summon a residue of strength and shove, it gives suddenly and I graze my knuckles on the rough wood. I lug the eiderdown to the floor and drag it over to where Emm lies. I tuck it round her and under her as best I can, feeling I shouldn't move her yet. I call her name over and over but she doesn't respond. The back of her head feels sticky when I slip my hand under it. Her mouth and nose are caked with blood. I stroke her cold cheeks and kiss her forehead, willing her to come back.

'You're safe now,' I murmur. She moans and her eyelids quiver and she trembles. I want to lie down and sink into oblivion with her. I feel beneath the eiderdown for her hands. The shock of their icy touch seems to motivate me. I stagger to my feet.

I am cold too but at least I'd been on the bed. Emm has been lying naked on the flagstones for I don't know how long.

I stumble around looking for my dressing gown. I wrap the harsh wool tightly round me, covering the stickiness of my body, the stench of Henry that seems to saturate me and permeate the cottage. I have to make the decisions now, there is no one else to rely on.

Heat – that is what we need. I have to warm up Emm, and keep myself from getting any colder. I tease the fire back to life with kindling and add drift-wood and logs until it starts to roar. Drifter crawls out from behind the armchair, wild-eyed, and rubs herself against me, appreciative of the heat. I feel so glad to see her, a little scrap of companionship. I shove my leaden feet into Emm's tartan slippers and push the armchair back so that the warmth of the fire won't be obstructed. I shuffle to the kitchen. Thankfully the range is still alight and I stoke it up. Trying not to retch, I carry the bucket containing Henry's urine into the outhouse and empty it down the lavatory, flushing it with another bucket of water. Then, holding my breath, I force myself to sluice his vomit from the kitchen sink. Each time disgust threatens to overwhelm me I turn my thoughts to caring for Emm. I can't allow myself to think about any of that yet.

I put water on to boil and hang towels on the range. I go back into the outhouse and search for the back door key that we never bother with. I end up jamming the wooden workbench against the door, knowing that it won't stop him if he chooses to come back. I feel my limbs beginning to warm up and with the warmth comes stinging and dull aches.

As soon as the kettle starts to sing, I fill a basin and try to bathe Emm's face, worrying whether I am doing more harm than good. Where has all this blood come from? As some of the clots come away I see that her nose has been bleeding and she has a deep cut in her top lip. And then I realise that embedded in her lip is a tooth. I pull it gently away and it rattles into the basin. Tears run down my face – poor, poor Emm. How could her own brother have done this to her? Both her eyes look puffed and bruised underneath. She must hurt so much. I kiss her forehead again and again, calling to her. Her eyes keep flickering open and she lets out little groans. I put my hands under the eiderdown. She is still so cold. I feel panic-stricken – what if I can't warm her up? I ought to try and get a doctor, but how can I leave her? Supposing she sinks deeper and –

'Emmeline!' My panic gets the better of me, I find myself shrieking her name. Her eyes open and stay open, staring at me blankly. She tries to lick her lips and winces with the pain.

'So . . . cold,' she whispers.

'I know, Emm. I know. But you'll soon be warm again, I promise.' I pull back the eiderdown thinking that the direct heat of the fire might be better. I rub her arms and hands and legs and feet, wrapping each limb in hot towels. 'Move,' I command her. 'Move your arms and legs.' She does as I tell her. I make her turn her neck gently from side to side. She whimpers but at least I know that nothing is broken. Eventually I manage to get her propped into a sitting position so that I can see the back of her head. I bathe it, causing the bleeding to start again, but now I can see that she has a gash about two inches long. It probably needs stitches. I place a wad of cotton wool on it and tie a bandage around her head. Then I get her to swill her mouth out with warm water. This is the worst part, the most painful. Her lip has swollen alarmingly. She spits into the bowl and out comes another tooth. She stares at it in horror and I see her running her tongue around her mouth to find out where it has come from. She looks up at me, her eyes brimming with tears.

'Oh, Emm,' I say, helplessly.

She reaches out a hand to me. 'You . . .' she whispers, 'you all right?'

I nod, avoiding her gaze. I hold a mug of warm milk for her to sip.

'The best place for you is in bed, my girl,' I say briskly. I get up and strip the sheets and pillowcases blindly, roll them into tight balls and feed them to the blazing fire. I get fresh bedding from the linen chest and remake the bed. I help Emm get up and pull a warm nightgown over her head as if she were a little girl. She feels less frozen now and crawls gratefully into the bed. She lies propped against the pillows while I make hot water bottles and help her swallow some aspirin. She seems drowsy. I feel scared to let her drop off to sleep, unsure whether she might lapse into unconsciousness again. What a fool I am, knowing so little about first aid. Drifter resumes her usual position on the bed and I notice Emm reach out to stroke her. Heartened, I go to the kitchen.

I heave the tin tub down from the outhouse wall, put it in front of the range and fill it with hot and cold water. I don't want to take off my dressing gown. I don't want to have to confront my own body, make it all real. Slowly, I undo the gown and let it fall to the ground. I close my eyes and hold my breath, trying not to breathe in my own smell – Henry's smell. I step into the few inches of water, wishing it was deep enough to cover me completely, over my head. I want to be under a waterfall that will dash over me and through me until I am scoured clean. I stand shivering and trembling, willing myself to open my eyes.

I look down at my legs, white and thin – they are streaked with mud from Henry's shoes and dotted with the reddish-mauve beginnings of large bruises. My knees are bleeding, punctured by splinters of glass. My thighs and pelvis are bruised and grazed from his remaining buttons and braces. My breasts feel tender, dotted with blue finger marks. My upper arms are more mauve than white and I have little cuts around my chest and neck which must have been caused by his starched collar. Worst of all is between my legs, where the light hair glistens with Henry's stuff and my delicate skin looks almost black, streaked with blood.

I double up my body, glad that I am so small, and lower myself into the water. It stings and I feel something deep inside my belly throbbing. But the heat feels soothing. I reach for the bar of coarse green soap and the scrubbing brush that Emm and I use to wash our clothes. I scrub every inch of my body making the grazes bleed and the bruises more livid. It doesn't hurt; it seems like someone else's body that I am washing. I rinse myself down with jugs of water from a bucket until the floor is awash and my stinging skin feels clean again. I rub myself dry with a coarse towel and put on a thick winceyette nightgown.

I brew tea and make a warm mouthwash for Emm. I stand by the bed looking down at her. She is staring at me, her eyes look puzzled in her strange, swollen face. I climb into bed and sip my tea. I don't want her to ask me anything. I don't want her mouth to hurt making words or her heart to break forming questions. But I can feel her eyes on me still. Her hand touches mine; it feels cool but not cold. She reaches up to my face, so that I have to turn towards her. Her eyes are insistent.

'Lilly,' she whispers, 'tell me . . . did he . . . ?'

I place my mug carefully on the floor and sit for a while looking at her hand in mine. My head nods slowly as if making its own decision to tell, and then my body allows itself to feel the shock. I feel myself jerk deep inside and then start to shake as if I have unleashed an earthquake. I push Emm away from me and fly out of bed, back to the kitchen. I hoist my nightgown, grab the scrubbing brush and shove it between my legs, trying to force it inside myself. My throat feels as if it might rupture with sobbing. And then Emm is holding my wrists, prizing the brush out of my hands. She guides me back to bed and holds me as best she can. It seems that we shake and weep together until daylight glimmers through the windows and we finally fall asleep.

I wake as Emm struggles out of bed. Her mouth has been bleeding again during her sleep and with the bandage around her head and her two blackening eyes, she looks like a war casualty.

'Sorry,' she manages to whisper. 'Need to wash and wee.'

'Wait, Emm. I'll help you.' I start to sit up.

'No, you rest.' She pads off to the kitchen. I know she will be looking for the bucket. This weather we do most of our necessary functions indoors. I hear her rummage under the sink and then pull back the blanket that covers the outhouse door. I hear the squeal of the pump handle and the rush of water. I feel warm now but I can't bear to be lying in bed knowing how she must be hurting. Perhaps she is looking at her face in the mirror, inspecting the damage.

I get out of bed and stack up the fire. Drifter rubs around my legs, demanding food. I go to the kitchen trying to avoid being tripped up by her. My body is stiff and aching with a sharp pain deep inside as I move. I fetch some fish from the larder and fill her bowl and top up the kettle on the range. I notice the large pan of turkey stew that we'd made yesterday, waiting to be heated up for tonight. I lift the lid; the rich smell of meat makes my stomach heave. It is midday already and we've invited Woody and Neptune for a New Year's Day supper. We can't let them see us like this. What on earth are we going to do?

I look around desperately, realising it is Emm I am looking for. She always knows what to do, laughing away problems, making them shrink, thinking of solutions that I could never come up with. Emm embraces life, sails along with it, she says. But Emm is hurt. A gust of wind rattles the windows and hurls gritty rain at the latticed glass. Perhaps it will be too stormy for Neptune and Woody to get the boat out. But then they will walk up the cliff path and across the fields. They are resourceful those two – like Emm.

She comes back into the kitchen holding up a large iron key.

'Under flowerpot . . . locked now,' she mumbles. She walks over to the sink, pours hot water from the kettle into a bowl and sluices her face. I flinch while she does it. She pats herself dry with a towel and then unwinds the bandage from her head. She fetches her cedarwood box of medicines and sits down at the table. Using two mirrors she inspects the back of her head and then her face and mouth. I watch her closely, feeling her horror, but she doesn't break down.

She gingerly puts on her wire spectacles and begins to select an assortment of potions. She'd always grown herbs in the hotel garden, brewing up different concoctions, consulting her thick reference books. Her jars are labelled with Latin names, stored with care. She tries to teach me too, telling me stories about the remedies – how mountain goats seek the yellow stars of arnica if they tumble over rocks, and marigolds absorb so much sun they just have to give some back to warm and soothe. But when faced with suffering my mind goes blank and I sink into a state that I don't understand, seeking something obscured by a layer of fog. I can't always penetrate it but if I do, I feel lightness and relief and so does the person or animal that needs healing. I wish I was clever like Emm, but she says both ways have value.

I help her apply her selected ointments, and then I cut a patch of hair from around her head wound with nail scissors and she soaks a pad of lint in a lotion and I fix it to the back of her head with sticking plaster. She dampens her flattened hair with camomile and I brush it back into its halo of light brown curls. She inspects her mouth again in the mirror. She's lost two of her front teeth, one top and one bottom. I try hard to stop my tears falling, watching her being so brave, but fail hopelessly. I put my arms around her.

'We'll make it better, Emm. We'll get you some false ones made,' I sob.

She hugs me back and I wince. She holds me at arm's length as if inspecting me. Not much of me shows, engulfed as I am in the big nightgown.

'Your turn.' She gestures at me to take it off.

'No, I'm all right, honestly.'

But Emm undoes the buttons and slides it down so that it drops around my ankles. Her face freezes and then contorts as if something inside her wants to burst out through her eyes. She puts her hands on my shoulders and turns me round examining me. I feel her shaking with rage. When I face her again, she looks like someone I've never seen before. For the first time, I feel frightened of her.

'He will pay for this,' she says, and her voice seems to come from deep in her throat. She then dabs and smears me with her ointments and lotions, picking out tiny splinters of glass from my legs and hands with tweezers. Finally, we both get dressed in slacks and thick jumpers and socks as if protecting our injured selves from further harm and cold.

The wind howls and the rain turns sleety, clattering against the windows. It rarely snows or stays freezing for long on this mild southern shore. Emm agrees with me that Woody and Neptune won't be deterred by a spot of blustery weather from having supper with us.

'We'll tell them we slipped last night coming back up the cliff stairs,' I say.

'Won't believe us – never done that,' Emm replies, in her strange new voice.

'We could say we were drunker than we thought.'

Emm shrugs. 'We could tell them the truth,' she mumbles.

'No, Emm! They'll go mad, they'll go after him.'

'Well?'

I remember Henry's parting threat to me as he left. He is a powerful man. It is our word against his – a respected doctor. Of course nobody will believe us. 'It won't do any good, Emm. Woody and Neptune will end up in serious trouble. There'll be a terrible scandal and we'll be ridiculed. We'll lose – women always do, you know that.'

'I'll go to the police then.'

'That will be just the same. Don't you see?'

'You'd let him get way with it?' Her eyes flash in their swollen flesh.

'No.' I put my head in my hands. 'But we have to think of something else. Some other way.'

'It'll be too late if we don't do something soon.'

'Just wait a while, Emm. Until we're both feeling a bit stronger.' I can see she is exhausted and so am I. I can't think any further than getting through the next few hours.

We manage to put the cottage to rights between us. We sweep up the glass and Henry's mud, rearrange books and shells, fold the bed back into a settee and sweeten the air with lavender. We heat the turkey stew and warm the bread and the remains of the

Christmas pudding. We make brandy punch and a jug of custard. We tidy each other and Emm combs rosewater into my hair, teasing out the tangles. We try to look sheepish as if we'd been rather silly.

Woody and Neptune arrive about seven, windswept and breathing fresh clean air into Wraith Cottage. Booty rushes around sniffing every corner, wagging his whole body as if he's never been here before. Drifter retreats behind the armchair, less pleased to see him than he is her. Despite my exhaustion I am glad to see them and I can sense that Emm is too. They dump waterproofs and boots in the porch and bottles of beer and a bag of broken biscuits on the table. They swig the hot punch, and tell us there have been several minor slips along the cliff-edge and our steps will need inspecting before we venture down to the beach again.

It isn't until Emm comes out of the kitchen and into the lamplight – which we'd kept purposefully dim – that they both stop talking and stare in horror at her face. She'd tied a flowered scarf around her hair, gypsy-style, to hide her head wound. She looks quite jaunty from the back. We both have on rollneck jumpers so nothing much shows on me apart from my pallor, some bruising on my bottom lip and my grazed knuckles.

'My God, Emmeline. What happened to you?' Neptune takes her by the shoulders and turns her towards the light. Woody's jaw drops, he turns pale and sits down.

Emm tries to laugh. 'Tell them, Lilly.'

I launch into our prepared story of too much gin and slipping on the cliff steps. My laugh sounds contrived even to my own ears.

'Have you seen a doctor?' Woody asks.

Emm shakes her head, carefully.

Neptune turns to me. 'Why on earth didn't you come and get us?' His voice sounds angry, for him.

I shrug. 'In this weather?' I go to stir the stew, trying to look casual. 'Emm's okay. We've got our own medicine and we'll go to the dentist when she's better.' I attempt a giggle. 'To tell the truth we were ashamed to admit to anyone that we were so tipsy.'

There is a lull while I ladle stew and Emm lights candles and opens the beer. I glance at the men and see them looking at each other, passing silent messages. We've known each other too long for them to be fooled by our flippancy. I am aware of their questioning eyes fluttering over our faces and hands as we attempt to eat, trying to make sense of it all. Poor Emm can hardly eat and I try to find her a straw. I open drawers and cupboards, prattling on and all the time I feel as if I'm crying inside. After we've eaten we sit slumped, while the men roll and light cigarettes. Woody suddenly slams down his beer bottle and looks at me.

'Why didn't you go up to the hotel and phone Henry? He's a doctor for Christ's sake.'

I feel as if he's blaming me for Emm's injuries. My eyes fill with tears. Emm puts her hand on mine.

'I wouldn't let her, that's why. The last thing I

wanted was Henry around me, moralising and lecturing.' She speaks firmly and the effort shows. She puts her hand to her mouth.

Neptune stubs out his cigarette and gets up. 'I think we ought to go, Wood, and let Emmeline rest.' He pats her tenderly on the shoulder. 'You shouldn't be talking at all.' His face is full of concern. Dear Neptune. He is the same age as Emm, but looks older than his twenty-five years with his gaunt weather-beaten face and thinning hair. They have always been close. I wish again that he was her brother instead of Henry. He turns to me and squeezes my arm. I gasp as his thumb presses into one of my bruises. He looks at me quizzically. 'We'll call in tomorrow evening to see how you both are and if you need anything. Get some sleep.' I nod and look away.

They pump water for us, filling our containers, then bundle themselves into their outdoor clothes and carry in piles of logs from the woodstore. Booty rouses himself from his hot spot in front of the range. After they've gone we stand and look at each other, relieved to be on our own but sad that we've deceived them. We wanted to protect them but it seems they've gone away feeling mystified and shut out by our strange behaviour. With our last bit of strength we unfold our bed-settee and for the first time we walk around Wraith Cottage checking the window catches and locking the doors. We heap up the fire and stoke the range. We lie in the firelight, Drifter purring at our feet.

'Why did Henry come here?' Emm asks, her voice thick.

'I suppose he went to the hotel first and thought you must be here.'

'No, Lilly. There's no reason why he should drive out to see me after leaving a party in the early hours of the morning.' She shifts in the bed, turning to look at me. 'He had this all worked out. He didn't go to the hotel at all. He planned to sneak out to the cottage, and rape you. But he didn't count on me being here.'

It sounds so blunt and final now that the word has been spoken. Like a life sentence. Rape. I'd been raped. 'Why . . . but, why?' I ask lamely, knowing that she is right.

'Because he's always wanted to and saw his chance. Victoria packed off home, him driving alone full of alcoholic bravado. Why not take a little detour and call in on Lillian – wish her a happy New Year? He could say you seduced him if you complained – made out you'd given him the eye. What can a poor chap do – men can't help themselves you know. And then he arrived and discovered you and me together. He must have felt he'd hit the jackpot. He could let out all his hatred and frustration and lust in one go.'

What she is saying makes me feel worse. Had he really been thinking like that about me all along? Had he thought that I wanted him to do that to me? I always felt he regarded me as a soppy girl – his sophisticated wife's little sister. He smirked if she called me Silly Lilly in front of him.

'Emm. I never led him on. I –'

She puts a finger to my mouth. 'Ssh, Lilly. I know you didn't. Don't ever think you were in any way to blame. He's a monster. And he's going to regret this for the rest of his life. Now let's sleep.'

I lie awake sensing the atmosphere of the night. There is nothing unfamiliar, apart from Emm's snuffly breathing, and an absence of light where my glass angel had been . . .

Emmeline came back to herself feeling disorientated. The side of her face was pressed against the stone wall of the terrace. She felt stiff and suddenly frightened, wondering if she had the strength to get up and walk home. She eased herself away from the wall. A shadow fell on the ground in front of her. She looked up and there was Marguerite, beloved Marguerite, wearing her sapphire blue dress. She bent towards Emmeline, her long silver hair slid forwards over her arms as she held them out. She took hold of Emmeline's hands and eased her to her feet.

CHAPTER 7

I spent the afternoon at Ventnor Botanic Gardens, dawdling through aromatic plantations of southern-hemisphere exotics. I buried my nose in flirty flowers until I felt as drowsy as a bumblebee. How mild the climate must be on this fringe of the island for these plants to survive the English winter. No wonder this site had been chosen for the chest hospital. I could imagine ashen-faced, wispy people with crimson coughs, drifting along these paths, beginning to blossom, their lungs sprouting fresh supple branches.

I sat on the grass here and there, tuning in for my birthplace, a gasping of air, an invisible slap on my bottom, but I couldn't locate it. I watched green wall lizards basking in the sun, flicking their tongues. I ate a tuna sandwich and drank tea in the airy visitor centre, wishing my fairy godmother would appear, wave her wand and grant me retro-cognitive powers. I browsed through more photographs of the old hospital – rows of cottages with verandas facing the shore, stretching for half a mile. But nobody knew about physicians' houses – if they still stood, or where they had been. The woman in the gift shop advised me to go to the local history society, they would have records, she said. I decided to leave that and the Coastal Visitors' Centre for another day. I bought a book on Wight wildlife and a jellybean plant for my garden and headed back to the flat.

I opened the windows and lay on the bed, sleepy, listening to sounds from the other apartments, replaying my visit to Wraith Cottage, wondering whether I'd been too hasty telling Emmeline she could stay there indefinitely, but I really had no choice. I wanted to get my hands on it, sort it out, maybe use it as a writing retreat – if I could cope with the fear of living life on the edge. Emmeline looked frail and must be well into her seventies, but she was pretty agile, she might live another twenty years. Chas would be mad at me for rushing into things. He would have found out about the viability of the property first and the question of rent. I must try to be a bit more forthright with her tomorrow if I was going to loan her my inheritance. After all, who exactly was she? Did she have any relatives or was she a loner like Lillian? If so, what would happen when she died? Would I have all her stuff to sort out too?

The truth was that I'd been deeply moved by Emmeline and her description of Lillian. Beautiful, gentle, loving, a sensitive, she'd said. And my father had called her a strange, mad thing. He must have been so baffled and shocked by her. But I sensed Emmeline's love and pride in their relationship.

Would it have been so shameful fifty years ago to be a lesbian? Yes, of course it would, judging by the intolerance that was still rife today.

I was looking forward to returning to Wraith Cottage tomorrow now the surprise had calmed down. I wanted to take it all in – the view and the garden, the strange sculptures. I wanted to find out more about my mother and her sister. What were they like when they were young? Emmeline said Victoria had been different before she met Henry, so perhaps they'd known each other as young girls. It was as if my mother had suddenly come to life, all this time after her death. Emmeline indicated she had more to tell me or show me. Perhaps she had some old photographs. She might be able to fill in the gaps – where my parents lived and I was born.

I wondered if there was more to this inheritance than just the result of a solicitor's search. Lillian knew I existed. She had my novels. If she'd read them she must have known that I had open views on all types of relationships. She could have contacted me through my publisher who forwarded mail to me. This family feud obviously ran deep. Perhaps there was too much bitterness on both sides or maybe gentle Lillian simply couldn't face any more contact with her prejudiced sister and brother-in-law. Why did I always have to look for something more than the obvious? But perhaps that was a good sign – my imagination might not be stone dead after all. I dozed, planning to shun the fridge and go for fish and chips and a glass of wine later.

I was woken by someone tapping at the door. I jumped up to open it, feeling disorientated. Erin and Rhian's mother stood there, looking uncertain. Had she come to tell me off for talking to her girls, touching them?

'Sorry to disturb you, but are you Jane Newcombe?'

I nodded. Surely I hadn't been recognised by a fan. That didn't happen, except at literary festivals or book launches.

'There's a phone call for you, down in the hall. I hope they're still there – I had to knock on lots of doors.'

I thanked her and ran down the stairs. Who would be phoning me this time of day? Nobody knew the number here and I'd arranged to phone Chas in the evenings. But it *was* Chas.

'I've been trying to ring you on your mobile.' He sounded annoyed.

'But, Chas, I told you there's no signal here. I haven't even got it switched on.'

'Obviously. Look, Janey, there's nothing to worry about, but it's Henry –'

'Dad? What's happened?'

'He's in hospital. Nothing serious, they think. He seems to have had a stroke.'

'Nothing serious! A stroke!'

'Well, it might be serious. They want to run some tests on him. I didn't want to alarm you, but I knew you'd want me to tell you.'

'Oh, Chas, of course. When did it happen?'

'Mrs Watkins found him this morning, slumped on his desk. It could've happened last night, I suppose.'

'And he'd been there all night?' Poor Dad. My stomach lurched, imagining his fear and helplessness. Thank goodness the weather was warm – if it had penetrated Winter Wood.

'Maybe. He, er, can't speak. His speech has been affected.'

'Didn't you call in on him last night?'

'I couldn't. I had to work late – a meeting.'

'Right. I'm coming straight home.'

'Don't rush. He's in good hands. Tomorrow will do.'

'Tomorrow? No, Chas. I'll come now. I'll see you in about four or five hours.' I put the phone down before he could lecture me about concentrating on my driving. I had to go straight away. What if he should die before I got there? I had to tell him that I knew about Lillian and Emmeline. That I knew about all that wasted time based on prejudice and ignorance. I didn't know why. It was as if there was something I needed to sort out with him before it was too late. My mother was gone, and now Lillian. Dad was the only one left to confront.

I hastily packed my things and threw them in the car. I said goodbye to Erin and Rhian, who were even more energised after their Plughole experience, and gave the contents of my fridge to their mother. I left a message on the landlord's answer-phone and set off.

As I drove through The Undercliff I fought a strong urge to stop and battle my way through to Wraith Cottage to tell Emmeline what had happened. But that would take time, and she might not be there. But how was I going to let her know that I wouldn't be able to come tomorrow? What would she think when I didn't show up? It was no good; I had to put Dad first. I could come back any time but I would never be able to make my peace with my father if he died before I got there. I would write to Emmeline and explain. She must have mail delivered, or perhaps she picked it up from the village post office. I'd noticed an old bike with a basket on the front, propped against the cottage wall. Presumably she went shopping and paid bills.

Tears of frustration rose in my eyes. Why did everything always happen at once? I brushed them away, trying to concentrate on the narrow road ahead. It was as if Dad was doing this on purpose to thwart me. He'd told me not to come over to the island. That was ridiculous – he didn't even know I was here. Was he wondering where I was, why I hadn't rushed to see him?

I willed the ferry to sail fast and drove through the New Forest feeling my spirit sinking, not noticing ponies or pigs. I switched on the radio to try and take my mind off my disappointment and anxiety. There was yet another programme on about the royal family. Yesterday was the fiftieth anniversary of Elizabeth's coronation. Chas would enjoy it if he'd time to listen, he loved British history, he was quite patriotic really, although he wouldn't like to admit it – regarding himself as a liberal European. June second, nineteen-fifty-three – the year that I was born. I would be fifty in September.

It occurred to me then that all this family drama was happening at that time – fifty years ago on the little Isle of Wight – the disowning of lesbian Lillian, my protected birth and my parents' frantic flight to the mainland. Lives changed because of something which must have seemed insurmountable at the time. It had really very little to do with me and my life, but it was as if I'd been called in to witness its ending – the revelations, confessions and demise of the principal players. How strange that it had affected me so much.

Marguerite handed Emmeline the drawing she'd been working on. Emmeline knew this was a study of Henry. She had seen others of him over the years. She examined the swathes of colour, the intricate oval of many shades.

'Has something happened to Henry? Is he dead?' Emmeline asked. Marguerite shook her head. 'But he's ill?' Marguerite nodded and made expressive gestures with her hands, pointing out an area of dark colours on the drawing. She put a hand to her head, bending her neck to one side.

Emmeline put the drawing down and leaned back in her chair. So that was why Jane hadn't come. She had been called back home. It must

111

have been urgent for her not to come and explain. But why should she? Emmeline had waited and waited, pacing backwards and forwards, getting more and more distraught, until Neptune and Marguerite had sat her down and made her tell them what was going on. Neptune had offered to go into Ventnor and see if he could trace her but Emmeline knew that would be futile. She could have been staying anywhere.

'Damn Henry!' Emmeline shouted, making Marguerite jump. 'He always wins!' She felt she'd played a game of cat and mouse with him all her life. And although she'd fought his manipulations, he always managed to win because of his deviousness and power.

Emmeline felt her energy draining away again. She got up and gave Marguerite a hug. 'Thank you for the picture, darling. I think I'll go to bed now.'

She hauled herself up the stairs, pulled off her clothes and sank gratefully onto her bed. 'Damn you, Henry,' she said again. What if he should die now, just when she felt she was getting somewhere? What if Jane didn't come back – just sent her solicitor, or that lad that had been poking around the outhouse? She'd wanted to shout at him to clear off, but knew she'd better keep quiet. She hid in the bushes and made rustling noises to scare him. He'd seemed very anxious to run away.

What was going to happen to her and Marguerite?

She couldn't think any more. She wanted to drop into a dreamless sleep and never surface again.

When she woke it was dark. She could feel Lilly's presence in the room.

'Don't give up, Emm,' she was saying. 'Jane will come back. She has to, now that she's seen Wraith Cottage. I promise I'll carry on with the remembering. We'll call her back, you'll see.'

Emmeline sighed deeply. 'Yes, Lilly. We have to go on.'

'Janey, come on now, let's go home.' Chas was stroking my hair. I was falling asleep holding Dad's flaccid hand, the anaesthetising atmosphere of the hospital heavy in my head. 'Henry's okay. The doctor said he probably won't wake up until morning.'

'Your husband's right, Mrs Newcombe.' The ward sister loomed, blue and white, at the other side of Dad's bed, tweaking tubes, twitching sheets. 'Go home and get some sleep. We'll call you if there's any significant change in his condition.'

I looked at Chas for confirmation. He nodded confidently, as if he was the doctor. 'But supposing we can't get here in time?' I said.

'He's not in any danger,' the nurse continued, as if she'd seen the Grim Reaper pass through the room and give Dad the thumbs up. 'Believe me, if he was I would advise you to stay.'

I wasn't convinced. Dad looked to me as if rigor

mortis was about to set in. His grey face seemed collapsed underneath the oxygen mask. His jaw was slack, his lips puffing as he breathed. I'd hardly recognised him when I arrived. I thought the nurse had sent me to the wrong patient. At least he was in a single room. He would detest being penned in with the common herd. I noticed they'd written his name with its full title over his bed – Doctor Henry Rampling. That should please him.

I let go of his hand and got up stiffly. 'I'd prefer to stay,' I said. 'I'll go and have some coffee and come back.'

Chas surveyed me over his cup. 'Do you so desperately want him to go on living, Janey? He's eighty-five you know. He'll have to go some time.'

'Oh, I don't want him to suffer unnecessarily, Chas.' I grinned. 'Sounds like deciding whether to have a pet put down. But there's something I want to sort out with him and I don't want him to go until I've had a chance.'

'The Isle of Wight stuff?' Chas sighed and glanced at the cafeteria clock.

I could see he was exhausted and anxious about work, but I just had to tell him about Wraith Cottage and meeting funny little Emmeline who loved Lillian and the imminent scandal that had resulted in my mother and father fleeing, with reputation intact, from the island. I didn't go into all the details – like the fact that Emmeline was living in my cottage. I'd leave that for another time.

114

He listened with interest about the state of the property and land but without portraying much enthusiasm for the emotional content.

'So, what is it you want to confront Henry with, exactly?' he asked.

'Well, the fact that I met Emmeline – he's got to remember her, surely – and that I know about the family skeleton.'

'Is that fair on him, do you think, given all this happened fifty years ago? Why not just leave him be? Chances are he's forgotten it anyway.'

I felt deflated. It had seemed so important to me a few hours earlier to talk to Dad about it.

'I mean,' Chas continued, 'your parents only did what they thought was right, didn't they?'

'What, disowning Lillian for being a lesbian?'

'Jane. That's simply how things were in those days. Parents were still throwing daughters out onto the street for getting pregnant out of wedlock.' He laughed. 'Can you imagine the uproar Henry and Victoria must have seen coming – in a tiny community on a small island?'

Chas was right. But, there was something in me that didn't want to let this go. 'I just need to tell him that I know – and to see his reaction, if any.'

'Why? Isn't that just for your own benefit? He's ill, poor old chap. Don't try to make him feel guilty too. It will only push you further apart and what's the point at this stage?'

'It's more complicated than that, Chas.' I was having trouble trying to explain this. Yes, on the one hand, it was silly, let it go. But something deep inside me had been disturbed. And this disturbance wouldn't be laid to rest. It had started at New Year when Lillian died and it had got a grip. It had affected my writing and my feeling about my life. It felt like the walls of my world had collapsed, exposing something inside myself that I could no longer ignore. Everything seemed greyed-out now except the discovery of Wraith Cottage and the meeting with Emmeline which seemed to stand out in my mind with a luminous glow. I couldn't let it go. It wouldn't let me go. And I needed to ask my father about his memories.

I smiled at Chas, realising this was something I would have to do without his support. Chas was on the side of not getting involved in family aggravation if there was any possibility of avoiding it. That's why he never asked his relatives how they were with any real conviction that he truly wanted to know. 'Go home to bed,' I said, and saw relief relax his face. 'I'll sleep in the chair in Dad's room.'

Dad was still sleeping. I sat listening to the night noises of the hospital. I found myself missing the drag and hiss of the sea, the push of wind against water. I wondered what Emmeline was doing. Was she tucked up in bed in Wraith Cottage under patchwork shawls like a little doll in a dolls' house? Maybe on a night like this she would be in her cave in the cliff, wraith-watching. I looked at Dad, flat out in his hospital bed. How well had those

116

two known each other fifty years ago? They'd probably been around the same age. Dad would have been thirty-five then and my mother thirty, Lillian only twentyish. I supposed Emmeline could have been anywhere in that age group. Perhaps she'd been regarded as the older woman, leading young Lillian astray. I had the feeling that Emmeline wasn't as old as Dad though. She was certainly more agile and bright-eyed, even though they were both wizened and skinny. There was a similarity in their freckled, balding scalps too. But it was difficult to compare ages. They had led such different lives – Dad, deskbound, Emmeline leaping up and down cliffs, weather-beaten and nimble as a mountain goat.

At that moment I yearned to be back on the island. I slid down in the vinyl armchair, trying to relax. I would have to go back. As soon as Dad was well enough and I could leave him, I had to return just to make sure I knew everything there was to know. Until I'd done that, I felt I wouldn't be able to get back into my old life.

I woke up struggling for breath. Once again I felt as if I was being hauled up by my hair through murky water. This time I broke the surface. I couldn't see anything; my eyelids seemed glued together. Then my ears popped and I could hear someone calling, Henry! Henry! I leaped out of the chair, startling the night nurse who was taking Dad's pulse.

'What's the matter?' she whispered.

'Is he all right?' I asked, my heart thumping.

'He's sleeping like a baby, Mrs Newcombe. There's really no need for you to be here.' She left the room.

I pulled my chair closer to the bed. I'd been so convinced that I'd heard someone calling him. Did I cry out his name or was it my mother's voice I'd heard? Perhaps she was calling for him to join her. But I didn't believe in all that spiritual stuff. I had a vivid imagination as far as thinking up a good story, but I considered myself to be a very rational person with no time for ghosts and heavenly clouds.

I got up and opened the window. I could hear the wind sighing through the trees. I felt it cooling me down, calming me. And then, I realised quite clearly that my creativity hadn't deserted me. It had simply changed direction and refocused, that was all. It was now gazing at itself, me, its source. It had turned inwards and was searching out its own story at the very heart of me. I had to allow it. What it would discover would be the truth, not the fantasy world of my imagination. I had no idea where all this was leading, but go there I must.

The following morning, I went for a walk while Dad was being bathed. When I got back he was propped up against a stack of snowy pillows which made him appear sallow. But he did look better than yesterday without the oxygen mask distorting his face. I took a bunch of pink and white daisies, dusty mauve grapes and *The Times* – although I knew none of these were likely to excite him. I needed to collect his pyjamas and some personal belongings from Winter Wood but I didn't have a key. I'd asked him for one several times but he said there was no need as he was always there. It occurred to me though, that Mrs Watkins must have one, or she would never have found him.

'Dad,' I called softly. His eyelids flickered but he was breathing as if he was fast asleep. The left side of his face was drawn down, the corner of his mouth oozing saliva. His few strands of grey hair had been arranged over his speckled scalp as if it were an incubating egg. I picked up a tissue and wiped his mouth. I felt a wave of tenderness towards him. I'd never done anything like that for him before and he certainly wouldn't have let me if he was awake. How vulnerable he seemed. All those years that he'd kept me, my mother and the world at bay, and now he was helpless at last. I could do or say anything to him. He couldn't walk away or silence me. 'Dad,' I said again, but he remained resolutely asleep. Perhaps this was his last line of defence.

You and I are going to communicate if it's the last thing we ever do, I thought. I pulled my chair close, leaned over the bed, picked up his limp hand and rubbed it.

'Dad,' I called. No response, not a flicker. I leaned over him, my face close. His chin and cheeks were covered in fine silver stubble, his breath smelt stale,

I could hear a slight rumble deep in his chest. 'Dad,' I spoke sharply. I saw a small jerk of his body, the pull of one eyelid. 'Dad!' His right eye opened, his left eyelid raised slightly leaving a slit of eye exposed.

'It's me, Jane. How are you feeling?' The right eye slid towards me, his mouth contorted.

I backed off, knowing how he would hate me to have my face so close to his. 'You're looking better today,' I said brightly, jiggling his hand, trying to rouse him further. 'Look, I brought you some flowers and grapes.' His eye slid backwards and forwards as if he was trying to follow my words. 'Would you like a drink?'

I could see his tongue moving dryly inside his mouth. I picked up the plastic beaker and put the spout to his lips. The water ran into his mouth and trickled out again. 'Swallow,' I commanded. I wedged some tissue under his chin and tried again. He gulped down a few sips. His right eye had started to move backwards and forwards again and his hand shook as if he was feeling agitated. Good. At least he was awake now. I took the tissue away. His eye drooped. Oh, no you don't, you old bugger, I thought. You can't escape that easily.

'Guess where I've been, Dad?' I fixed his eye with mine.

His mouth stretched and his tongue felt around for position.

'L . . . L . . . L,' he struggled.

'London?'

He nodded.

'No. Thought I'd surprise you. I've been to the Isle of Wight.' I smiled cheerily, watching for response. Sure enough, I felt his hand grip mine and saw his throat convulse. His right eyeball oscillated as if seeking escape. 'It's a lovely place isn't it?' His right eye was now fixed on mine. 'All that tropical vegetation and rugged coastline. I went to the Botanic Gardens at Ventnor. Did you know that's where the Royal Chest Hospital used to be – where you worked?' He was gazing at me transfixed; I could feel his hand trembling. I hoped I wasn't overdoing it. What if this triggered another stroke? But I couldn't stop now, not while I had his attention. 'What a wonderful place to work,' I mused, 'facing the sea, lovely climate.' I gave him a few sips of water to wash this down. 'Oh, and I met old Bill Allain. He remembered you and your father. I had no idea that Grandfather Rampling worked at that hospital too. You never told me. You both seemed to be very highly thought of, you know. I felt very proud.'

I got up to let him rest and digest. I messed about with the daisies for a bit, humming jauntily. When I glanced at him I could see him watching me. I perched beside him on the bed. 'But the most exciting thing was, I found Wraith Cottage.'

Dad's body jerked and he started to cough, short painful spasms. His eyes were watering, tears and saliva running down his face. I wondered whether to call a nurse but I bathed his face with a cold flannel and administered water. His breathing sounded a little noisier now. But his eye was still riveted on me.

'All right now?'

He nodded.

'Yes, unbelievably, it's still there. The cliff has crumbled away, almost to the front door. The solicitor and the estate agent both advised me to wait for a while before making any decisions. There's a lot of coastal renovation work about to commence along that stretch of cliff and there may be a compulsory purchase order or, you never know, they might make it safe enough to live in. It's so lovely there – I could have a writing retreat. What do you think?'

He shook his head a little, side to side.

'Doubtful? Well, we'll wait and see.' I faked a yawn. 'I must go soon, let you sleep.' I laughed. 'You must be worn out after all this talking.'

My heart was beginning to race. I was trying to slow everything down but my mind wanted to bludgeon ahead, get everything said. But I knew that wasn't the way with my father.

'There's a nice little beach down below Wraith Cottage. I expect you remember it. I suppose it must be Wraith Cove. Anyway, it's practically cut off now by the cliff falls, so it's like a private beach. I climbed down there to explore. Very sheltered, lovely.' I picked up the newspaper and flicked through a few pages but I could feel his attention still with me. His hand twitched on the sheet impatiently.

'Oh, I forgot to tell you. When I was down on the beach I bumped into this strange old woman. She mistook me for someone else at first, I think she was a bit – you know – but then we got talking. And do you know what, Dad?' I looked at him. He held my gaze like he'd never done before in his life. 'She remembered Aunt Lillian.' I nodded slowly, reinforcing my words. His jaw dropped, his tongue fumbled around his lips. He held up his right hand as if to stop me. 'Did you want to say something?' I asked.

'Nay . . . nay . . .' he stammered.

'Her name? Oh, it was Emily, I think. No, Emmeline, that's right, she told me off for getting it wrong, said she was named after Mrs Pankhurst.'

Dad seemed to shrink back against the pillows.

'She said she would tell me her memories of Lillian. Apparently they were old childhood friends. She remembered Mother too. And you. Unless she was just senile and making it all up. I was going to call on her the next day but then you were poorly so I came home. Do you remember her, Dad? Emmeline?'

He was staring at me, mouth lax, his breath sounded quite creaky now. I began to feel alarmed. Had I exhausted him? I thought of going to fetch a nurse but then the door opened and one appeared.

'I've just come to do Doctor Rampling's obs. You can stay if you like. He'll be having some lunch afterwards.' She took Dad's blood pressure and

123

pulse and temperature, laid a hand on his fore-head. 'How are you feeling, Doctor?' she asked. He was lying with his eyes closed. I noticed there was a line of pink across his cheeks, making him look slightly healthier than usual. The nurse glanced at me. 'I think I might get Doctor Phipps to pop in and take a look at your father. His temperature is up a little and he sounds a bit chesty. I'm sure it's nothing, just a precaution. Why don't you go and get some lunch in the cafeteria and come back later?'

I walked around the hospital grounds, absorbing the smell of the cedars. I whiled away a bit more time sitting by the pond watching the Canadian geese teaching their bolshi manners to four fluffy grey goslings. I didn't want to rush back in too soon and upset Dad's lunch. He'd certainly reacted to what I was revealing to him about my discoveries. Perhaps I should drop all this cloak and dagger stuff and simply tell him that I would like to talk to him – when he was feeling better – about the past.

I wanted to know about Mum and her wild painting and her sensitive little sister, Lillian, and the supposedly grand hotel that was the family business. And I wanted to hear more about Dad's childhood, and my suffragette grandmother and the renowned Doctor Henry Rampling senior of The Royal National Chest Hospital. And I would love to hear – and understand – his version of the Lillian and Emmeline affair. And where did

Emmeline come from? She was named after the most famous of suffragettes – perhaps her mother had been a close friend of Grandmother Rampling then. My storyteller teeth were into this one.

When I walked back into the ward, the sister stopped me.

'Mrs Newcombe, before you go back in to see your father, Doctor Phipps would like a word with you.' She showed me into a room behind the nurses' station. Doctor Phipps had a long dark plait of hair. She perched on the edge of the desk, swinging her legs, showing blue jeans beneath her white coat. I wondered if she was going to lecture me about persecuting the frail and sick.

'Hi, there,' she said, 'nothing to worry about. But your father has developed a bit of a lung infection. This sometimes happens in the elderly because of shallow breathing, lung secretions stagnate, get infected. And he had a couple of cracked ribs didn't he, a while back? That would also have affected his breathing.'

'Has he got pneumonia?' I asked. Oh, God. That was the end wasn't it? Didn't they call it the Old People's Friend?

'Basically, yes. You're his sole relative aren't you?' I nodded.

'Well,' she said, flicking through notes. 'We have started him on a course of antibiotics – hopefully that will do the trick, we've caught it early. But,' she looked up at me. 'We do need to ask you – given his age and condition – about your feelings . . . if he

125

should need resuscitation. You see, it's our policy – unless relatives request otherwise – that we let the elderly slip away peacefully, rather than try to keep them going indefinitely.'

She ended this last sentence on an upward note as if it were a question. A habit of the young which annoyed Chas intensely. I sat looking at her. She was indeed very young. I wondered how she would feel if it was her father. Come on, I thought, she's a qualified doctor, doing her job.

'It may not happen,' she added. 'He might pull through just fine. But we need to know your wishes.'

No, I couldn't let him go, not yet. This wasn't fair. He would have to hang on in there. 'He does lead a very active life,' I lied. 'He was still seeing patients himself before this happened. Could you have a go? I mean, I wouldn't want him to suffer, but just a gentle attempt?' I didn't have a clue what I was talking about. I had flashes from films of people being punched in the chest. Dad's ribs would crumble to dust under that force I was sure. 'You know, not go on too long . . . if he doesn't respond.' My sentence ended on an upbeat like hers as if I was batting back the question. But she seemed to understand what I was saying. She nodded and scribbled in her notes.

'That's fine. Just so long as we know. Get a nurse to bleep me if you want to chat about anything. I'm usually around. You can go back in to see him now.'

126

Dad looked terrible. He had a drip into an arm vein and his face was covered with the oxygen mask again. His eyes were closed and I could hear his chest rattling. Guilt settled over me like a lead blanket. I felt he could never recover from this. And it was my fault – I had pushed him too far.

CHAPTER 8

Emmeline lay in bed, her breath rattling in her chest. She didn't know if she could muster enough strength to recover from this infection. Why, oh why, had she left it so late to sort this out?

Maybe she and Lilly should have had the courage to confront Henry years ago. But it had never seemed quite the right time somehow. It could even have made things worse. But was she to die now without achieving her aim? Even if she recovered would Henry die and escape retribution? Perhaps she should just let it all go and slip away quietly, be with Lilly. But what about Marguerite? Neptune was an old man now.

She felt herself sinking and then something touched her fingers. She opened her eyes. Marguerite was standing there putting something in her hand. It was a photo. She struggled to sit up and Marguerite helped her to put on her glasses. She was looking at a picture of Lilly. Woody must have taken it. Lilly was standing thigh deep in the sea wearing her navy-blue, school swimming costume. Her long hair was wet at the ends, darkening its fairness. She had just caught up some water to splash someone and the drops were captured in mid-air. Lilly was a slender little girl, laughing, innocent.

Tears sprang to Emmeline's eyes. Lilly had trusted in the goodness of life and the people she knew. Even after Henry's brutality and Victoria's cruelty she had recovered that trust. But she had never been the same laughing girl. Something had closed down inside her and diminished her joy and love of life.

Emmeline kissed the photo and closed her eyes. She felt Marguerite's healing hands on her chest as she fell into a deep sleep.

My father. Eighty-five years old and still in control. He hovered behind his barricade while I sat, vigilant as a sniper, waiting for him to peep out. His pneumonia fluctuated, so did my stamina. Doctor Phipps said he had guts. The nurses said he was strong-willed. The physio hefted his passive limbs and cajoled him to cough up that nasty stuff for her. Chas came and spread the *Financial Times* across Dad's legs, muttering over the share index, as if encouraging Dad to cash in and quit. I was torn between my desperation for him to recover and my repressed anger, which wanted to screech at him to piss off and have done with it.

I sat by his bed for aeons reading to him from newspapers, my novels – which seemed boring, even to me – and the geological history of the Isle of

129

Wight, along with assorted tourist guides. Each time I mentioned The Undercliff or Botanic Gardens, I emphasised the words and glanced up to see if any part of his anatomy would twitch, but there was no response. The nurses got to know who I was and brought in various copies of my books for me to sign. One of the cleaners ventured into a spot of literary critique and told me her views on what she thought worked and didn't work. I listened politely and told her I valued her feedback, but quite honestly I wasn't even registering which novel she was talking about. I was too immersed in my own story.

I wrote a letter to Emmeline, explaining why I hadn't shown up to meet her and that I would return to the island as soon as I could. Then, I was unsure where to send it. I did think about mailing it to the solicitor, Bill Allain, but I thought he might investigate who this person was, living in my 'hovel'. It was the same with the estate agent. I didn't want them to know about Emmeline occupying Wraith Cottage. I was sure she wouldn't welcome any snoopers. I thought of sending it undercover to the nearest post office but if Emmeline didn't collect mail then an adventurous postman might go forth. And the cottage seemed to be almost midway between Niton and St Lawrence, so which post office anyway? I decided to leave it unsent in the end and aimed to get back there as soon as I could.

After a week of bedside tension, Chas picked me up at the hospital to take me out for a meal.

We sat on a terrace above a looking-glass lake on the west side of the Malvern Hills. I slumped in my chair, watching swans drifting and willows weeping, feeling like a newly released prisoner. The air felt soft and easy to breathe.

'Any change with Henry?' Chas asked, tucking into his garlic mushrooms.

'None.' I picked at a prawn. Why had I chosen these? They were too much effort.

'Is that good or bad?' He wiped his mouth on his linen napkin and sipped his chilled white wine with enjoyment.

I shrugged. 'Good, I suppose, in that he's still hanging on. Do you want these prawns?' I pushed them across. 'The staff are surprised at his tenacity.'

'It sounds like he can't make up his mind whether to go or stay.' Chas dipped prawns into the remains of his garlic sauce.

'Precisely.'

Chas glanced up at me between mouthfuls. 'Weary?' he asked.

I nodded, hoping he wasn't going to be too sympathetic. I could easily succumb to tears given a kindly word.

'You look pale,' he commented.

'I feel like a hospital flower.' I kicked off my sandals, feeling the cool flagstones. It was nice to be eating outside even if I wasn't hungry. 'Anyway, tell me what's happening at work.' Tales of the office had become a welcome diversion for me since my incarceration. It seemed there was a whole other world out there where people added up columns of figures and worried about them. It felt quite interesting to me at the moment.

Chas sighed and launched into details. I started to refocus from catheter bags and sputum samples to the bank rate, fund management, and the price of a barrel of oil. 'Remember the eighties, Jane, with new business and property all booming?'

I laughed. 'You were a bit of a yuppie, Chas, weren't you?' In fact, he had started calling himself Chas rather than Charles around that time. It seemed rather trendy.

We ate in silence for a while. Under stress, Chas ate more and I ate less. I slid my salmon around the plate, wondering if swans liked it.

'Sometimes,' Chas said, between mouthfuls of homemade steak and ale pie, 'I wonder what life's all about. I mean, why am I working like this? I don't seem to have that drive any more. I keep wondering if I should do something different.'

'Really? Like what?'

'Go fishing.'

'Fishing? A holiday, you mean?'

'No. Retire and potter about in a little boat.'

I put my fork down. We'd stretched our finances to the limit on our architect-designed home. Not suspecting that Chas's business would be destabilised by the aftershock of terrorist attacks, or that my flow of words would dry up like a river in the desert. Chas eyed my uneaten salmon and salad, obviously considering lean times ahead.

'How would we manage? I don't want to risk losing our home,' I said.

Chas sighed. 'Well, couldn't you write a bit while you're sitting around at the hospital – take the laptop in?'

I pushed my plate towards him. 'I can't possibly write under those circumstances. But we can't sell Birdsong – we'll need the space if Dad has to move in with us.'

Chas choked on a mouthful of food and I had to ask the waiter for water. While he was recovering I realised what I'd just said. It was an insane thing to say without thinking it through. I would probably kill my father in a week if he lived with us.

'Can't quite see that working,' Chas said, twiddling his wineglass. He ordered a brandysnap basket for pudding.

I returned to Dad's bedside, resigned to another frustrating vigil. Suddenly, he opened his eyes. He looked around bewildered, his left eyelid drooping. He saw me and grabbed my hand, grasping it with all his might. It took me so by surprise that I yelped.

'Jane! Jane!' he cried out.

'It's all right, Dad, I'm here.'

He started to struggle in the bed and dug his nails into my hand.

'Thith-der . . . thith-der . . . thith-der . . .' he said, his eyeballs moving, searching.

I sat on the bed and held his hand tightly in both

of mine, putting my face as close to his as I dared. His eyes looked wild. 'What is it, Dad? Who do you want?' He continued repeating his word. 'Are you saying, sister?' He nodded. 'What sister?' I asked. He pulled his hand out of mine and grabbed me by the shoulder. I was amazed by his strength.

'Jane, Jane. Thith-der,' he implored over and over. I felt helpless, near to tears. He had never held onto me, spoken to me, needed me like this before and I was letting him down.

'Do you mean the nursing sister, Dad?' Tears spilled from his eyes and mine. I wiped his away with my fingers. He shook his head, released his grip. His eyes closed and at last he fell silent.

I felt my own internal split – a disappointment that the pneumonia hadn't carried him off and the anticipation of knowing that our battle wasn't over. We hadn't finished with each other yet.

For the first time in her life Emmeline resorted to antibiotics. Neptune, ignoring her protests, had half-carried her across the field to the road where they caught the bus to the village. The doctor reprimanded her about missing her hospital check-up and told her he would rebook an appointment for her. She nodded meekly. There seemed no point making a fuss at this stage.

'Thanks, Nep,' she said, falling exhausted into an armchair when they got back.

'Just make sure you take them,' Neptune mumbled as he nodded off in the other chair.

'Oh, I will. I can't give up now.'

Emmeline felt dazed, her mind scattered after the anxiety of the visit to the doctor. The cottage felt stifling in the summer heat. She wished she had enough energy to go outside. It seemed ages since she'd managed the climb down to the beach. She visualised the sea splashing cool spray onto her as it met the rocks. She could hear Lilly's voice calling to her.

'Are you ready, Emm, to remember more?'

Emmeline felt her head nodding against the back of her chair. Or was it the wall of their cave? Lilly's voice echoed in her mind . . .

We stay in bed for most of the next day, dozing, listening to the moan and surge of wind and waves, occasionally getting up to make drinks or rescue the fires. We don't speak much or cuddle each other. I feel we are submerged in our own separate worlds, not knowing quite how to surface. I can sense bouts of rage rising up in Emm that she is trying to hold back. I don't feel anything except the physical soreness and bruising of my injuries. I am glad; I need something external to focus on. It is the internal that is so frightening. I tense between every lash of rain, listening for the different sounds that Henry would make if he returns.

In the evening we sit at the table trying to eat warmed-up stew. Emm's eyes are glittery slits in her swollen, multi-coloured face but I know she will heal quickly with the help of her remedies.

The south-west wind is droning without pause and we both jump when someone bangs at the door. My heart knocks at my ribs. Then I hear Booty's sharp yap.

'Neptune,' Emm confirms, peeping out of the window.

'Just Neptune?'

She nods and unbolts the door. Where is Woody? They nearly always turn up together. But I know why he hasn't come. Pain and injury trigger terrible flashbacks for him. Poor Woody, normally I'd be the one to help him get through it but not today. Neptune stands in his dripping oilskins looking us up and down, frowning; his face scoured red by the wind. We don't try to smile. I give Booty a quick rub over with an old towel before he can dispense damp mud over the cottage. Neptune opens his coat and produces a string bag containing half a loaf, some mackerel and a bottle of milk. He dumps it on the table and goes outside to fetch wood. He comes back in smelling of sawdust and wet earth. Emm tries to thank him but he holds up his hand.

'Don't try to talk, Emmeline.' He turns to me. 'Is there anything else you need today?'

'No, Neptune. Sit down for a while and have some tea.' We have a big enamel pot simmering on the range. He sits warming his hands on the mug. 'How's Woody?' I ask.

'Upset. He'll be okay – give him a day or two.'

I nod. The atmosphere feels strange. We've never been like this with each other before. I sip my tea, toying with a spoon. Neptune's eyes are searching the room. He scrapes his chair back and clears his throat.

'Look, I know something happened here after our New Year's party. Woody and me – we have our suspicions.'

I glance up at him. I must appear frightened. He takes my hand in his. It feels rough and reassuring.

'I know you don't want to tell us because of what we might do. But I promise you we won't do or say anything without your permission.' He rubs my hand between his callused palms. My grazes and cuts sting. I don't mind the pain. He is trying to get me to look at him. 'We only want to help.'

I gaze at Emm. Concern creases her forehead. We stay silent.

'Look,' Neptune catches hold of Emm's hand now, 'Woody and I know what it's like to be persecuted. We've been threatened and beaten up more than once, as you know.'

I remember Woody coming home from the war, initially hailed as a hero. There was even a bit in the local newspaper about our very own carpenter's triumphant return. And then he'd moved into Neptune's cottage and overnight they became known as queerboys, perverts. It had all died down eventually but not before the local yobs had shown their distaste.

'We know you didn't fall,' he continues. 'So, either some thugs were waiting for you – and we think that's pretty unlikely considering nobody knows about your relationship – it's not as if you live together openly like me and Wood. Or, it was Henry – he found out somehow and thought you might benefit from a good hiding.' He looks at each of us in turn. 'And we go for the second version.' His eyes continue to flick backwards and forwards between our two faces, looking for reaction. 'And you're trying to keep us out of it because you think we'll end up in trouble. Is that it?'

There is no point pretending. 'Neptune, listen. Henry could have you arrested if you so much as question him. You know he could. It would be senseless to get you both involved.' There, I'd admitted it now, no going back. Emm's hand is pressing my arm. I'm not sure whether she wants me to stop or go on.

'We understand that. And you're right – my first impulse is to rush over there and beat him to a pulp. Wood is more restrained. We've talked about this. We promise we won't confront Henry. But we need to support you two. To be different takes courage. You've always accepted us. We want to help in whatever way you want us to.'

I can see Emm's eyes overflowing. She sighs and nods.

'Thanks, Neptune.' I take a deep breath. 'All right. It happened because Henry came looking for Emm at the hotel and then came down here. We were in bed. He went berserk – knocked poor Emm flying against the door latch.'

'And you, Lillian? What about you?'

'I took a few blows trying to protect her. He blames her you see. Emm being older, plus all the pent up feelings he's had for years.' I hadn't planned that I wouldn't tell him the whole truth. I just can't. I can't get the words out. I can feel Emm watching me. I don't know what she wants.

'But why was Henry looking for you at that time of night, Emmeline?'

Emm starts to speak. I hold up a hand. 'He says he was worried about the hotel, all that old wiring, another fire.'

'And he drove out here from Ventnor, out of concern for his sister's safety? Doesn't sound like Henry. Why didn't he phone the hotel?'

I look at Emm for inspiration. She shrugs.

'Perhaps he did – and there was no answer,' I say. 'He didn't sit down and explain himself.'

'Sorry. I don't mean to go on at you. Just doesn't add up. Henry knew the fire brigade had disconnected the electricity and he never forgets anything.' He gets up. 'I'll go now and let you get some more rest. Keep the door locked. I would offer to stay but Woody –'

'We'll be all right.' I help him into his coat and give him a hug. He smiles down at me, his eyes so full of concern, it seems to me that he and Henry must be two entirely different species of male. I reach up to kiss his stubbled cheek. 'Thanks, Neptune, for everything.'

The wild weather wears itself out during the night

and we wake to sunbeams sneaking their way in through the salty panes. On a day like this, Emm and I would go hunting, picking our way along the littered sand, over slippery rocks, finding the treasures the sea had delivered to our beach. I want to be out there, breathing lungfuls of briny air, stretching my huddled limbs, feeling the wind raking my hair. But Emm isn't well enough to let the smallest breeze near her face and I feel scared to go out alone. I think I would feel nervous even with Emm, strong and fearless, beside me.

So, we sit beside the fire, staring at the glowing logs. Emm has Drifter on her lap, stroking her endlessly. I know she wants to talk but every time she attempts to speak I tell her to rest her mouth. It looks so painful for her to move her lips but, if I am honest, I don't want to talk anyway. It means I will have to start thinking, allowing my mind to delve into itself. Instead, I turn on the wireless and we listen to crackly music and doze. Occasionally I have to get up and wander around picking up shells and staring out of the windows. Emm prepares calendula mouthwashes for herself and guts Neptune's fish and stores it in the larder.

Mid-afternoon we are startled by a tap at the door. It doesn't sound like Neptune's hefty thump. I get up and tiptoe to the window.

'My God, Emm. It's Victoria.' She is the last person I expect to see. She never comes down to Wraith Cottage, not wanting to muddy her shoes or get her hair blown by the sea wind. She knocks again and calls out my name. I look at Emm, not knowing what to do.

'You'll have to let her in,' Emm mumbles.

I unbolt the door. Victoria practically falls in.

'Good gracious, Lillian. It's bitter out there.' She looks annoyed as usual. She has on her belted grey coat and a silk headscarf. She stares down at her fur-trimmed boots, frowning at the mud. 'How long does it take you to answer the door for heaven's sake? I expected you to be at the hotel. I thought I'd call in to see how the clearing up is going. Emmeline wasn't there either. I'd like to know where she's got to. She is still being paid as manageress.' She peels off her grey leather gloves and bends down to take off her boots, standing them neatly by the door. 'I came on the bus, and then I had to walk all the way down here. I dread to think what this will do to my chest,' she complains, moving towards the fire. It is then that she spots Emm in the armchair. 'Oh, my goodness. Who's that?' She steps backwards, narrowly missing my toes.

'Emmeline,' I say. 'It's Emm.'

'Emmeline? Look at your face. Whatever's happened to you?' She takes a few steps forward again and stops, staring at poor Emm.

I try to get in front of her to head her off. 'Try not to make her talk please, Victoria. She's in a lot of pain. She's had an accident. A fall.'

'I can see she has.' She turns to me, unbuttoning her coat and untying her headscarf as if she is preparing to sort us out. 'Why didn't you call Henry?'

'Because Henry wouldn't have been sympathetic.'

'Why wouldn't he?'

I attempt to look contrite. 'To tell you the truth, Victoria, we'd had a bit too much to drink and Emm slipped on the cliff path. Henry wouldn't approve of that now would he?'

She sits down in the other armchair and crosses her legs. 'You'd better tell me what's been going on here.'

Victoria always speaks to me as if she is my mother even though it is a role she detests. She sits, tucking stray hairs into her heavy chestnut chignon, while I feel compelled to recite the story of the beach party and the fall. I can tell by Emm's glower that she thinks I should just tell her to clear off. But I slip into the role of obedient child with Victoria just as she plays mother with me. It is all we know.

'I might have guessed,' she says, 'fooling around with those two fellows.' She leans towards Emm. 'You, Emmeline are old enough to know better, even if Lillian refuses to grow up. Why couldn't you have got dressed up nicely and gone to a respectable party? Henry would have driven you. Instead of which you mess around on the beach with those two chaps, drinking. Do you know what sort of reputation they have locally?'

'Victoria, they're our friends. It wasn't their fault. They'd already left when we slipped.'

'Any decent men would have seen you home. That's what I mean, Lillian. If you had let Henry –'

Suddenly, Emm leaps up from her chair; Drifter drops onto the hearthrug with an annoyed squawk. Victoria jumps. Emm towers over her, shaking with rage.

'You little prig, Victoria Rampling,' she shouts.

I can see her lip reopening. I hold out pacifying hands but there is no stopping her.

'Do you really want to know what happened at New Year?'

Victoria's face goes pink, her hands are trembling. Emmeline, although outspoken, has never lost her temper with her quite so violently before.

'Well, I'm going to tell you, Mrs Self-Righteous. My dear brother, Henry – your gentleman doctor of a husband – burst in here during the night. He knocked me senseless and raped your sister.'

Emm is literally spitting blood. Victoria puts her hands up to protect herself from Emm's fury. All three of us freeze while the implications of this sink in. Then Victoria makes small whimpering noises like a frightened animal. She shakes her head in a few rapid bursts as if trying to clear it.

'No,' she says. 'How dare you say that. How wicked you are, Emmeline.'

Emm lets out a hoot of laughter. 'Me? Wicked?' She sits down abruptly in her chair, reaching for her handkerchief. She dabs at her mouth.

Victoria looks up at me, her face now a pale oval. I am still standing, my legs shaking.

'You're making this up between you, aren't you, Lillian? Why are you doing this? Do you hate me so much?' Her voice is tremulous. Her dark brown eyes fill with tears and she starts to cry.

'Oh, Victoria. We don't hate you.' My legs feel unsupportive. I kneel down on the hearthrug between them. I try to put my hand on Victoria's arm but she pulls away. 'But Emm's not lying to you. It's true.'

Victoria's sobs grow desperate, her full bosom heaves under its beige cashmere. 'I don't believe you.' She glares at Emm. 'You and Henry – you never got on. He always said you hated him, ridiculed him when you were growing up. You and your mother. What are you trying to do, destroy him? And why are you dragging Lillian into this?'

'How was he then, on New Year's Day? Did he appear normal to you?' Emm's voice is muffled behind her handkerchief.

Victoria's face is red now. 'Of course he was normal.'

'He's even more callous than I thought. So, what time did he get in after the party?'

'I was asleep.' I can tell she is trying to think hard behind her answers. Her tears have stopped and she snaps open her crocodile handbag to find a handkerchief. A strong smell of violets wafts into the tense air and hangs there as if unsure where to go. She dabs at her eyes and nose. 'He stayed on with some colleagues after the party.'

'And you didn't notice the state he was in the next day? His muddy clothes and the stink of him? Bitten fingers? Maybe a scratch or two?' Emm demands.

'I didn't see him. He left early for work.' She uncrosses her stockinged legs and crosses them the other way. 'I won't be questioned like this. I don't know why you're doing this but you won't succeed.' She unfolds her handkerchief, smoothes it over her knees and refolds it, matching the lace edges.

I catch hold of her hands. She tries to pull them free but I won't let go. 'Victoria, why would we lie about this?'

'I have absolutely no idea.'

We sit for a while, me still clasping her hands. I feel something inside her cease struggling and let go as if she is giving in. Her desperate eyes look into mine and the pain in them feels overwhelming. 'Please tell me it isn't true, Lillian.'

I shake my head, 'I can't, I can't.'

'But, he's always thought of you as my little sister.' Her voice is hoarse, strangled. 'He wouldn't – you must have encouraged him in some way.'

That does it. I stop feeling sorry for her. I thrust her hands away from me. 'Victoria! I've never thought of Henry in that way and I'd no reason to think that he ever thought me more than his sister-in-law. I can't believe you would think I was flirting with your husband.'

'But –'

'Henry's cold and cruel. He's the last person on

145

earth I would want to go to bed with. He's repulsive to me now.'

Victoria breaks down completely, sobbing wildly. I look across at Emm; she nods, evidently pleased that I have spoken up at last.

'It's all my fault,' Victoria howls. 'I should never have married him. I . . . I just wanted someone. I'm not a good wife. We hardly ever . . . you know. And I can't have a baby – I don't know why.'

'You could have tests done,' I venture, taken aback by this sudden outpouring of my sister's private life.

'No! I don't even want a child now. Not by him. Anyway, I'm too old – nearly thirty.' She gulps and starts coughing. I pat her here and there, until she gets her breath back.

'What will you do?' Emm asks, not unsympathetically. 'You can't stay with him.'

'Please, please, don't tell anyone. I'll make it up to you both somehow.'

Emm lets out another bellow of laughter. 'What could you possibly do, Victoria? What can anyone do to repair this damage?'

'I . . . I'll pay for your teeth and –'

'Go away, Victoria,' Emm growls.

She looks at me in despair. 'Oh, Lillian, I don't know what to do.'

'No, Victoria. Neither do we,' I say flatly. I watch her while she staggers to her feet and fumbles with her outdoor clothes. Her breath comes in wheezing gasps. I open the door and she stumbles out, tottering down the path like an old woman . . .

Emmeline woke feeling disorientated. It took her a few moments to recognise Neptune sitting opposite her in the armchair where Victoria had been sitting just now. He was watching her with those deep shrewd eyes of his, that she had known most of her life.

'What's the matter? Was I snoring?' she snapped.

'No. Mumbling.' He continued to stare at her. 'What are you plotting, Emmeline?'

'I'm not plotting anything. Just preparing, that's all.'

'Then you should prepare yourself for the fact that he might not come. If Henry's very ill he is likely to die at his age. Even if he recovers, why do you think that he would even consider coming back here? I would think it was the last thing he'd want to do.'

'Lilly's been calling him – we all have in our way. Even you, Neptune. You've always wanted to confront him, haven't you?'

'Yes, but we're all so old now. I don't want you to get too wound up with all this. I want us to spend our last years in peace here with Marguerite.'

'I haven't got a few years, Nep. Even if Henry doesn't come, I'm counting on Jane. That's why I'm trying so hard to recall everything. Maybe, if Jane knows, she can confront him.'

'Have you considered that Jane might be like him? What if she doesn't believe you?'

'I know it's risky, but I have to do this. It's the only way to put an end to it all.'

Neptune got up stiffly and shuffled to the kitchen. Emmeline could see by the stoop of his shoulders how much this was weighing on him.

CHAPTER 9

I could feel my father's bony fingers pressing into my flesh. I couldn't free myself from his grasp however hard I wriggled. His hands seemed to be searching for my throat. I gasped and woke with a start. Chas was shaking my shoulder.

'Janey. Sorry to wake you but I'm off to work. I've brought you some tea and the post.'

He dropped a kiss on my forehead and crept out of the bedroom as if he was trying not to disturb me when he already had. I was glad he'd woken me from my dream though. I sat up and reached for the mug of tea, my heart still beating rapidly. What was it with these dreams? I'd had some discussions with the older nurses at the hospital, waiting for Dad to surface. They reported sensations of choking and breathlessness during the night and were divided about the benefits and risks of HRT. I finished up none the wiser.

I sifted through the pile of mail lying on the bed. The usual annoying circulars and bills and also a small padded bag. I opened it and a bunch of keys fell out. There was a note inside from Dad's house-keeper saying that as she hadn't heard to the contrary, she assumed that her services wouldn't be needed at the present time and would I kindly let her know when she was to resume. Meanwhile, she thought it best to return Doctor Rampling's keys to me. Oh, dear. I'd forgotten all about Mrs Watkins. I should have kept her informed.

I sat staring at the keys to Winter Wood. It struck me as strange that I'd never owned a key to the house which had been my home. I'd grown up there, but I thought of it as my parents' home, not mine. Birdsong was my home. Some of my women friends talked about going home when they were visiting their parents, even though they had long left and established their own territories.

I had access to Winter Wood now. That meant I could call in on my way to the hospital this morning and check the place. I could collect some of Dad's personal stuff, maybe something to read to him to stimulate his memory. Perhaps I should ask him first. He wouldn't like it if he knew I was poking about his house. But that was stupid. I was simply going to collect his pyjamas and if I asked him he would only say, 'thith-der.' Dr Phipps explained it might not be what Dad thought he was saying, that was why he was so upset. It was best just to nod and smile until he regained some strength.

Two hours later, I was letting myself into Winter Wood. The day was gloomy, but then it always was, under this louring hill with its dank vegetation and shadows. Whoever designed the house must have been sun phobic. The only aspect that faced south

150

had few windows. Even as I drove up the driveway I had the intrusive feeling that I was tunnelling into something that was trying to hide away. I stood in the dim hallway for a while, listening. All I could hear was the slow tock, tock, of a clock. I felt paralysed by freedom. There was a pile of mail on the doormat that had been pushed aside by my entrance. I bent to pick it up and stacked it on the hall table.

I opened each of the oak doors off the hallway in turn. Everything seemed clean and ordered, thanks to Mrs Watkins. I must remember to contact her. The sitting-room was as it had always been with its striped cream wallpaper and polished mahogany furniture. The dining-room likewise, the long table gleaming, silver candelabra precisely central.

The unmodernised kitchen had a quarry-tiled floor and a rambling oak dresser along one wall, its warped shelves laden with fussy bone-china tea and dinner services. What must Mrs Watkins think, cleaning all this with no one to use it? I moved on to the next room, a small library from which I'd stolen books when I was a girl and which doubled as a waiting room for my father's remaining patients. Next to this was a downstairs cloakroom with a white china cistern big enough to bath a child in, and then the holy of holies – Father's study.

I had expected it to be locked but then realised, of course it wouldn't be. This was where Mrs

Watkins had discovered Dad slumped over his desk. I stepped inside, smelling the familiar papery must. I glanced around; no sign of a drama. Mrs W must have sneaked in for a quick tidy, even though she wasn't allowed. It was odd standing in this room alone. I couldn't recall ever being in here without him glowering at me over his specs. I looked around for suitable reading material but it all looked the same to me. Would he want me to take him piles of files and journals to read? I went out again, closing the door quietly as if the room might register an intruder.

I went upstairs. The bathroom wasn't leaking water; the claw-foot bath was scrubbed. I collected his washing and shaving things and looked in vain for a wash bag. I supposed he'd never gone away anywhere. I went into his room next. The double bed still had the same burgundy eiderdown and bedspread and one central pillow.

Little memories were starting to nudge at my mind of being small and frightened, edging my way into this room at night and being ushered back to my own cold room by my mother. I looked in one of the walnut wardrobes. My father's clothes took up little space, dangling on their wooden hangers. I put his hairbrush and comb on the bed and opened drawers looking for pyjamas. I added these to the pile and his maroon dressing gown which hung on the back of the door. Everything was so old and worn. Didn't he like spending his money or did he just not notice or care? I was tempted to throw the lot out and just buy everything new. But he would be offended, and so would I if anyone had done that to me.

I opened the other wardrobe, looking for some sort of bag and was taken aback to find it full of my mother's clothes. The violet smell of her still lingered. I sat down abruptly on the bed which gave a surprised squeak. Dad had told me he'd got rid of all her things. I offered to help when she died and he said he'd already done it. I was upset because I'd wanted to keep something of hers. Why had he done that? She'd been dead for almost thirty years and I could still smell her. The violets were getting stronger as if they'd been let loose and were determined to make up for their long period of imprisonment.

Something in my chest felt tight and heavy. I got up and tried to open a window, pushing the rotten wood with the heel of my hand until it burst open, sending woodlice and small spiders scurrying for their lives. I breathed deeply. Would I ever understand this father of mine? Had he cared about her so much? Or had he just left it all and then forgotten? I pulled open the drawers of her dressing table. Sure enough, there were her yellowing lace handkerchiefs and underwear, a gold powder compact, dried-up leather gloves and a casket of her jewellery – pearls and rings and brooches.

I shunted out the stiff bottom drawer. It was

empty apart from something wrapped in tissue. I lifted it out. The tissue crumbled as I unwrapped it, releasing a dust of dried rose petals. It was a white lacy shawl – worn and ragged. But I recognised it immediately as my own baby shawl. I buried my face in it, evoking an avalanche of unnameable feelings – so intensely familiar, yet intangible. It seemed for a moment to be alive, speaking to me with a language of its own. It had always smelled of roses however grubby it became. This shawl had been my constant companion, an extension of myself, until I'd been packed off to school. Why had my mother kept it? Of all my baby things – why had she kept this tatty old moth-ridden shawl? I shoved it back in the drawer hurriedly, feeling overwhelmed with memories battling to surface. I closed the bedroom door before the violets and roses could escape and follow me through the house.

I peeked into the two spare rooms, one of which Chas and I had stayed in a few times before we bought Birdsong and lived close enough not to have to stay overnight. They both contained the same heavy, dark furniture, anonymous and cheerless.

Next was my own small room, the only bedroom which was on the south facing side of the house, managing to lure a little sunlight. My parents had wanted me to have one of the big scary rooms but I'd managed to get my own way. My single bed was still there. I hadn't slept in it since I was eighteen and left to go to university. Even before then I was seldom here, away at boarding school or staying with friends. But I did have some fond memories of it, lying on the bed reading for hours, or sitting at my little desk writing my fantasies. The window looked out on some gnarled apple trees, my enchanted orchard in which fairies and elves lived. My childhood books were still here on the shelves. I'd been planning to fetch them – if the day arrived when I knew I was going to have a child. Perhaps I would keep them, when the time came to clear the house.

There were some old dolls and teddy bears too, and a rather beautiful dolls' house – probably worth a fortune. My favourite doll, Daisy, was sitting on a shelf, her little rubber legs dangling over the edge. Her once bright blue eyes which opened and closed were staring, colourless. I tried to pick her up but her legs were stuck to the shelf. I prised them gently away. They were split at the knees and elbows and her china head was almost falling off its rotting neck. Daisy had been so special with her soft limbs and body. Every night, after my mother turned out the light and I heard her footsteps fade, I would get out of bed and tuck my dolls and bears, two by two, into drawers and shoe boxes, wrapping them tightly together so that if one woke in the night they wouldn't be alone. I'd kiss them all goodnight, then clasp Daisy to my chest, wrap my shawl around us both and whisper to her as I dropped off to sleep. When I was sent to boarding school it was absolute heaven for me to go to bed knowing that I was sleeping in a row of girls – one on either side of me that I could reach if we stretched out our arms.

I pressed disintegrating Daisy to my heart briefly then sat her back on the shelf, propped against a stiff china doll with moth-eaten hair, whose name I couldn't remember. My father asked me once to take them away, but for some reason I'd resisted. Perhaps I thought it was tempting fate to bring children's things into Birdsong. I sighed; there was no reason why I shouldn't take them now. Or maybe I would throw them away.

I went back out to the landing. I still hadn't found even a small suitcase. I decided to try the attics. Narrow wooden stairs led up there. I was always frightened of these rooms when I was small; convinced they were inhabited by toothless goblins and plump dwarves with hatchets. The door was stiff and I was showered with dust as I opened it – obviously Mrs W didn't get this far with the Hoover. There were a few cardboard boxes and bits of discarded furniture.

I went through another door into a room which had been made into a studio for my mother. There was a large skylight letting in the northern light that she needed for her intricate work. Her drawing desk squatted heavily under the window. The shelves still held her files, the labels faded and peeling. My father must have wanted to keep all her work too. What on earth was I going to do with it all? Perhaps I would have to bring in an expert to look at everything.

I pulled open some narrow drawers in the desk. They were filled with the dusty remains of her leaf specimens, crumbling at my touch. There were drawing boards and easels and boxes of pens and pencils, bottles of dried-up ink. Against one wall was a built-in cupboard. I opened the doors. It was full of moth-eaten sacking. I pulled some of it away, shuddering at the big spiders that I was disturbing. There seemed to be a stack of large drawings in here. I managed to extricate the first one, which was smaller. I laid it on the desk and carefully brushed away the dust. It was a watercolour, a child's painting, the standard house with a chimney and square windows, a path and a gate. I blew on the picture, removing more of the dust and some of the flaky paint. There was her neat name in the corner – Victoria Walding July 1933. The little house was perched on top of a cliff with the sea rolling at the bottom. And then I realised, with a jolt of recognition that sent shivers through my body, that I was looking at a painting of Wraith Cottage with its low thatched roof. The surroundings were different – the cottage set back from the cliff-edge, proper steps with a rope rail leading down to the beach, but there was no mistaking it. Was this why I'd experienced the feeling of familiarity when I'd confronted Wraith Cottage? I must have seen these paintings before, when I was a child.

I hauled out the larger canvasses. There were several more of Wraith Cottage painted in oils, around the same time. One of them was from the top of the cliff. There was another building in the background – it must be the old hotel that was now part demolished. It had a veranda running the length of the ground floor and fairy-tale turreted roofs, the whole thing festooned in wisteria and ivy.

I recalled Bill Allain senior mentioning that my mother's family had owned one of the grand hotels in Ventnor. Could this have been the one? It was possible, seeing as they owned Wraith Cottage. But there must have been dozens of hotels in and around Ventnor in those days. There was another painting of the hotel from the road, the one which had now collapsed, with the dilapidated sign that I had seen in the neglected garden. The paintings lacked perspective but there was a certain wildness about them, in the way the trees slanted in the wind and the sea curled and the clouds flew. I must take these, I kept thinking. I must have them. I will ask Dad, but I'll have them even if he says no.

I pulled out more of the paintings. These were bigger and bolder. Some violent storms were raging. They were dated over the next few years. No more Wraith Cottage or hotel – just wild seascapes, thrashing and heaving, tumbling and roiling. This is what Emmeline must have meant when she said Victoria once had spirit and talent. My mother. It seemed I never knew her at all. What had happened to her to subdue all this passion and brilliance?

I had taken all the large canvasses out of the cupboard now. There was one small one left behind, caught in the bottom of the sacking. I closed my eyes and delved down, trying not to think about spiders. I placed the fragile painting on the desk and brushed it off carefully. It was a beach scene. This one had some people in it – the only one of her paintings to contain humans. I turned it over. It was signed and dated nineteen-thirty-four. It was of three children playing on the sand. The oldest one was a boy. He was standing, wearing a white shirt with the sleeves rolled up and knee-length trousers like plus-fours. He was holding a fishing net and looked in his mid-teens. Crouching on the sand was a girl of about five, with light brown curly hair, her thin arms and legs bent as she concentrated on making a sandcastle. Sitting on the sand was an infant with white filmy hair, looking up at the two older children. Surely this boy was my father, Henry Rampling, as a youngster. There was something in his stance as he stood looking down at the two little kids and his black hair which waved back from his forehead. It was him, I was certain. He would have been about the right age. And the curly-haired girl? Who would that be? It couldn't be Victoria. My mother would have been eleven in nineteen-thirty-four and she wouldn't have painted herself. And the baby – might that be Lillian? She would have been about one year old. So who was the other little girl? My heart was palpitating with excitement. Could it possibly be Emmeline? She had told me she had known Victoria and Lillian since they were very young. I laughed at myself – I was making up stories again. The picture was too vague. These kids could be anybody, even children that my mother had imagined.

I looked through the pictures again, putting them into date order. I could see how they progressed from childish sketches and paintings into the huge tempestuous landscapes that Emmeline had talked about. And she had painted my father when he was a boy. They must have known each other since childhood. Did she know she was painting her future husband? I was beginning to form a revised picture of her in my mind. Something had changed her around the time of painting the children. I picked up a watercolour of Wraith Cottage and compared it to a bold oil painting of the sea and cliffs tumbling. Why hadn't I talked to her more when I had the chance? I looked at one of her framed leaf drawings on the wall, fading, spidery. My poor mother. I felt tears running down my face and land on the watercolour, blurring the edges, freeing the colours which had been held captive – just like the violets and roses – for such a long time. How would she feel if she knew I was doing this?

I gathered up the paintings and struggled down the attic stairs with them. I discovered some string in a kitchen drawer and tied them together. I found a carrier bag too and gathered up Dad's toiletries and pyjamas. As an afterthought, I ran back up the stairs, retrieved my baby shawl from my mother's drawer and collected Daisy. Then I put the rooms back as I found them, closed the bedroom window and left, taking my treasures with me.

Emmeline could only watch now when Marguerite and Neptune went out fishing and tended the garden. Her chest felt clearer but she couldn't summon the energy to do more than a few light chores – picking the vegetables and fruit, preparing the fish for supper. She spent a lot of time sitting in the shade of the sycamores, browsing through Lillian's old journals that she'd kept since she was a child. The past seemed more vivid and alive to her than these present sun-filled days spent in her chair. Sometimes she wondered if she should just throw all these exercise books away and let go, but then she looked at Lilly's careful writing and became involved in their old lives together and knew she couldn't. They weren't hers to destroy.

And Lilly no longer needed persuading to recall the past. When Emmeline showed reluctance to invoke those intense days, she would encourage her to go on, as if she was reading over Emmeline's shoulder . . .

The reluctant days of January enfold us in a dusky cocoon in which to curl up and recover. Our bruises start to fade from purple to bilious yellow. We grimace at ourselves in the mirror as Emm's face bulges and shrinks like an autumn fruit and my ribs resemble a piano keyboard. Her head wound scabs over and sprouts a track of fuzzy hair like a caterpillar. Emm consults her medical text-books and I lie on the table with a lamp between my legs while she examines me. I'd been bleeding ever since the attack and we want to find out where it is coming from in case I have an internal injury. She discovers several tears in my external flesh, probably made worse by my attempts with the scrubbing brush. She makes lint pads for me, steeped in herbs, the bleeding gradually stops and I feel better.

Each day our preoccupation with ourselves peeps outwards a little more and we begin noticing things about the cottage that need our care. We take down the Christmas decorations and start sleeping upstairs again but we still lock the doors. We venture out for walks when the wind drops. We pick a bunch of hazel twigs dangling yellow catkins and look for snowdrops under the crispy gold bracken in our garden.

Woody reappears, needlessly apologising for his absence. I cling to him like a limpet, absorbing his smell of sea and fish, tobacco and dog. I know he and Neptune are watching over us. We often spot them in the fishing boat out in Wraith Cove, scanning the land with Woody's army binoculars.

I begin to feel restless and decide to do some

more clearing up in the hotel. There are decisions to be made about its future but that will mean contact with Victoria and Henry and I can't cope with that. One morning Emm and I go up there with Woody and Neptune. The men drain down the water system and assess the damage to the electricity. Emm spends time in the office, dealing with the remaining business. Woody and Neptune carry the boxes of salvaged kitchen equipment down into the cellars.

I go on a tour of inspection through each of the rooms to make sure nothing of value has been left lying around. We'd stripped all the beds at Christmas and the linen was laundered and stored. Emptied of holidaymakers and their cheerful paraphernalia, the rooms expose faded wallpaper, damp patches of plaster, worn carpets and stained mattresses. The smell of neglect is already gathering in the corners of the airless rooms. The Wraith Cove Hotel had once been the finest place to stay, nestled in the lush vegetation of The Undercliff with its south sea view. It had escaped being taken over by the war-machine and survived the bombs which had demolished another large hotel further along the coast at Niton.

This place had seemed like a palace to me when I was growing up. The carpets were thick and springy as moss, the brass fenders gleamed, impassioned Victorian oil paintings in curly gilt frames paraded up and down stairways and lined corridors. Aspidistras flourished in elaborate china pots on carved tables in every niche and my father was king of the castle. He prowled the place with pride, pinching maids' bottoms, flicking cigar ash at the polished grates and joining in any conversation as if he were part of everyone's family.

I begin to feel nostalgic; wandering through these passages leads me back to my childhood. Victoria and I were born here, thrown together in our perplexing sisterhood. I can hear my father's rumbling laughter as I stand in the lounge. There would be a lot of memories here for Victoria of our mother that I'd never known. I open the door of Victoria's old room, used for guests after she married Henry and moved into the physician's house. No trace of her remains; no lingering whiff of her young years. She's been covered over by seasons of pleasure seekers. My room still contains some of my belongings – beach treasures, child-hood books and a china doll with a head injury. It's as if I couldn't quite leave, although I've lived in Wraith Cottage for a couple of years.

It is strange how the cottage has become mine. I loved it so much that I gradually assumed posses-sion of it. Once, the whole family had used it, escaping from the demands of the hotel for a break. But Dad always wandered back up here, missing the company of his guests. Victoria had come to think of the cottage as a shabby hovel. She'd wanted Dad to spend money on it, plumb in a bath and toilet, install a telephone. But he couldn't see the point – we had all that at the hotel. He did have an electric pump for the well installed in the outhouse but it was always breaking down. I often resorted to the tin bath in winter instead of using the hotel facilities. It doesn't bother me; it's cosy in front of the kitchen range. Wraith Cottage is my passion – the thunder and sigh of the wild shore and the wind that whispers and howls, the strange shapes that the blackthorn assumes in its wrestle with the gales. Every time I go outside something has changed – the sea and the sky and even the beach shift endlessly. I never want to leave. And I know Emm loves it. I'm glad it's now her home too.

The Ramplings came into our lives before I was born. Henry Rampling Senior was my mother's doctor when she was suffering from tuberculosis – consumption it was called then. I often wondered if he'd been in love with her – sweet Beatrice – my pale, frail mother. Did he lay his hand on her delicate breast while she gazed up at him with eyes of fragile blue? There must have been some reason – other than photography and old malt whisky – why he and my father became such unlikely friends; Henry Senior frequently came to the hotel when he wasn't at the hospital. He would bring Emm and Henry Junior with him when their mother was away on her suffragette campaigns in London. He'd sometimes forget all about them and leave them behind when he went home.

Eventually, Henry Junior disappeared to the

mainland to boarding school but Emm and I were constant companions when we were little. Sometimes she got left behind for days on end. She was five years older than me but never scolded like Victoria did. She reminded me of a fawn even then with her fluffy hair, big eyes and long skinny arms and legs. She was so daring, always up to something. She would grab me by the hand and we'd run off to the kitchens to get petted and fed by the cooks and then we'd clamber down to the beach to explore the rock pools and collect shells and wood. We took them into Wraith Cottage which was our playhouse. Nobody seemed to worry about two small girls, treacherous tides and crumbling cliffs. Everybody assumed that someone else was taking care of us. And we had no sense of danger. We'd get chided for the state of our clothes when we got back but that was all. Victoria never came with us. She liked to stay in her room to draw and paint. She didn't fancy getting dirty. I think she was glad Emm was around so she could stop having to keep an eye on me for a while.

I go into my father's room. My mother's too really, although I'd never experienced that. I'd stood in this room several times since his death, sensing his presence whilst trying to accept his absence. His clothes are all gone, bed stripped, possessions distributed. His smell still pervades the emptiness as if he'd just lit up his last cigar. I remember snuggling into his camel-hair coat, that night on the beach when I'd felt so ecstatic. I had no suspicion of what was being planned for me that night. It seems like the end of my girlhood. I have to be a grown up woman now in order to carry on.

I go over to the window and stand watching the winter sunlight dancing on the sea. A few gulls swoop on a shoal of fish beneath the waves. I can see the misty shape of a large ship on the horizon on its way into Southampton. The hotel garden spreads below me filled with green even at this time of the year. The energetic ivy shins its way up the tallest of the Scots pines. Rhododendrons, tree ferns, flax and palms, hydrangeas still topped with masses of pinkish-brown flower heads, surround the lawn dotted with snowdrops. The garden slopes down in a succession of terraces to the mole-riddled croquet lawn and the disused tennis court – now in layers due to a landslip. There are rickety stables and paddocks in which Victoria and I once trotted our ponies. And then two little orchards of stunted fruit trees. I can see the scarlet caps of a couple of bobbing pheasants pecking at the rotting windfalls in the winter grass. A stone wall separates the hotel grounds from the garden of Wraith Cottage. I can just see the chimneys, and wispy spirals of smoke, swirling in the breeze.

I turn back to the room, checking all is in order before I close the door. A few framed photographs still hang on the wall. I start to take them down. Autographed photos of Dad – Old Father William – at the hotel bar, his arm round the shoulders of music hall stars and famous visitors. One of him

167

and my mother on their wedding day, sepia tinted; even then she looked almost translucent, like a shadow – her hair as fine and light as her wedding veil. I used to ask Victoria to tell me about her but she wouldn't share her memories. It was as if Mother was hers and I had no right to ask. She would just say that Mother was ill and needed to rest a lot. Once, she blurted out that I looked just like her and then she rushed out of the room. I thought I'd better not ask again. But it is true, I do look like her. No wonder my father used to gaze at me, his eyes moist with tears, after he'd downed a few whiskies.

I reach for a larger family group higher up and lift it down. This must be a gathering of ancient relatives. I rub my sleeve over the dusty glass and realise it is of my family and Emm's family – the Waldings and the Ramplings together, how strange. A formal black and white studio photograph. But then my father and Henry Senior had shared an interest in photography. That was one of the things they had in common, beside my mother and old malts.

I turn the photo over. The date is written faintly on the brown paper backing – nineteen-thirty-three, twenty years ago – the year I was born and my mother died. I turn it over again – yes, I can see, I am sure I can – my mother was sitting on a straight-backed chair and she had a distinct swelling under her shapeless crepe dress. The rest of her was slender and transparent as ever. But there I

168

was – my mother and I together. I did have a mother, even if I was at that very moment threatening her life. I hold the photograph against my heart for a moment and then look at it again. My mother was resting a hand against her belly – over me. This photograph is coming back to Wraith Cottage with me. I take out my handkerchief and spit on it, giving the glass a quick polish. The material turns yellow with dust and cigar smoke. The picture becomes clearer. My father stood behind my mother, he looked slimmer then and unusually serious in his dark suit, one hand on her shoulder, cigar poised in the other. In front of them on a footstool sat Victoria, aged ten, wearing a dark velvet dress with a white lace collar, her hair dressed in shiny ringlets. Her eyes seemed to gleam at the camera and she was smiling. I hadn't yet arrived to shatter her world.

The inevitable aspidistra in an ostentatious pot separated us Waldings from the Ramplings. Doctor Henry Senior looked officious, as if about to do a ward round. His black hair was sleeked back and he had a small moustache which made him look like David Niven. Beside him stood Florence his wife, chin and bosom thrust forward, her wavy light hair swept back from her face, secured behind. She looked as if she'd rather be off on a rally instead of wasting time on this tomfoolery. In front of them stood Henry Junior aged fifteen, hair oiled back like his father, handsome and arrogant even then, one hand holding the lapel of his striped school blazer. And sitting on another footstool was five-year-old Emmeline. She was wearing a white dress with a dark sash, her hands were clasped around her knees and she gazed at the camera with interest as if she would like to have a go.

I sit down on the bare mattress of my father's bed. Here it is, in black and white, the strange entanglement of the two families for all these years. Each one of us is depicted in this old photograph. How would my mother have felt if she could have seen the future – her daughter, Victoria, married to Henry Junior; her husband, William, dead; Wraith Cove Hotel falling into disrepair? And what would she have made of me? Would she have considered me an abomination? How would she – and Dad for that matter – have taken the news that Emm and I wanted to live together? Strangely, Florence Rampling, Emm's mother, would probably have been quite understanding, staunch as she was for the rights of women. She'd given Emmeline *The Well Of Loneliness* – a banned book about lesbians – for her sixteenth birthday.

But now, everything has changed. Not one of these four parents would be looking down on their children with approval I am sure. They would all be devastated to know that Henry – my brother-in-law whom I should be able to trust – the senior male of the family, had raped me. And that he'd seriously injured his sister and deceived his wife. I look again at the picture – perhaps I should throw it away after all. What deception photographs were

170

capable of. Look at this – two happy, respectable, wealthy families, educated and privileged – such a pretence. But then, I gaze down at my mother, her thin hand draped over her unborn child – me. She had unwittingly given her life for me. Surely that is worth something. I take the photograph and leave the room, shutting the door quietly behind me.

I go to find the others. Woody and Neptune have nailed a closed sign at the hotel entrance. I pile their arms with bottles of brandy and whisky – not caring about Victoria's share of the inheritance – and we padlock the gates and go home.

Emm had collected the last of her possessions from her room at the hotel and brought them down to the cottage. I tell her that means she's officially moved in with me. This evening we had a celebration – the first time we'd celebrated anything since New Year. Emm made fish pie and we toasted each other with a small gin and orange. Emm had to drink hers through a straw so that it wouldn't sting her healing lip. Later, we sit by the fire and I show Emm the photograph. She'd never realised I was in it although she'd dusted it a few times over the years. She too seems saddened by the false picture it presents of our two families.

'I don't know how it all went so wrong,' she says. 'I don't understand it, Lilly.' She looks at me; her eyes open wider now the swelling has almost gone.

'I suppose we'd have to be trained as psychiatrists to make sense of it all,' I say.

She puts the picture down on the floor. Drifter, awaiting her chance, settles herself on Emm's lap, purring loudly. 'I don't remember that my mother and I used to laugh at him or ridicule him,' she says, gazing into the distance.

I assume she is talking about Henry. 'I remember that he always seemed frustrated because he wanted you to do as he said and you never would. You'd laugh and stick your tongue out at him.'

'But all kids do that. It doesn't explain such violence, Lilly.'

'Perhaps it was because – I don't know – your family was a bit different. On the one hand it was conventional – your father was at least. But you and your mother weren't. I mean, he must have seen his friends' families being dominated by the males. He wanted to be like your father but however much he strutted, you and your mother took no notice.'

'But, Lilly, times were changing, women were standing up for themselves.'

'Maybe, but not in his circle. Emm, this is an island. Your mother spent most of her time in London, among radicals. She tried to bring back her ideas to a small community of people. It was great for you but it must have been difficult for Henry. Your father didn't help – he was either working or propping up the hotel bar with my dad.'

'You sound as if you're defending him.'

'No. Just trying to understand, like you are.'

Emm sounds irritable. I know she wants to talk about what has happened. We'd skirted round it many times and I'd always avoided going deeper. Perhaps this is the time. I feel stronger now that our lives are returning to normal.

'Emmeline,' I venture. She looks up sharply. I seldom call her by her full name unless I am joking or upset. 'There's something I need you to understand about that night.' She continues to look at me as if urging me on. 'I know what happened was brutal and disgusting but I don't feel tainted – not the real me, the essence of me.' She opens her mouth to speak, I hold up my hand. 'My body felt polluted and abused and dirty but – when it was taking place – I wasn't in my body. I was with you. I felt I was floating with you, untouched by what was happening to the physical me on the bed.'

She nods slowly. 'I know, Lilly.'

'You know?'

'Yes, because I felt you with me.' Her eyes slide away from mine and she begins stroking Drifter. She lets out a long sighing breath. 'But I haven't wanted to hear you say it.'

'But, why? I thought you would have been pleased, relieved.'

'Oh, Lilly, I am. Believe me I am so glad that you feel like that.' She draws her brows together. 'But it also makes me feel that Henry is getting away with it. As if you've forgiven him. And I can't bear that.'

'I haven't forgiven him, Emm. I don't even want to talk or think about him.' I can feel myself trembling just having this conversation about that night.

'Lilly.' Emm pushes Drifter off her lap and gets down on her knees in front of me, grabbing my hands. 'Let me confront him.'

'No!'

'But why?'

'For the same reasons as before. It will only make things worse.'

'Lilly, I'm frightened this will come between us. I can't just let it go. I'm scared my anger will eat me up.'

But I can hear Henry's threat ringing in my head – I can have you both certified and, believe me, I would do just that. I feel myself break out in a cold sweat. I rush to the outhouse and am sick in the lavatory.

I am sick several times during the next two weeks. The first week in February, Emm and I sit and look at each other across the breakfast table after I return, white-faced, from the outhouse.

'I think you're pregnant,' she says.

I put my head on the table and weep. Emm strokes my hair and lets me cry. Later we try to work out my period dates but they'd always been erratic, which has never bothered me knowing that I could never get pregnant sharing my life with Emm. I thought that I'd bled after the rape but we conclude it was blood from my injuries.

'What am I going to do now, Emm?' I whisper.

'It's early days. Maybe it's not what we think. Perhaps everything is just upset inside you, re-adjusting.'

I shake my head. 'No, I'm pregnant. I know it.'

Emm puts on her spectacles and delves into her books. She keeps glancing up, asking me questions. I confirm that I have tender breasts and want to wee more often. She goes on reading and looking things up.

'Well, we could try a herbal mixture.'

'For the sickness?'

'No, Lilly – to put an end to it.'

I push my chair back with a screech and stand up shocked. How could she even think of such a thing? I grab my coat and storm out of the cottage, heading for the cliff steps. I clamber down, buffeted by the wind, blinded by my hair in my eyes. I stride along the beach, tripping on pebbles, kicking out at bits of wood. After I've exhausted my anger I sit down on my stone and try to think rationally. I let the rhythm of the sea calm me, feeling the spill and suck of the water deep inside my mind. Of course Emm would want me to get rid of it. I'd known all along that she was harbouring the fear that I'd be pregnant by her detested brother who'd so cold-heartedly raped me. I suddenly realise I am facing facts squarely now. I can think the word rape without flinching.

'I'm pregnant,' I say over and over, imagining the words being carried by the waves to wash up on a foreign shore where someone might hear their whisper and wonder what they meant. 'I am expecting a baby, a child,' I call to the diving gannets as they hit the water. I imagine a tiny, fully-formed infant floating inside me, like one of the dolls' house children I still own. I close my eyes allowing my mind to probe the inside of my body. Yes, I can definitely sense an energy there. A daughter, I think. Imagine me having a daughter. I'd never considered that I would be a mother. This is such a new feeling, totally unexpected and somehow joyous, as if it has nothing to do with Henry and violence and disgust. This is pure and innocent.

I get up and start to walk slowly back. I want to describe all this to Emm, but I know I cannot, must not, expect her to feel the same. Perhaps she is right; perhaps this is going to come between us. What if she asks me to choose? No, she wouldn't do that. I will have to be very gentle and careful with her.

When I get back I am surprised to hear Emm talking as I open the door. Victoria is sitting at the table sipping tea out of one of our chipped cups, rejects from the hotel. Their faces look strained. Oh, God, surely Emm wouldn't have told her. Victoria turns to me and looks me up and down without smiling.

'How are you, Lillian?' she says, her voice uncertain.

'Recovering. And you?'

She pats her lips with her handkerchief. 'I've

come to see you about something.' She glances at Emm. 'Emmeline, would you mind awfully if I had a private word with my sister?'

Emm shrugs and gets up. 'Don't mind me. I'll go and chop some wood.'

I take Emm's place at the table and Victoria opens her handbag. She pulls out a large brown envelope and puts it in front of me.

'Lillian, I know I can't make it up to you – what happened. But I want you to have these.'

'What are they?'

'I've had the deeds to the hotel and Wraith Cottage put in your name. I don't need them and I thought it would give you some security for the future. Father wouldn't have wanted us to sell them and well, as I say, I don't need them.'

I don't know what to say. I run my hand over the envelope. Wraith Cottage – all mine. I don't think much about the hotel.

'But, Henry, does he know?'

She nods. 'What you decide to do with the hotel – that's up to you. I suppose you'll want to keep this.' She gestures around the room.

'Are you and Henry trying to pay me off, Victoria? Whose idea was this?'

'Mine. But Henry agrees.'

'Have you confronted him – about what happened?'

She nods. 'He denied it of course. He says he simply called at the hotel to check up, found it empty and came to see if you and Emmeline were all right. He told me he suspected you and she were up to something. He said he arrived and found you both drunk and Emmeline had fallen. He offered to help but you tried to get off with him. He was worried about his reputation, did what he could for Emmeline and left you to it.'

'You believe him?'

She looks down at her hands. 'I'm so confused I don't know who to believe.'

'It doesn't add up, Victoria. Why would he come out here at that hour?'

'He wanted to catch you and Emmeline . . . at it. He thought he should put a stop to what was going on.'

'He denies raping me then?' She nods, biting her lip. I leap up, knocking my chair over backwards. I wrench up my jumper and unfasten my slacks and let them drop. She tries to avert her eyes but then she looks at my body, at the fading grazes and bruises and scabbed-over cuts. She puts her hands over her face and rocks backwards and forwards. I do up my clothes.

'I can't believe he'd do that to you, Lillian. Not Henry. He must have thought, I don't know, that you wanted him to.'

'I think you'd better go now, Victoria.' My voice is shaking.

'Oh, Lillian. I'm so sorry,' she wails. 'I didn't mean that. It's just that sometimes you look so innocently at him with your wide eyes – like you worship him or something.'

178

'That's not true, Victoria, and you know it. I love Emmeline. We are lovers. I have no desire for men. There! I can't put it more clearly than that.'

'I'm just trying to make some sort of sense out of it all.'

'Well, whatever sense you make of it, don't try and excuse him. Why don't you leave him?'

Victoria's face registers shock. 'How can I? What would I do?'

'Get your old job back at the gallery. Paint – sell your wonderful pictures. Move into the hotel or in here with Emm and me.'

'What?' Her face shows clear disgust. 'What would everyone think? Live with you two? But you're –'

'Not normal? Not normal like you and Henry?'

'Lillian, I didn't mean . . . you're still my sister.'

'You'd rather live dominated by that cruel man than be free and live your own life?'

She sits with her head bowed for some time. She picks up her gloves, smoothing the leather fingers, placing them palm to palm as if they were praying. Then she gets up and buttons her coat and puts on her boots. I want her to say something, to make a sign that she will think about what I'd said. But she goes, without looking back, leaving behind the sad scent of violets . . .

Emmeline closed the journal. The notebooks were starting to get blotchy with the tears she had dripped onto them.

'I'm sorry, Lilly,' she whispered. 'I'm sorry I told you to get rid of your baby. Was that when you decided to have secrets? Did you think I would leave you?'

CHAPTER 10

My father had changed. When I appeared in his hospital room now, he immediately became agitated and grasped my hand as if he had something urgent to tell me. He would stare at me as if seeking eye contact and repeat my name over and over. I wasn't used to this. It felt quite unnerving. I'd spent my life with him trying to catch his eye, get him to notice me, and now I was wishing he would go to sleep for a while. I didn't know how to communicate with him. He couldn't answer my questions and I couldn't understand his.

I tried to soothe him, like a baby, stroking his hands and hushing him until his head would sink forward on his chest. That head of his. I found myself staring at it. I wanted the contents, his memories. Were they irretrievable now, lost with the damaged cells? Or was his mind still whole, continuing its own existence beyond his brain, aware, detached, with no instrument through which to express?

The hospital staff thought he was a marvel. How he had recovered from his serious bout of pneumonia they would never know. He was off all medication now, de-catheterised and able to shuffle to the toilet with the aid of a zimmer frame. His left side was weak but his face less drawn down. His speech was lacking and he got angry when we tried to get him to write or even point to letters. He still seemed to think that what he was saying was quite clear. The physio was pleased with his progress, however, and said not to try and rush him, after all it had only been a few weeks since he was at death's door.

Doctor Phipps asked me, whilst flicking through the Sunday colour supplement, if I thought my father had something to sort out with me.

'What do you mean, exactly?' She had caught my interest.

'Well, he could have gone, couldn't he? But he pulled back. It seems to me he wants to tell you something before he goes. But part of him is resisting. It's like there's a battle going on inside him.'

I laughed, 'I wish he'd spit it out and put me out of my misery.'

She laughed too. 'Do you know what I would do, Jane?'

'What would you do, Doctor Phipps?'

'I'd take him home, wheel him around his house, confront him with old memories, photos and junk. Natter on about your childhood – you know – do you remember this and that, type of thing. Get it out of him before his head explodes again. He might be quite peaceful then.'

I thought about this for a while, wondering how I would manage him. Doctor Phipps was obviously thinking this through too. She sat on the edge of her desk as usual, she seemed incapable of sitting in a chair as if it might be too much effort to get up again. She pulled her long plait of dark hair over her shoulder and inspected the tuft for split ends.

'Your nice big husband would help you, I'm sure. I mean with manoeuvring the wheelchair.' Her bleep started to sound and she slid off the desk. 'Take him out for a day, see how you get on. Then we can start to assess what he needs with a view to discharging him.'

I ambled along to Dad's room where the physio was finishing his session, praising him for his progress. He was smiling at her, when I went in. The smile drooped when he saw me and I saw the look of agitation return. I started to speak before he could commence his chant of Jane and thith-der. I took his hand.

'How would you like to go home for a day, Dad? Chas and I could take you.' He stared at me as if trying to remember what home was and then he nodded his head.

'But he won't be able to live on his own at Winter Wood,' Chas said, as we drove to pick up Dad the following Saturday. 'I thought he was going to come and stay with us.'

'I haven't plucked up enough courage to ask him

183

yet. Let's see how he gets on today at Winter Wood. The doorways and corridors are wide and there's a downstairs loo and plenty of space to make a bedroom on the ground floor. Maybe it would be better to hire carers from an agency.'

'Expensive . . . full-time care.'

'He can afford it, Chas.'

'Surprising how quickly it goes,' he muttered.

'Well, have you got a better idea?' My voice sounded sharp, I was feeling nervous, taking Dad out of hospital. What if he should fall or have another stroke? Chas turned the cricket on to change the subject and I leaned back against the soft leather, watching the dried-up verges whizz by, wishing I could hear the sea.

Dad was ready and waiting when we arrived. He was wearing his grey trousers and a striped shirt with a frayed collar which I'd returned to Winter Wood to collect. He'd looked at me strangely when I took them in as if he was trying to work out where I'd got them and what I'd been up to. I wondered what the nurses had thought about the state of Dad's old clothes. Did they think I was a neglectful daughter? But perhaps they understood the pride and privacy of the elderly better than I did.

The wheelchair fitted snugly into the back of Chas's Range Rover, along with the zimmer. It was relatively easy strapping Dad into the front seat too; he was so thin and light. Chas was great, talking in his deep, slow voice all the way to

Malvern, pointing out where we were and constantly asking him if he was all right. I sat in the back, trying to prepare myself for the day ahead. I planned to make a light lunch and then send Chas off for a few hours.

At Winter Wood there was one awkward moment while Dad fumbled for a pocket, obviously thinking that he should have the keys.

'Here we are,' I said brusquely, and opened the door. Chas wheeled him around the ground floor to reassure him that everything was as he left it. And then we hoisted him out of his chair and attached him to his zimmer and Chas – husband from heaven – shuffled him to the toilet. I heated mushroom soup and made dainty minced chicken sandwiches and dutifully mopped up Dad's dribbles as we ate. I was beginning to think a full-time nurse was a very sound idea. Chas and I made cheerful small talk throughout the meal, trying to include Dad without overtaxing him to provide answers. When we finished I suggested Chas went off for a couple of hours while Dad rested. Chas didn't need asking twice. He took Dad to the toilet again and settled him in his wheelchair.

Right, I thought. Here we are, alone. I had no intention of letting him sleep, not yet. I wheeled him into the sitting-room and parked him in the centre while I wandered around picking up ornaments and regaling him with little reminiscences from my childhood.

'Look, Dad. See this vase? I knocked a handle

off it once with a tennis ball and Mother stuck it back on. We were so scared you would notice.' He nodded his head and gave a slight smile. 'I bet you did though. And look at this.' I picked a silver-framed photo of myself from the top of the piano that nobody ever played. 'I look so pleased with myself don't I?' I took his glasses from his jacket pocket, popped them on his nose and showed him me at my graduation ceremony, in gown and mortarboard, clutching my certificate. My chestnut hair was sleek and shiny, cut in a long pageboy, my brown eyes shining. 'I look just like Mother, don't you think?' He raised his hand and tapped the glass a couple of times. I moved over to the mantlepiece and lifted the photo of my parents' wedding. It was polished, dust free. Good old Mrs Watkins. 'Where did you and Mother get married?' I asked, bringing the picture over to him and squatting down beside him. He lifted his hand again. I waited.

'Ven . . . Vent . . .' he sighed.

'Ventnor? On the Isle of Wight?' I rested the frame on his knees. He nodded. 'I went there,' I said. 'I liked it.' We both stared at the photo for a while. 'You both look so nice.' Actually, Dad reminded me of a mean, slick-haired Sean Bean, and Mum, wide-eyed and oval-faced under her lace veil looked as if she'd just been captured by Rudolph Valentino. I put the photo back. 'Dad, have you got any photos of your childhood – yours and Mother's?'

He was quiet for a time and then nodded. He

gestured to the hallway. I pushed him out of the room. He pointed to his study. It was a bit tricky manoeuvring the wheelchair. I had to sit in his swivel chair, a reversal of roles. He gazed around for a while as if he'd forgotten why we'd come in.

'Dad?' I prompted. 'Photos?'

Suddenly, his eyes alighted on his walking stick, which was propped against the side of his desk. I realised how much he must have missed it. He reached out his hand eagerly as I handed it to him, as if it were an old friend. He raised it to tap at one of the drawers in his desk. I pulled it open. Inside there was an old leather album. I gave it to him and he turned the pages with difficulty. I was itching to help. In fact I was dying to grab it and look for myself.

'Can I see?' I knelt down in front of him. The pictures were very old, sepia and black and white. I recognised his parents, my Rampling grand-parents, in Victorian or Edwardian dress, standing on the steps of a grand house with the Royal National Hospital in the background. 'Is that the physician's house?' He nodded. 'Where I was born?'

He didn't answer; I'd have to come back to that. He seemed absorbed in turning the pages as if he was searching for something. I wanted him to slow down, give me time to ask questions. He stopped at a page which appeared to be an infant's christening.

'Is the baby you?' I asked. He nodded. There were a few more of stern-faced adults and Dad as a serious young child. Then followed a schoolboy in a dark suit, his baby curls flattened. I could easily recognise him now, that arrogant look down his narrow, straight nose, developing well. And then more baby photos. 'Who's this?' I asked. His hand started to shake violently. I grabbed the album before it went flying. His hand shot out and grasped mine.

'Jane, Jane!' he cried out.

'Dad, what is it? Tell me,' I said firmly.

'Thith-der, thith-der,' he wailed.

Oh, no, not again. 'Sister? Are you saying sister?'

He nodded miserably.

I looked again at the photo. 'Do you mean, this baby was your sister?'

He nodded hard. 'Thith-der.'

'Is that what you've been trying to tell me? Did you have a little sister that died?'

'No, no.'

'She didn't die? Then what happened to her?'

He gestured for the photo album again. I kept hold of it this time and started leafing through to where we were before. The infant did indeed appear to be a girl as far as I could tell, in those days when baby boys wore dresses. And there was another family group, with Henry about ten years old holding the new baby. A large photo in a folder fell out of the back of the album onto the floor. I picked it up. It was a formal studio photograph in black and white of two groups separated by an aspidistra in a grotesque pot. On one side stood a large man in a dark suit, cigar in one hand, his other on the shoulder of a pale, thin woman, her hand resting on her pregnant abdomen. In front of them sitting on a footstool was my mother aged about ten. She was wearing a dark velvet dress with a white lace collar and her hair was in shiny ringlets. She was smiling straight at the camera, her dark eyes gleaming. So these were my mother's parents – the Waldings – who possibly owned an hotel. And the photo was taken just before Aunt Lillian was born.

On the other side stood my father's parents – Doctor Henry Rampling Senior, black hair sleeked back, small moustache, reminding me of John Cleese, and Florence, his wife, chest thrust out, looking every bit the suffragette. In front of them stood my father, Henry Junior, about fifteen, handsome, snooty, holding the lapel of his school blazer. Sitting beside him on a footstool was a small girl with light curly hair in a white dress with a dark sash, gazing at the camera with curiosity.

I turned the photo over. On the back was an inscription. *To my dear friend, Henry Rampling, from your companion at the bar and the lens – William Walding. September 1933.* So, my mother's and father's parents were good friends, a long way back, when Henry Junior and Victoria were children, before Lillian was born. It seemed almost like an arranged marriage.

'Tell me about them, Dad,' I commanded.

He tapped the photo. 'Friends,' he stuttered.

'Always.' He pointed at William Walding. 'Hotel – Wraith Cove.' He rested his finger on the fair woman, 'Beatrice. TB.' He jabbed at his father. 'Her doctor.' He paused, wiping his mouth.

'I see. Grandfather Rampling was Grandmother Walding's doctor. That's how they came to know each other?' I asked.

Dad nodded, his eyes were glistening. He bent over the photo again. He indicated pale Beatrice Walding. 'Died . . . birth of Lillian.'

'My God, so who looked after Victoria and the new baby?'

Dad pointed at smiling Victoria. So, that was it. My poor mother, ten years old and looking after her baby sister with her mother just dead. No wonder she was such a tortured soul pouring all her emotions into her paintings.

'Me,' said Dad suddenly, pointing to himself. 'Boarding school.'

'Yes, I can see that's you. And who is this?' I indicated the small girl in the white dress.

Dad's agitation seemed to be returning full force now. He poked at the photo and knocked it to the floor. I retrieved it and held it firmly in front of him.

'Thith-der.'

'Your sister? So what happened to her, Dad?' Then a curious thing occurred. My father burst out crying. He wept and wept, his shoulders shook. I patted him on the back, found tissues to mop his tears. He looked up at me. His eyes swimming.

'Emm,' he said. 'Emmeline.'

I sat silent, while my mind did all sorts of rapid retakes and computations. I could feel him observing me, his sobs quietening. If this was true and not just the confused ramblings of an old sick man, then it meant that not only had my mother disowned her sister but also my father had done exactly the same with his. That would make Emmeline my aunt as well as Lillian. It couldn't be true, she would have told me. But she said she had a lot more to tell me the next day, and then I didn't show up.

'Is this true, Dad?'

He nodded. I could see that it was by his expression. For the first time in weeks, he looked calm, as if he was all there, concentrating.

'Did you know that Emmeline was still alive before I told you I'd met her?'

'No.'

'So you and Mother assumed they were both dead, Lillian and Emmeline?'

He nodded. What a shock it must have been to him, hearing about them after all this time. Perhaps now I could offer some reassurance.

'Dad . . . Emmeline told me – about her and Lillian – that they loved each other. They lived together happily for all those years you know – fifty years.' He looked exhausted. I took his hands in mine. 'I do understand how difficult it all was in those days. I suppose time went by and the past seemed buried.' He didn't respond, his hands were slack in mine. 'Look, I'm glad you told me. I'm going to go back and see Emmeline when you're better. Perhaps, I don't know, you could write her a letter or something. I could take it to her. You two could forgive each other before it's too late – like it was with Mother and Lillian.'

His eyes were closing with fatigue. I heard Chas drive up in the car. Enough, I thought. Enough.

Emmeline kept her next appointment at the hospital. She knew her strength was failing fast and she felt she would try anything that might enable her to hold on. Neptune went with her, helping her across the fields to the road and onto the bus. The doctor told her she should have a course of radiotherapy. She could have had it weeks ago, he said, to supplement the chemotherapy. But he was a sympathetic man and told her to go away and think about what she wanted to do.

There was still no word from Jane. 'What shall I do?' Emmeline asked Neptune and Marguerite after supper that night.

'If you promise to go for that treatment I'll make some telephone calls and try to speak to someone at her publishing place. They might be able to give us her address,' Neptune said.

Emmeline reached across the table to squeeze his hand. She knew how Neptune hated dealing with strangers and telephones. His world consisted of The Undercliff, fishing and occasional trips to Ventnor.

Emmeline, weary from the day, got into bed and wondered how they had managed to get themselves into this reclusive life. It had seemed vital at first when Lilly realised she was pregnant. She had been terrified that Henry would find out and try to do away with her. He might try to push her off the cliff or at least capture her and get rid of the baby. That was how all the hiding away had started and they had dug themselves in deeper and deeper until the world seemed like an alien place. And Wraith Cottage had allowed them to do that. Every year it became more and more closed off with the cliff falls and the closed down hotel and the overgrown grounds and fields.

'Poor Lilly,' Emmeline murmured. 'How frightened you were . . . the dreams you used to have . . .'

I have nightmares in which Henry is watching me, waiting for his chance to grab me. I don't tell Emm, but she knows. Sometimes I wonder if we can read each other's mind too easily and I try to close mine down. But it has become a habit now. At least Emm and I seem to have got over our difficulty in talking about what has happened. Now, we spend endless amounts of time going over and over it, trying to come to terms with our newly-shaped lives. In the old days – before Henry's attack – we loved to cuddle up and chat about our future together, living in Wraith Cottage, sharing our lives, our ideas, and interests. We'd planned to be like Woody and Neptune, allowing gossip to rise and fall, letting it take its course. We aimed to keep the hotel running, gradually modernising it, attracting younger people, families. But first we had the fire and then came Henry and now everything is different. We have no income, no employment. But Emm has some money that her parents left her and at least I now own Wraith Cottage and the hotel. I had feared that Henry would convince Victoria that the whole lot should be auctioned off.

We can also talk about my pregnancy. I am still being sick, and as we move into March, Emm grows concerned and suggests I should visit the doctor.

'It's only morning sickness, Emm, nothing to worry about.'

'But we don't know, do we, Lilly? What experience has either of us had?'

I feel reluctant to consult the doctor. It might get back to Henry through medical circles. The thought of him finding out fills me with dread. What would he do? He could have our well poisoned or arrange to have me pushed off the cliff. I have all sorts of fantasies about how he might plan to get rid of the baby and me.

Emm still isn't happy about the baby, but she's stopped making any references about trying to rid me of it. She sometimes has outbursts when her feelings get too much for her.

'What if it looks like Henry?' she shouts at me one day. 'How are we going to live with that?'

'It's a girl,' I yell back at her. 'And it's not her

fault.' I catch hold of her and hug her close. 'Oh, Emm. Just think, we would never have had a child to raise. She'll be our daughter.'

'Henry's daughter!'

'She'll have your blood in her veins too, Emm – your family's line as well as mine.'

'Well I hope to God she looks like you, Lilly. I just feel that every time I look at this child I'll be reminded that Henry raped you.'

'Not me, Emm – my body, but not me.'

After we calm down we walk. We both feel better for the lively air. Emm's eyes are bright again and her cheeks rosy. March is mild and sunny. Optimistic yellow flowers shine from shrubs and grass. The sea entertains us with shades of blue and green obliterated in a moment by smoky mist. There'd been several cliff falls during the winter storms and the revealed strata are streaked rusty-gold and white in the spring sun. Woody and Neptune have made temporary repairs to the cliff steps and we are glad to see that our cave is unaffected. The beach is littered with fossils and shells. We gather new treasures and sit on a boulder feeling the spray from the frisky sea dampening our faces.

'Okay,' Emm says, renewing the conversation we'd started at breakfast. 'I agree we should try and prevent Henry knowing. But tell me how, Lilly. You'll start to show in a few weeks. And another thing – I think we should tell Woody and Neptune. They're going to know anyway and they might be able to help us.'

'Help us how?'

'I don't know. But if you want to keep this pregnancy hidden then you can't go anywhere can you? They might be able to find out things for us without raising suspicion – legal things. You can't just give birth to a child without registering it and being under the care of a doctor or a midwife, I'm sure.'

Emm's tone is brisk as if she needs to present all the obstacles that she can think of to make me realise what I am taking on. She sounds a bit like Victoria. I glance sideways at her. At least she doesn't look like Victoria in her baggy trousers, navy fisherman's jumper, a red and white striped scarf round her head and neck. I smile, imagining my sister in that get-up.

'I don't mind telling Woody and Neptune. They'll have to know soon anyway, like you say.'

My chance comes in the afternoon. They arrive in the boat to take Emm to Ventnor for a dental appointment. I go along for the outing. It is such a glorious day to be tossed about on the sea and I don't feel at all queasy. In fact I feel the tension of the last few weeks washing away. We moor up and Woody spreads his army great coat against the sea wall and we sit sharing a bottle of lemonade and a jar of cockles, laughing at Booty's antics with the waves. Neptune walks up to the town with Emm.

I tell Woody about the rape and the baby. He holds my hand, letting me speak without interruption. I can feel his response by the tightening of pressure on my fingers, the changing rhythm of his breathing. He sits for a long time, gazing out to sea, his face inscrutable amongst the wilderness of dark curling hair and beard. This is his way, a slow pondering of facts. He is less impetuous than Neptune, especially since his war experiences. Before then they were both likely to hit out first and think afterwards. He sighs and nods his head.

'This doesn't come as a surprise, Lillian. Nep and I, well, to be honest, we've chewed this over a few times. We found it hard to believe that Henry hadn't gone for you that night. But we could understand why you wouldn't want to talk about it.' He rubs my hand. His touch is like Neptune's, rough and strong. 'What are you planning to do?'

'I want to keep it quiet. I don't want anyone to know, especially Henry. I'm scared of what he might do to me if he finds out. And then, I suppose, I'll have to invent a story, a fictitious father – a Christmas party fling. I'll have to brazen it out and take on the stigma of unmarried mother.'

'And Emmeline?'

'She's not happy. You know how she feels about Henry. But what can she do? I know she'll support me.'

Woody conjures one of his roll-ups from some sheltered spot behind his ear. He lights it and I lean back and close my eyes, the smell reminding me of Dad. Supposing it was him I was confessing to – would he order me from his door? Woody produces a flask from his pouch and offers it to me. I take a tentative sip not quite knowing what sort of concoction is going to hit my throat. It is brandy. I feel the hot trickle of it wander down to my stomach. Woody takes a large swig and wipes the back of his hand across his mouth.

'Well, Lillian. If it's of any help to you, I'm quite willing to be cited as the baby's father.'

I feel a shiver of shock run through me, more potent than the brandy. Is there no end to this man's kindness?

'But, Woody, you can't do that.'

'Why not? I've developed a thick skin against gossip over the years.' He smiles. 'And you and Emmeline will have to as well.'

'But what about Neptune?'

'Nep won't mind. We know we belong together just like you and Emmeline. If we can help each other out I think we should do so.'

'But everybody knows that you and Neptune are –'

Woody laughs. 'There is such a thing as liking both sexes. Who's to say you and I didn't have a New Year's fling down on the beach? If we both say we did, then we did.' He takes another gulp of brandy. 'We could even get married if you like. Then it could have a legal father. After all it's not the kid's fault is it?'

'It's a girl. Oh, Woody. I need to think about all

this.' I lean against his shoulder. 'You really are an amazing man. There's no one I'd rather be married to – given that I can't marry Emm. I do love you.'

He turns to me and puts a hand to my cheek, his dark eyes searching my face until they lock with mine. He leans forward and touches my lips with his. I feel a little dart of heat flash through my body as if I'd taken another sip of brandy. In that moment I can imagine being loved by him, like Emm loves me.

'I love you too,' he says.

Emm is as surprised as I by Woody's startling offer but she stops short at marriage.

'Putting his name down as the father would certainly solve a lot of problems. But getting married seems a bit unnecessary. It might raise all sorts of issues about living under the same roof and sharing legal stuff. Just paternity will be enough, I think.'

She goes outside and splits some logs rather ferociously. I wonder if she is feeling a bit threatened. But when she comes back in she is smiling cheerfully as if she's made sense of it all. After that, things seem to lighten up considerably, as if we've found a way to cut Henry out of the picture. We find ourselves planning a surprise supper for Woody and Neptune, starting to look ahead, even talking tentatively about our baby.

'Why are you so sure it's a girl?' Emm asks as she brushes leaves down the garden path.

'I just know. I'm a witch,' I laugh.

Emm stands leaning on her broom, looking like a witch herself with the gaps in her teeth. She is waiting for her new plate with one top tooth to be made. She isn't going to bother with the bottom one. 'Why don't we do that dowsing thing? You know, holding a pendulum over your tum and see which way it revolves.'

'I can't remember which way is for what sex though, can you?'

'Come on. I'll look it up.' She drops her broom and runs inside. She gets out her books and I lie on the settee with my jumper pulled up while she threads a gold ring of my mother's onto some cotton. She holds it over my belly trying to let it settle. But Drifter gets quite excited by the swinging ring, trying to swat it with her paw, and we have to put her outside. We wait, scarcely breathing as the ring starts to gather momentum and then begins to circle slowly.

'There,' I cry. 'I told you. It's a girl.' We both find ourselves laughing with delight.

'What are you doing?'

We both jump. Victoria is standing in the doorway. I pull down my jumper and sit up. 'Victoria! I didn't hear you arrive.'

She marches over to the settee. 'What are you doing?' she demands, her voice shaky.

Emm stands in front of her, hands on hips, jaw thrust forward. 'What business is it of yours?'

Victoria holds up a hand. 'I know what you're

200

up to. I've read about that. Some of my friends have tried it.' She pushes past Emm and looks at me as I struggle up. 'Are you pregnant, Lillian?' Her voice is harsh and insistent. 'Tell me at once!'

'No,' I say feebly. 'I'm not.'

'You're lying.' She turns and looks at Emm. Emm shakes her head. Victoria's face is growing red, her mouth shaking. 'Liar! You're both liars!' she yells, then turns and rushes out of the door.

We stand staring after her, astonished. 'She didn't even say what she came for,' says Emm.

Henry arrives two hours later. He takes us by surprise. Emm and I had been certain that Victoria wouldn't tell him. We are in the garden weeding, a bit subdued after her visit and its implications. Henry appears from behind the cottage. Emm sees him first. She shoves me in the doorway and stands there brandishing her garden rake. He looks smart in his black suit, well groomed, as if he'd just left his consulting room. But his face looks haggard. He steps back and holds up his hands. His heavy gold signet ring glints on his finger. I realise it is this ring that has caused so much damage to Emm's face. I shudder. Had he gone home, washed the blood out of it and put it back on?

'I want to talk to you, Lillian,' he says, as if Emm isn't there. 'I won't come in.'

'You certainly won't,' snarls Emm.

I stand behind her in the doorway. I can feel

myself trembling all over. This is the first time I'd set eyes on him since he raped me and all sorts of reactions are going on in my body. 'What do you want?' I manage to say.

'Victoria tells me you're pregnant. Are you?'

What is the point of denying it? He will know soon enough. But now I have a plan, I can stand up to his bullying. 'Yes,' I say, trying to speak boldly. 'But it's nothing to do with you, Henry. I was already pregnant when you raped me, so you can go now.'

'And who is the father?'

'Woody,' I say, raising my face to look him in the eye.

Henry gives a snort of laughter. 'I don't believe you. Everybody knows he's a queer.'

'Ask him.'

'I wouldn't give him the time of day. It's just a conspiracy you've cooked up.'

'This is none of your business, Henry. You have no right –' begins Emm. I see his eyes flicker over her face. Has he noticed the livid scar on her lip, her missing teeth? But then he ignores her as if she isn't there.

'You can stop all this damn silly nonsense. I want your word that you will not name me or involve me in any way.'

'The last thing I want is your involvement,' I manage to spit the words out through chattering teeth. I see a look of surprise flit across his face as if he'd been expecting me to beg for his support.

I try to hold myself together by holding onto Emm. 'I'll do what you want if you give me your word that you will not harm me or the baby or come near me ever again.'

'I can't think why you imagine that I'd care to. I don't want anything to do with you, or it. If you refuse, then the consequences will be dire. Notes have been made on your medical records – and hers.' He nods towards Emm.

'You swine,' she hisses.

'Anyway.' His hand toys with the chain of his fob watch as if he's spent enough of his time on this mundane task. 'I came to tell you something of importance. Victoria is pregnant.'

'How did you manage that?' Emm spits. 'Did you go home and rape her after you'd finished here?'

'Victoria is my wife,' says Henry, not looking at her.

'That doesn't make rape more acceptable.'

Henry ignores her but his face starts to turn red. I will Emm to keep quiet, not to antagonise him. All I want now is for him to go. I try to sound calm.

'She didn't say anything to us.'

'She's only just had it confirmed.'

I can't believe it. Victoria pregnant. After all these years, after her confession about not wanting a child with him. Perhaps she'd already been pregnant then, and didn't know it. That's what she must have come to see us about earlier – she was going to tell us. Poor Victoria, how we must have ruined it all for her. 'I want to see her,' I say.

'She's gone away.'

'Gone! But she was here a couple of hours ago.'

'She came to say goodbye. I've sent her away to some friends in Scotland. I don't want her to be in contact with disease at the hospital.'

'Scotland. But that's such a long way.'

He takes a step nearer. I catch a faint whiff of his cologne and my stomach heaves. Emm brandishes the rake.

'Put that ridiculous thing down,' he snaps, and turns to me. 'I expect she'll write to you.' He puts his hand to his forehead and rubs it as if he is trying to remember something. 'Look, Lillian. I'm, er, sorry about what happened – this, er, misunderstanding between us. I know Victoria has signed over her share of the property to you. Also, I've arranged for a weekly sum to be paid into an account. But I do insist that you keep this quiet for your sister's sake. Her reputation depends on it.'

'Bloody cheek you've got,' yells Emm. 'Anybody would think you were the injured party here. You and your precious reputations –'

'You two will have no reputations – except sordid ones – when people realise what you are.'

'I don't want your money, Henry. I'll sell my father's hotel if I have to. I want nothing from you and I don't want to see you ever again.'

Henry stands and stares at me. I think he is going to spit on the ground. Then he turns abruptly and walks away. I grab the back of Emm's jumper to prevent her from going after him. We watch until he disappears. Emm throws the rake at the garden gate and puts her arms around me. We cling to each other, shaking and I don't know whether to laugh or cry.

We sit up late drinking hot milk. Emm gets up to lock the doors.

'I don't think you need to do that, Emm. He won't be back.'

She is restless, pacing up and down the cottage. 'We just can't let him get away with this, Lilly. He actually confessed to tampering with our medical documents. That must be illegal.'

'He might have been making that up to frighten us.' But I don't feel frightened any more. I catch hold of Emm as she walks by. 'But, don't you see? We're free of him now. You and I. We can bring up this innocent child together and people will gossip and speculate. Woody doesn't mind being implicated and after a while it will all die down.'

'What about the baby? What about medical care? The authorities might check up if Henry really has written something detrimental about us. They might take her away, imply we're unfit to look after her.'

'They won't if they don't know. Woody will sign his name. We can get books and study about the pregnancy and birth. I can lie low down here. As long as everything goes smoothly nobody need find out.'

'What if something goes wrong?'

'If the worst happens then we'll get the local midwife or doctor or go to hospital. Woody and Neptune will help us, I know they will.'

Emm reaches her arms out to me. 'I couldn't bear it if anything happened to you.'

'I'm strong and healthy. I know I don't look it. I may have inherited my mother's frail looks but I'm like Dad – strong as an ox. I know I'll be all right.'

We lie in bed holding hands. The sea and wind are so placid we can hear the rustle of our resident mouse in the thatch. I know, like me, Emm is turning over the events of the day.

'I have the feeling I might never see Victoria again, or her baby,' I say. 'I'd really like to know how she is. She said she didn't want a child. Poor Victoria.' I hate to think of her all those miles away in chilly Scotland. She is probably still on her way, all alone on a bleak steam train chugging through snow-capped mountains. It isn't her fault, all this. She is weak, that is the trouble. Maybe she will defy Henry and come back and live here with us after all. We could bring up our children together. But Henry would never permit that. I sigh. 'Poor Victoria,' I say again.

'Hmm,' grunts Emm.

'Isn't it strange though, Emm? My sister and I expecting babies by the same father – your brother.'

'Some father,' she says. 'And he's no brother of mine, Lilly. I have no brother . . .

Emmeline wondered about her brother. Like it or not, that's what he still was. She pictured him lying in a hospital bed somewhere, hovering between life and death. 'I have to see you, Henry,' she muttered into her pillow. 'You must come.'

CHAPTER 11

'Well, well,' Chas said when I told him about Emmeline and showed him the old family photographs and my mother's paintings. 'It all seems like a lot of fuss about nothing really, doesn't it? I do like some of these seascapes, Janey. We could get a couple of them framed. And you got a living auntie in the end too. Not quite the one you expected – Emmeline instead of Lillian – but nevertheless a bona fide blood relative.' I put Daisy and my baby shawl on a shelf in my study.

The summer was slipping away. It was now August and I seemed to have spent all my time involved with my father. I'd asked him if he would like to come and live at Birdsong with us. Not only had he said no, he actually shook his stick at me. He was back at Winter Wood now with a team of carers tending him round the clock. His chest was only slightly wheezy, his rib healed. Mrs Watkins had resumed her duties and his elderly gardener doddered about outside.

Chas and I had shifted furniture around and

208

made a comfortable bed-sitting room for him downstairs in the lounge. He could totter from here to his study where he liked to spend some of his day sifting through his archives. We'd had disability aids installed for him and I called in to see him every day. He seemed content but subdued. His former agitation had disappeared after his confession to me that Emmeline was his sister. But it seemed as if that was as far as he could go. I tried to draw him into talking about the past but he closed his eyes or said he couldn't think or had something important to see to in his study. I told him I'd taken Mum's paintings and borrowed his photo album to show Chas and he waved me away as if he had done with it.

I was beginning to feel I was no longer needed. Dad was being cared for. Chas was busy trying to keep us solvent. I was concerned about him – his hair seemed greyer and thinner and he was piling on weight. In fact he'd been so stressed that he seemed to have forgotten about supervising my life for me. He hadn't thought to inquire if my writer's block was showing signs of dissolving.

I wandered up to my study and blew some dust off my files, wondering if I was going to end up like my father in a room full of musty paper. I went out on the deck and stood looking down the valley at the scorched grass from the dry summer. The sunshine had been good for the fruit and grapes but not for lawns and gardens. Autumn was arriving early, leaves fading, grey squirrels hoarding hazelnuts. I thought of the dainty red squirrels on the Isle of Wight and felt a pang of longing.

I sat down in my white armchair feeling vaguely dissatisfied. Was that it then? Was that the end of the little drama I'd unearthed about my parents and their subversive sisters? If so, where had it left me? I looked around my room. Time was running out for the deadline on my novel. And I still had no inclination to switch on the computer and get on with it. I knew I could do it if I applied myself. Writer's block was just a convenient label I was hiding behind. This story was all drafted out – a thirty-something couple moving to France to pep up a floundering marriage. She has affair with local cad, thinks it's for real until she catches him with someone else, chaos, reconciliation with husband etc.

I wanted to write with more depth, that was my dilemma. I yearned for something which eluded me. I understood that my creativity had turned inwards and was disinterested in fabrication now. But I felt as if I hadn't quite got to the centre of myself.

I didn't know how to do this. I didn't feel drawn to psychotherapy like some of my peers and I didn't relate to religion – ancient or new age. I'd begun to avoid the evenings spent with my friends, eating out, discussing relationships, kids, work, diets. I'd always enjoyed this so much, gathering information, sharing intimate details, laughing fit to burst. But now it all felt superficial, as if it was a layer we were all caught up in that marched blindly over something vast, deep and untouched that we ignored.

I got up and paced around my room restlessly. What did I want then? I had always trusted in my own innate creativity and now that it seemed to be taking a different course surely I should go with it. Where did it want to take me?

I sat down in my armchair again and leaned back. I took some deep breaths and relaxed. I felt myself letting go of the questions in my mind, feeling deeply into the moment of being here. The inside of my eyelids glowed golden. And then into my inner vision there drifted a thin woman with long pale hair. She paused to look at me, then faded. Like a wraith, I thought, opening my eyes. And then I knew exactly what to do. I had to go back to Wraith Cottage and talk to Emmeline, my Aunt Emmeline.

I went downstairs to make myself some coffee. My thoughts drifted to the beach at Wraith Cove and Emmeline's little Gollumy face with its gappy grin. I smiled and picked through the morning mail. There was one from Bill Allain. Some new information had come to light on Wraith Cottage. He'd dug out some old plans and deeds that had been needed for the coastal management scheme and it turned out that my area of land included the grounds of the old hotel – Wraith Cove Hotel. Only the building had been sold for demolition and the company had taken everything it wanted years ago. In fact they were no longer in existence. So, I now owned approximately six acres of land as well as Wraith Cottage and a half-demolished hotel. He went on to say that when the coastal work was completed the land might have more value. There was the possibility that a new building could be erected on the foundations.

Well, I thought, I'm a landowner, that'll please Chas. Then I suddenly thought with horror, I might be liable for all sorts of taxes. I shoved the letter back in its envelope thinking I must pay Bill Allain a visit when I was over there.

The next letter was from my publisher asking how my work was progressing and inquiring after the health of my father. It also contained several other letters from readers who wanted to express various opinions on my books. One of them was written in a rather childish hand. It began quite personally – *Dear Jane,* and then I realised it wasn't from a reader. *I am a friend of Emmeline,* it continued. *I am sorry to write to your publisher but I did not know where else to write. I want you to know that Emmeline is very ill now and could you come to see her please. She has things she wants to tell you and wonders if you will ever come back. Yours, Neptune.*

Neptune! Was somebody having a joke with me? Wait a minute, I'd heard Emmeline mention Neptune coming to visit Wraith Cove. I'd assumed it was a figure of speech, as in things being thrown up by the sea. I never dreamt she meant a real person. But joke or not, Emmeline was ill and

212

wondering about me. I would have to go. I didn't want to lose another aunt before I had a chance to get to know her better.

I packed some clothes, phoned Chas, and didn't let him talk me out of it. I drove over to see Dad. He was dozing on a comfortable sun lounger under the chestnut tree on the south side of the house. The carer that was sitting with him looked half asleep, bent over her knitting. They looked very peaceful in the dappled light, the two of them, with a little fold-up table holding drinks and fruit and books. The woman roused herself as I approached.

'I'll go and make Doctor Rampling's lunch while you're with him. Can I get you something?'

'No, thank you. I won't be here long today.' I followed her toward the house out of earshot of Dad and explained that I was going away for a few days, telling her to get in touch with Chas immediately if anything went wrong.

'Dad,' I shook his shoulder gently. He opened his eyes and smiled.

'Jane?'

I bent and kissed him. I decided in that moment to be honest with him. No more deception. 'I'm going back to the Isle of Wight. Emmeline's ill and asking for me.'

His eyes darted a little and he grasped his stick tightly so that it shook. But then he sighed and squeezed my hand. 'Give her . . . give Emmeline . . . my regards.'

★   ★   ★

I arrived on the island at the end of Cowes Week. Dusk was falling as I crossed the Solent and I could see party lights and fireworks and hear music way out at sea. Yarmouth was once again bursting with boats and revellers. I knew I wouldn't be able to get to Wraith Cottage that night and managed to get bed and breakfast in a pub. The noise went on until late, or early, but I couldn't sleep anyway. I felt overwhelmed with excitement at being back here, picking up on my adventure, all mixed with concern for Emmeline, worrying that I might be too late to talk with her. I lay in bed realising that I could hear the wind on the sea and the slurp of waves against the pier stanchions as the human noise died. The sound lulled me and I dozed, not sleeping deeply enough to be pulled under water by dreams.

I couldn't face the full English breakfast and had croissants and coffee instead. Then I embarked on my journey south; I remembered it this time. The Military Road was still closed to the West. The coast road was relatively quiet considering it was August. The sun glinted on yachts, skimming the sea. The fields were parched like everywhere else. The holiday camps looked cheery with tents and caravans parked in the fields near the chalets. Bright kites whooped and soared and hang-gliders rode the thermals like giant birds of prey. Gore Cliff loomed and soon I was in the shady green Undercliff, bracken flouncing down the banks, ivy wandering the walls and nettles reaching out into the road, making it even narrower.

I parked in my usual spot and found my way into the grounds of Wraith Cove Hotel. It seemed even more tangled now with ivy and honeysuckle and roses climbing and tumbling over each other. Plums and greengages were falling off the trees, lying pecked and pungent in the grass of the orchard. I noticed things I hadn't seen before – the skeletons of greenhouses, remains of stables, the odd metal fence post where maybe there'd been a tennis court. I stood and looked at the faded sign and saw it now with a different depth. It had become part of the story – my history. This was my mother's childhood home and Lillian's, of course. Their parents, my grandparents – the Waldings, had lived and possibly died here. And even my other set of grandparents – the Ramplings, had stayed here and been family friends. I wondered if suffragette Florence Rampling and tubercular Beatrice Walding had been friends or whether it had just been their husbands that had welded the families together with wedding plans for their offspring. And this was my land now, how strange was that?

I fought my way through the garden and tramped across the field. The going was easier this time as much of the vegetation and tall grasses had drooped and settled in the drought. I soon found myself at the gate of Wraith Cottage. The garden was a rainbow of colour and had been cared for, watered. Everything was quiet. I peered over the edge of the cliff. The tide was half-way out, rock pools forming, sea glinting blue on the dark golden sand. A few dazzling white gulls waded at the water's edge and a grey heron stood motionless among the stones. A small blue and white boat was pulled up on the beach. I wondered if it was Neptune's. I suddenly felt like an intruder. Maybe there was nobody here. Should I let myself in? It was my cottage but I couldn't just walk into someone else's home.

I crept towards the porch, images flooding into my mind of my mother's paintings. The door was ajar and for a moment I thought I heard voices but it was the tinkle of shells blowing in the breeze. I rapped on the wood with my knuckles. I heard footsteps and the door creaked open. There stood an elderly man in khaki shorts and a grey vest. He was tall and thin, slightly stooped, his white hair cropped close either side of his bald head. I imagined him to be in his seventies. He had an aura of wellness about him, maybe because of his deep tan. An expression of something like relief crossed his face.

I held out my hand. 'You must be Neptune,' I said. 'I'm Jane. I got your letter yesterday. I came as fast as I could.'

He grasped my hand in his dry, leathery one. He smiled and his weathered face creased into dozens of lines. I felt an instant liking for him.

'Please, come in,' he said. 'I'm glad you've come. I'll make some tea. Sit down, sit down.'

I sat at the kitchen table where I'd talked a few months before, briefly, with Emmeline before she hurried away. Everything looked much the same, piled books, and the black cat, Surfer, sleeping on the sagging armchair, the kettle warbling. I felt happy just being here, absorbing the smell of lavender and herbs and fresh logs. Where was Emmeline, I wondered, upstairs in bed? I wanted to rush in with questions, but thought I would wait for Neptune to make the tea. At last he sat down opposite me. I sipped the strong brew out of the heavy mug.

'How is Emmeline?' I ventured at last, as Neptune didn't appear to be eager to tell me.

'Not well, not well at all.' He gazed into his mug, frowning.

'Where is she?'

'Oh, in the hospital. But she wants to come home.'

'Tell me, Neptune. What's wrong with her? I thought you said she wanted to see me. I thought she might be –'

'Dying?' He looked up at me. I thought I could see tears in his deep-set eyes. 'Yes, she is. She has cancer.'

I realised now why she'd looked so jaundiced and bald. 'She's having treatment?'

He nodded. 'But she doesn't want any more. She's told them that. She wants to come home to die.'

'Does she? But, who will care for her?'

'I will.' His voice rose and his head came up. 'She's my friend. I've known her since I was a boy.'

'I see.' He obviously had this all worked out. 'So, where do you live, Neptune?'

'In the next bay – Puck's Bay – I've fished there all my life.'

'Will you be able to manage?' I asked.

He nodded. 'I couldn't leave her, could I?' he said simply.

'Maybe I can help in some way?' I said. Here I go again, I thought, speaking before thinking. How could I help, living so far away? But, my impulse was to help. After all, she was my dad's sister. 'Did you know that Emmeline is my aunt?' He nodded. 'Why didn't she tell me, Neptune, do you know?'

'She was going to. That's one of the reasons why she wanted to see you.'

'One of the reasons?'

Neptune shifted in his seat, looking uncomfortable. 'She has a lot of things to tell you, Jane.'

'Well, I want to hear them. So, what can I do to help?'

'Have you got your car with you?' I nodded. 'You could go to the hospital to fetch her, then.'

I didn't expect this. 'Will they let her leave, just walk out? You will come with me, won't you?'

'I, er . . . I have to do something here.'

'But I can't go on my own, Neptune. I don't know the staff or the situation. Please come with me.'

'I can't. I told you, I have to do something.'

'Well, can I help you do it and then we'll go?' What could be that important here – more important than

218

picking up Emmeline? Perhaps he suffered from agoraphobia.

Neptune put his head in his hands briefly as if thinking, then got up abruptly. 'Come with me,' he said. He led the way out of the cottage and through the garden and we clambered down the slope to the beach. He was agile, like Emmeline, and I had difficulty keeping up with him. I stood on the sand, hot and panting beside him as he looked around. For a minute I thought he had to do something with his boat. But then he put two fingers in his mouth and let out a whistle. What on earth was going on here? Had he lost his dog? Sure enough, around the rock-strewn edge of the cove, a small brown and white terrier appeared and let out a couple of sharp yaps.

'Loot!' Neptune called. 'Fetch Marguerite! Go.'

The dog wagged its tail, turned and disappeared back the way it had come. I looked at Neptune for an explanation but none was forthcoming. A few moments later, Loot reappeared and to my astonishment I saw a figure picking its way through the rocks. It was a girl, wearing a blue dress. She was small and slim and her hair was pale blonde flowing right down past her waist. She waved a slender arm at Neptune and then paused as she saw me.

'Neptune,' I said. 'Who is this?'

'It's Marguerite,' he said. 'She's Emmeline's adopted daughter. I can't leave her for long, you see, not on her own. She's safe down here with Loot, but I couldn't go too far away.'

I sat down on a boulder as Marguerite threaded her way through the rocks. My mind had gone into a sort of limbo. So this was why Emmeline had kept rushing off saying she had to be somewhere. As Marguerite grew closer I could see that she was a lot older than she looked at a distance. Her hair was silver, her thin face mature.

'She can't hear or speak,' said Neptune, 'but she understands everything you say – and more,' he added, and smiled at me proudly.

'Did you say she's Emmeline's adopted daughter? How did that come about?'

'Emmeline will explain when she gets home,' Neptune said, holding out a hand to Marguerite as she approached. 'Marguerite, dear, Jane has come to visit.'

I stood up. Marguerite walked right up to me and stood looking at me. She was very beautiful, fragile like some sort of ethereal creature. Her eyes were large and palest blue with fine lines at the corners, her face and limbs tanned light gold. It was impossible to tell how old she was.

'Hello, Marguerite,' I said.

Marguerite continued to look at me intently as if she was listening to something. And then she smiled. To say her smile was radiant sounds corny, but something inside me felt as if it was dissolving, making me want to cry. She put out a hand and stroked my face and I could see that her eyes were full of tears too.

'Jane is going to fetch Emmeline from the

hospital,' Neptune told her, taking her hand. 'Come up to the cottage now. We must make sure everything is ready. You can pick some flowers for the kitchen table.'

He led her up the cliff path, talking to her all the while, Loot bounding ahead of them, leaving me to follow. I could see now, walking behind, that Marguerite held her left hand curled against her side and she dragged her left leg a little. How had Emmeline managed to adopt a disabled child? It seemed every time I came to Wraith Cottage a surprise awaited me.

I suggested we take Marguerite with us to fetch Emmeline but Neptune seemed startled at the idea.

'She's never been out like that,' he said. 'She only goes in the boat.' He gave me directions to get to the hospital in Newport. This was still feeling very difficult for me. How could I just go and collect a seriously sick woman that I hardly knew and fetch her back here? But it seemed I had no choice.

Emmeline wandered along the hospital corridor feeling lost. She could see some grass outside and trees but she couldn't find a door to get out there. People passed her by in both directions, seeming to know what they were doing, where they were going. She felt invisible. Perhaps she wasn't really here, perhaps she was dreaming or dead. She didn't even know how to get back to the ward or remember what it was called. She found herself in the reception area. There was a big desk and some seats. She thought she would rest for a while and recover. Just as she was going to sit down she collided with a young woman who was heading for the same seat. She was about to turn away but the woman spoke.

'You have that one,' she said. 'There's another one over there.' She smiled and Emmeline felt as if she was going to pass out. She half fell onto the seat. The woman stood there looking down at her, concerned. She was pregnant, her belly protruding from under her skimpy white tee-shirt. She looked so young. She pushed her blonde hair back behind her ears.

'You okay?' she said. Emmeline nodded and she walked away.

Emmeline watched her, reminded of Lilly. She remembered observing Lilly's thin frame fill out with her pregnancy. She didn't want her to be pregnant. But there was something intensely beautiful about Lilly then. She wanted desperately to hold her and make love like they used to. But she sensed Lilly's private joy in her communion with her unborn child and Emmeline couldn't share in it. It kept her at arm's length. She tried to think of something she could do to break down the barrier between them, to show her love was undiminished. She had gone to the market in Ventnor to buy some material to make her something. It was silly really, she was hardly showing yet. She could see

Lilly trying to stand still like an impatient child, hear her giggling . . .

I try not to laugh but I have that irrepressible feeling bubbling up inside me.

'Keep still, Lilly, please,' Emm mumbles. She is kneeling on the floor, pins sticking out of her mouth, holding a piece of gingham material against me. She spits the pins out, sits back and sighs. She frowns up at me, her round wire spectacles teetering on the end of her nose. 'I suppose the front ought to be longer than the back to allow for your expansion.'

I feel jittery, as if something is running along my nerves, waking them up, making my limbs want to fling themselves about. I smile down at her. I long to tell her that I won't need a maternity top for ages. We live in fishermen's smocks and slacks now that we don't have to dress in black skirts and white blouses for our hotel duties. But I know she wants to do something for me to show her support. I sense she is struggling – her hatred and anger for Henry still dangerously near the surface, ready to erupt at any mention of him. I am scared sometimes that she will give in to her rage, hunt him down and plunge a knife into his cold heart. I feel the only thing that is stopping her is the thought of prison and what will happen to me without her.

'Why don't you leave it for now, Emm?' I say. 'There's plenty of time and we can make clothes in the evenings.' I ruffle her curls. 'It's such a beautiful day, I wonder what's on the beach.'

'Mm, you're right, Lilly.' She sticks the pins back in the pincushion and takes her glasses off, looking relieved. 'I think I'm better at gardening and mending gutters.'

I bend and kiss the top of her warm head. Her hair smells of camomile daisies. 'You're good at everything, Emm.' I giggle. 'Except maybe, dressmaking.'

'Cheeky minx,' she laughs, slapping my arm. We are getting easier with each other again, feeling our way back into our old sense of fun. It isn't the same though; nothing could ever be the same. A reserve has crept in between us as if I possess something that keeps me apart from her. And I do, there's no denying it. However much we talk about it and what the future might bring, there is the stark fact that this is Henry's child I am carrying.

I've been forced to mature in the past few months, like a tender plant in a hot house. I hadn't really understood the extent of the hatred and persecution that lay in wait for those who happen to love somebody of the same sex. And I don't think that I'd truly considered what it would mean to go through life childless. How perfect it would be if by some miracle of biology, Emm was the other parent of this child. But our relationship is lopsided now and however hard we try we can't balance it. I don't think she loves me less than she did – or I her. If anything, our devastation has sunk our roots deeper, entwining our lives like the wisteria in the thatch. But there is a new tendril now that clings to me as its sole support.

But I am feeling well again. It is the end of March, spring is surging through The Undercliff and as I reach the end of my third month of pregnancy I stop feeling sick. My appetite returns along with my energy. Emm reads about the minerals and vitamins that I should be eating for my health, and that of the baby, and begins feeding me spinach and liver.

We buy some clucky grey hens and a proud cockerel with bouncy orange feathers, so that I can have an egg every day. Woody and Neptune help us collect sea timber and we hammer together a run and fox-proof house for them. Woody stands with his hand on my shoulder laughing at Booty's bewilderment as the unreachable chickens scratch around their new home. He mentions that he's noticed a wooden cradle in the attic of the hotel and wonders if I'd like him to do it up for the baby. He says it shyly, as if I might think he is trying to intrude. If only he knew how lucky I feel to have him offer his skills for my child. I give him the keys and he goes to retrieve it. Underneath the dust and grime is dark gold oak carved with rambling roses. No wonder it had caught Woody's eye. It must have been Victoria's and then mine, perhaps even the previous generation had slept in it.

I wonder if Victoria would mind. Would she want it for her own child? But knowing my sister, she will order a satin-lined one from Harrods. She wouldn't care for one that had been used. I haven't heard from her. I long to know how she is. I can't imagine her being pregnant and losing her figure. Does she have morning sickness too? I want so much to talk to her, but how could we possibly chat about our pregnancies when our babies share the same father? It is all so strange. But I miss her. Even though we are so different, she is my sister, my only blood relative. And our children – they will be half-siblings, I suppose. Anyway, no letter has arrived from Scotland and I don't know how to contact her.

Emm sometimes rides off on her bicycle to Niton or St Lawrence to pick up post and do some shopping. Sometimes, on a calm day we sail to Ventnor with Neptune. I am becoming reluctant to go far from Wraith Cottage. Although my pregnancy doesn't show yet, I feel protective towards my unborn daughter and need to keep within sight of home. I think underlying all this is the fear of bumping into Henry. I am certain he won't come back to Wraith Cottage, but just sailing within sight of the chest hospital, knowing he is in there walking the wards, fills me with fear.

Emm and I head for the beach, breathing deeply, forgetting about pins and smocks. Spring always comes early to The Undercliff. Green woodpeckers yaffle through the woods; jackdaws, crows and rooks rise in clattering mobs from the tops of the elms and poplars. Gulls fight over the choicest nesting places on the cliffs and so many small birds flutter in the blackthorn that the bushes seem alive. The vibrant air charges us with energy. We soon shed our coats and begin piling driftwood against the cliff. We inspect our cave. It seems relatively undamaged by the winter storms, protected as it is from the prevailing south-westerly winds. We clear out debris and prune the honeysuckle vines, which are already sprouting tender green leaves. Snowdrops, primroses and cowslips grow down here on small grassy ledges, amazing us with their strength of character in the face of the wind and sea.

The falls from the cliffs have been minor this year. And the rainfall light, preventing the treacherous slither of soil over the slippery blue gault clay. My beloved Wraith Cottage is still safely perched many yards back from the edge. The steps need a few repairs. Emm forbids me to heave any boulders.

I wander off, picking around like a sea bird amongst the debris, looking for shells and treasure. Upstairs in Wraith Cottage there is a tiny room off the main bedroom. The ceiling slopes right down to the floor in one corner and it has a sea-facing window. It is full of books and dried herbs and jars of preserves. But Emm and I have plans to clear it out and whitewash it for the baby. I want to find special shells and driftwood to hang from the beams for her to look at. I can imagine my precious child lying there in Woody's polished cradle, her tiny hands reaching out. I hope that she will love this place like I love it.

I sit down on my stone to rest in the sun. The sky is a dazzling blue. A raven cronks its way across to Gore Cliff. Far out on the horizon, I can see a grey warship heading for Southampton. I wonder where it has been. A whole vast world lies out there. But, it doesn't entice me. This is the best place on earth that I can imagine.

Emm is still shifting large stones, wedging them under the wooden steps on the cliff, which are starting to sag here and there. I watch her strong agile body, her angular arms and legs. How I love her. I hope her emotional strength is going to equal her physical over the next few months. I see her pause in her task and look out to sea. There is a boat chugging past, fairly close into shore. It isn't Neptune. I can see two people in it; they seem to be looking our way. Emm gallops down the steps and hurries across the sand to me.

'Hope they're not thinking of landing,' she says, shielding her eyes with her hand.

'They wouldn't attempt it, not this time of year, would they?' I say. Occasionally couples haul boats in here, or anchor out in the bay and swim ashore in summer. They usually make love in the shelter of the rocks or potter about the pools, soon getting bored. But it is treacherous, unless you know the shoreline like Neptune and Woody. The boat putters by slowly. I see a glint of sun on what looks like binoculars. I feel a moment of fear deep down inside me, like a threat. Silly, they are just a couple of people enjoying themselves on this bright spring day. But they don't usually come so close in to the shore. I move nearer to Emm, watching as they disappear round the cove.

'Are you all right?' she asks.

I nod. 'I don't like people intruding on us, that's all. Not after –'

'I know, Lilly, I know. But this isn't a private beach. Anyone could land here if they've a mind to. But look,' she gestures around the cove, 'it's getting more inaccessible every year. It's really hard to clamber around from either side – even Neptune and Woody prefer to walk over the top. And now the hotel's closed, no one walks down from that direction any more. Only the foolhardy or very good sailors would risk mooring here. And if it's lovers – well, no harm in them is there?'

I smile. 'I just had the feeling they were two men.'

'So?'

We both laugh and she puts her arms around me and nuzzles her face into my neck. 'How about celebrating spring in our cave?' she whispers.

I feel confused suddenly. We haven't made love, not since my injuries and knowing about the baby. I sense she can feel my tension.

'We won't if you're worried,' she says. 'We can just cuddle.'

'Oh, Emm. I do want to, really I do. It's just

that – it's all different now, isn't it?' I finish lamely. I'd been dreading this moment. Wanting it but fearing it too. What would she think, making love with me? Would she be thinking of what Henry did to me? Would I be thinking that too?

She lifts my chin so that I have to look at her.

'We need to be tender and understanding, that's all,' she says. 'It will come right in the end, you'll see.' She strokes my face. 'Besides, our baby needs to know about love, doesn't she?'

I nod, realising that I'd been worrying that Emm wouldn't want me any more. I might seem repulsive to her, however hard she tries not to let it affect her. I look at her eyes that seem soft with love, her wide mouth with its scarred top lip. I kiss the scar gently and see her eyes fill with tears. I find I can't bear it. I am unable to receive the full impact of the pain she is enduring. I have to turn away from her, just for a moment.

I look out to sea. It is empty now, just a glittering expanse of water. A few pearl-grey clouds are gathering in the west. Emm stands motionless, waiting. Everything seems hushed, the birds, the breeze, the waves. With a clap of wings a solitary pigeon flies from behind us out over the sea. It swoops and soars as if rejoicing at having all this vastness to itself. I can see the sun glinting on its iridescent neck feathers. Something in me seems to attach itself to its spirit and I feel a glorious elating freedom. And then a dark shape scythes from on high and, for a second, the sun goes out.

I feel the impact as if it was me being plucked from mid-air. Emm grasps my hand and we watch as the peregrine flies back to its ledge to share its prey with its mate. I imagine their bloodied talons holding it down, lethal beaks tearing at the warm breast. A shiver runs through my body as if the inside of my blood vessels were scraped raw. A few pale feathers waft down to rest on the water.

I look at Emm. I want to feel her aliveness, the pulsating softness of her body against mine. I need to touch her vitality, to connect with the heart and soul of her.

'Let's go home,' I murmur. 'Let's celebrate spring at home . . .

'Miss Rampling.' Emmeline felt a hand on her shoulder. The staff nurse from her ward was bending over her. 'We wondered where you were.'

Emmeline blinked rapidly. 'I was with Lilly, on the beach,' she stammered.

CHAPTER 12

I found my way to the hospital, trying to concentrate on driving, while my mind wanted to dwell on Marguerite. I couldn't believe that she never went anywhere. Surely that couldn't be right in this day and age. A person with special needs should have help and support.

When I got to the ward I decided I would try and speak to the medical staff before making off with Emmeline. I knocked on the door of the sister's office and introduced myself.

'Ah, yes. Emmeline Rampling,' she said. It gave me a shock when I heard her called that. I hadn't taken on board that Emmeline would have the same surname as my father – my single name. She told me the medical staff were aware of the situation and seemed quite resigned to the fact that Emmeline had discontinued her treatment and wanted to go home to die.

'It happens,' she said. 'And to be honest, who could blame her? She's endured so much. I think I'd do the same myself.' She piled me up with medication for Emmeline and lots of advice leaflets and phone numbers of the cancer care team that would help any time we needed it. I found myself asking questions as if I was taking on the role of chief carer. What was I doing? I had no idea how long all this was going to take and what about Dad back home? One step at a time, I told myself. And there was Neptune to help her too.

The sister took me into the ward to find Emmeline. She didn't look as bad as I thought she might. She was dressed in her baggy tee-shirt and trousers and canvas hat. She had her back to the television and her head moved from side to side like a trapped animal desperate to escape. She practically flew out of her chair when she saw me.

'Jane! I knew you'd come. Take me home, please,' she begged.

I drove carefully, trying to avoid potholes, not knowing if she was in pain. We didn't talk much; she seemed to be dozing. I wondered how I was going to get her across the fields to Wraith Cottage. I parked and loaded my things and hers into my backpack. We wandered slowly through the hotel grounds, stopping for frequent rests. I told her that I knew the hotel had belonged to my Walding grandparents. I also told her about my father's illness and that he'd admitted she was his sister. She listened intently, her forehead creased, her mouth puckered.

'That makes you my aunt,' I said, after a lengthy silence.

'It does, my dear, and I'm glad he told you.' She patted my arm.

'I'm glad too,' I said. 'When I found out about Lillian and that she'd died before I had a chance to meet her, I was so upset. I thought she was my only relative, you see.'

'I know,' she said. 'I know.'

'And, Emmeline, Dad asked me to give you his regards. I think he's genuinely sorry about what happened.'

She muttered something which I couldn't catch and struggled to get up. Perhaps she hadn't heard me properly. I would mention it another time.

We set off again. When we got half-way across the field, I spotted Neptune coming to meet us. Loot, trotting beside him, broke into an ecstatic run to greet Emmeline. Neptune quickened his pace and then holding Emmeline by the shoulders, kissed her tenderly on her forehead.

'Marguerite is asleep,' he said, his voice hoarse. He brushed a hand across his eyes, turned around and bent down. 'Get on,' he commanded, and Emmeline climbed onto his back. I watched the two of them, tottering across the field. An elderly man carrying a dying woman. I had to wait for a while before following them, to let the constriction in my throat pass.

Back at the cottage, we all had to rest for a time to recover. Neptune supplied us with a jug of cold well water and they both dozed in the armchairs. Surfer jumped onto Emmeline's lap, kneading her with her paws, purring deeply. There was no sign of Marguerite. I wondered where I was going to sleep tonight. I had a few things with me in my backpack. I supposed I could always drive into Ventnor, but I couldn't face the trek back to the car again in this heat. I would have to stay until it cooled down later this evening.

Emmeline woke and came to sit opposite me at the table. She looked better, relaxed under her own roof again. I explained in more detail what had happened to Dad last time I was here, why I had disappeared so suddenly. She nodded.

'I thought Henry might call you back,' she said. 'I expect he didn't want you finding out things about him.'

'To be fair, he didn't know I was here,' I said.

'Not consciously maybe,' she said, 'but he knew all right. You can't mess about with people's lives to the degree that he did and not stay connected.'

I had no idea what she meant but didn't want to question her. I told her I had found my mother's paintings and an old photo of the two families.

'Yes, Lilly had that photograph too. She liked it because she felt it connected her with her dead mother that she never knew. She loved her father too – Old Father William, he was known as locally. He was a good man but neglectful. He didn't mean to be. He just had no idea of the care that children needed. He thought that Victoria could cope with raising Lilly, simply because she was a girl.'

She paused and put her head on one side, inspecting me. 'Victoria looked like him; you do too – that heavy brown hair, robust. But in fact,

Lilly was the stronger of the two sisters. I think I told you that Victoria had TB when she was a baby. But William idolised Lilly; she looked so much like poor Beatrice, his dead wife, fragile and fair. After she died he just lived for the hotel. Him and Henry Senior, they just hit it off. Old malt whiskies and cameras. But my father was a good doctor, never neglected his patients. He used to bring Henry Junior and me over to the hotel when our mother was off on her rallies. She always wanted to take me with her but I pleaded to be left here by the sea, with Lilly.'

She sighed. 'Our four parents between them were a dead loss.' She laughed. 'Everybody used to think that someone else was looking after us. Lilly and I didn't mind but Henry and Victoria were always angry.'

I smiled. 'Was their marriage arranged for them from the cradle?'

Emmeline shrugged. 'Might as well have been. They deserved each other.'

I thought she was being a bit hard on them. I changed the subject. 'And Marguerite? Where does she fit into all this?'

'She's my adopted daughter.' Emmeline looked away. I knew there was more. Maybe I should mind my own business. But for once I'd got someone talking freely.

'How did you manage to adopt a daughter? As a single parent that would be difficult. Believe me, Emmeline, I've looked into adoption procedures.

And we're talking what, forty-something years ago?'

'This is difficult,' she said. 'I was going to tell you last time.'

'You don't have to, Emmeline. It's none of my business really.'

'In a way it is.'

'It is?' Oh, God. Not another family skeleton about to be trotted out of the cupboard.

'Marguerite is Lilly's real daughter, my unofficially adopted daughter. We raised her between us.'

'Lillian's actual daughter? She gave birth to her?'

'Oh, yes. She looks just like her.'

'But, I thought –' this was astonishing news to me.

'I know. That we are . . . were . . . lesbians.' She took a deep breath. 'The truth is that Lilly was raped and got pregnant.'

'Raped! Oh, no. Poor Lillian.' I couldn't believe it – not gentle, sensitive Lillian.

'Yes. Well, we put it all behind us and just got on with caring for Marguerite. She almost died. She was very frail and weak and needed lots of attention.'

'But who was it? Did he get arrested?' I felt hot anger rising up in me.

'A drunk who burst in on her. No, he was never caught. Please, Jane, I can't talk about it any more right now.' Her hands were shaking and she looked pale and withered.

'Oh, Emmeline, I'm so sorry.' I jumped up and gently put my arms around her shoulders. She leant against me and I could feel her trembling. 'I think you're so brave.' I was aware then that Neptune was watching us from his chair. He got up.

'It's about time you had some of your medicine,' he said. He looked at me, his face haggard. 'Perhaps you could go upstairs and see if Marguerite is awake.'

I nodded, remembering the little staircase beyond the red blanket near the fireplace. I went up the stairs, trying not to bang my head. Neptune was obviously using the landing bed. I went into the bedroom. The bed was empty, neatly made, a jug of sweet peas standing on the bedside table, filling the room with their fragrance. Where was Marguerite? Had she vanished into thin air, a figment of my imagination? Was I going to wake up in a minute and find this was all a hallucination under an anaesthetic or something?

In the absence of anything else to do I opened the cupboard door and found myself in another tiny room. It was tucked right under the eaves, the ceiling sloping down to the floor. There was a bed underneath the open window and Marguerite was lying on it asleep, like something from a fairy tale. I stood mesmerised, wondering how anyone so seemingly pure could be the result of a rape. As I stared she seemed familiar to me. I supposed she resembled her grandmother Beatrice, pregnant with

238

Lillian in Dad's photo. If Marguerite was Lillian's daughter then she must be related to me too. She would be my cousin if Lillian was my aunt. I seemed to be collecting relatives all over the place. But, it seemed, no sooner had I found them than I lost them again.

Marguerite opened her eyes and looked at me. There was something so profoundly innocent about her, totally without guile, I felt fearful for her. She was so vulnerable. Those who loved and understood her were going to be abandoning her soon. She would be taken away, cared for in some sort of home. How would she cope with that? Marguerite sat up on her bed with a question in her eyes, as if she could read my thoughts. She got up and took my hands and put them on her chest. I could feel her heart beating. Her hands felt cool. I calmed down. She smiled at me, and I felt that dissolving feeling inside again as if she had made everything all right. She handed me her hairbrush and turned round. I brushed her long silver hair for her, feeling tender as a mother.

That evening, our mood seemed to change and Emmeline suggested we have supper outside to celebrate her homecoming and my return. She wanted to go down to the beach but Neptune wouldn't hear of it. Marguerite went out with him to pick salad and Emmeline and I prepared fish and potatoes and put them in the range. We carried a comfortable chair outside for Emmeline and we sat eating, and drinking elderflower wine until it

239

got dark. Neptune played softly on a little concertina, pausing to stare out to sea and Marguerite stood perilously close to the edge of the cliff, her face tilted to the sky, looking like a wraith in the firelight. Loot padded around foraging for scraps of food.

I felt contented sitting there, breathing the salty air, smelling roses and herbs, the sweet taste of elderflowers on my tongue. Mars gleamed in the southern sky, dwarfing the glittering stars. Cruise ships sauntered past, fairy-lit and intriguing, disturbing the lazy sea. I realised I wasn't worrying about Dad or my work or feeling homesick for Chas and Birdsong.

Emmeline's head fell forward onto her chest and she jerked it up again. Marguerite took her hands to help her up and take her inside. Neptune and I cleared up. Back in the cottage, Neptune picked up his torch and announced he was going to push his boat out and go home but Emmeline wanted him to stay.

'You need the bed for Jane,' he said.

'Jane can sleep on the bed-settee,' said Emmeline, indicating the ancient sofa in front of the fireplace. 'I don't want you out on the sea at this time of night at your age, Nep.'

'I know that sea –'

'Yes, I know, like your own arse,' Emmeline retorted.

I smiled at their bickering and attempted to open the sofa-bed. It took all four of us in the end to prise it open and by the look of it, I think I would rather have slept on the floor. But Marguerite fetched sheets smelling of lavender for me and brought down one of the patchwork covers. The night was so warm, I didn't think I would need it anyway. We sat drinking tea and then Marguerite went up to bed, dropping a kiss on each of our heads on her way.

The three of us sat on. They asked me questions about my life. I noticed that if I mentioned Dad they went quiet and I wasn't sure what they were thinking, so I regaled them with funny stories about my antics at boarding school and my travels with friends and Chas.

Emmeline told me that she and Lillian had tried to trace Henry and Victoria after they had left the island. They'd even written to some Scottish hospitals. I couldn't think why. As far as I was aware my parents had always lived and worked in Malvern. Years later Emmeline chanced upon a book of mine in the library. The first two books I'd had published were under my maiden name, Rampling, and she had read the bit of blurb about me. From then on she and Lillian had kept track of my writing career but had never known where I lived. I felt sad at what I'd missed by not knowing them.

'I would have loved to have come here and got to know you all,' I said.

'But you're here now, that's the important thing,' said Emmeline. 'It's not too late.'

'But –' I wanted to ask her how long she'd got

241

left. They were both looking at me across the table. Suddenly I felt my stomach clench with anxiety. Why was it so important for me to be here? Emmeline blinked and Neptune looked away. I realised then, I was being set up. They must have seen the truth dawn on my face. Emmeline started up from her chair and doubled up with pain. Neptune supported her under her arms.

'We just wanted you to meet Marguerite, to get to know her, that's all,' he said. 'We're not expecting anything of you.'

'You think that I'm going to take over the care of Marguerite, don't you?' I said slowly. I could see it all now. Lillian dying, leaving me her cottage, knowing that Emmeline was on her way out too. Me, the unsuspecting lost cousin, probably quite well off, lured into the trap. Bingo!

'We don't want you do anything, Jane,' she gasped. 'We just wanted to give you the chance. You two deserve to know each other.' Emmeline was leaning heavily on Neptune now. He looked concerned and lowered her into the chair.

'I'll get your medicine and you must go to bed,' he said.

Emmeline and I sat opposite each other. I glowered at her. Her protruding eyes swam with tears.

'I can't bear it, Jane. She's such a sensitive soul, like her mother. She won't survive if she's taken away from here.'

I said nothing. I couldn't believe how I'd walked into this one. How could I just turn my back now without feeling guilty for the rest of my life? It seemed I'd inherited a cottage about to fall into the sea, several acres of doubtful land, a rotting half-hotel and a middle-aged disabled woman who'd never been further than Wraith Cove.

Neptune helped Emmeline up to bed. I visited the basic bathroom, off the kitchen, tacked onto the back of the outhouse that I'd once mistaken for Wraith Cottage. I lay sweating on the lumpy sofa-bed in my knickers and tee-shirt with Surfer purring at my feet. I wished I was back at Birdsong, tucked up with Chas and this had never happened to me. I lay there for what seemed like hours. The cat stopped purring and I could hear the little creaking noises of the cottage and the sound of the wind sweeping the sea. It was so peaceful here. Something inside me, deep down, despite all this turmoil, was at peace.

I heard a slight rustling noise close by. I opened my eyes. Marguerite was standing looking down at me. Her silver hair gleamed in the moonlight. I realised that it was her I had seen in my mind at Birdsong when I'd entrusted my own wisdom to show me my way. She didn't startle me. It was almost as if I expected her to be there. She lay down beside me on the bed, her feather weight hardly making it creak. I felt her small hand creep into mine. I moved closer to her. Her hair smelled of fresh air. Cousins, I thought, daughters of estranged sisters. I could feel her breath on my face as I drifted off to sleep.

★　　★　　★

Emmeline lay awake, her body shaking. What have I done? she thought. She'd let her tongue run away with her. She had felt relieved to be home and so relaxed listening to Jane, enjoying her stories and her sense of humour. She didn't appear to possess any of Henry or Victoria's characteristics that she could detect, as yet. And she seemed full of enthusiasm for the island and Wraith Cottage. But Emmeline had forgotten her plan and Jane had sensed that there was more expected of her than a simple reconciliation with an aunt and a cousin.

'Silly old fool,' she chided herself. If she'd alienated Jane there would be no chance of getting Henry here. She pressed her hands into her aching stomach, almost glad of the pain. 'Lilly,' she groaned, 'I've let you down.'

She heard a slight noise and Marguerite came out of her room. She crept past her bed and went silently downstairs. Emmeline felt her tension ease, she could rest for a while now.

CHAPTER 13

'No!' I woke with a gasp and sat bolt upright. Who was that yelling? I swallowed hard and put my hand to my throat. It felt sore as if I was getting a cold. Had I been shouting? I'd been having that terrifying dream again of someone trying to pull me up through bloodied water. And I was choking as if I was being strangled. I ran my tongue around the inside of my mouth trying to get some moisture to flow and peered about the shadowed room. Day was breaking. I was alone on the sofa-bed. Marguerite must have gone back to her own room during the night. Or had I dreamt that too? I listened. No one was stirring; even the cat was still sleeping at my feet. I couldn't have cried out then – I would have woken everyone.

I slid off the bed and pulled on my jeans and trainers. I lifted the heavy iron latch and opened the door, shutting it as silently as I could behind me. The morning felt delicious with that little bite of departing night. I smelt salt and dewy grass and wasp-bitten apples. I picked my way along Emmeline's pebbled paths, avoiding collisions with hanging shells, driftwood sculptures and speckled spiders poised in the middle of glistening webs. I was getting used to the cliff edge and the sand and boulder clamber down to the beach. The tide was receding, leaving a few feet of darkened gold, permitting rocks to display their enhanced colours, ivory, amber, rust, before drying off, flattened by the sun. The sea was striped; dark blues interspersed with green and hazy turquoise and a layer of cream along the horizon like a mermaid's birthday cake.

I wandered the shoreline of Wraith Cove, allowing my mind to flow with its own current. I noticed it kept drifting towards Marguerite, the comfort of her hand in mine. Had that been real? Everything about her seemed to have an ethereal edge that I couldn't quite grasp. My rational mind wanted to burst in, demanding explanations. Wasn't it dangerous to keep a person isolated like this? Suppose she was ill and had to go to hospital, wouldn't she be prey to infections? Had they had her vaccinated? Could she have been taught to speak? What had Lillian and Emmeline been thinking of keeping her sequestered like this?

I spotted an inviting stone and sat down, kicking off my trainers. I wondered what it had been like for my two aunts, ostracised and then one of them raped. Had my mother and father known about Lillian's rape? They couldn't have done, surely they would have dropped all their silly prejudice and rushed to her aid. It must have happened after they'd left the island and lost touch with their sisters. So, they would never have known about Marguerite. It was just as well really. If my father had found out about her he would probably have committed her into some institution, thinking he was doing the right thing.

So, these two young women, lesbians, had just knuckled down and raised the disabled offspring of a rapist. I had to hand it to them; they were an extraordinary pair of females. I wished I'd known Lillian. I wished I had met them years ago. I might have been able to help them then. What a nerve! They had managed perfectly well on their own. Who was I to think they might have benefited from having me around? I sighed. The truth of the matter was that they did need my help now. And instead of feeling honoured I was feeling used and tricked. And they hadn't actually asked me for anything. It seemed they just wanted me to know the truth. And the truth was that Lillian was dead and Emmeline was dying. Marguerite was losing her carers. There was Neptune, equally elderly and anyway, he couldn't possibly take on the care of an unrelated woman with feminine needs and all that implied. I could sympathise with their dilemma.

I got up again and began pacing, not noticing the glory of the morning any more. They should have seen this coming. They must have discussed what would happen to Marguerite. I felt my anger starting to rise again. Had they really thought they could haul me in at the eleventh hour to take over the care of a dubiously related cousin that I'd never met? They'd been living in some sort of time warp down here, a fantasy with me as the saviour in the wings. Perhaps they'd read too much fiction in damn silly books like mine.

I stopped and looked up at the cliffs oozing down to the sea as if yearning for liberation. The sparkling water winked and nudged at the stones whispering gossip from unknown shores. Had I made a mistake with my life and been distracted by stories whilst some deep truth evaded me? But perhaps it wasn't evading me at all and I simply ignored it, tempted away by the siren call of fiction. And I'd spent my life not only immersed in my own drama but inventing bookloads for others to escape into. There had to be more than this, what was it I was missing?

I couldn't face the others yet. I wasn't ready to talk or make decisions. I brushed the sand off my feet and pulled my trainers back on. I climbed the cliff path and skirted round Wraith Cottage, thinking what an atmospheric picture my mother had painted of this place when she'd been so young. I heard a sharp yap from Loot, detecting my movements. Oh, well. They'd realise I would return sooner or later – I'd left all my belongings.

I tramped across the field, my shoes soaking up dew. I wandered around the grounds of Wraith Cove Hotel for a while, running my hands over the lichen-encrusted stone walls, sitting on ivy-invaded steps, imagining guests taking tea at tables on the lawn, gazing out to sea. Perhaps little motherless Lillian being petted by them before she was hauled away by Victoria and reprimanded for being bothersome. This must have been a holiday paradise, before the war and rationing sucked the life out of it. I brought myself back to the present. If my father managed to leave me some money – after paying his carers vast sums for sitting beside him knitting jumpers for their grandchildren – then I would look into the possibility of rebuilding something here.

I walked up to the main road. It was still early, not many cars about. I turned left towards Niton. I had to walk and keep going until I found a way through all this. Chas would say, 'It's simple, Janey. Just tell them it's not your problem and let them sort it out. Marguerite may well have to go into some sort of sheltered environment. You can visit her, keep in touch. It's tough, but so is life.' And he wouldn't give it another thought. But he was used to evading family issues. I'd never had a family to side-step before. Just walk, I told myself.

I turned left at St Catherine's Road just in time to see a red squirrel scamper across and leap up into a hazel tree. I felt my spirit lift. The houses down here were interesting individuals with wynd and clyffe names. The pavements and road were cracked and creeping inexorably towards the sea. I walked down sun-dappled lanes until suddenly everything opened up and I stood in an area of National Trust land overlooking summer-scorched meadows. Centre stage was the lighthouse, an astonishing white in the southern sun. The beam flashed round and round, dazzling, even on this bright day. It had small minarets around the top which gave it rather a Moorish look. I half expected a muezzin to sing out the call to prayer.

I wandered down to it, avoiding cowpats, and sat, leaning against a white wall looking out across the English Channel – next stop Cherbourg. I imagined rambling here with Chas, thinking he would like it. I usually suggested our foreign holidays, craving hot sun. Maybe he just humoured me. I smiled. Chas would be more at home in an English deckchair really, trousers rolled up, socks and sandals, handkerchief knotted on his head. I could imagine him fishing, chugging around the bay with Neptune. Dear Chas, I felt a pang of home-sickness. I wanted to be back at Birdsong, on top of my hill, above this dilemma.

I got up and kept on walking along the cliff until it disappeared into a gorge and I had to clamber up a steep slope and found myself at the foot of a stunning inland cliff, like a mini Grand Canyon. Birds soared and rode the thermals. I wished I'd got my binoculars with me. I could make out the stiff winged flight of fulmars and hear the shriek of hunting peregrines. Fishermen made their way down to the shore, rods slung on their backs. I was beginning to lose touch now with how far I'd gone and exactly where I was, but I shrugged, this was just a little island, I'd soon find myself. Rabbits scooted over the hills and excited dogs panted about waiting for their owners to catch up. Friendly walkers paused for an exchange of potted life histories.

It was nearly lunch time before I found myself back on familiar territory and I sat outside The Buddle Inn for orange juice and crisps, glad that I had a fiver in my pocket. Little kids rattled buckets and spades, eager for sand and sea while parents lingered over their Ploughman's and local brew, reluctant to move. I wondered what it would be like to live here with this old smugglers' inn as my local, getting used to a new way of life, a different set of people.

I turned my mind again to the dilemma of Marguerite. What would it be like for her to be taken out of her secluded environment and placed among people not of her choosing, people with different ideas of how she should lead her life? My walking hadn't brought me closer to a solution. I couldn't move down here and leave everything I knew to look after her. But how could I take her away? Imagine packing up her belongings, strapping her in my car and arriving back at Birdsong. Besides, I wasn't qualified to look after her. I didn't even know what kind of disabilities she had.

Suddenly, I felt clearer. Of course, I didn't have enough information to make any kind of decision. I'd got caught up in yet another drama. Poor Jane, having all this thrust upon her, however will she cope? That's how my storyline was going.

251

I needed to talk to Emmeline. She was the one who had spent the last forty-odd years living with Marguerite. Maybe she and Lillian had thought up all sorts of contingency plans and I just happened to figure in one of them.

I wandered down to Castlehaven and whiled away some time picking my way through rock pools, watching a slender little egret fishing the shallows, kids messing about on body boards and a couple of men pushing out their boats to inspect the lobster pots. I lay on the warm sand watching amiable clouds and turned over to view the scene from beach level. Whole miniature worlds clung to the rocks, dealing with their own life issues, oblivious of mine.

I fell asleep and woke feeling chilled and hungry. The tide was coming in fast and I had to paddle through the shallows. I soon warmed up on the climb to the road and found I was nearer than I thought to where I'd started. My car stood where I'd left it the day before and it hadn't been vandalised. By the time I'd cut through the hotel grounds and the field I was feeling tired and in dire need of a cup of tea.

Before I opened the gate of Wraith Cottage I looked over the cliff. I could see Loot scampering at the edge of the waves. Marguerite was there, standing on a rock out in the sea, wearing her blue dress. She stood motionless, watching. Then in one fluid movement she slipped her dress down, raised her arms and tipped naked into the sea. I felt the cold shock of the water like a baptism, as if I was being immersed. I stood mesmerised. The waves rolled and tumbled with her as if they were part of something synchronous. I saw flashes of darkened hair, limbs and buttocks made pale by the blue-green water as it carried her in to the shore.

She stood up, thigh deep, glistening. She held her arms out at each side, caressing the sea and raising her arms to the sun like an offering. She threw back her head, the tips of her silver hair touched the waves. Stars from her fingers fell upon her face. I felt the tingle as if the droplets rained down on me. My mind felt wide open, wordless. I was aware of a profound feeling that I couldn't put a name to. It wasn't anything like joy or sorrow. It was something different, as if there existed inside me a place that I had never known. I felt tears running down my face but they had no reason attached to them – they just flowed out of the nameless feeling as if they were part of it, expressing it perfectly. Marguerite waded to the shallows. Loot bounded to her feet. She placed a hand on his plastered head and he panted up at her. Then she picked her way carefully across the rocks to retrieve her dress.

Emmeline slept most of the day and woke feeling calm, until she remembered last night.

'She'll be back,' Neptune said. 'She's left all her things here and her car is still parked up on the road – I checked.' Emmeline looked at Marguerite for reassurance but she was busy, making bread. She wandered outside and looked over the cliff and along the edge of the garden to the field, but there was no sign of Jane. Of course she'll come back, she said to herself. She just needs some time to think. She stood looking down at the vegetable garden. So tiny compared to the one that they'd had in the hotel grounds. And her herb garden up there – it must be overrun with weeds by now. She hadn't been able to get up there to tend it for ages.

She sighed and sat down on a tree stump by the lobster pot table. Such plans they'd had for the future, the four of them, all those years ago. But she should never have left Lilly alone like that, every day at Wraith Cottage, thinking she was contented and safe. She listened to the wind rustling the leaves, tinkling the shells.

'I thought I was doing the right thing, Lilly. I wanted to create some security for us. But I got caught up in the project too much. Did I neglect you?'

'No, Emm. Don't keep blaming yourself. I wanted to be alone. I felt free to concentrate on my pregnancy when I was by myself. I couldn't explain that to you.'

'I should have understood.'

'How could you have? I was glad you had something to occupy you. You were happier, more like your old self. I can recall that summer as if it were yesterday . . .

★   ★   ★

I remember aching backs and muddy hands. The four of us get into a discussion one night after a crab supper at Puck's Cottage. We are sitting outside on the wooden veranda. Neptune is throwing a stick for the tireless Booty to retrieve from the shallow waves. The evenings are longer now but still with the slight chill of not-quite-summer. I am glad of the freshness. The men's cottage makes me feel a bit queasy with its strong smell of tobacco and fish and dog. The sea is a delicate shade of lilac, the horizon lost in a pink mist. Emm and the men are all smoking, adding a drifting haze to the evening. I seem to have lost my taste for cigarettes.

Neptune's old blue and white boat is hauled up on the sand looking tiny against the side of their big yellow fishing vessel. They earn little these days from their fishing and carpentry skills. They put it down to a mixture of post-war hardship and a certain amount of ostracism due to prejudice. They ask us how we are going to manage without an income from the hotel. We are fortunate, I own the roof over our heads and we live cheaply. But there are still bills to pay for electricity and rates. Emm has an inheritance from her parents and has looked at different ways to invest it so that we can have a small income to live on. We also think we might be able to sell our surplus home produce.

'Will you sell the hotel, Lillian?' Neptune asks.

'Not at the moment. We don't want anyone looking around, or living too closely.'

'We'll see how it works out when the baby is here and then maybe I'll get a job or Lilly will sell the hotel just for its demolition value,' Emm says.

'This is just an idea,' says Woody, pouring brandy into our glasses. 'But supposing we all muck in and make a market garden. We could use the old plots in the hotel grounds and we could buy some more chickens and breed rabbits and what with our fish supplies and free wood – well, we could live on next to nothing.'

Emm and I look at each other. I can see her eyes sparkling with excitement. This would be just up her street – an outdoor project – getting her hands dirty, studying the best way to do things, working it all out. And with the men to add their support and help with the labour. All four of us are soon bursting with enthusiasm. New ideas are pouring out of us. Even Booty is stirred, going from one to the other, wagging his tail.

'We could renovate the greenhouses and have a market stall – out on the road,' Neptune says. He smiles at Woody. 'You can make it, Wood, but I'll have to trim your hair and beard if you're going to sell the produce, you'll scare everyone off.'

Woody cuffs him round the head. 'I think this calls for another drink,' he says.

So, most of April is spent digging and planning and plotting. I am given the task of ordering seeds and plants and comparing price lists from growers and nurseries. There is plenty of choice.

The island is full of keen gardeners because of its climate. I am enjoying all this so much that the fear of Henry is receding further. I can walk out of the door now without glancing around. I sit in the garden at the lobster pot table with my catalogues and price lists, dreaming about how it is all going to be, listening to the sea. In the evenings, we sit by the fire. I knit pink and white bootees and mittens and tiny coats and hats while Emm reads out loud to me until her voice starts to slur with tiredness after her hard day's work. Then I take the book out of her hands, tip Drifter off her lap, and we go up to bed. We still lock the doors at night. It has become a habit now.

One morning I realise, however hard I breathe in, the hooks and eyes on the waistband of my slacks will no longer meet. I look at myself sideways in the outhouse mirror. My waist is disappearing and there is a definite protrusion around my belly.

'Look,' I shout, running back into the kitchen with my top pulled up and my trousers hanging open. Emm admires my bulge, placing her cool hands on my abdomen.

'I'd better get on with that smock,' she grins.

'You've got enough to do. A piece of elastic will be fine.'

From then on I expand rapidly. Emm finds me some elasticated trousers and large shirts on a second-hand stall in Ventnor market. Woody and Neptune tease me and I love it, but I can feel Emm's eyes on me from time to time, pondering, serious. I wonder what she is thinking but deep down I know. I see less of her. She is working in the hotel gardens much of the day now, planning things with Woody and Neptune.

I prepare meals and whitewash the nursery and start knitting a delicate shawl from fine white wool that Emm had spied in the market. I read the book on labour and childbirth that she had bought in the second-hand shop. It scares me stiff. It is a medical book and outlines all the possible complications for mother and infant. There are graphic photographs of Siamese twins and malformed infants. I try to skip over those bits but get myself caught up in fascinated horror. I am near to tears when Emm comes home. She snatches the book away.

'You aren't supposed to read that,' she says, holding me. 'It's for doctors and midwives.'

'But I need to know. I should know, Emm,' I sob.

She holds me firmly by the shoulders. 'Look, Lilly. Nothing is going to go wrong. Do you hear me?' She holds a handkerchief to my nose as if I were a little girl. 'Blow!' she commands. I do as I am told. She sits me down and makes some tea, even though she has been the one working so hard.

'Better now?' she asks after a while. I nod, still giving the occasional sob. 'Little Water Lilly,' she teases. 'I've never known anybody cry as much as you.'

I am glad that I'd read it though. I sometimes think how naïve I am. I read a lot but I know little of the world. We hardly ever listen to the wireless and I never go anywhere, not that I want to.

I wander the beach most mornings and sit in the garden in the afternoon, peeling potatoes and chopping vegetables. Occasionally I notice a creeping sensation down my spine, almost as if there is someone watching me. I know there can't be. Anyone coming down to Wraith Cottage is bound to call at the hotel first and the others are working up there. I think it must be the remnants of my fear that sometimes come to the surface when I feel drowsy as if I am off guard.

And then, one day, I feel a jolt, like an electric shock and I know he has come. I jump up, spilling my bowl of beans.

'Lillian, it's all right.' He is standing several feet away from me. His dark suit and black hair look menacing against the light sky. 'I won't come any nearer.'

I start to shake from head to toe. I grab my paring knife. 'D . . . don't, Henry,' I stammer. 'Don't.'

'I promise.' He takes a step back. 'I just wanted to know how you are? I've been concerned about you.'

'G . . . go away!' I mutter, my teeth chattering.

'I am going,' he says. 'I just wondered if you need anything?'

'No. I don't. Please go now.'

'All right. I'm sorry, I didn't mean to scare you.' He stands there, looking down. He speaks quietly. 'It's just that I wondered if you wanted to write to Victoria. If you do, I'm going to see her soon and could take it.'

'Give me her address.'

'She . . . she doesn't want that. But, I thought if I took her a letter, she might read it.' He shrugs. 'That's all I wanted to say. I don't want you two to lose touch because of this.' He takes another step back. 'But, if you'd rather not –'

'Where . . . how will I get it to you?'

'Send it to the hospital, if you like.'

'I can't. Emm takes our letters to the post office.'

'Then leave it in the hotel postbox and I'll collect it. I'm going in two days.' He turns and walks out of the garden. I watch him skirt along the edge of the field. He'd obviously crept through the bushes and shrubs of the hotel, avoiding the vegetable plots on the other side of the garden where the others were working. I sit down, still trembling. Have my feelings been right then, has he been watching me? I should run and find the others, tell them. But then I will miss my chance of contacting Victoria.

I go indoors to get myself a drink of water, letting my fear settle. I find myself stroking my abdomen, reassuring my daughter that all is well. Henry won't mean me any harm now, will he? What would be the point? We'd both agreed we didn't want anything more to come of this. And he has his wife and child to think about. He isn't interested in my baby or me. But why does he care if I lose touch with Victoria? Maybe he thinks it is a small way of making amends. He'd looked shrunken somehow, diminished. Perhaps guilt is eating him up and this is all he can think to do.

I go back outside, gather up the beans. Well, I'd faced him alone and survived. My worst fear had happened and I am all right. I'll write to Victoria and see what comes of it. I can't give up this last chance at reconciliation with my sister. But I'll have to keep this a secret from Emm. She'd be furious if she knew.

The next day I write the letter. It is quite short. I tell her how I am and of the plans we have for the market garden. I tell her I miss her and want to know how her pregnancy is going. I ask her what she is going to do. Did she plan to come and live back on the island? It would be nice, I write, to have our children know each other. They needn't know about what happened. I explain about Woody's paternity offer. I send her my love.

That afternoon I stroll over to the hotel to see how the gardens and the greenhouses are progressing. After the inspection, I say I need a walk and wander off through the grounds. I walk up the drive to the road. The wooden postbox is full of cobwebs. I put my letter inside. I lean on the padlocked gate for a while. The shady road is quiet. Not many people own motorcars here yet. The sound of hooves is still more common than the roar of an engine. I turn and look at the hotel. Its paint is flaking badly, tiles slipping. Perhaps I should sell it for demolition. My stomach clenches at the thought. Poor Dad, what would he say? But it is just nostalgia. Things are different now. I touch my belly. I am moving into a whole new kind of experience. I am going to be a mother. I wander back through the grounds and join the others for a flask of tea.

'I've been thinking,' I say. 'I could have the hotel cleared and the contents auctioned. That would raise money for the garden but we will still have our privacy.'

'Won't you mind? All your past disappearing like that?' asks Woody, concerned.

'That's exactly it – the past. Time to let go of it.'

Emm seems happier since she has got her teeth into the gardening. It is what she loves most. I see much less of her but I can't complain. I know she is doing all this for us and I need to play a part. I write to a firm of auctioneers to come and assess the contents of Wraith Cove Hotel.

A week has gone by since Henry's visit and I wonder if he might have returned and left a letter from Victoria for me in the postbox. I walk up there but the box is empty. Perhaps he isn't back yet. I try again a week later but still there is nothing. But maybe he is still away; it is a long journey to and from Scotland. I wonder who Victoria is staying with. I don't recall them having any Scottish friends. But then, Victoria didn't confide in me about her social life. She met a lot of people through Henry's medical circle.

A few days later, I am writing at the garden table and I can feel the familiar sensation along my spine and the back of my neck. I turn to look towards the gate. Henry is standing there watching me. He is smoking a cigarette. I feel the trembling begin but I get up slowly. There is no knife on the table this time. 'Stay there,' I say.

'I've just come to tell you something,' he says.' He grinds out his cigarette and stands looking down at it. 'I gave Victoria your letter, but, she, er,' he looks up at me. 'I am sorry, Lillian. She said she doesn't want any contact with you. I tried to persuade her but she was adamant.'

I sit down slowly. 'She can't mean it,' I say. Victoria was always getting angry and stalking out of rooms. But I knew she would come back. 'Did she read my letter?'

Henry nods. 'I am sorry, Lillian,' he repeats softly. 'She said she thought it was for the best – for both of you, and the . . .' He nods vaguely at my middle.

My eyes fill with tears. 'How is she?'

'She's well. Everything's as it should be.'

'Who is she staying with?'

'Some old friends of mine from medical school. I've known them for years.'

'Will she be coming back here – to the island – after the baby is born?'

Henry opens the gate and comes towards me. 'That was the other thing I've come to tell you, Lillian. We think it best if we move away permanently. After all that's happened – a fresh start.'

I feel the tears running down my cheeks. 'Then, I might never see her again – or her baby.'

I hear Henry sigh. I look up at him. He wipes his hand across his eyes. 'I will do my best to try and persuade her, Lillian. Perhaps she will feel differently when the baby is born.'

I nod. 'Will you send me a note . . . to let me know when she has the baby and where she will be?'

'Lillian, I will of course.' He blows his nose on his handkerchief. 'I'm so terribly sorry about all this. I should never – I've been a real swine.' He turns abruptly and walks out of the garden, leaving the gate swinging behind him.

I sit with Emm that evening trying to pluck up the courage to tell her about Henry's visits. But I can't. If I tell her he's been today I will have to tell her he's been before. She will be angry and hurt and I can't blame her. But what good will it do? I know now, about Victoria's silence – it is what she wants. I can stop wondering. Henry is going too. Soon it will all be over. They will be gone. Emm need never know about this. I will grieve over Victoria and her child in silence. One day – who knows, she might relent and get in touch with me. She knows where I am at least.

Suddenly, I become aware of a little fluttering sensation inside me. I sit still as a statue. There, it comes again. 'Emm,' I whisper. She looks up sleepily. 'Emm, she's moving . . .

Emmeline sighed and ran her hands over the table top. This was where Lilly used to sit and write or prepare vegetables while they were working on the garden project. Neptune had repaired the old lobster pot table many times over the years.

A movement caught her eye. Jane was standing at the edge of the garden looking down on the beach. Emmeline knew Marguerite was down there, bathing. She was going to call out, but something in the way Jane stood, watching, kept her silent.

CHAPTER 14

The following morning, stiff-muscled, I wandered out to sit in the garden with Emmeline. Marguerite was caring for her, draping a lilac crochet blanket over her hunched shoulders and lifting her flapping feet onto a lobster pot. Surfer, ever vigilant for her place on Emmeline's lap, jumped up, causing her to wince. Marguerite attempted to lift her off.

'Don't fuss,' Emmeline snapped, holding onto Surfer. But she was smiling. Marguerite kissed her and set off with Neptune to fish in the bay. I could see them out there now, the red beacon of Marguerite's life jacket amidst the white flurry of scavenging gulls. Neptune's fishing boat was a sturdy yellow vessel with a motor, much larger than the blue and white dinghy that he rowed around the cove.

I sat on a patch of prickly grass, smelling crushed camomile. Emmeline was silent, stroking Surfer. We'd hardly spoken since I'd stumbled back last night. All three of them seemed to understand that I'd needed time alone. I told them I'd been walking, following the coastal path. They nodded thoughtfully and didn't question me. Neptune left after supper and rowed home and I helped Marguerite to clear up. She ran me a welcome bath and I lay in it for ages, surprised how hot the water was, heated by the ancient kitchen range. And then I'd slept deeply, upstairs, undisturbed by drowning and strangulation.

The air was warm, the sun softened by sea-haze. Emmeline seemed relaxed; her hand had ceased stroking. I wondered if she was sleeping. I glanced up at her, disconcerted to meet her yellowed eyes as if she was waiting for me to speak.

'Are you going to write any more books?' she asked.

This took me by surprise. 'I don't know. It's been difficult with Dad being ill.' I picked up a pebble and began turning it over and over.

'Things change, don't they?' she said.

I wasn't sure whether this was a question or not. I nodded. We sat quietly. Even the soft swoosh of the waves below us seemed to fade. I felt the silence become tangible, drawing me in, pulling something out of me. Words seemed to form themselves in my mind and tumble from my mouth telling her about the change in myself since the beginning of the year, how I'd been questioning everything, unable to write like I'd done all my life. It felt a relief as if I was in the confessional. Every time I glanced up at her she seemed to be listening intensely, teasing it out of me as if she had hold of the end of a skein of thread. When I came to the end of my outpouring, I laughed, self-consciously.

'Dad calls my books damn silly stories,' I said. 'That used to upset me but now I think maybe he's right.'

'No, Jane. He has no right to belittle your talent. He did that to Victoria too. I'm sure your books have given pleasure to many people. You have a gift for storytelling. Lilly and I read them all with great enjoyment.'

'But I feel I never faced up to reality. My whole life seems to have been a fiction.' I hoped I wasn't tiring her with all this stuff. She should be resting. But she was still gazing at me with her bulbous blue eyes, keeping hold of the thread. 'I wanted children you see, Emmeline. My life would have been different if I'd had a child.'

'You think you would have been fulfilled if you'd been a mother?'

'Yes, part of me feels empty . . . a sort of longing.' I felt tears welling up in my eyes, I thought I was over all this.

'But, Jane,' she said gently, 'perhaps that is also part of your fantasy.' She leant forward slightly. 'Look, we all have this yearning. If you had been a busy mother you might have blamed the yearning on the fact that you had no time to fulfil your ambition to be a writer.'

'I would've liked the opportunity to find that out,' I sniffled.

'Oh, I'm not meaning to trivialise it. I'm just trying

268

to say that the feeling you mentioned – emptiness, longing – might not have magically disappeared if you had been a mother.'

I nodded. I wasn't completely sure what she meant but her words gave me comfort.

'You're no different from anybody else, my dear. We all make up a story, a world, for ourselves. We have to do it to survive. But at any moment it can collapse around us and we have to, well, concoct another drama or take a look at the debris.'

I felt astounded. I stared up at her. How could I have thought this old woman was a bit senile, an old eccentric, cut off from the world?

Emmeline laughed. 'I know what you're thinking,' she said. 'What does this crazy old woman know about anything? What experience of life has she had?'

I laughed with her and shook my head. 'Is that what I have to do then, Emmeline? Take a look at my debris?'

'But that's exactly what you are doing, Jane. You started doing it when Lilly died.'

'I did?'

'Of course. Didn't you say that you felt a change in yourself at New Year?'

'Yes. But wasn't that just a coincidence? I mean, my age and a running out of ideas. It all just happened to collide.'

Emmeline shook her head. 'Why do you suppose you are here? Why did Henry have a stroke? Why am I dying?'

She'd lost me. I shrugged.

'When Lilly died it affected an energy pattern you could say. Look, all of us are connected. When a major change happens – death for instance – the reverberation is felt by everyone close to that person. It depends on our sensitivity how much we feel it. It might be just a vague feeling of disquiet. Someone as sensitive as Lilly – or Marguerite – would feel it like a sledgehammer.'

'But, that can't be true. I never knew about any of you –'

'Oh, but you did. Not consciously. But your family and mine are deeply connected. When intense emotions and events happen between people then strong bonds are formed – not always positive – even if they have no further contact. When something happens to one person it's as if they twitch the web of connection and everybody is affected to one degree or another. That's why you have been so disturbed since Lilly's death. We all have.' She grinned. 'You said yourself that even Chas has been questioning his way of life.'

'Yes, but –'

'You've changed – so must he.'

'How do you know all this is true? Isn't it just a theory? A psychic thing or one of those New Age myths? I really don't go along with all that stuff.'

'Well, I have read a lot. But it isn't the reading that's important. It's my experience because of living with Lilly and Marguerite.'

'What sort of experience, Emmeline?' Despite my scepticism I was getting intrigued. Her eyes glittered in her shrunken face. 'Are you sure you're not getting too tired?'

'Tired? I've been waiting to tell you all this.' She shook the blanket off her shoulders as if she was warming up. 'Lilly was always sensitive. She could feel other people's pain and understand why they were suffering. She would have to write it down in order to let it go. It gave her a great capacity for forgiveness. Although she didn't see it like that.'

She sighed and paused as if reflecting on Aunt Lillian's goodness. I wondered if that was it, but then she brushed a hand across her face and continued.

'And then, as Marguerite grew, we realised she was experiencing a different world. She needed to draw, loved colours. We didn't understand at first. She drew things and people, but all blurred – a bit like wraiths.' She smiled. 'Good name for this place. She used lots of colours as her pictures became more detailed. Sometimes she used to get very agitated and she'd draw scenes. In those days we listened to the wireless and we realised she was drawing pictures of earthquakes or other disasters. Sometimes she would draw them before they happened. It was as if she possessed antennae that picked up disturbances in a much vaster network of energy.'

'You say she used to. Doesn't she do it any more?'

271

'She got distressed. We tried to find ways of helping her. She was more relaxed just being here quietly, with Lilly and me. We stopped listening to the wireless and Neptune ceased taking her into town.'

'Into town?' So she had been further than Wraith Cove.

'To the fish market, every week. He used to tell people she was his niece – deaf and dumb. We couldn't isolate her down here, could we? We needed to expose her to the usual childhood diseases and to see how she coped with the world. But she would stare at people and see things that we couldn't. Some times she would be all right, other times she would be terrified.'

'So she stopped going?'

'Lilly tried to teach her ways to protect herself.' She smiled, and a radiance spread across her face as if a light had come on inside her. 'You should have seen the two of them, Jane. They'd clasp hands and Lilly would talk quietly to her and then they'd both grow still for ages, looking into each other's eyes. I had no idea what they were doing. I wasn't on their wavelength. I just look up things in books. Their methods worked up to a point. But she still got very disturbed amongst certain outsiders. And gradually we let the outings slip.'

'Doesn't she go anywhere at all now?'

Emmeline shook her head and sighed. 'We were wrong, Jane. We should have persevered with her. That's the dilemma we're facing now.'

'And she's never seen a doctor, a dentist?'

'We've always treated her with herbal and homoeopathic remedies. She's very healthy.'

'What about school? You must have registered her birth. Didn't anyone ever call to check?'

Her head drooped and she bit her lip, like a guilty child.

'But, Emmeline. She could have been given specialist help. What about her speech?'

Her eyes blazed and I caught a glimpse of her young, fearless self. 'If you get to know her you will understand that she is a peaceful, joyous woman. She is in touch with whatever it is that we all yearn for. Who are we to suppose we have something better to offer her?'

'But she has to live in this world. How will she cope when –'

Emmeline's hands fluttered in the air like birds with nowhere to land. A noise like a groan came from her throat. 'We hoped . . . Lilly and I . . . that if you met her you might want to come and live here with her.'

'Live here? But, Emmeline, that's utterly impossible. I have a home and a husband and – well, I have a life.'

She held out her hand towards the scene in front of us. I could still see Neptune and Marguerite far away, a little yellow dot on the hazy blue sea. 'This is life too,' she said. 'And Marguerite is the most precious gift that anybody could be entrusted with.'

I put my head in my hands.

'How long can you stay for?' Emmeline asked me after a deep silence.

'A couple more days. I don't want to leave Dad for too long.'

'How is Henry?'

'Better than he was. But depressed, I suppose. It's as if he's given up. He tries to read his journals but I can see he's lost interest.'

'Why do you think he's still alive?'

'I don't know. I thought that once the truth had come out about you being his sister he might let go. His agitation calmed down.'

'He's sifting through the debris too. Trying to find peace, a resolution.'

'He seems quite peaceful.'

'Is he happy?'

'Happy?' I laughed. 'I've never seen my father happy.'

'Then he's not at peace.' She put a hand on my shoulder. 'Bring him here.'

'What?'

'Bring him here.' She said it slowly, like a command.

'That's impossible. He wouldn't come. It would kill him.'

'I want to resolve this before I die and I know he does too. I have no wish to carry this hatred into my next existence – whatever that means.'

'Hatred, Emmeline? Do you and Henry hate each other so much?'

'You don't know the truth yet, Jane. He must tell you before he dies. Bring him here. He will come.' She sighed heavily and pushed Surfer off her lap. Her hands moved restlessly over her thin belly. She looked white and waxy. I clambered up.

'I'll get you some water and your medicine. You must sleep now.'

Emmeline felt better after she talked with Jane. At last she felt there was a possibility that her plan might work. Jane seemed surprised by her suggestion that she bring Henry to the island, but open to the idea. Almost as if she sensed the need to resolve this lifelong feud.

Emmeline was eager to be alone now, glad to rest on her bed, so that she could tune in to Lilly and get on with the recounting. The more Lilly told her the more she could remember herself. The way Lilly was reliving it enabled the past to become vividly alive once more. Emmeline felt the pain of this but knew it was the only way she would be ready to confront Henry.

'Tell me more, Lilly, I want to know what happened between you and Henry. I want to know everything he said to you . . .'

Once my baby starts to move it seems like she is communicating. I feel her fluttering and butting up against me. I love it. I talk and sing to her and imagine she is listening and responding with her movements. I lose interest in the market garden project. I'm unable to concentrate on what the others are saying when they sit around the table discussing their plans. They laugh and say I've become even dreamier than I was before. But I'm not really dreaming, I am communing with my child. Her energy intrigues me. She is strong and inquisitive, longing to be out in the world, exploring it. But sometimes she grows quiet, as if she is attending to something too fine for me to comprehend.

At the beginning of June, Neptune and Woody surprise Emm and me with an outing. They borrow a horse and cart and take us for a ride along the south of the island. We go all the way to The Needles and back again to Shanklin. Woody, with his shaggy hair and beard, spurs the elderly mare on with wild whoops of encouragement which she ignores. Emm and I sit behind the men with a tarpaulin draped over our heads to keep off the drizzling rain. Booty sits at the back, growling at anyone on the road. I wonder if the people we pass think we are rag and bone men.

The villages look festive, decked with red, white and blue bunting and balloons to celebrate the coronation of Queen Elizabeth. Trestle tables are set up in the streets and children are eating sandwiches and cakes undeterred by the showers. A few television sets are sheltered under awnings and people stand around drinking orange squash and frothy pints of beer, staring at the blurry images on the screens. The bigger towns have stages for dancing, music plays through loudspeakers and boys and girls run about wearing gold cardboard crowns.

I am so touched that Woody and Neptune have thought to do this. Emm tells me later that they're concerned because I seem so withdrawn and they thought the trip might take me out of myself. How can I explain to them that I am involved in an internal process more compelling than anything I've ever experienced? I love them for their kindness and hug them with gratitude, but I long to be back in the peace of Wraith Cove.

As we move further into summer, my fear of Henry recedes more and more. I am certain that he means me no further harm and I can venture down to the beach and wander around like I used to. While the others are busy with the garden or fishing, I collect the newly laid eggs and feed the rabbits and prepare food. And then I go down to the shore, kick off my shoes and paddle in the lacy fringe of the waves, listening for the silent beat between each one. I can feel this hush right through my body and I know my daughter can feel it too and she grows still.

I sit on my warm stone to rest and read. Emm and I have been reading Virginia Woolf's books. I love the way her mind works – a flowing of thoughts, fluid as water finding its own natural channels, connected but diverging, only to connect again. I have always felt my mind is odd, the way it weaves in and out of itself, the way it changes and doubts, but can also receive something complete and clear like a gift without wrappings. She helps me realise that perhaps my mix of scatter and coherence is normal after all. Virginia, perhaps I will call my daughter Virginia.

My drowsiness flees as if an errant wave has washed over me. A man is paddling out of the shallows. A small boat is anchored out in the cove with another man sitting in it, leaning on his oars. I'd been so immersed in my reading and my drifting thoughts that I hadn't noticed them arrive. I drop my book and pull my skirt down over my knees. I wish I had Booty with me, he would have barked and warned me. The man has on a navy jumper and black trousers rolled up to his knees. He picks his way through the rocks onto the sand, stumbling on sharp pebbles. His dark hair is hanging forward over his forehead. He runs a hand through it to push it back and looks up. I try to pretend that it isn't Henry.

I feel the thud of my heart; my eyes seek out the nearest fist-sized stone and I pick it up. He stops several yards from me. Surely he won't hurt me, not with somebody out there in the boat, watching. Henry stands looking at me, his eyes flicking over my body as if taking in my size. He smiles.

'Hello, Lillian, how are you?'

'Don't come any closer, Henry.' I point to the cliff behind me. 'I only have to shout. The others are just up there.'

'I just wanted to know how you are getting on.'

'I'm well.'

He squats down on his haunches as if to make himself less threatening.

'Look, Lillian. I don't want to intrude, but have you seen a doctor or a midwife yet?'

'That's none of your business.' How dare he come here questioning me like this?

'I am a doctor, Lillian. I know about these things. There are certain checks you need to have done at various stages.'

'I'm not stupid, Henry.'

'I know you're not. I'm concerned that's all.' He stands up and stares down at his sandy feet; the wet hairs glint on his calves. I don't want his bare flesh so near to me. I grip the stone in my hand. 'I've been to see Victoria,' he says, his voice blunt.

Something in my chest seems to tighten, forcing my breath into my throat. 'How is she?'

'Very well. But she has been seeing a doctor and midwife regularly and so should you.'

'Did she mention me at all?' My voice feels strangled.

Henry shakes his head. 'I'm sorry, Lillian. I've done all I can, but she won't relent.' He takes a couple of steps forward. I fold my arms across my belly. 'I've got something for you,' he says. He pulls up the front of his jumper. I feel myself cringing as memories flash. He has a waterproof bag underneath, from which he takes a parcel. He now has to walk up to me and pass it over. I snatch it and he sits down near me on a boulder.

'What is this?' I say.

'Some advice for expectant mothers. I thought you might find it helpful.'

I want to throw it back at him but don't dare. We sit for a few moments staring out to sea. I feel my energy pushing at him, urging him to go. His companion sits out there waiting, smoking.

'Who is he?' I ask.

'A friend of mine. A doctor from the hospital. Likes sailing, invited me along. Don't care much for it myself though.'

'When are you leaving the island?' Why am I asking him questions, delaying him?

'I'm working my notice. I've got a new position to go to.'

'In Scotland?'

'Up that way, yes.'

He continues to sit, bowed forward, his hands hanging between his knees. I look anxiously up at the cliff path. Supposing one of the others comes back for some reason. This feels all wrong, I am betraying their trust.

Henry must have noticed me glancing up. 'I ought to go,' he says. He stretches and looks around. 'This is a nice place. Do you remember coming here as a child?'

I nod.

'I remember you as a baby with fluffy white hair. I used to carry you down here. You crawled around knocking down our sandcastles and we fished in the rock pools and Victoria painted pictures of us.'

He smiles and sighs. I notice he doesn't mention Emmeline by name. 'You were such a happy little thing,' he continues, 'everybody loved you.'

'Except Victoria,' I comment.

'She loved you in her way.' He gets up. 'She was trying to be your mother and exercise a little discipline. She did her best.'

'Oh, I know that, Henry. I know how hard it was for her.' I can feel my eyes welling up. 'I miss her. Tell her I miss her.'

'Of course.' He squats back down. 'You know, when you were little I was always telling her to be more gentle with you.'

'Were you?'

'Oh, yes. You see, I'd experienced a harsh mother myself. I didn't want that to happen to you.' He picks up a handful of sand and lets it trickle through his fingers. 'Do you remember my mother?'

'A little. She wasn't around much, was she? I remember being a bit scared of her.'

'Florence was a terrifying woman,' Henry says, brushing the sand off his hands. 'In fact, knowing what I know now, I think she was mentally deranged in some way.'

'Emm never said –'

'It was me that suffered at our mother's hands, not her.' He sounds angry. He puts his hands over his face. My anxiety is growing. But when he speaks again his voice is so quiet I have to strain to hear it. 'Oh, Lillian, if only you knew what that woman did to me, what she put me through.' He gets up abruptly. 'What am I doing? You don't want to hear all this.' He shakes sand off his trousers. 'I'll get word to you when I'm leaving the island and I'll give you our new address so that at least you'll know where Victoria is.'

In the evening Emm and I sit outside until late. The air is warm and still. It will soon be the longest day. The waves are sweeping the beach. We have candles burning on the lobster pot table. Moths and June bugs buzz and dive around us. I can see Emm's eyelids drooping.

'Emm, what was your mother like?'

Emm rouses herself. 'Florence the Formidable?' she laughs. 'She was all right. Her bark was worse than her bite. She had a dry sense of humour. If you didn't know her you could take it the wrong way.' She pushes her chair back so that Drifter can jump up. 'Don't you remember her, Lilly?'

'Hardly at all. I do recall being a bit frightened of her.'

'Well, let me see. You must have been about sixteen when she died. I suppose you wouldn't have seen her much. She was always away in London, involved with the Women's Movement.' She laughs again. 'Do you know, Lilly, I often wonder if she had a female lover up there. How many mothers give their daughters banned lesbian literature to read?'

I smile. 'But what about her husband and son?'

282

'Father was content with his work and his hobbies with your dad. Who knows? Maybe he had a mistress, although how he found the time I wouldn't know. Henry was away at school, trying to lord it over his peers.'

'Was your mother ever cruel to him?'

'Good heavens, no! She put him in his place a bit, but God knows he needed that.' She looks at me. 'What makes you ask?'

'I just wonder how somebody from a good family can turn out to be so —'

'Violent? Arrogant?' She sighs. 'Lilly, please don't get into trying to understand Henry.' Her voice turns sharp. 'You'll be telling me you've forgiven him next.'

'No, Emm, I could never forgive him. That's not what I'm doing.'

'Well,' she says irritably, 'analysing then.'

'I don't think of it like you do. I'm not thinking of it in terms of understanding or forgiveness. I just feel things that make sense to me.'

'Like what?' Her voice sounds full of tension. I should change the subject but something drives me on.

'Pain. I feel other people's pain. You know that, Emm. I've told you before. You've read things that I write down. It's like a flowing of something through me. I can't help it.'

'You feel Henry's pain? Is that what you're saying?'

'No. I won't allow myself to. But I know it's

283

there. It's there with everyone. It's what makes us do what we do.' My eyes well up, as they do so often these days. 'Being human is so very hard,' I add, as if that explained everything.

Emm reaches out and catches hold of my hand. 'Don't think about him, Lilly. I couldn't bear it if you felt his pain. I want you . . . I need you to hate him as much as I do.'

'Hate will destroy us, Emm,' I say in a small voice, choked with tears. 'I'm not sure if I can feel such hatred. Not like you do.'

'Then I will hate him enough for both of us,' she growls.

I gaze at her face. I can see how her pain has etched tiny lines in her skin as if her tears have formed tracks. I can see it in the way her mouth turns down at the corners and her eyes haze over with hardness when she sits thinking. It has changed her movements too. I see it in the way she tips Drifter off her lap or pushes her with her foot when she fusses around her legs. It is as if her body is mapping out what goes on inside her. I can see similar changes in my own face when I look in the mirror. Behind the bloom of my motherhood – my pink cheeks and shining hair – my eyes seem less wide open, my lips unable to part so easily to allow laughter.

'But what about our child, Emm? She will feel our hatred for her father.'

Emm suddenly puts her head on the table and starts to weep. 'I'm not sure I can love this child,

Lilly. I'm not sure I can live with this. But, if I think of losing you, I can't bear it. I would die without you.' She looks up at me her face contorted with anguish. 'Sometimes I wish the baby would die or be born dead.'

'I know you do. But she has nothing to do with hatred and violence.'

'How do you know that? She's chosen you and Henry as parents. Why? And supposing you are wrong and it is a boy after all. It might look like Henry and be a constant reminder.'

'We've been through all this. If she chose me then she must have chosen you too. She could have reasons that we don't understand.'

Emm bashes her fist down on the table. Drifter jumps off her lap and flees. 'I just want you to hate him, Lilly.'

'But then we would become like Henry. Don't you see that, Emm?'

'Maybe I'm like him already. Is that what you mean? Perhaps it runs in our family.' She glares at me, her eyes flooded, her mouth quivering. 'Why don't you feel it like I feel it? I don't understand how you can't. Please hate him, Lilly. Hate him for me and for you and for this child.'

'I can't pretend to you, Emm. You would know anyway, because of our love.' I reach out to her, catch one of her flailing hands. 'It's just that I feel where anger and violence come from. I don't always want to but I can't help it.' I feel her hand pulling away from my grasp but I have to go on. 'It's a place of blind wordless fear that just wants to hit out.' I try to hold her eyes but I see them slide away from mine. I want to tell her about the agony of a human without love, with no recognition of worth, with no creative outlet for a spirit buried beneath the anguish of life.

Emm turns away from me. 'Quite the little philosopher aren't you?' she snaps. 'Maybe you should look a bit harder at your own pain, and mine, and stop feeling sorry for the devil that caused it.'

I sit back, stung. I was struggling to express my feelings, I hadn't expected this. We sit in silence for a while. Emm gets up.

'I'm going to bed,' she says, and goes inside.

I continue to sit, stroking my belly, waiting for the responding flutters to calm my feelings. I begin to get chilly. I blow out the candles and go in. I take my book out of my basket and notice the package underneath it that Henry had given me. I open it. Inside there are booklets on pregnancy and birth and feeding the newborn. Beneath that there is a thick wad of twenty-pound notes. I remembered shouting at him that I didn't want his money. I didn't want anything from him. But what if Emm leaves me? I will need things for my baby; I have to think of her. I hide the notes underneath my knitting wool.

I make the cottage safe and go up to bed. Emm is breathing deeply but I know she is pretending. I climb in beside her and put my arm across her back. She makes no response. I lie awake wondering if she will relent and turn to me but she doesn't. Fear nags away beneath my ribs. What if I should wake up one morning and find her gone? Maybe I should be the one to leave and allow Emm to have a choice about what she might do with her life. But she said she would die without me. Perhaps I will die in labour and take my daughter with me. I can feel my tears soaking the pillow. I'm not ready to die yet. I'm not ready to let go of Emm's gentle touch, her mischievous smile. And never again to feel my hair tugged by the wind or watch the mesmerising change of the sea teased by the sun and moon. I want to share this with my child, to offer it to her soul so that she can carry it with her wherever she might journey.

Emm's breathing has become natural. I stroke my hand lightly down her spine and then wipe away my tears. I'll make it up to her tomorrow. I'll make it all right between us again. I feel the baby move and settle . . .

Emmeline shifted and turned over in her lonely bed. She would have given anything to feel the touch of Lilly's hand on her spine at that moment.

CHAPTER 15

The next day Marguerite sat beside Emmeline's bed for hours watching her sleep. They were both perfectly still. Emmeline's eyes were closed, Marguerite's open, unfocused. I fretted around downstairs wondering if I should take responsibility here and fetch a doctor or call one of the cancer care organisations. But I didn't like to interrupt their reverie.

Emmeline hadn't had any of her medicine – which I presumed was morphine – but she didn't appear to be in pain. I tiptoed into the bedroom a couple of times with a fresh jug of water and a clean towel. Marguerite's eyes followed me around the room but she continued to sit motionless. Perhaps Emmeline was going to die soon and I wasn't doing anything. I had no idea how capable Marguerite was. She might have supernatural perception but could she cope with this? Perhaps she was sitting there because there was nobody to tell her what to do. But that wasn't the impression I had of her. I felt it would be an imposition to interfere. I went back down the stairs.

I whiled away a bit of time browsing through my

288

aunts' impressive library. I could see that Emmeline's main interest was science. If she had read and absorbed all these tomes, I reckoned she could teach Stephen Hawking a few things. And it looked as though she had read them too. Every book I picked up was well-thumbed and had underlining and notes in the margins. It seemed like she was a real egg-head, this amazing little aunt of mine.

'The interface.' That's what she'd said to me last night over supper. 'The interface between science and mysticism, that's where the answers lie, Jane.' She had looked exhilarated when she said it. 'You can keep all the religious nonsense,' she added. 'Nothing but trouble, all that.' And it seemed she'd read all the religious nonsense too, judging by her dog-eared collection.

I plonked the iron kettle on the range for more tea. The electric kettle was working but I'd become fond of this big black stove blasting out heat. Even in August there was a certain comforting feel about it. Loot and Surfer scorched themselves on it and there was always a pile of boots and shoes around its bottom and drying clothes draped above it. Not exactly the shiny Aga of my imagination, but just as embracing.

I stood in the doorway waiting for the kettle's steamy song. A sea mist had rolled in this morning and I felt as if I was drifting up in the clouds. I heard a crunch of footsteps and Neptune appeared like an old sea-dog returning from a voyage, with Loot snuffling along behind. I was so relieved to see him; he would know what to do. I practically dragged him in the door.

'Emmeline's in bed. She's not had any medicine. Marguerite is sitting with her. Should I get a doctor?' I poured it all out.

Neptune smiled. 'They know what they're doing. Just leave them be. They'll stay like that until it's done.' He put his bag on the table and took out a newspaper parcel of fish.

'Until what's done?'

'The healing, as much as Emmeline can absorb. That's what they're doing. Best thing. She'll be much better afterwards.'

I made no comment. I was out of my depth again. I made the tea and sat down at the table hoping he might talk some more. I'd learnt that it was best to wait for him. He reached for his mug. I could see fish scales glistening on his hands. He filled the kitchen with the smell of the sea. I breathed deeply.

'What's your cottage like?' I asked him, unable to wait any longer.

'Ordinary. Lower down than this, nearly on the beach, raised up on a bit of a ledge. Wood and stone.' He laughed. 'Just about hanging on.'

'That's not ordinary. Don't you get scared – in storms I mean?'

'There's been times. But the sea hasn't beaten me yet. Me and Woody – we built a good bank of concrete and boulders.'

'Woody?'

'He lived there with me – died a long way back.' He sipped his tea, his eyes looking into the past. He got up and rummaged on one of the shelves. He handed me an old photograph, cracked and faded. I could just make out the face of a young man with dark eyes and a heart-throb smile. It was one of those photos where the gaze seemed to latch onto you.

'He looks nice,' I said.

Neptune nodded. 'We were together, you know, like Emmeline and Lillian were.'

'Oh, I see.' Another little bit of the past coming into the present. 'So, you all knew each other? You were friends?'

'We were – and a great support to each other. Things weren't easy in those days. Some folk were quite hostile.'

I sighed. 'You know, Neptune, sometimes I think things haven't changed much.'

I looked at the photo again. 'What happened to Woody?'

'He got called up. Went off to war. Saw terrible things. He was never the same again. Drank a lot. One night he fell from the cliff and drowned. Or at least that was the verdict.'

'You don't agree?'

'No. Woody knew every inch of this coastline. We first met down on the beach. He was a carpenter but spent his spare time beachcombing. We hit it off straight away. I taught him to fish.'

'So, what do you think happened to him?'

'Someone pushed him.' Neptune stared long and hard at me and I felt suddenly chilled as if he thought I might know something about it.

'Why would they do that?'

'They didn't like what he was doing.'

'Oh, Neptune. Surely not.'

He shook his head slowly. 'There's no doubt in my mind.'

And I could see by the set of his jaw there wasn't. We sat drinking tea. The silence felt strained.

'Did you know my father – Henry – at all well?' I asked.

Neptune's head shot up. He banged down his mug, ground his chair across the flagstones and started to pull on his waterproof coat. 'That man has a lot to answer for,' he growled, and slammed out of the door.

I felt startled. Was it something I said? My poor old dad seemed to be the focus for a lot of animosity around here. Okay, so he hadn't approved of gays and lesbians and he'd done a runner to avoid being associated with them and never looked back. But it seemed to me like he was getting blamed for everything that had gone wrong since. His name always seemed to trigger a response like he was a serial killer or something. Emmeline implied yesterday that I didn't know everything. Was I missing something here? Did Neptune think that Dad had pushed his lover over the cliff because he didn't like gay men?

Suddenly I longed to be back at Birdsong again

with Chas's down to earth, straightforward sanity. I wondered how Dad was faring at Winter Wood with his knitting circle. I would have to drive out of The Undercliff tonight and try and get a signal to phone home.

I took Neptune at his word and decided to leave Marguerite and Emmeline to get on with whatever they were doing in peace. The sea mist seemed to have cleared and I wandered out into the garden and picked some lettuces and tomatoes and broad beans. I gathered a large bunch of sweet peas and sat down on a log, inhaling their fragrance and watching dozens of bright butterflies busy on the buddleias. The departing mist seemed to have skimmed off the haze of the last few days and everything appeared crystal clear. The sea seemed bigger and nearer as if I could reach out my hand and touch it. The horizon was a darker line of blue. I watched a heron flap its lazy way across the sky and tingled with pleasure. This place was getting under my skin in more ways than one.

I felt a light touch on my shoulder and Marguerite was standing there. She smiled down at me; her pale blue eyes seemed to be lit from within. I reached up and stroked her hand. She rested her cheek on my hair briefly. She scooped up the vegetables and went inside. I followed her and she made a salad and put bread and cheese on the table. I arranged the sweet peas in two jam jars and took one upstairs to Emmeline. She seemed to be sleeping soundly; her breath was slow and deep. Marguerite looked up at me as I came down and I smiled and nodded to reassure her that Emmeline was okay.

It was relaxing, eating with silent Marguerite. I became aware of just how difficult it is to talk and eat at the same time and do both well. I thought about the number of meals I'd had with friends, Chas even, and hardly noticed that I'd eaten and yet there was my empty plate. This was so restful. In fact everything about Marguerite was peaceful. When we'd finished she put our plates on the draining board and handed me an apple.

'Marguerite,' I smiled. 'I like your name. She got up, went to one of the bookshelves and handed me a paperback. It was *The Well Of Loneliness* by Radclyffe Hall. I wondered what that had to do with what I'd said. She took the book back from me and opened it at the blurb about the author. Could she read then? She pointed to a word. Marguerite, I read. Radclyffe Hall's first name had been Marguerite. 'I see, you were named after her.' She nodded. 'Your mother must have really liked this book, this writer.' She nodded again and went back to the shelf. She brought over *Mrs Dalloway* by Virginia Woolf and pointed at me. I didn't know what she meant, I shook my head. Marguerite pointed to the word, Virginia, and then at me again.

'Virginia?' I asked.

She nodded and pointed at me. I shook my head. 'Jane,' I said, remembering that Emmeline had called me Virginia – along with a few other names – when I had first met her down on the beach. It was my turn to get up then and fetch one of my novels. I pointed to my name on the cover. 'That's me,' I said. She smiled and shook her head and pressed her finger firmly on Virginia. I laughed. 'You think Virginia suits me better?' She nodded. 'Well, I wish I could write like her.'

Marguerite cleared away the rest of the lunch things and fed Surfer, who was rubbing around her legs. She seemed very capable, as if she had adapted well to her slight physical disability. In fact I realised that I wasn't really noticing it any more. She lifted a big mixing bowl down from a shelf and measured out flour and mixed yeast to make bread. She left it on the range to rise and made a pot of tea which she brought back to the table.

'Marguerite,' I said. She looked at me expectantly. 'Did you know we are cousins?' She gazed at me, a look of puzzlement on her face. 'Our mothers, they were sisters – Lillian and Victoria.' She frowned; her eyes moving backwards and forwards across my face as if she was trying to read me like a book. Then she shook her head. I thought I'd better not pursue that one. Perhaps it was beyond her comprehension. After all she'd never met Victoria and maybe Lillian had cut my mother out of her life with finality too.

But, something inside me was beginning to rebel against all this deception. Why shouldn't Marguerite know who I was and that our mothers were sisters? 'Did you not know about your Aunt Victoria?' I asked gently.

She sat for a while gazing at me and then got up and went over to a carved wooden chest under the window. She opened it and I could see her searching through what appeared to be books and papers. She closed the chest and handed me a drawing. I assumed she'd given it to me the right way up but I couldn't make head nor tail of it. I remembered what Emmeline had said this morning about Marguerite's wraith-like pictures.

The figure bore no resemblance to a human except that it was vaguely oval. It was composed of many shades of grey and violet and slatey blues. Underneath it all somewhere in the centre seemed to be something red but deeply hidden. Coming out of the top of the figure there was a pale spiral of grey shading into a pinkish-gold. It was very intricate as if she had worked on it for hours. And although it was just a blob, the more I looked at it, the more three-dimensional it became, as if I was looking into the heart of something very subtle and hidden – like one of those Magic Eye pictures that had been all the rage a while back. I looked at Marguerite over the top of the picture. She took it out of my hands and turned it over. There was some writing in the bottom corner. Victoria, I read, May 29th 1973.

I felt strangely disconnected then, as if I couldn't quite get a grip on where I was. That was the date of my mother's death. So, Marguerite did know about Victoria. I turned the paper over and looked again at the wraith. Had Marguerite perceived the death of my mother and drawn it?

'Whose writing is this?' I asked, my voice shaky. 'Emmeline's?' She shook her head. 'Lillian's?' She nodded. 'You drew this and Lillian – your mother – wrote the date on it?' She nodded. No wonder Emmeline had come to believe in this web of connection as she called it, living with these two. I was feeling a bit freaked out. I had never had any experience of this sort of thing before. It felt like one of those television shows where confused people are confronted with a personal possession in an inappropriate place and you know it's a complete set up. Except this wasn't.

'How did you know Victoria had died, did someone tell you?' She shook her head and closed her eyes and put her hands to her chest, breathing deeply.

'You just felt it?' She nodded. I sat back in the chair. I felt amazed and strangely pleased. I wondered what else this enigmatic woman and her apparently mystical mother had been capable of. I felt brimming with curiosity. I wanted to know what else Marguerite knew. But how was I going to do that? I wanted to know about Aunt Lillian and what they had been up to during all those years of seclusion.

I looked at Marguerite, she was smiling, her silver hair shone, caught in a ray of sunlight. Her wide mouth reminded me a little of Emmeline's.

I shook my head slowly at her, feeling a smile spreading across my face. She got up and put her arms around me and rocked me like a baby. I knew I was going to have to learn to communicate with this mysterious woman.

'Please, go on, Lilly,' Emmeline urged. Her body felt relaxed and comfortable after Marguerite's healing. She knew that she could more easily bear the pain of what Lilly was telling . . .

Henry comes again in July. It is a blistering day and I feel stretched and heavy. I struggle down the steps to the beach in search of a cooling breeze but nothing stirs. I sit on my hot stone shading myself with a parasol. Even the waves are creeping onto the sand as if they can hardly be bothered. The horizon is blurred and I can't tell where the sea ends and the sky begins. A cormorant poises on a rock offshore, its wings half raised as if it were its own sunshade. Its black silhouette seems abnormally solid in this hazy world of misty blues and shifting sand.

I feel sweat trickling down my back. Emm plaited my hair for me this morning and I've wound the two long braids around my head to cool myself down. She told me I look like a Norwegian princess. I laughed and said I looked more like Humpty Dumpty. I heave myself up and plod down to the shoreline. I hoist up my skirt and paddle out into the waves. The contrast on my hot legs makes me gasp, but I soon feel the warmth of the water. I look down at my swollen belly. It seems huge, bulging out from the rest of my thin frame. I can't believe that I still have a couple of months to go. I'll have to ask Woody to make me a platform on wheels to support it.

I'm not at all embarrassed in front of the men. They often sit with their hands on my bump, grinning when they feel a kick. Woody has finished the cradle and it stands, waiting for her, glowing under the window of the tiny white nursery. Emm and I have made small sheets and blankets out of some of the posh embroidered linen from the hotel. I have also taken an antique chest with a matching cupboard which Woody has polished and they now hold piles of tiny knitted clothes. Neptune arrived one day with a bundle of towelling napkins. He wouldn't tell us where they'd come from but they hadn't been washed up by the tide.

'All above board,' he said. 'We don't want anything but the best on our little 'un's backside, do we?'

We had thought of replacing the shabby furniture in the cottage with smarter stuff from the hotel but it was too big and had now been auctioned. Our investment and project money had got a good boost instead. I was relieved. I love our familiar assortment of battered chairs. I was worried that Wraith Cottage would lose its special atmosphere if we changed it too much.

I feel cooler now. The waves are lapping round

my thighs. I am tempted to let myself sink down in the water. I would soon dry off in the sun. Maybe I would just slip out of my skirt and smock first. I turn around to wade back to shore and there is Henry. I jerk with the shock and let my skirt drop so that it spreads out on the water and is immediately soaked. I walk out of the sea, cotton clinging to my legs.

'I'm sorry, Lillian. I should have called out but I didn't want to startle you. Can I get you a towel or something?'

I shake my head, turning away from him in embarrassment. How long had he been watching me?

'I've just arrived, I only just spotted you,' he says quickly.

I look at him coldly, remembering the trouble it had stirred up between Emm and me the last time he was here. 'I thought you would have left the island by now.'

'There's been difficulty getting my replacement,' he says. 'I can't just leave. Medicine isn't like that.'

I start to walk up the beach. I have a sudden irrational fear that he might try and drown me. I need to put some distance, some firm ground, between us.

'Victoria must be missing you,' I say.

'I doubt it.' He sounds bitter. I stop walking and turn to look at him. 'She's better off without me.'

'I expect she needs you now, Henry – with the baby due soon.'

He stops and loosens his tie, undoes a button. I look away, I can't bear to see some of his movements. I walk towards my stone where I'd left my basket and sandals. I look back, he is staring down at the sand. His shoulders droop. He seems to have lost some of his arrogance and pride. He usually holds his head high, giving the appearance of looking down his narrow nose at everyone. I want to remain standing but I feel exhausted and sit down.

'Did you want something in particular?' I ask.

'I wanted to let you know that I hadn't left. I didn't want you to think I'd disappear without giving you an address. We haven't yet decided on a house.'

'I don't care if you disappear, Henry. It's Victoria I want to stay in touch with. You can send me your new address. Emm would understand that.'

He sits down on a boulder a few feet away. 'Lillian, to be honest, I really wanted to see you. I wanted to know how you are, if you need anything.'

'I've already told you. I don't need anything. I'm with people I love and they care for me.'

He looks at me so fervently then that I have to look away. 'You are so fortunate, Lillian,' he says.

'Fortunate! How can you say that after what you did to me – and Emmeline.'

He puts his hands to his ears. 'Please, Lillian. I'll regret that until I die. I mean that you are fortunate to be so loved.'

'You have a wife who loves you and you will soon be a father.'

He shakes his head hard. 'No. Victoria doesn't love me, she never has. And I don't love her.'

Why is he telling me this? Does he expect me to feel sorry for him?

'Then why did you get married?' It is all I could think of to say.

'It was expected of us, that's why. My parents, your parents – it was joked about since we were toddlers. We never stood a chance. It was an arranged marriage.'

I look at him, aghast. 'But they wouldn't have forced you. You could have refused.'

'It doesn't work like that. After years of indoctrination, you hardly question anything any more.'

'And Victoria? Does she feel the same?' He nods miserably. 'Well, your parents are dead now. Why don't you get divorced?'

'The stigma. My reputation. My career. It isn't looked upon kindly, is it?'

I don't know what else to say. He looks up at me and catches my gaze and seems to hold it. In that moment I sense his genuine pain and misery. I try to shut it out but it is too late. Images flash through my mind of a sad and frightened little boy. I see him trying to please his mother who only laughs at him. I see him running to keep up with his father who is too busy. I see him bullied at school for his pretentiousness. And I see him standing naked in the bathtub with little Emmeline sitting at the other end laughing while their mother lifts his penis and says something scathing.

My hand involuntarily reaches out to him. Just in time, I manage to retract it and pretend I am picking up my parasol. I blink to dispel the images and prevent my tears. He is still gazing at me but I won't meet his eyes, not again.

'Lillian,' he says softly. 'If I divorced Victoria, would you come away with me? Would you marry me?'

I can't believe what I'm hearing. I look at him, amazed.

'I've always loved you, Lillian. Ever since you were a child. You're so beautiful and gentle. I think maybe I married Victoria so I could be near you. I'm sorry for what I did. But I love you and I want to make it up to you and our baby.'

Sweat pours down my body and for one moment I think I am going to faint or be sick as a wave of nausea sweeps through me.

'We could move away, start again. Just the two of us and our child.'

I struggle to my feet, shaking my head.

'Lillian, think about it. It would be better for everyone.'

'Please go now,' I stammer.

He holds up his hands. 'It's all right. I'll go. But I want you to think about what I've said. Victoria and I have talked about divorce and it's what she wants.'

'But, your child . . .' I whisper.

'I will support her financially, of course.'

'You can't do this to her, Henry —'

'I beg you to think about it, Lillian.'

'I don't need to.'

He turns away from me, towards the cliff steps and stops again. 'Will you promise me one thing?'

'What?'

'That you'll put my name on our child's birth certificate. I want it to know the truth of who its father is.'

'You gave up all rights to this child when you raped me.' I spit it out.

'So, you're still planning on naming that Woody fellow as the father?'

I nod.

'I'll come back once more, Lillian, to see if you've changed your mind. I expect this has come as a shock to you. If you still refuse me, I'll go and you'll never see or hear from me again.'

I stand and watch him climb the cliff steps. I hope at that moment he will bump into Neptune or Woody, but I know they are busy in the vegetable garden around the other side of the hotel and Henry will slip through the shrubbery. I sit down and search in my basket for my flask of water. I pull out a brown paper package. Henry must have put it in there before he walked down to the sea. I open it. Inside is another bundle of money, some leaflets on diet and some bottles of vitamins and minerals with hospital dispensary labels on them.

I wait for a while to calm myself and give Henry time to be well away. I wring the sea from my skirt and sip some water, shading myself with the moth-eaten Victorian parasol. It makes sense to me now. It always does once I've received the full force of someone else's pain. Not that I condone his actions. I could never do that. But at least I know from what source it has taken seed, festered and wormed its way deep into the mind of a small boy who only wanted love. Wasn't that what we all wanted, the only thing that could truly nurture us?

I long for Emm in that moment. I want to feel her tenderness and look into the depths of her love-filled eyes. I want to kiss away her pain and confusion of these last few months. I haul myself up the cliff steps and tramp through the garden and across the fields.

Emm and the men are sitting under the sweeping shade of the cedar, having a rest. I stand looking at them across the lawn. They are laughing about something and Woody gives Neptune a shove. I send a bolt of love towards them, Emm looks up and I burst into tears. She comes running to me.

'Lilly, darling, what is it?' She takes me in her arms as best she can with my great lump between us.

'I don't know,' I sob. 'I just wanted to be with you.'

Neptune and Woody come towards us looking concerned. I wonder if they think I am going to give birth.

'Lillian?' says Woody.

'It's just . . .' I sob. 'Life is so hard, sometimes, isn't it?'

'You're soaked,' says Neptune, feeling my skirt.
'I . . . fell over in the sea,' I wail.

'Oh, Lilly. You shouldn't go down there any more on your own. You're too unstable,' says Emm.

I begin to laugh hysterically. They lead me into the shade of the cedars, where I laugh and cry until I fall asleep. That's exactly right, I think, I'm unstable . . .

Emmeline sat up in bed watching the moon through the open window. But her eyes were unseeing. 'If only you had told me, Lilly,' she said.

CHAPTER 16

Neptune was right; Emmeline was much better the next day. I could hear her chattering to Marguerite in the bathroom when I came downstairs. I went outside to greet the dazzling day. A jaunty breeze tinkled the shells hanging from the blackthorn. The sea was flouncing and yachts with rainbow spinnakers scooted along, taking advantage of the fair wind home. I breathed deeply, stretching my back and arms, sparing a brief commiserative thought for cramped commuters.

I went back inside and laid the table for breakfast. Every item of crockery and cutlery was comfortably mismatched. Some bore the inscription of Wraith Cove Hotel. I found butter and eggs in the antique fridge and unearthed Marguerite's loaf from the bread bin, crusty and dusty with flour. There were jars of homemade jam and marmalade on a stone shelf in the walk-in pantry. No sign of a tin or a packet. No wonder Marguerite had stayed healthy, living on home-produced goods, breathing pure air. I put eggs on to boil and the kettle to sing.

I heard Loot scuffling up the path and Neptune

walked in, looking like the world's healthiest grandfather, lean and brown in his khaki shorts and white vest. I smiled at him:

'You're just in time for breakfast.'

He grinned back. 'Timed it right then, didn't I?' He came over and patted me on the shoulder. 'Sorry I left in a huff yesterday, I still get angry about the past – can't bear to see her suffer, you know. I'm glad you're here.'

I nodded and squeezed his arm. I took the eggs off the hotplate and made tea in a brown pot that looked as if it had been requisitioned from the civil defence.

Emmeline and Marguerite emerged from the bathroom giggling like a couple of adolescents. I noticed that I'd heard Marguerite laugh before and wondered why she couldn't speak if her vocal cords were intact. But what did I know? It was probably more to do with neurones than her larynx.

We carried our plates of toast and eggs and mugs of tea outside. Breakfast lasted a long time. There seemed no reason to hurry it. Emmeline and Neptune talked about the market garden they and Woody and Lillian had planned fifty years ago and how the partly restored greenhouses had fallen back into disrepair after Woody's death. Neptune reminisced freely about Woody as if he'd been thinking about him a lot over the last twenty-four hours. He and Emmeline kept looking at each other with joy and sadness trembling in the lines of their faces.

Marguerite's hair shimmered down the back of her leaf-green dress. I could imagine her as a wood elf flitting across a film-set for *Lord of The Rings*. I noticed that all her clothes were of the same design – two lengths of material sewn together leaving holes for her arms and neck. Emmeline probably made them for her. They emphasised her slender frame and delicate face. She listened avidly to what we were saying, communicating with fluttering hands and vivid facial expressions. But it wasn't like the usual signing I'd seen before. I guessed this was their own homebrew. I noticed once again that she responded even if she hadn't been looking directly at whoever was speaking. Perhaps she wasn't totally deaf. How could I ask without seeming patronising, overriding their years of skilful communication with supercilious questions?

But I couldn't stop watching her. She was so expressive; I felt I knew what she was feeling just sitting close to her, observing her. I remembered what Emmeline had said yesterday about the web of connection. Perhaps if I stayed here much longer I would become more sensitive too.

'Why don't you come out in the boat with us?' Neptune asked me. 'It's such a glorious day.' Marguerite's fingers pattered along my arm like a mouse. I glanced at Emmeline. She nodded encouragingly.

'You go, Jane. I'll be fine here sitting in the sun. I can catch up on some reading.'

We left her surrounded with shawls and drinks

and books, Surfer on her lap and Loot at her feet. She looked like a small bag-lady.

Neptune rowed us around Wraith Cove into Puck's Bay. It was tiny, just a crescent of sand and fine shingle and boulders and Puck's Cottage just as Neptune had described it, set upon a rock and concrete platform above the slope of the beach. It was an archetypal fisherman's cottage, festooned with nets and floats and pots.

'My family have been fishing here for several generations,' he said. 'I'm the last of the line.'

'Isn't there anyone to take over, Neptune?'

He shook his head. 'Can't give it away. This bit of the coast won't last much longer see, and there's plenty of folk fishing these waters now.'

'It seems sad, the end of something so old.'

'Time to let go,' he said. 'Everything has to come to an end.'

'Well, that's very philosophical,' I said, doubtfully.

He laughed. 'That's what comes from having these wise old women as friends.' He gave Marguerite's shoulders a squeeze. 'You learn to see that some things are only relatively important.'

'You do sound like Emmeline.' I laughed.

'See what I mean?'

He showed us around the cottage which was basic and masculine with an elderly range and items of furniture crafted by Woody. It smelled of fish and dog but looked clean. Sailing paraphernalia hung from the beams, ships' lanterns and other bits of nautical equipment. I found myself wondering yet again what was going to happen to all this when Neptune died. I sighed, there seemed to be so many end of the road situations going on around me. Why hadn't I been summoned back here years ago?

'When I go, anything salvageable can be sold off and the money given to Marguerite,' he said, as if he'd been reading my thoughts.

Neptune rowed us back out to where his yellow fishing boat was anchored and we took off to the wider stretch of Ventnor Bay. I felt exhilarated ploughing through the glittering water. I could see the beach at Ventnor with people sunning themselves on the sand. I noticed Marguerite staring at them intently, sitting very still and I wondered what she was seeing. Was she perceiving them as little ovals of coloured lights? Is that how she saw the world all the time? How different everything must be for her.

We moved further along the coast and I could make out Puck's Bay and Wraith Cove amongst the tumbling cliffs. I wondered if Emmeline would be able to see us – Marguerite and me – in our red life-jackets. We trailed lines over the side of the boat, fishing for mackerel while Neptune zigzagged here and there, checking his pots. Marguerite seemed very at home on the water, Neptune said he'd been taking her out with him since she was a toddler, strapped to the boat.

'Could you swim?' I asked her, worried for her

life all those years ago. She nodded, deftly unhooking a writhing mackerel from her line. I gave up on my fishing, they obviously preferred being skewered by Marguerite. I sat back, relaxing, listening to the bomp and slap of the water against the boat.

I would have to go home tomorrow. I'd walked up to the main road last night and managed to pick up enough signal to give Chas a brief call. Everything was as usual but I gathered from him that Dad still seemed down and was asking for me. He'd even remembered that I'd gone back to the Isle of Wight to see Emmeline. That had to be a first – my father aware of my movements – he'd be remembering my name next. The knitting ladies were taking good care of him but he seemed bored, no longer even interested in shuffling around his study.

Neptune had finished his pot inspection and we were heading back to shore.

'Might as well go straight back to Emmeline's,' he said. He winked at Marguerite. 'See how the old girl's faring.'

We had lunch in the garden and Emmeline and Neptune dozed off under their sunhats, snoring and grunting like any two ordinary old people having an afternoon snooze. Except, I thought, they're not ordinary at all. I looked at Marguerite wondering if she was going to have a nap, but she was looking at me bright-eyed. Later that afternoon I had to go and see Bill Allain to sort out the tax situation on Wraith Cove Hotel, but there was time to relax before then.

'Will you show me how you draw, Marguerite?' I said.

She got up without hesitation and went inside. She came back carrying a stack of paper, wooden boxes and tins. She laid them out on the table and opened the lids. They contained dozens of coloured pencils, crayons, felt tips, watercolour pencils and chalks. No paints, I noticed, she wasn't another Victoria. She looked at me expectantly.

'What would you like to draw?' I asked. She pointed at me and her hands moved like lightning, reaching for colours and textures and before I knew it there I was, a curving oval full of yellows and oranges and pinks. There seemed to be no firm outline to the oval, the colour just faded out. I laughed.

'I look very happy,' I said. She nodded and made a gesture towards the sea and lifted her face to the sun. 'So, do people's colours change then, with their mood?' She nodded and spread her hands over the vast array of pens and pencils. 'That's why you need so many?' She nodded.

I asked her to draw Emmeline. She hesitated for a while and gazed at Emmeline. Then she drew another curve, slender and delicate, full of blues and greys with pale gold at the centre and filtering through at the edges. She seemed subdued when she'd finished it, her eyes sad. She put the drawing under the one of me and then her expression changed and she looked mischievous. She turned my face away with her hand and I could hear her pencils brushing the paper. She tapped my arm and showed me a small oval, full of reds and oranges and browns.

'Neptune?' I asked. She smiled and shook her head. I knew it couldn't be Lillian. She would be delicate, silver and white perhaps. Marguerite pointed to Loot, asleep at Neptune's feet. I laughed.

'Do Neptune,' I said.

I noticed she was drawing Neptune's shape on the same paper as Loot. The finished Neptune was dark greens and blues with some yellow but there were strands of colour coming out of him which connected him with Loot.

'What are these?' I asked. She looked at me for a while and then she lifted her hands and felt the air in front of her delicately, as if she was feeling for something. She held my eyes with hers and continued her movements as if she was playing an invisible musical instrument.

And then I had the strangest sensation in my chest and solar plexus. My mind clamoured for words, none came, but for an instant I felt as if I was her. The air around us seemed to shift and I lost sight of her outline as if she was dissolving. Where her hands were poised in the air I saw floating filaments of a shimmering substance and I felt overwhelmed with happiness and the knowledge that everything was perfect. The feeling was gone almost as soon as it came and I was left stunned. I felt her place her hands on my chest. I closed my eyes and felt peace wash over me and through me as if every cell in my body was having a cool drink. I heard her get up and go into the cottage. She came back after a while with a tray of tea. I opened my eyes and she smiled.

I drank tea while Marguerite doodled away having a guessing game with me. I was amazed that she could even draw the energy pattern of the teapot.

'So everything has a pattern, even inanimate objects?' She nodded. 'And the colours have meanings?' She frowned and put her head on one side and then interlocked her fingers. 'The way the colours are put together have meanings?' She nodded. I was intrigued. 'What about sounds?' She looked around. The afternoon was very still. She seemed to be listening intently. Did that mean she could hear? She reached for her colours and did a lightning quick series of squiggles. She looked at me quizzically. I couldn't hear anything. She pointed to Neptune. He was giving a little puff with each out breath. I hadn't even noticed it. I laughed and hummed *Baa Baa Black Sheep*. And there it was, in a series of coloured blobs and squiggles that somehow looked just like the words.

'Marguerite,' I said. 'You are amazing.'

Emmeline woke up and Marguerite made her some camomile tea. I remembered my appointment with the solicitor.

'I must go,' I said, getting up. Marguerite looked

up at me; I thought her eyes showed disappoint-ment. On the spur of the moment I said: 'Why don't you come with me?' I saw her eyes widen.

'No!' said Emmeline abruptly, sloshing her tea and waking Neptune up with a start.

'What's the matter?' He peered around, disori-entated.

'Jane wants to take Marguerite with her to Ventnor to see the solicitor.'

Neptune pushed his sun hat back. 'Well, why not?' he said gruffly.

'You know why. It's difficult for her, Jane. She hasn't been in a car and she gets overwhelmed. I told you.'

'Okay, maybe going to the solicitor is too much but –'

Marguerite got up and caught hold of my hand. She patted her chest and pointed at me. It was obvious she wanted to come. I should have thought this through, not been so impetuous. But if I was to be involved with the care of this woman then I was going to have to prise her out of The Undercliff. There was no way I could transfer the whole of my life to Wraith Cottage. I went over to Emmeline and squatted down beside her. I could see she was very frightened and near to tears.

'Emmeline,' I said. 'I have to do this. I promise I will look after her.' Emmeline shook and Neptune reached for her hand. I looked at him for support and he nodded. 'There is no other way through this. You know I can't drop my life and move in here.'

'She's not somebody you can just play with like a toy, you know.' She caught me quite roughly by the front of my tee-shirt. 'She's not a circus act.'

'I know that, Emmeline,' I said, startled by her ferocity. 'I'm nervous too. I have no experience of this. But if you want me to help, then some things have to be on my terms. You can't ask me to give up my life. There's got to be a compromise.'

Emmeline burst into heart-wrenching sobs. 'I'm sorry,' she gasped. 'I'm scared.' Marguerite came over and put her hands on her shoulders.

'I'm scared too, Emmeline,' I whispered. I looked up at Marguerite's concerned face. 'I think we're all scared.'

'Jane's right,' said Neptune. 'We are all going to have to make changes. We need to work it out together, just like we've always done.'

I could see Emmeline nodding even though her poor little shoulders were still heaving. Marguerite was nodding too. In fact we were all nodding away. Well, that's a start, I thought.

'Do you want to go, really?' Emmeline asked Marguerite. Marguerite walked towards me, smiling.

'Right, then,' I said brightly, trying to cover up my anxiety. 'Let's visit the girls' room for a wash and brush up and we'll go.'

We walked across the field and through the hotel grounds. I could feel the light touch of her hand on my arm as she steadied herself on steps and

317

rough ground. When we reached the closed road she held my arm more tightly. My scarlet mini glowed, unmolested, under a large sycamore, dusty and sticky with pollen. I wondered if she had ever been in a motorised vehicle before or if her sole means of transport had been Neptune's boats.

She didn't seem perturbed by the car. I guessed she must have seen lots of pictures, maybe stood in the grounds of the hotel, watching them go by. And of course she would have seen them in Ventnor on her excursions with Neptune. I felt a bit like an explorer finding a jungle child raised by wolves, not knowing how she was going to react to civilisation.

I unlocked the doors and helped her in and pulled the safety belt across her which appeared to confuse her a bit. But she seemed to be enjoying herself, she had a little smile on her face and her eyes were darting about over the dashboard. I tried to do everything as gently and quietly as possible, starting the car and driving up to meet the main road. I drove slowly through The Undercliff to Ventnor, glancing at her from time to time to see how she was coping. She was gazing out of the windows with interest, leaning forward as the trees gave way to houses. She laughed at the traffic lights and pointed at the shop windows. I parked down on the esplanade and we sat watching the holiday-makers for a while. She seemed alert and curious. I began to wonder if Lillian and Emmeline had kept her isolated at Wraith Cove unnecessarily.

I glanced at my watch. It was nearly time for my appointment with Bill Allain. 'Marguerite, I have to go and see the solicitor now. Do you want to come with me or would you rather stay here and watch the sea?'

She looked at me blankly. I wondered if the decision was too much for her to make. I could see that this was going to be the difficult bit. How could she make a choice when she didn't know what was involved?

'I tell you what,' I said. 'It might be better if you stay with me as this is the first time we've been out.' I released her from the car and locked it up and we set off up the hill.

In the waiting room, Marguerite seemed intrigued by the old pictures of Ventnor and the seascapes and watercolours of boats that adorned the walls. Bill Allain came out of his office to fetch me. I introduced Marguerite as my cousin. She nodded at him and returned to her scrutiny of the pictures. I indicated to Bill that she was deaf, feeling uncomfortable, as if I'd made an excuse for her, where none was needed. Well, I was having to learn here too. I touched Marguerite's arm. 'Do you want to stay here and look at the pictures?' I indicated the room I would be in. 'I won't be a minute.' She nodded.

Bill informed me that he'd looked into the tax and rates position for the hotel and discovered that there had been an account set up years ago to cover any expenses that were needed. The account was in the name of Doctor Henry Rampling. I was astounded. My father hadn't relinquished all his connections with the island after all then.

'There has been very little tax or rates to pay anyway,' Bill said, 'seeing as there is hardly anything left of the hotel. The account is still open. But there's another strange thing. While I was investigating this I came across references to an additional account, from which this one was to be topped up, if necessary. This one is also in your father's name and contains money left in trust for Lillian Walding, who left you Wraith Cottage. She should have had it years ago. It's as if she didn't know it existed. I presume your father is aware of her death?'

I nodded, puzzled.

'Well, I have written to inform him. I presume, as you are the only beneficiary, that the money will go to you.' He sat back. 'It's most odd how all this has come to light in dribs and drabs. Almost as if nobody knew what anybody else's intentions were. Or things were put in motion and then forgotten about. It does happen when people live to a ripe old age. They forget just what they've got and where.' He laughed. 'Wish I had a senile rich relative somewhere. Anyway, as I say, I've written to your father. I'm not able to disclose how much is in the fund at the moment as it is confidential between your father and his solicitor, but it is a substantial amount. He's been paying into it weekly for fifty years.'

'Fifty years!' I nearly fell off my seat.

Bill then went on to ask me if I was still planning to hang on to the Wraith property and thought I was doing the best thing to wait. I was only half listening, my mind on Marguerite. I got up. Bill held out his hand. 'I'll write as soon as I hear something. But rest assured you haven't been building up any debts.'

I dashed out into the waiting room. Something was wrong, I could feel it. Marguerite wasn't there. But there was now a receptionist behind the desk, intimidating in her black suit.

'There was a woman in here,' I said, my voice rising in panic, 'green dress, long silver hair.'

'Oh, was she with you? She was touching the pictures. I asked her what she wanted and she ignored me. Weird. I told her to go.'

'She's disabled,' I shouted at her. 'You insensitive –'

'You shouldn't have left her.' I heard her say as I fled out the door.

'Stupid, stupid, stupid,' I aimed at myself as I rushed this way and that, not knowing which way to go. Calm down, calm down, she can't have gone far. I took a deep breath. She would have gone back towards the sea. That's where she'd be. I ran down the hill to the esplanade, threading my way through the crowds walking up from the beach. I asked a couple of people but they shook their heads. I leaned over the railings, scanning the beach, searching for a green dress and silver hair. She wasn't waiting by the car. I asked people in the café and ice cream parlour. Oh, God. Supposing she'd walked up the other way and got herself killed on the road. How would I live with myself? I thought I was so bloody clever, didn't I? Knowing better than Emmeline. This would finish her off too, on the spot. How could I have been so irresponsible? I would have to go to the police. I pelted up the stairs to the top of the bandstand and leant over the edge.

'Marguerite!' I yelled at the top of my voice. 'Marguerite!'

I felt as if I'd stopped the world. A hush seemed to fall on the beach and the traffic. And then I saw her; a huddle of silver and green. She was curled up below me against the wall of the band-stand. I hurtled down the stairs and rushed around the base. She was in the foetal position. I gently called her name and wrapped my arms around her. She looked at me, her eyes caverns of terror, tear stains on her cheeks. What had I put her through?

'Marguerite, Marguerite,' I sobbed, brushing her hair back from her face. 'I'm sorry. I'm so sorry. I should never have left you.' It seemed to take a while for her to focus on me. She put her hand out to touch my face. Her eyes flickered over me and then she gasped and her mouth spread in a rapturous smile. I felt forgiven.

I took her to a toilet and washed both our faces and combed our hair. I talked to her all the while, telling her how stupid I'd been. She kept shaking her head and smiling at me. She seemed to have regained her composure. I was amazed, considering the trauma she'd been through. I asked her if she wanted to go back home but she shook her head. We walked slowly along the esplanade, her arm in mine, me holding it tightly. We were going to get through this. I bought strawberry ice-cream cornets for us and we sat on a bench and ate them. I asked her if something had frightened her. She pointed to the other end of the esplanade and held her hands out in front of her with a swaying movement. I had no idea what she meant. She got up and swayed from side to side. I laughed, feeling such relief that we'd gone from panic to laughter in such a short space of time.

'Shall we paddle?' I asked, feeling suddenly childish. She nodded and we scampered across the sand. I rolled up my jeans and she held up her dress. The sea was warm after the day's hot sun. Afterwards we sat on the beach, drying our feet before putting our sandals back on. 'Let's have some chips,' I said. She looked puzzled. She'd had ice-cream before but not chips, obviously. I was going to contaminate her healthy system now. What a good parent I would have made. We sat with our little greaseproof bags. She couldn't eat many, neither could I after the ice-cream, which was just as well – I didn't want her to throw up in the car. I talked to her about Birdsong and Chas and the books I had written. She nodded and made hand gestures and her expression was so fluid that I forgot that she couldn't speak. I felt I was having a conversation with her. I looked at my watch.

'Perhaps we ought to go home now. Emmeline might be worried. What do you think?' She nodded seriously this time. We walked back along the esplanade to the car. Suddenly she stopped and pointed to a group of boys coming towards us. She looked at me and made the swaying movement with her hands again. I understood then. They were skateboarders. They'd probably scooted past her on her way down to the shore after she been ticked off by the scary receptionist. Enough to frighten the pants off anybody on their first journey out of solitary confinement.

'Marguerite, it's a game,' I said. 'A kind of sport that youngsters play these days. They have great fun.' She was listening intently. 'They don't mean any harm. But it is noisy and you have to keep out of their way. They didn't mean to frighten you.' I stood still with her and let the kids pass us by. They were talking animatedly and laughing together. I felt her relax and regard them with interest. 'Okay?'

We arrived home in time for supper. Emmeline, charged with nervous adrenalin, was feeling lively enough to serve up jacket potatoes and salad. I could tell she was relieved to see us safely back. She kept scrutinising Marguerite's face for signs of damage. But Marguerite was showing none, except for a delicate flush on her cheekbones and a slight bout of indigestion.

★   ★   ★

Neptune sat beside Emmeline's bed stroking her hand. She always felt comforted by the feeling of his rough palm. She remembered her hands were once as rough and calloused as his. But lately, since she'd been unable to chop wood and dig the garden, her skin had become softer again, but without the suppleness of youth.

'She managed, didn't she?' Neptune said.

Emmeline nodded. 'I just can't help worrying.'

'Well, it's understandable. You've not exactly had a worry-free life, have you?'

'Nor have you, Nep. We always seem to have been worrying about someone – the two of us.' She looked at him, knowing they were both thinking about Woody. What would Woody look like now? Grey? Bald? It was hard to imagine – he would always be dark and wild in her mind. She sighed. 'Maybe we should have told Lilly sooner. She seemed to be the one who could help him.'

How Lilly had loved Woody. Emmeline sometimes felt a prickle of jealousy, watching them talk and laugh together. She wondered what Lilly's life would have been like if she had never met her. Would she have got married and lived an acceptable life as a wife and mother? Would Emmeline have travelled and trained to be a scientist as she'd dreamed? Emmeline had been older, had she led her on? But their love had happened so naturally. Lilly had always been the one who wanted to snuggle up. There had seemed to be no doubts, no choice.

'It was a long time ago,' Neptune said, gruffly. 'Get some rest.' Emmeline closed her eyes . . .

There is something going on with Emm, something she isn't telling me. It has nothing to do with the baby – she isn't looking at me with the shadow of hurt before her eyes that separates us when we talk about the impending birth. I know she wants to tell me, but I will have to wait until she is ready or else she will swallow it down and become very busy. I watch her pushing toast crumbs around her plate, gathering them into a pile and scattering them again. Her hands, which always seem too large for her thin arms, are ingrained with dirt. I sit silent; mentally weaving threads of gold around her which blend with the sun's rays dancing across the table. She pushes the plate away from her, sits back and blinks as if she has just woken up.

'Neptune and I are worried about Woody,' she says.

And then she lets it flow as if a rock has been lifted out of a stream. His drinking bouts were becoming more frequent and consequently he was pulling his weight less and less in the market garden. They hadn't been able to set up the roadside stall to sell produce as Woody hadn't got round to finishing it. The greenhouse renovation had fallen way behind schedule. It was as much as Emm and Neptune could do to tend the garden and the animals – which now included pigs and goats – and go to the market. Neptune was still fishing every day too, as he wanted to keep supplying his existing customers.

'Why didn't you tell me before, Emm?' I feel cross that they'd kept me in the dark about this. I'm not a child. I see her bite her bottom lip, realised how torn she must have been.

'He made us promise not to because of your condition. He didn't want to worry you.'

I can see her dilemma, but I still feel irritation rising out of my anxiety for Woody.

'Oh, for heaven's sake – this isn't exactly a worry-free pregnancy. I might be able to help him, I've always helped him in the past.' Poor Woody, he needed me and yet he was trying to protect me.

'Precisely. And that's why Neptune and I decided we would say something to you. We knew you'd want to help him. His difficulty is, he's having more flashbacks which makes him drink more and now he seems to be in some sort of downward spiral where it's hard to know which is causing what.'

I realise that I have noticed how frequently he seems to take a swig from his flask but haven't given it much thought. As usual, I am completely wrapped up in myself and my unborn child.

'I wish I hadn't given him all those bottles of spirits from the hotel. I didn't think about it at the time.'

'Oh, Neptune says they disappeared months ago.'

'What?' I am aghast, there seemed to be enough to last for years. 'So, where does he get it from now?'

'He goes down the pub. He spends money they can't really afford.'

'But, I thought he hated the pub – all the comments that he gets.'

'I suppose the need for a drink gets the better of all that. Nobody seems to take a lot of notice of him now apparently. He didn't respond to their comments, so Neptune says, eventually they just got bored and stopped.'

'Poor Woody.' I can't bear to think of him sitting all alone in the bar getting drunk to avoid his nightmare visions. I imagine him, huddled in a corner in his army greatcoat, his huge black leather boots, his dark hair and beard tangled. If only those who judge him knew what he'd been through in the war. 'I want to go and see him, Emm. I can help him. I know I can.'

'But you need to be careful, Lilly. I know you can let Woody's pain run through you, but what about the baby? Won't she feel it?'

'As long as I can write it down it doesn't affect me.'

'But can you be sure it won't be too much for her?'

I have to think about this and I am unsure. I do these things intuitively, I can't rationalise it. I put my hands on my belly. If only she could tell me. I shake my head.

'Then you mustn't do it, Lilly. You can't take that risk.'

'But, there must be something we can do. We can't just leave him to drink himself to death.'

'We'll get him over here in the evenings for

supper with Neptune, try and divert him. And it won't be long now until the baby comes and that will change things, I'm sure.'

'Won't he listen to Neptune?'

'Up to a point. But then his addiction takes over and he can get quite aggressive, even with Nep.'

I decide to try and see Woody on my own. I think I might be able to talk to him without absorbing his pain. I keep waking up in the night and seeing his face, gaunt behind his beard, his dark eyes haunted. I remember that face, open and laughing as he ran along the beach with Neptune and they splashed into the sea, swimming out until I could hardly see them and I cried to Emm that they might get lost in France and never come back.

The next morning after Emm has gone to work and I know Neptune will be doing his fish deliveries, I set off to walk over the top of the cliff and down to Puck's Bay. If it becomes too much for me I will just have to turn back.

I reach the second field gate beyond the gardens of the hotel when I see Henry coming towards me. So this is the way he comes. He must leave his car parked some way up the road to avoid anyone seeing him. It is pointless trying to turn back. Whichever way I go, he could catch up with me in a few strides. I stand and wait. I rest my hand on the gate, keeping it closed between him and me. The air is heavy with bloated mauve clouds. I have my umbrella with me; I grasp it tightly.

'Lillian, what are you doing up here?' he says.

'Walking.'

'I was coming to see you.' He pulls out his handkerchief to wipe his forehead. I feel a pang of revulsion. I stand still, gripping the gate so that he can't open it.

'What do you want?' I feel the familiar tremble in my legs and wish I could sit down.

'Could we . . .' he looks round, 'is there anywhere we could sit and talk?'

'No. You can talk to me here.' I can feel drops of sweat beading on my top lip.

'Well, Lillian. I've come back to ask if you'd thought about what I'd said.'

'And I said there was nothing to think about.'

He sighs. 'Please, Lillian. I've told you how sorry I am. What else do you want me to do?'

'I just want an address for Victoria – which you can send me.'

'Then let me give you more money. At least have a telephone installed, a bathroom. For God's sake, Lillian, think of the child.'

I stand silent, looking past him. I don't want to anger him and he seems frustrated by what I've already said. He runs his hands through his oiled hair several times and wrenches open his stiff collar. I try not to shudder. I don't want him to see that I am afraid.

'Please, Lillian, come away with me. We can work this out. I will be so different if you'll let me.'

I look down at the grass and shake my head. We stand in silence. I can feel his eyes examining me.

'Have you seen a midwife?' he demands. I don't answer. 'You might have high blood pressure. You look flushed.'

I feel startled. High blood pressure, that sounds frightening. Emm hasn't mentioned that.

'Has the child moved into the birth position yet? Can you feel its head pressing down?' He continues to stare at me. 'You see, Lillian. You don't even know that. It might be breech. What will you do then?'

'I have it all planned. We're not far from hospital here.' But I suddenly feel anxious about the birth. More than I have ever felt before.

'Have you been taking the pills I gave you? You mustn't get anaemic.'

'I'm not anaemic.'

'How do you know?' he hisses.

'Please stop this, Henry.' He moves nearer the gate.

'Lillian, let me bring someone out to the cottage to examine you. I promise I won't come inside. I can get a colleague of mine to attend the birth if you like.'

I shake my head, feeling near to tears. Why doesn't he just go away and leave me alone?

'Very well, Lillian. You're being damn silly, but it's your decision. Just promise me that you'll register the child in my name – if it survives.'

'Why? I don't understand.'

'Because we . . . I . . . owe it that much. A child needs to know the truth about who its father is.

Look, it doesn't have to know until it's grown up, but at least it will know the truth. When it's old enough to understand.'

'Understand?'

'Oh, I don't know, Lillian. I can't think. It seems the best thing to do. Do you have a better suggestion?'

'Woody –'

'No! Everyone knows he's a queer. No one will believe that. You'll be branded as an unmarried mother. Why don't you say you are married to a sailor and that you've come back here to live while he's overseas? Later, you can pretend to be a widow.'

'But, Emm –'

'Don't talk to me about her!'

'What has she ever done to you?'

'I hate her and all she stands for.'

'I'm no different.'

'You are! You could be – Lillian, please reconsider – come with me.'

'No, Henry. Don't ask me ever again.'

He puts his hands over his face briefly as if he doesn't know what to do next. I feel exhausted, as if I could drop onto the grass. The baby drags at me like a ton weight strung around my middle. I put a hand on my belly. He is watching me. He feels in his pocket and brings out another package.

'I want you to take these,' he says. 'They will help tone up your womb and make for an easy confinement. All the mothers take them these days.

It's a preparation for the birth.' He turns away. 'I might not see you again, Lillian. Please take care of yourself.'

'You will let me know about Victoria, won't you?'

He nods and walks away.

I stumble back across the fields towards home. I can't make it to Woody's.

The next day, Woody is missing. He didn't return home the previous evening from a drinking bout at the pub. Neptune endured the sneers and called in at the local to ask the regulars if anybody remembered Woody leaving and what state he was in. Emm and I wander the beach in case he has slept it off in the cave. No work is done in the gardens. The animals are tended and that is all we manage to do.

The following day, Neptune asks around the neighbouring villages and pubs.

'He's never stayed out for two nights before,' Neptune says, looking from one to the other of us, his deep eyes even more sunken with fatigue. He gets up from the table. 'I'm going out in the boat again.'

I catch hold of his hand. 'Please take care, Neptune. It's squally today.'

'I need to scan the cliffs again now that the light is in a different place.'

He has spoken to the coastguard who he and Woody know well. A boat had gone out earlier for a preliminary search but to no avail.

'He'll turn up, old Woody.' The coastguard had

tried to reassure him. 'Sleeping it off somewhere, he'll be.'

But we aren't reassured. It is out of character for Woody to do this. None of us can eat or sleep. We want Neptune to stay with us but he says he needs to be at Puck's Cottage in case Woody turns up there. Booty is restless, he keeps whining at the door, raising our hopes.

'I should have tried to help him,' I keep saying. Damn Henry! If he hadn't waylaid me, I might have seen Woody and prevented all this. Emm sits and strokes Drifter. The waiting seems interminable. After a while we give up talking and just sit. Occasionally one of us goes and looks out to sea. Neptune is out in his boat all the daylight hours, scanning water and cliff faces. He went to the police in Ventnor but nobody had sighted him. He wasn't in any of the hospitals.

At midnight, on the third day, Neptune sits at our table and weeps.

'Maybe he just decided to go away,' he sobs. 'He often said he was letting us all down. But I never thought he would leave me.' He wipes his red, rough hands across his face and over his light hair. 'Perhaps I was too hard on him. I thought if I got angry he might pull himself together. We had a row, that last night, you see. I told him he needed to think seriously about what he was doing, that it was affecting us all. He glared at me and went out. I shouldn't have said it.'

'You did the right thing,' Emm says, stroking his

back. 'Perhaps he has gone away to sort himself out. He might come back cured.' She looks at me over Neptune's shaking shoulders but her eyes look hopeless.

Five days later, Woody's body is washed up on Ventnor beach. The longshoremen find him early and call the police who come and inform Neptune. He stumbles over to Wraith Cottage to tell us what has happened as soon as he gets back from identifying Woody's body. He lies back in the armchair and tells us, almost as a matter of fact, as if he has been expecting this all along. Emm sits weeping, holding his hand; he dozes for a while, exhausted.

I go outside and struggle down the steps to the beach and sit on my stone and howl into the blustering wind like a banshee. I can't believe it, not my Woody, my lovely gentle Woody who had lived through the horror of war and loved Neptune and had been like a big brother to me. I had looked into his eyes and seen obscene cruelties inflicted by humans on each other. If he had survived that, why couldn't he survive flashbacks and the curse of alcohol?

'Why, Woody, why?' I yell into the droning wind. And then it comes to me. He hadn't meant this. He hadn't meant to leave us. He'd promised to give his name to my child and I knew he intended to keep his word. That wasn't the nature of Woody, even with the blight of the alcohol; I knew this was not what he would do. What then? An accident?

Had he fallen from the cliff in the dark? But he knew the cliffs like he knew the sea. Had he been followed by a mob, attacked? The police would find out if his death was suspicious. Who or what was behind this?

I glance around me, see the wink of the lighthouse, the flash of gulls, feel the salt wind scour my wet cheeks. A fishing boat bobs far out on the waves. A vision of Henry wading darkly from the sea breaks into my mind. Henry! Oh, God, no. Not Henry. He'd always detested Woody for being different. But could he hate him even more for offering to father his unwanted child, child of his rape? But that was ridiculous, Woody was doing him a service, wasn't he? What am I thinking of? I am accusing Henry of murder. But even as I try to exonerate him, I know deep down that he is involved in Woody's death. Somehow, Henry is involved . . .

Emmeline felt Neptune's hand shaking in hers. She knew he was remembering too. She looked at his familiar face. Grooved now, worn by the weather and the years, but just as beloved. Tears were tracking their way down through the deep furrows. She put her arms around him and they clung to each other for a long time.

CHAPTER 17

Chas sat at he kitchen table which was heaped with paper. His fair hair, flopping over his forehead, seemed thinner and greyer. He looked as if he'd just experienced the Wall Street crash and might rush upstairs and hurl himself out of the bedroom window.

I switched on the kettle, gasping for tea. I'd just arrived home from the island and this felt like a culture shock. A few hours ago I'd been involved in a surreal world of forgotten women who communed with the supernatural. I fought back the urge to yawn and switch off. Chas needed me and so did Dad. I made the tea and hunted around for food which seemed to be rather scarce. I put a plate of water biscuits and cracked cheese on top of a pile of accounts.

'Accountant's block?' I said.

He smiled, mournfully. 'Could well be.'

'Perhaps Dyno-Rod would do us a two-for-the-price-of-one deal.'

We sat, nibbling dry biscuits like a couple of hamsters. Chas stared into space with red-rimmed eyes. His skin looked pale and flabby. I had a sudden vision of Neptune's brown, clear-eyed face. I leaned forward and took one of his big soft hands in mine.

'I don't want you to clog up your coronary arteries with the share index.'

There followed a two-minute silence. Then he gave an enormous sigh, papers fluttered in the draught. 'It was all right when I was younger. Now I wake up at night with my heart pounding and my guts churning.'

'Oh, Chas. That's no way to live, is it?' I thought of Wraith Cove and the sigh of wind on sea, Neptune chugging about in his boat, Marguerite wandering in the shallows. 'Couldn't you go back to being simply an accountant? You used to enjoy that. Let go of all the financial wheeling and dealing. Work the hours that you want.'

'But how would we manage? It would take time to get established again.'

'I bet you have loads of loyal clients. And we could downshift. There's only the two of us – we have everything we need. You could work from home, cut out all the overhead expenses.' I got up and put my arms around him. 'You could take up fishing.'

'You know, Janey. That's not a bad idea.'

I didn't feel it was a good time to launch into the Isle of Wight saga. But I did mention that I'd inadvertently acquired a cousin on my latest visit. I also told him about my visit to Bill Allain and the property update.

'Chas, why do you think Dad would have put money into a trust fund for Lillian?'

'A tax dodge, I should think.'

'But why Lillian and not Emmeline, his sister?'

Chas shrugged. 'Well, you said yourself how much they hate each other. Perhaps he had a conscience about leaving them with the headache of the hotel, so he put it in Lillian's name as a cop out.'

'But what was the point of it, if she never knew it existed?'

'I really don't know. Perhaps he genuinely forgot about it. You know what Henry's like. He's always had his head buried in diseased lungs. I suppose he just left all that to his accountant.'

'This money might possibly come to me.'

'Might it?' Chas perked up.

'So Bill said. Because I'm the beneficiary of Lillian's will.'

'But Henry's still alive. Why don't you ask him about it?'

'Oh, Chas. You know I can't talk to Dad about money.'

'But this does concern you. Tell him your solicitor asked you.'

'I might. I'll see how he is after his check-up. Talking of which, I had better go and pick him up.' I dropped a kiss on Chas's head. It felt hot, as if it had been over-revved. 'We'll talk about fishing later. I have missed you.'

★   ★   ★

It was hard for Emmeline to believe that almost fifty years had gone by. Lilly's vivid recall of that devastating year made it seem such a short time ago. She had never truly understood the depths of what Lilly had endured from Henry. After Lilly died, Emmeline was lost in grief and then bombarded with drugs until she felt she was going out of her mind. She couldn't remember what had happened an hour ago let alone fifty years. But now everything was sharpening, coming back into focus. The drugs were clearing from her body with Marguerite's help, her memory returning as she listened to Lilly. And with the remembering she felt the pain anew – and her hatred of Henry. She wanted to finish it. 'Come on, Lilly,' she urged . . .

Woody is being buried today – the tenth of September. The coroner reported that the post-mortem had revealed no signs of foul play, no stabbing, shooting or strangulation. His body had been battered against the rocks by the tides. The landlord of the pub had noticed Woody lurch out after last orders in a state of inebriation. Nobody had seen him stumbling along the coast path and there had been no recent cliff subsidence. There had been no evidence to indicate a struggle and his personal possessions, including his money and his watch, were still on his person. The verdict was accidental death.

I can't go to the funeral. I don't want curious eyes staring at me, sparking another topic of local gossip.

Neptune and Emm arrange everything, and have been surprised by the number of local fishermen and trades-people who have come forward to offer their condolences. Apparently, Woody had been well thought of amongst a certain class of society. Some folk had great respect for his carpentry skills and his fishing prowess. Others could relate to his postwar distress. It seems he wasn't the only one who suffered from flashbacks and nightmares and tried to blot them out with drink. I wonder why he never sought solace with them, but maybe they could only compound it for each other.

I think Neptune is heartened by this support and kindness. It helped him through the bleak days after Woody's death when he seemed to be in limbo awaiting the release of his body. Woody is being laid to rest in a small graveyard overlooking the sea where other longshoremen and seafarers are buried. I plan to go there with my daughter when she is born. I want her to know about the goodness and love of this man.

I sit alone in Wraith Cottage while the burial is taking place. I set a glass jug of roses and a fat beeswax candle on one end of the long table. Against the jug I prop the only dog-eared photograph of Woody that we possess. I light the candle and the cottage fills with the sweet scent of the flowers and the spicy smell of the burning wax. Outside the air is heavy with moisture which refuses to let go and I can hear a distant rumble of thunder echoing across the Channel.

I sit and contemplate Woody's image. The snap had been taken with Emm's old Brownie, he must have been about twenty-four. He was smiling, pleased to be home, but I can see the strain in his expression, the drawing down of his heavy brow, that might have forewarned us of his torment. Dear Woody, we have a gap in our lives now that will never be filled. He did things quietly, surprising each of us with his gifts, a polished curve of wood, an endless supply of kindling, a stack of logs, a repair to the crumbling cliff steps to make our path safe. His dark eyes gaze steadily back at me.

I wonder how we will manage without him. We can't afford to employ anyone to help out, and the greenhouse and produce stall schemes have come to a halt. Vegetables are waiting to be harvested. The ground is dry from lack of rain. Emm rushes around trying to keep everything going. Neptune is still dazed and we know he won't be able to function until after the funeral. And I am hardly able to move – I am enormous.

Every time I stand up I feel as if the baby is going to fall out of me. I know she is in the right position for birth. I can feel her head pressing down hard and she has dropped lower, making my breathing and digestion easier. Her movements are less, as if she has little room for acrobatics now. My womb is tightening up frequently, sometimes painfully and I know that is as it should be too – Braxton Hicks contractions, Emm calls them, peering at me over her spectacles like a professor.

Yesterday and this morning the contractions are happening every few minutes. I hadn't mentioned it to Emm; she has enough to do and the baby isn't due until the end of the month. Emm and I have studied all the books, although I have kept Henry's literature hidden at the bottom of my wool basket, reading it when she is away.

I look again at Woody's face. My tears have dried up and I am left with a deep yearning for him. I think back to our New Year party on the beach when we were so carefree and happy. None of us would have believed what lay ahead in the coming months. How could we have known that I would be raped and pregnant by my brother-in-law, disowned by my sister, Emm attacked, Woody dead, our market garden project failing? And my relationship with my beloved Emm changed, not lessened in strength, but different nevertheless.

'Oh, Woody,' I say to his photo, 'how did all this come about?' His eyes burn into mine and tell me the answer. 'Henry,' I say. 'It's all because of Henry.' Henry had stored his own hurt and pain and thrust it upon us. We have paid a price we didn't deserve. I can feel my anger running inside my veins like venom from a snake's bite.

I heave myself out of my chair and lunge at my basket of knitting wool. I throw the skeins and balls around, Drifter bounds after them. I unearth the pile of booklets and the bottles of medicines that Henry has given me. I put them all in a heap on the armchair. Lastly, I pull out the wad of twenty-pound notes. Why have I kept this tainted money? It will poison anything I spend it on, even if it is for his child. I pile the money and books into the grate and light a match. The paper flares. I open the bottles of pills and empty them on top. They ignite with lurid chemical colours. Thank heavens I hadn't taken any. Poison, everything of his is poisonous. I throw the glass bottles into the waste bucket and stand, panting with the exertion.

Why had I allowed Henry to come anywhere near me again? I had let my sisterly feelings for Victoria take over and he'd wormed his way back in with his self-pity and false declarations. I'd been so naïve. I should have told the others straight away. Neptune and Woody might have been able to warn him off. Weren't all bullies cowards at heart?

I hold my belly, feeling it contract tightly. 'It's all right, my little one,' I whisper, 'you are not tainted. Your beautiful soul has not been poisoned by him.' I wait for her answering movement, her response, but none comes. My heart starts to pound, sweat runs down my face. Oh, God. Supposing all this is too much for her, what if she's changed her mind and decides she doesn't want to be born into this world of pain? I lean over the table breathing heavily. And then I feel an almighty lurch inside me and a great flood of water cascades down my legs. This is it! She is coming and I am alone.

Emm won't be back for hours. She is helping Neptune with Woody's wake. But I don't care. This is between my daughter and me now. It is right that I should be on my own. I feel suddenly exhilarated, powerful. Strength seems to flood into me. I pull open the bed-settee easily, usually it takes both Emm and me to do it. I spread the bed with the rubber sheet and old towels that Emm and I have stored. I put water on to boil and wipe the floor. I have to stop every few minutes as the pain grips me like a pair of giant hands. I don't want to lie down; I pace around the cottage feeling strong and full of energy. I talk to Woody's photo and Drifter, who watches me from the armchair, her ears on alert. I strip off my drenched clothes, wash myself with cool water, brush out my hair and put on a white cotton shift. I lay out my brown paper parcels of cotton wool and sterilised scissors and string on a table next to the bed. I clamber upstairs to fetch the shawl I'd knitted. I unwrap it from the tissue paper and shake out the rose petals. I hold it to my cheek; it feels as light and soft as summer morning mist and holds a mote of love woven into every stitch. I put it with a set of tiny clothes in a basket near the range. Happiness tingles through my body.

And then, a shadow seems to fall over Wraith Cottage. I am leaning over the table, panting, when it falls. I raise my eyes. Henry darkens the doorway, taking away the light, draining my joy. What a fool I've been. Had I really thought I could escape him? I gaze at him through my jagged pain and feel a deep recognition of my defeat, as if I'd always known I couldn't win. He stands staring at me as the contraction subsides and I can straighten up.

'Lillian, you're in labour.' His eyes seem to glitter out of shadows.

I shake my head. 'No. I have another three weeks to go.'

A strange look passes across his face, something sly, like a suppressed smile. 'How long have you been having pains?'

I stare at him, anger courses through my body again. 'Did you kill Woody?' My voice sounds like an animal growling. His jaw drops.

'What? Are you mad? Why would I want to kill Woody?'

'To prevent him claiming paternity.'

'You really think I'm that bothered? What nonsense. Woody was drunk and fell off the cliff. It was that simple.'

The death of Woody – simple! I pick up the jug of flowers and hurl it at him. It takes him by surprise. He ducks but it catches him on the shoulder. Glass and roses fountain through the air in slow motion as it hits the flags. I realise too late what a stupid thing it was to do. His face suffuses with blood and he snarls with rage. My mind floods with images of him bursting into the cottage at New Year. I feel myself start to shake and another pain grips me. It goes on for several minutes. I groan with the force of it. I will have to lie down soon; my legs are turning to jelly. I don't want to lie on the bed, not with him here.

'Go . . . go and fetch Emm,' I pant.

Henry ignores me. He has his black bag with him. He thumps it on the table and opens it. 'I came to get you to sign some legal papers,' he says. 'The solicitor needs them to finalise the deeds of Wraith Cottage and the hotel.' He pushes some papers towards me. My head is beginning to spin and I feel faint.

'Sign,' he commands. 'Sign. And then I'll go and fetch Emmeline and leave you to it, if that's what you want. I've warned you of the dangers. I can do no more.'

He pushes a pen into my hand. I can hardly grip it, I am trembling so much. I scribble on the forms where he indicates. He stands watching me as the pain seizes me again. I can stand up no longer. I stumble towards the bed and half fall onto it. I yell out loud with the force of the pain. I am dimly aware of Henry's hand touching my back. I try to tell him to stop, to shrug him off, but I am completely overwhelmed with the pain. It starts to recede but almost as it ceases it begins again. I feel Henry trying to lift me further onto the bed. I try to shout at him but then I am overtaken by an incredible urge to push. I hear a noise issuing from my throat.

'Wait!' He says. 'Not yet. Breathe deeply, Lilly.'

I don't want him to call me Lilly. I strike out and feel my hand connect with his face. 'Go,' I shriek. 'Get Emm. You promised.'

'I can't leave you like this,' he says.

My mouth has gone completely dry. I long for water. I can hear heavy drops of rain falling, tantalising me. Sweat is running down my face. I want to pull up my shift to wipe my face. But Henry is here. How dare he be here! The need to push is coming back. I feel myself completely at its mercy. I pant and gasp trying to resist the urge, knowing I might damage the baby's head. If only Emm was here. She would tell me what to do. She would give me cool water and talk quietly to me. When the pain lets go, I realise that Henry has pulled my shift up and is looking between my legs. I want to kick him in the face but then it dawns on me that maybe my life and that of my child depend on this man. I try to detach from him emotionally, use him as a necessity. I try to make him faceless, just a person with medical knowledge.

'I can just see a patch of head when you push,' he is saying. 'It won't be long. I'll go and scrub my hands.' I hear him moving about the kitchen, pouring water, opening the parcels of scissors and string.

He comes back, a dark shadow looming over me. He has taken off his jacket, rolled up his shirt sleeves. He looks at me for a while and then kneels down beside the bed. He takes hold of my limp hands and brings his face close to mine.

'Lillian,' he says. 'Listen to me. Let's get our child born and then I'll carry you to the car. Come with me, I'll take care of you.'

I shake my head from side to side on the wet pillow. 'She's not your child,' I just manage to whisper, before the pain engulfs me again. I hear myself cry out. Henry puts his hand over my mouth. I smell something sweet and suffocating. My head starts to swim. Pain recedes and builds again immediately. I hear Henry's voice as if he is far away.

'Push now, Lillian. Push hard.'

I push with all my might. I can hear myself screaming with each push. It seems to go on for ever.

'Stop! Stop,' he commands. 'The cord is round its neck.'

I feel Henry's fingers probing me, forcing me open. I feel his hands groping inside me, twisting and pulling. I think I am going to split apart. I hear the clink of metal, feel it cold against my flesh.

'Push again now,' he says. 'Gently, gently.'

I feel the slither of something leaving my body, hear small grunting noises, a squeak, a yell. She is here! I reach out heavy arms. I can't speak, my tongue is like dry leather. Henry places his hand over my mouth again. I struggle against the sweet stench, battling to stay conscious. His face looms close to mine distorted, grotesque.

'You didn't think I was going to let you keep my daughter, did you?' he hisses the words at me. I feel his spittle hitting my face. 'Say anything to anyone and I'll tell them about your insanity. I'll say you gave birth and got rid of it – threw it into the sea.' I try to scream but my mouth and throat

349

seem paralysed. Flashes of light blind my eyes and a thunderous noise reverberates in my head. I seem to be spiralling, as if I am travelling at top speed through a dark tunnel. I can hear my voice yelling from further and further away.

'No . . . no . . . no . . .'

Emmeline opened her eyes. Her heart was thumping so hard she felt fearful it might burst. 'If only I'd been there, Lilly,' she cried.

I asked to speak to Doctor Phipps after Dad had his check-up. I liked her more and more. I detected underneath her casual air a genuine interest in people as humans and not just medical cases.

'He really is doing well,' she said, 'physically, that is.'

'Not psychologically though,' I said.

'Well, he's very subdued isn't he? It's as if he's lost in his own inner world.' She swung her stethoscope backwards and forwards like a pendulum as she perched on her desk. 'Did you manage to get him to open up?'

'I did. I wheeled him around his house evoking the past. He confessed to having a sister – thith-der – that he'd disowned along with his sister-in-law. They were in a lesbian relationship.'

She cocked an eyebrow. 'Interesting. Are they still alive?'

'His sister is. I've met her. She's on her way out too – with cancer.'

'Oh, what a pity. Any chance of them getting together and dropping the old family feud?'

'That's what she said – his sister.'

'Maybe that's what he needs then. Now that he's let it come to the surface, perhaps he's full of regrets.'

'They're both so old and ill that I don't know how either of them would stand up to the journey.'

'Well, your father's not exactly ill, Jane – just frail. Ask him if he wants to go. I should take him if I were you. What does he have to lose?'

'Can I ask you something else, Doctor Phipps?'

'Fire away.'

'I discovered that I have a cousin on the Isle of Wight. One of my lesbian aunts was raped and became pregnant. She had a daughter and my two aunts raised her between them.'

'My goodness. It all happens in your family doesn't it?'

'Seems to. I met her – my cousin. She's extraordinary. She appears to have been born with some sort of disability. She's a bit weak down her left side and doesn't speak.'

'A degree of cerebral palsy due to birth trauma, maybe oxygen deprivation, I should think. Have you spoken to her doctor?'

'Strangely, she's never seen a doctor or been medically diagnosed. She's kind of isolated in a little cottage by the sea.'

'Amazing. A genuine wild child. Go on.'

'She draws what she sees – people are like swathes of colour – animals and objects too.'

'Well, some children view the world like that, before it gets conditioned out of them. How old is she?'

'I'm not sure. In her forties I would think. She's very beautiful and fragile looking but seems strong and healthy.'

'You said she doesn't talk. Is she deaf?'

'No. She looks round when you speak to her and hears minute noises – she even draws sounds.'

'Ah, she may well be deaf but very sensitive to vibrations. She might sense the world in a totally different way to most of us. That ability to see sounds – synaesthesia it's called – it's always fascinated me.' She laughed. 'Ever smoked marijuana, Jane?'

'I have, but I just end up giggling stupidly. I've never had beautiful psychedelic visions. My cousin seems to have other abilities too. She picks up events at a distance. Sometimes before they happen.'

'Pre-cognition. She sounds intriguing. It's as if she's been allowed to slip through the net and develop in her own way without outside interference.'

'I was wondering – if I could ever get her to travel this far – if I might have a private appointment with you to assess her, find out if she is deaf or if there is something wrong with her vocal cords.'

'I would be happy to see her. But, she sounds rather unique and special. Maybe she should be left alone. Would you say she was happy?'

'Happy? I think she's the most profoundly joyful

and peaceful person that I've ever met. Just to be around her has a calming effect.'

'Then why interfere?'

'I just wonder if she should have been given a chance at speech or something. I don't know really.'

'It sounds to me as if she speaks with her soul.'

'Her soul?'

She laughed. 'It's the great unknown, isn't it? What and where is the soul?' She looked thoughtful for a moment, stopped swinging her legs. 'If she is at peace with her world why alter anything? After all, how many of us can claim that? Unless you think she is being deprived in any way or really needs medical intervention, I should leave well alone.'

I nodded. 'I think you're right. I suppose a bit of me feels like I should do something.'

'Take your father to see her – she'd be his sort-of-niece, wouldn't she? Perhaps she can pass on her peace of mind to him.'

She laughed as we said goodbye. 'Plenty of material there for a novelist I should think. Don't they say truth is stranger than fiction?'

I laughed with her. 'I haven't got time to write any more. I've got too many lame ducks to look after.'

Dad dozed on the way back to Winter Wood. His head drooped forward on his chest, reminding me of Emmeline in her chair. I wondered how she was. I'd left Neptune my telephone numbers in case of emergency and he told me Emmeline always had any mail sent to his address and he collected it at St Lawrence post office. I was feeling pretty tired myself after my early start from the island, listening to Chas's woes and then this hospital appointment.

Dad hadn't said much. He seemed vaguely pleased to see me which was quite something for him. But then he'd lapsed back into his lethargy. I was hoping that I might be able to unload him into the arms of his present carer when we got back and then escape, but he seemed as if he wanted me to stay. He kept beckoning me with his gnarled old hand. I felt as if I was being summoned.

We got him settled in the sitting-room with a rug over his knees. The carer went off to make tea. He looked very pale. His left eye and the corner of his mouth still drooped slightly, more so when he was tired. He could move his left arm but it seemed very shaky. His speech was much better although he talked in a very monosyllabic way now. I wasn't sure if that was a result of the stroke or just that he couldn't be bothered to make the effort. He'd certainly given up on his brief attempt at smiling. I wondered if the physio would still be able to tickle one out of him.

I considered how I might approach the subject of my visit to the island without upsetting him too much. Property rather than people might be a good start.

'Dad, I went to see the solicitor about Wraith

Cottage and the land. He seems to think it's worth hanging onto for a while. Did you know that Lillian still owned all the hotel grounds?'

He shook his head.

'Oh, and another thing. The solicitor said there was some money put by for hotel rates and taxes, that sort of thing – in your name.'

He nodded. 'I believe so. My accountant deals with all that.'

'And er, he mentioned there's another account too – a sort of trust account for Lillian.'

'May have been. I can't remember.'

'Why didn't she ever have the money, Dad?'

'Can't think.'

'Why did you provide money for Lillian and not for Emmeline?'

He was starting to stir now. His hand shook alarmingly. I rescued his cup and saucer. 'It was for the hotel. Help her out.'

I let him have a rest, asked about his carers.

'Fed up with them, silly women. Always talking about their families.'

'Well, I seem to have acquired some family now that I didn't know I had.' He was looking at me; his left eye still slightly veiled. 'What with discovering Lillian and then Emmeline.'

'Emmeline?' he said.

'She's not well, Dad. She has cancer.' I heard him draw in his breath, almost like a sob. 'She said she would like to see you.'

'She said that?' He shifted forward in his chair.

I nodded. 'Would you like to go?'

He wiped a hand across his chin, lost in some sort of reverie for a while.

'Dad.' He looked up, startled. 'Something terrible happened to poor Aunt Lillian, after you left the island.' His hands gripped the arms of his chair. 'Someone – a drunk I think – broke into her cottage and raped her.'

'No, no,' I heard him whispering.

'She had a child – a daughter.'

'Lillian, Lillian,' he whispered, like a rustling of dry leaves.

'Lillian and Emmeline raised her between them. I met her, Marguerite, her name is.'

His head jerked up and he stared at me, piercingly, like an old hawk. 'No,' he said, shaking his head. 'No.'

'It's all right, Dad,' I put my hand on his. 'It was awful, but it turned out okay because they adored Marguerite and she is the most beautiful person. Of course she is a grown woman, well into her forties I should think. But she still lives there, with Emmeline.'

Dad continued to shake his head, looking completely bewildered.

'You obviously didn't know about any of this? About Marguerite?' He continued to stare at me, transfixed. 'They have an old friend, a fisherman, they call him Neptune, who helps them out.'

Dad collapsed back in his chair. 'Go away,' he cried hoarsely. 'Go away from me!'

I left, locked back into my distant past, chastised, a small bewildered girl, wondering where I had gone wrong again.

The next morning Dad's carer phoned to say my father had seemed agitated after I left. She'd wanted to call me to come back but he wouldn't let her. But this morning he was demanding to see me. I was wondering how much more I could take of this. I'd spent last night mulling over the meaning of life with Chas. He had got very drunk and maudlin over his financial disasters. I seemed to be lurching from one life crisis to another. I suddenly longed for the calm presence of Marguerite who seemed to be the only totally sane, peaceful person I knew at the moment. What I wouldn't have given to be transported to Wraith Cove, walking along the sand with her.

I arrived at Winter Wood in trepidation, wondering if I was in for some more admonishing. The carer escorted me into the sitting-room as if I were the prime suspect. Dad was looking a bit livelier, apparently roused from his lethargy.

'Jane,' he said, and held out a shaky hand. 'Sorry, my dear. I'm sorry.'

This was a surprise. 'Oh, Dad, it's all right,' I responded gratefully. 'I do spring things on you, don't I? I get carried away with my discoveries and forget they can be a bit of a shock.'

He nodded. 'Sit down, sit down.' I sat obediently. 'Money,' he said. 'That money for Lillian.

You must have it, of course.' He held up his hand before I could interrupt. 'My accountant – he should have seen to it.' He peered around the room. 'Charles –'

'Chas isn't here, Dad. You want to see him?'

'Charles, yes. Want him to sort out my affairs. Don't trust that other fellow. Sacked him this morning.'

'I'm sure Chas would be happy to, Dad.'

'Time I put things right. Made things easier. It's all yours anyway.'

'Dad, I –'

He held up his hand imperiously. 'Tired, Jane,' he said. 'Had enough.'

'You want me to go?'

'No, no. I want to go – to die.'

'Don't, Dad.'

He patted my hand. 'For the best.' He looked at me, his eyes pleading. 'Take me back to the island, Jane. Have to see Emmeline, have to sort it out – the truth – before I go.'

I didn't know what truth he meant. Did he mean he wanted to find out for himself what happened to Emmeline and Lillian after he left? Did he think I was exaggerating about Lillian's rape and her daughter – another one of my damn silly stories?

'Dad, if you really want to go back, then of course I will take you. I'll ask Chas to come over later and talk to you about your finances and we'll make the arrangements. Maybe Chas would like to come too. We could make it a holiday, a tour of remembrance. You could show me all your boyhood haunts.' Why hadn't I thought of this before? It would be a lovely thing to do before Dad died. Hopefully he could make his peace with his sister and meet Marguerite – his sort-of-niece, as Doctor Phipps had described her. I felt quite excited at the prospect.

CHAPTER 18

Emmeline had sensed there was something wrong that day. Woody's funeral seemed endless and her anxiety increased by the hour. She hadn't planned on being away from home for so long, leaving Lilly all alone. But so many people turned up and Neptune needed her support. When the last person left, she helped Neptune clear up as quickly as she could. He had wanted to sit down and reminisce about Woody but Emmeline snapped at him to hurry. He'd looked at her with surprised and hurt eyes but then realised she was desperate to get back to Lilly. They had practically run across the fields from Puck's Bay . . .

'Lilly! Lilly! Open your eyes!'

I feel something cool on my forehead. I try to open my lips. My tongue is stuck to the roof of my mouth; it hurts to pull them apart. I had to have water. I try to speak but no words will come, and then I feel cold wetness trickle through my clenched teeth to my parched tongue. It is the only thing I need, these drops of water.

'Lillian! Open your eyes.'

Is that a man's voice? I feel the damp cloth wiping my face. I open my eyes a slit, the light is blinding. A pain sears through my head. I long to float back down the dark tunnel but the insistent voice is calling me. I feel arms lifting my shoulders and head and then laying me back on a cool surface. My chest and arms are being sponged. I attempt to raise my eyelids again. I see Emm's face waver above me. She stops the sponging.

'Lilly, thank God. Don't worry, my darling. I'm here now. Everything is going to be all right.'

What is happening to me? Am I ill? I close my eyes again. I can feel Emm wiping my legs, pulling wet sheets from under me. Perhaps I am dreaming, I will wake up properly in a minute. I start to drift and then I hear a man's voice. I feel a stab of fear.

'Henry!' I yell, and think my throat will burst with the pain. I open my eyes. There are two faces gazing down at me now. Emm and Neptune. Thank God, it is Neptune.

'Ssh, now, Lilly, it's all right. Henry's not here. Just me and Neptune.' I feel her arms lift me again and hold a cup to my mouth. I gulp it, dribbling icy water down my neck. Emm mops me up and I sink back on the pillow. She lays a cool cloth on my forehead. I can hear her whispering to Neptune.

'Perhaps you should go for the doctor, Nep. What do you think?'

'I don't know. What stage do you think she's at?'

'I didn't think there was meant to be so much blood so soon. I'm worried that some of the placenta has come away and the baby won't be getting enough oxygen.'

'Then I'd better get some help, don't you think?'

Something seems to click into place, as if I am re-connecting. My baby! That's what is happening. Images start to crowd into my mind as if my memory is trying to force itself back in a great jumbled mass. I put my hands on my belly. It feels taut under my fingers. And then Henry's face flashes before me, his hands on my body.

'Henry!' I scream. Emm rushes to me.

'It's all right, Lilly. Henry's not here, I promise you. Just me and Neptune.'

'He was here,' I yell, grabbing hold of her. 'He was here. He's taken my baby!' I try to struggle up. 'I have to go after him, get her back!'

'Nep, help me.' I hear Emm say. 'She's delirious, I think. Don't let her get up. I'll get my remedies.'

I feel cold water being splashed on my face. A great wave of weakness and nausea spreads through my body. And then the muscles of my belly clamp in the vice-like grip that I now remember. I groan and feel a great urge to push down.

'Thank God,' Emm says, 'something's happening.' I feel her bending my knees, opening my legs. 'Let me see, Lilly. I need to know what stage you're at. Do you want Nep to go?'

I shake my head as the pain recedes. I don't understand this. Henry has stolen my baby and nobody seems to be going after him. I feel the pain gathering momentum again.

'Push, Lilly,' Emm is saying. This must be the afterbirth then. I have to get it out and then I will make them listen and understand.

'I can see something,' Emm says. 'Push again, Lilly,' she urges, as the pain grips once more. Why is it taking so long? 'It's coming, it's coming.' Emm's voice is sounding hysterical now. 'Hold her other leg, Nep. Now push very gently, Lilly, gently, gently, nearly there.' What is she talking about? Why do I have to do this? I feel something warm and wet sliding out of my body. There, that was it. All over. Now let me up. I have to go after him.

There are a few moments of complete silence. Even my exhausted panting seems to cease. And then I become aware of Emm and Neptune staring down at the bed. Emm is pale and shaking. Neptune is open-mouthed.

'What shall we do?' I hear Emm whisper. Neptune bends down and lifts something off the bed, something small and bluish-red. Why is he removing the afterbirth? Why isn't Emm doing it? He picks it up slowly as if it is something precious. It looks so strange, dangling from his big hands, as if it has little arms and legs hanging down. I let out a strangled gulp of laughter. Neptune is being funny now. He rubs his hand over it and then holds it upside down and gently slaps it.

Emm reaches out her arms and takes it. I can see a wet blue rope that seems to be coming from me, it pulls at my inside as Emm moves. She puts the thing down on the bed and bends over it. She keeps straightening up, ashen-faced, to look at it. Neptune stares as if he's forgotten how to breathe. Why are they so concerned with this when my baby had been taken from me?

My mind stops working. I watch from a distance without making sense of anything that is going on. Then I hear a tiny squeak, like a kitten mewing. I see Emm looking at me and suddenly her worried face is transformed with delight, tears run down her face and Neptune is crying too.

'She's here, Lilly,' Emm is whispering. 'Your daughter's here.' She lifts the bundle and places it as high as she can on my front. I can still feel something pulling, attached to my inside. I look down at a face so tiny I can't believe it. Her eyes are tightly closed, her forehead covered in a whitish substance. Wisps of fine hair are plastered to her scalp with blood. Her minute hands are clasped together; her legs tucked tightly up. Her lips look blue, moving slightly emitting the little mewing sound. I can't make sense of anything. This must still be the dream that I am caught in. I look up at Emm; she is smiling and sobbing.

'This can't be true, it can't be,' I whisper. I look at Neptune; he is grinning and wiping his eyes. Then Emm seems to pull herself together.

'Nep, we must sterilise scissors and string. I can't find the ones I prepared. Get some more out of my workbox. Hurry.' Neptune scuttles away, knocking things over in his haste. I can't take my eyes off the tiny child. Emm goes over to the range and comes back with a large warm towel which she tucks over the baby and me.

'She's so small, Emm,' I whisper.

'Well, she's arrived early. She's very beautiful, Lilly. She looks just like you.' I look at Emm. She seems so happy; she doesn't seem to realise that something is wrong. 'But what about the other one?' I ask.

'Other what, Lilly?'

'The other baby.'

'What other baby?'

'I told you. Henry was here. He's taken my other baby.' I can hear my voice rising hysterically.

'There is no other baby, Lilly.' She puts her hand on my forehead. 'Your mind's been playing tricks. I expect it was the pain and the fear of being alone. You must have been frantic. There's glass all over the floor.'

Is that true? Have I imagined it all in some hallucinatory state? Before I have a chance to think any more, I start to feel another build up of pain, I groan. Emm jumps to attention.

'This will be the placenta. Nep, hurry up with the scissors and string. I have to tie the cord and cut it. Just a few more minutes, Lilly, and it will be all over and we can make you comfortable.'

I lose track of my thoughts again as they deal with the afterbirth and bustle about preparing hot water and clean bedding. I am still holding my tiny daughter to my chest, listening to her little squeaks, watching her stretch her exquisite fingers.

At last Emm takes her gently from me and lays her in a drawer lined with a folded blanket covered in a napkin. I look around for the basket I'd prepared but I can't see it. Emm washes me while Neptune clanks about in the kitchen making tea and I can hear him sweeping up broken glass.

At last I am clean and propped up in the bed in a fresh nightgown, drinking tea. I am feeling dazed and confused. I can't speak; I don't know where to start. Emm keeps glancing at me, smiling.

'Thank goodness we arrived back home in time,' she says.

'But you didn't,' I whisper. 'You didn't.'

Emm looks at me quizzically, her head on one side. 'You're absolutely exhausted. You must sleep. Let's put her to your breast first to encourage her to suck.' She lifts the baby and hands her to me. She is as light as a feather. I undo my nightgown and put her tiny lips to my nipple but she is fast asleep.

'Never mind, we'll try again later,' says Emm. 'We'll make her comfortable too and you can both sleep. She tenderly bathes the tiny head with warm water to remove some of the blood, then checks where she had tied off the cord. She tries to pin one of the nappies on her but it is enormous, Neptune cuts it in half. Then Emm dresses her in the smallest vest and nightgown we have, wraps her in a soft blanket and lays her back in the drawer. Neptune lights the fire even though it is only early September.

'We must keep you both warm,' Emm says, bending to kiss me. 'Now sleep.'

Yes, that's what I want. I long to sink back into that black oblivion and when I wake up the world will be real again and it will all make sense . . .

Emmeline remembered standing for a long time looking down at Lilly, hardly able to let herself dwell on what she must have been through alone. She remembered Lilly's white face, her eyes had mauve shadows beneath them. Her breath was so shallow that her chest barely moved. Thank God it was all over and she and the baby were safe. 'I'll never leave you again, Lilly,' she'd whispered.

Dad coped with the journey to the Isle of Wight quite well. He seemed almost eager, taking notice of his surroundings and where we were on the journey. We took frequent breaks and stopped at a posh hotel in the New Forest for lunch. Chas was so good with him, taking him to the toilet and keeping him up to date with our progress.

I was feeling excited. I wanted Dad and Chas to be on the island with me and to be with Dad when he revisited his old haunts. I couldn't wait for his younger day memories to resurface, and I was sure they would once he was back there. And if he and Emmeline could be reconciled and let go of their old animosity, what a bonus that would be. Chas had told me not to hold my breath. He'd known relatives of his go to their graves spitting in each other's eyes rather than forgive some old slight even if they'd forgotten what it was long ago.

I watched Dad as we crossed The Solent. He wanted to sit out on deck until it got too windy. He pointed out the sea forts and The Needles to me, as if I'd never seen them before. I was so pleased he was noticing things that I acted as if, indeed, I was seeing them for the first time. Chas was smirking at me but went along with my little game. As we drove south across the island I kept indicating things to Chas. In his Range Rover I could see over the hedges. I realised I desperately wanted him to like the island as much as I did.

Before we'd left, Chas had told his colleagues that he wanted to set up on his own and relinquish his partnership in the company. This had triggered the final breakdown of the whole firm and everybody seemed relieved that the decision had been made. Chas had walked out of the office at that point and said if he didn't take a holiday he would crack up. He'd been the one that had tried to hold it together for the last couple of years and now he felt no guilt letting others finalise the matter.

I'd written to my editor and told her I wanted to be released from my contract, if necessary paying back my advance. She'd been surprisingly agreeable and said she thought I'd come to the end of writing the type of novel I'd always written. I was so relieved, I just managed to restrain myself from dashing upstairs to my study and tearing up the pages of notes and typescript that I had produced so far. We'd agreed to meet when I returned and talk over the possibility of me venturing into a new area of work – given my maturity. I couldn't think what that might be; I didn't feel more mature. Visions of writing advertisements for stairlifts and denture-gripping gel came to mind. I frightened Chas by telling him I was going to let my hair go grey and have a perm.

So Chas and I had set off with light hearts. I sensed he was feeling easier after he'd spent a few days with Dad, going through his finances and realising what my inheritance involved. Winter Wood and its contents were worth a vast amount for a start. But more important to me was this quest with Dad. It felt like something really special that we were doing together before he died.

We'd booked into a hotel in Ventnor, next to the Botanic Gardens. We had a ground floor suite with two bedrooms and wheelchair access. After we'd settled in we had afternoon tea in a beautiful room with large windows overlooking the lawn and the sea. It reminded me of my little holiday apartment I'd rented the first time I'd been to the island. What a lot I'd uncovered since then.

I thought Dad might want to lie down after tea while I took Chas for a stroll in the Botanic Gardens but he insisted on coming. We bundled him into his wheelchair and off we went. This was probably the nearest Chas and I would ever get to pushing something around in a pram. The weather was still warm and sunny, lots of holidaymakers about. Dad began to get quite animated when we reached the visitor centre.

'It's all gone,' he kept saying. 'So many buildings gone.' He pointed to the long car park. I showed him the old photographs in the entrance of the centre. He got up out of his chair to look closely, holding a shaking hand up to the framed photos. He kept looking at us as if trying to impress upon us that it was really here. We took him down to the gardens in the lift and wandered around for a while enjoying the sunshine and the extravagant trees and plants. We sat on a bench and had ice-cream, helping Dad with his plastic tub and spoon. Chas was smiling and joking more than I'd seen him for months.

'Where was your old house, Dad, when you and Mother lived here?'

He looked disorientated for a moment and then pointed to the far end of the garden where the temperate house stood. 'Must have been there,' he said.

'Let's walk along there and see if you can remember it.' I got up and Chas wheeled while I chatted. Dad seemed to remember the old buildings which housed the smugglers' museum. He said there were lots of tunnels under there connecting parts of the hospital and staff buildings. I could sense the old history and atmosphere of this place. I'd read books on the haunting and smuggling heritage and shipwrecks that had abounded along this magical stretch of coastline and it really did seem permeated with mystery. No wonder it had inherited names like Wraith and Puck.

We went past a children's play area and Dad commanded Chas to stop and we stood staring at a grassy slope that led to the cliff edge.

'It was here,' Dad said. 'My house . . . here.'

'My word,' said Chas. 'What an amazing place to live, Henry. Look at that view.'

The view was indeed stunning. Chas pushed Dad to the edge which was now part of the coastal path and we could see Ventnor Town and the bay and beach to our left. To the right was beautiful wild coastline and glimpses of the rock-strewn sandy bays which, I guessed, must stretch right along to Puck's Bay and Wraith Cove.

'What do you think of it, Chas?' I asked, holding his arm.

He nodded. 'Very nice, Janey. I can see why you like it here. I suppose it's in your blood.'

I squatted down beside Dad. 'So, you and Mother lived here when you got married?' He nodded. 'And did your mother and father live here before you – my Rampling grandparents?' He nodded again. 'There really is quite a lot of family history on this spot then?' I thought he was looking rather sad and tired. I patted his hand. 'And was I born here too, the third generation?' He shook his head. I thought he must be reminiscing, but he grasped my hand.

'No,' he said. 'You weren't born here.'

I smiled, reluctant to contradict him. 'It's on my birth certificate,' I said, gently.

'Mistake,' he said.

I felt my heart sinking. Surely he wasn't going to tell me I wasn't born on the island after all.

'How could there be a mistake? Where was I born?' I spoke slowly, dreading his reply. He was beginning to look as if he was nodding off now. I had to catch him before he disappeared. He didn't answer me. 'Where, Dad, in the hospital?' His eyes were closing, I could feel Chas squeezing my shoulder, I shook him off. 'Dad! I want to know where I was born. Please tell me.' He opened his eyes briefly.

'Wraith Cottage,' he whispered.

I stood up, surprised. 'Did you hear that, Chas?' It was his turn to nod now. 'Dad says I was born in Wraith Cottage. Why on earth would I have been born there?'

Chas started pushing the wheelchair back towards to the hotel. 'Let's get Henry back for a lie down,' he said. 'Well, didn't they use it for holidays or something? I thought you said Victoria and Lillian used to practically live there when they were younger. Perhaps Victoria wanted to give birth there.'

'It was Lillian who loved it. Victoria lived in the hotel and then in the doctor's house here with Henry.'

'Yes, But Henry has always said he didn't want you near the chest hospital, didn't he? That's why they took you away as soon as you were born.'

I walked along beside Chas, silent for a while. No wonder I'd had such a feeling of familiarity the first time I'd seen Wraith Cottage. And I thought it had been my mother's paintings. I felt pleased. It was similar to the feeling I'd had when I returned to the island and absorbed the fact that I'd been born here. Now I could pinpoint the actual place and it was a place that I had already – I realised in that moment – grown to love.

Back at the hotel we got Dad settled on his bed and Chas went to have a nap before dinner. I felt restless and decided I would drive out to Wraith Cottage to see how Emmeline was getting on. Neptune had phoned me a few days ago, as he'd promised, to give me a progress report and her condition was much the same. I'd written to tell them when we were arriving but I had no idea whether Neptune had picked up my letter from the post office.

As I trudged across the field, wondering how we were ever going to get Dad here, I felt the presence of Marguerite and looked up to see her waving at the garden gate. My heart lurched with happiness to see her and I broke into a run. We hugged and kissed as if we hadn't seen each other for years. Emmeline was sitting in the garden in the early evening sun. I kissed her. Her face felt dry and papery.

'He's here,' I said. 'Henry's here.'

Emmeline jolted in her chair and dropped her book. Marguerite grabbed my arm, looking concerned. I realised Emmeline thought I meant that he was just out of sight, around the corner of the cottage, waiting to jump out. I laughed.

'I'm sorry, Emmeline. I don't mean right here. He's back at the hotel in Ventnor.'

I realised then the enormity of this situation for her. Meeting her brother who she hadn't seen for fifty years was going to be a traumatic experience – probably for both of them – especially as they had parted on such bad terms.

We sat and talked about her health and the dry weather. Marguerite joined in with her body language. But I felt Emmeline's anxiety. We weren't usually at a loss for words. We didn't normally stumble over small talk. I looked at Marguerite, her eyes didn't waver from mine but she seemed subdued as if she was worried, not for herself but for us.

'Have you changed your mind about meeting Henry?' I asked, after a few minutes of awkward silence.

She sighed and then shook her head. 'No, Jane. I haven't. It's just quite a hard thing to have to face now that he's here and there's no going back.'

'You don't have to do this, Emmeline. I could explain to him that you are feeling too ill and just can't cope with it.'

'No.' Some of her fighting spirit seemed to come back then. 'This has to be done. If I don't confront him then he will never do it.'

'Do what?'

'Tell the truth.'

'The truth about what?'

'Fetch me tomorrow, Jane. Take me to his hotel to meet him. I can't have him here. Not yet.'

'Okay, Emmeline. If that makes it easier.' I was beginning to be really intrigued by this meeting. What on earth could Dad have done to Emmeline that warranted all this drama? Had she blown it all out of proportion because his rejection of her had been simmering for years, or had Dad done something else dastardly in the dim and distant past? I looked at Marguerite. 'Would you like to come and meet my father, Marguerite?'

'No!' Emmeline said. 'Not yet she can't. She can stay here with Neptune. I have to see Henry and talk to him first.'

I shrugged. 'I'll come and get you tomorrow then, about eleven?'

She nodded. Marguerite walked back to the gate with me. 'Dad's not that bad,' I said to her. 'And you'll really like Chas, my husband. He's looking forward to meeting you.'

She looked at me as if she wanted to convey something very difficult. And then she relaxed and smiled her slow beautiful smile and we kissed goodbye.

Emmeline couldn't believe it. Henry was here, on the island. She had waited fifty years for this and now that he was here she almost wished he wasn't. She felt terrified. What was she going to say to him? She would have to go to his hotel. She couldn't confront him here, at Wraith Cottage. Not yet.

She lay in bed tossing and turning. 'Hurry, Lilly,' she said. 'We're almost there . . .'

I wake in the night to a strange glow. I lift my head from the pillow and realise I am lying on the bed-settee downstairs and the fire is alight. I wonder for a moment what I am doing down here and then I see Emm sleeping in the armchair, her feet up on a stool. One of her arms is stretched out, her hand resting on a little white bundle in a drawer lying on the foot of the bed. I let my head drop back. I feel hot and I ache all over. I move my legs slightly and a pain sears up into my belly from between my legs. So, it is real then. Everything is just the same. I've given birth and I have two different scenes in my head about that birth and who was present.

I lift my head again and look down at the drawer and the white blanket. But this is real. I have a baby, a daughter. I feel the first strange stirrings of joy. Why hadn't I felt like this when she was born? But I hadn't known what was happening to me. I long now to pick her up and look at her properly, inspect her from top to toe, kiss her and welcome her.

I try to move myself in the bed. I think I might be able to get up without disturbing Emm, go out to the toilet and wash my hands and face, and then I can try and feed my baby. I move one of my legs and groan with the pain. The old bed creaks and Emm's eyes shoot open.

'Lilly?' she says. 'Are you all right?'

'I need to go to the toilet, Emm.'

'You mustn't get up. Wait a minute.' She switches on a lamp and goes into the kitchen and fetches the bedpan that she'd borrowed from the Red Cross people in town. It is agonising trying to get onto it even with Emm's help. I am dismayed to see how much blood there is. But Emm reassures me that it is normal to bleed for a few weeks after the birth. She bathes me with hot water and calendula, pads me with a warm napkin and goes to make tea.

'I want to try and feed her again,' I say, after I've drunk my way through three cups.

'Do you think we should disturb her?' Emm says doubtfully.

'Yes,' I say. 'I think we should, and I need to hold her.'

Emm lifts her from the nest and hands her to me. I kiss her downy head which still bears traces of my blood. She is the softest thing I have ever touched. Her eyes are tightly closed but her face looks pinker now than it had earlier. I open the blanket to inspect her. I lift up the nightgown and touch her tiny legs and feet. She is still curled, her little knees held up to her tummy. I look at Emm, see her eyes shining in the lamplight. I smile. 'She's ours,' I whisper. Emm nods.

I open my nightgown and touch her lips with my nipple again. She stirs but doesn't seem interested in feeding. 'She's still sleepy,' I say.

'She's only a few hours old,' Emm says. 'You wait, in a few days she'll be gulping it down by the gallon.' She gets up. 'Shall I lay her back down?'

'I want to hold her for a while.'

Emm lies down beside me on the bed. She talks to me about Woody's funeral. He was buried under a small wind-blown hawthorn, with sea views; the sort of place where he loved to sit and stare. She and Neptune had been surprised by the number of people that turned up. Afterwards, they had gone to a pub for drinks and sandwiches and then a few had drifted down to Puck's Bay and sat reminiscing about the war and the old fishing community until the whisky ran out. All in all a good send-off, Neptune reckoned.

'Why didn't you tell me this morning that you were having regular contractions?' Emm asks.

'I thought they were those Braxton Hicks things that you said I should be getting.'

'Not every ten minutes regularly.'

'Well, I didn't know. Anyway, you had enough to do.' I look down at my tiny daughter, my heart expanding with love. Everything still possesses a quality of unreality which keeps making me wonder if I am still dreaming all this. Emm gets up to fetch me some arnica.

'The first thing we saw was glass all over the place. Did you drop the vase during a contraction, Lilly?'

'No.' I open my mouth for the arnica. 'Emm, please sit down, I need to tell you something. This is all so strange, but I don't know what's true any more, or if I dreamt something.'

'What is it, Lilly?'

'I think Henry was here.'

'Here!'

'Listen to me, Emm. I was having contractions and my waters broke so I got everything ready. I opened the bed-settee and prepared it with the rubber sheet and towels and got the baby basket ready with the shawl I knitted.' I see Emm look around at this point. 'I even got out the parcels we made – you know the scissors and string.' She nods, looking puzzled. 'Then, Henry came.' I see her shake her head in disbelief. 'He got me to sign something – I can't remember what – I wanted him to go and fetch you, but the baby was coming. He kept asking me to go away with him and then he put something over my face which made me feel dizzy. Emm, I'm sure the baby came then and he said he was going to take her. Then he put the pad over my face again. It smelled strong. I thought he was trying to kill me. That's all I can remember.'

Emm is shaking her head. 'But he couldn't have done, Lilly, she's here, safe and sound.'

'I know, but it all seemed so real. I can't believe I dreamt it all. Why would I have done that?'

'You must have been in such deep distress, my darling. Maybe all your fears came up to the surface.'

I nod. 'But I remember some of it so clearly – before he drugged me. I remember throwing that vase at him and hitting his shoulder.' I sit forward slightly, wincing at the pain. 'I remember he had his black bag with the papers in.' I look around the room. 'And where's the baby basket gone and the scissors?'

'I'll look for them in the morning. Don't worry now. You need some more rest.' She takes the baby out of my arms and lays her back in the drawer. She helps me to get comfortable and goes back to her armchair. 'Sleep now,' she says.

But I can't sleep. I lie listening to the dawn break, the sounds of the first blackbird, wood shifting in the fireplace. I hear a few creaks from upstairs and realise that Neptune has stayed the night. I remember him holding the baby up. He and Emm had probably saved her life, got her tiny lungs to suck in her first breath of air. Thank God they had arrived home when they did. I look at the little white mound in the drawer. I must name her. Emm and I have two names we like – Virginia and Marguerite after our two favourite writers. We'd decided to wait until she arrived to see which one suited her best.

I hear Neptune get up and move about upstairs. He is an early riser, always wanting to be up and outside on the sea. I hear him trying to creep down the stairs but it is impossible to do anything quietly in this creaky old cottage. He pulls back the red blanket and comes into the room, smiling when he sees that I am awake. He stands looking down at the sleeping baby for a while and then goes to make tea. He brings me a cup and sits beside me.

'How are you feeling?' he whispers.

'Sore.'

'Sore?' he grins. 'If I'd been through that I doubt if I'd ever be able to sit down again. I don't know how you women do it.' He gets up. 'Well, I'm going to cook up a great big breakfast. Want some?'

I nod, suddenly aware that I haven't eaten anything for about twenty-four hours. Emm stirs and opens her eyes. 'Did I hear the word breakfast?' she asks.

Neptune cooks us scrambled eggs and toast and makes more tea. Emm goes into the outhouse. 'I'll help you wash when you've had breakfast,' she says to me.

Later, when Neptune has gone off to fish and I'd been bed-bathed, Emm picks up the sleeping baby again and tries to get her to suck. But she screws up her face and steadfastly refuses. Emm changes her nappy which contains a tiny black smear.

'That's good, Lilly,' Emm says, peering at her books. 'That's meconium, just how it should look.'

'Don't you think she should be crying more?' I ask, feeling a bit anxious at my daughter's insistence on sleeping.

'Well, it does say here that they're sometimes very sleepy for the first couple of days, and don't forget that she is premature too.'

'Can I have a read?' I say, reaching for the book. She hands it to me and goes off to do some chores.

An idea has occurred to me. I keep telling myself I am being ridiculous but I have to check. I look up in the index for the section on twins. I read that twins can be monozygotic – developing identically from one fertilised ovum that splits and may have single or shared placentas. Or they can be dizygotic – developing from two ova and having two separate placentas. If my strange fantasy wasn't a dream there might possibly be two placentas.

'Emm?' She looks up from her medicine box. 'What did you do with the placenta?'

'I put it on the fire, Lilly. Why?'

'I just thought it would be interesting to see it.'

'Oh, I am sorry. I should have thought –'

'It doesn't matter.' I sit thinking. But just supposing I had given birth to another child earlier. Henry would have had to cut the cord and deal with the placenta, wouldn't he? Unless there had only been one placenta anyway.

'Emm?' She looks up again. 'What sort of a mess was I in when you arrived?'

'Well, there was quite a lot of blood. I was a bit concerned.'

'What sort of blood? Do you mean just watery stuff or what?'

Emm looks up at me sharply then. 'Well, no. It was red – quite a lot of it. I was worried, in case some of the placenta had come away. But it was

382

difficult to tell, it was all crumpled up with the newspaper.'

'What newspaper?'

'The paper you had put on the bed.'

I think about this. I don't recall putting any newspaper on the bed; I had just spread towels on top of the rubber sheet. 'Emm?' She is still looking at me, her brow creased. 'What did you do with it – the newspaper?'

'I screwed it up and put it in the outhouse to go on the bonfire.'

'I want to see it.'

Emm stood up. 'Oh, Lilly. What on earth for?'

'Please, Emm, just to put my mind at rest. I need to know that there wasn't another baby.'

'Lilly!' Emm sounds shocked.

'Please, Emm, I beg you. If you won't do it I'll get up and do it myself.'

'All right. I'll inspect it, if it will make you any happier. But it won't be pleasant.'

She goes into the outhouse and I hear her scrabbling about out there. Poor Emm. What a task. The things I ask her to do for me. I can't bear it any longer. I heave myself out of bed and hobble across to the kitchen, feeling as if my insides are going to pour out of me. I can hardly prise my legs apart at the top. I feel weak and faint. I pull back the curtain to the outhouse. The door is open and Emm crouches on the flagged floor. She looks up at me.

'There's nothing here, Lilly, except paper and blood.' She has the bloodied newspaper unwrapped on the floor in front of her. 'And you shouldn't be up.'

She leads me back to the bed and sits stroking my trembling hand. 'Look, darling, you must have been imagining things – hallucinating with the pain and anguish.'

'But where are the things then? Answer me that, Emm – where are the basket and the shawl and scissors?'

'We, er, we found hot ashes in the grate. You'd burnt something. Perhaps you were trying to light a fire and got confused. You could have burnt the basket and things without realising what you were doing.'

I flop back on the pillows, exhausted. Whatever Emm says to me I can't shake the vision of Henry's face out of my mind. It seems so real. I close my eyes and feel myself drifting away, Emm's cool hand on my hot head.

I wake to the sound of Neptune and Emm murmuring in the kitchen. I can smell bacon frying and bread baking. My stomach gurgles with hunger and for a moment I feel comforted, and then I remember Henry. I struggle to sit up so that I can see the drawer at the foot of the bed, containing my daughter. The voices stop and Neptune comes over to me.

'How are you?' His face looks concerned, I guess Emm has been telling him about my strange behaviour. I don't know what to say to him. I nod my head feeling near to tears. I can hear Booty yapping outside. Neptune squeezes my hand and goes to look out of the window. He calls to him to be quiet but the dog goes on barking. 'Must have seen a rabbit,' Neptune mutters and goes out.

Emm fetches me some fresh water and stands looking down at the baby. Neptune puts his head around the door and beckons to her. She follows him outside. I wonder if someone has come to call. I know that they won't let anybody in. And then Emm comes back. She has her hand to her mouth and her face is pale, her eyes wide. She comes over to the bed. My heart is thumping painfully. What is she going to tell me?

'Lilly . . . Booty's just pulled something out of the compost heap.'

'What, Emm?' I whisper. 'Please, don't let it be –'

'It's newspaper.' She clasps my hand. 'Lilly . . . there's scissors and what looks like another placenta – with a cord and everything. Oh, Lilly.'

So, it is true. Henry has stolen my first daughter. My God, what would he have done with her?

'He was really here,' Emm was muttering. 'He was here and stole your child not knowing that you were giving birth to twins.' She looks at me, her face white with strain. 'Is that what happened, Lilly? Is that possible?'

My mind seems to be clearer now that the doubt is receding. 'I heard a baby cry quite loudly,' I say. 'I remember him shouting something about not letting me have his daughter.'

I look towards the drawer. 'This little one didn't cry like that.' I struggle up and lift her out. She stirs and for the first time she opens her eyes. I catch a glimpse of darkest blue. 'This is Marguerite,' I say. 'Henry took Virginia.'

Emm puts her shaking arms round me. 'I'm so sorry. I'm so sorry I didn't believe you,' she sobs. She puts out her hand and gently strokes the tiny cheek. 'Sweet Marguerite, we'll get your sister back for you,' she says, her voice hoarse. 'We'll get Virginia back, if it's the last thing we ever do . . .'

Tomorrow, thought Emmeline. I'll see him tomorrow. I must be strong. She tried to imagine what he might look like now, but all she could see was his young face, watching her, trying to catch her out.

She and Lilly used to play truant. They would run hand in hand down the Old Blackgang Road to Windy Corner to watch the peregrines. And then they'd climb down to Chale Beach and play all day, stripping off their clothes, running naked. She knew that Henry sometimes followed them, and hid in the bushes on the cliffs, watching . . . watching . . .

CHAPTER 19

Emmeline seemed nervous as I drove her to the hotel to meet Dad. She looked tiny, strapped in the front of the big car. Her shrunken body made her feet seem even bigger as they flopped around the footwell seeking for somewhere to rest. She took her glasses out of her pocket and polished them twice on the short journey. I attempted a little light-hearted chatter but she only grunted back at me. As I helped her out of the car she grasped my hand.

'Jane, I'm sorry to put you through all this,' she said.

'It's no problem, Emmeline, honestly. I'm just glad that you two are getting together.'

'I hope so, my dear, I hope so.'

She took my arm as we went in and I was aware just how frail she had become since the first day I'd met her on the beach. Although she had been thin and wizened then, she'd had an agility about her which seemed quite gone now. I took her into the sitting-room which formed part of our suite and then went to find Dad and Chas. They were outside on the terrace; Chas was scanning the morning paper, reading out things to him.

'Emmeline's here,' I said.

Dad looked up quickly, an expression of alarm spreading across his face. I smiled at him. 'It's all right, Dad. She's just as nervous as you are.'

Chas wheeled him into the sitting-room. For a moment I thought Emmeline had gone but she was standing by the window, half hidden by the long curtain. She turned slowly as if she wanted to delay setting eyes on him. They looked at each other for some time as if they were both struck dumb. Finally I offered Emmeline a chair. She sat down and I sat beside Chas on the sofa, trying to keep in the background. Dad and Emmeline were still glancing at each other warily. I noticed that they were both shaking and they both looked rather watery about the eyes. In fact they looked quite alike as if age had somehow evened them out. I remembered the photo of them when they were young – Dad with his black hair and arrogant look, Emmeline with her light brown curls and intelligent curious gaze. Now they were both wrinkled, balding, speckled, trembling, dying. Two little old Gollums.

'Why are you dressed like that?' Dad asked, abruptly.

'Like what?' she snapped back.

Here we go, I thought. Why couldn't they have started with a hello, how are you after all these years? Okay, so Emmeline had on her baggy khaki shorts and faded tee-shirt, did it really matter? I could have knocked their heads together. Why didn't they just give up and have a hug and say sorry? I started to get up.

'I'll go and arrange some tea,' I said.

'No, please stay, Jane,' Emmeline sounded panic stricken. Chas squeezed my hand and I sat down again.

'I'll go,' he said and went out. I wished I hadn't mentioned it now, I wanted Chas to stay. The silence was getting tense. I started to chatter about taking Dad to see the Botanic Gardens on the site of the old hospital.

'It's all changed so much, Dad, hasn't it?'

Dad nodded and coughed. 'Yes,' he managed.

'You never came back to the island?' Emmeline demanded.

'No,' he mumbled. 'Never.'

'Not since you ran away with Jane?'

'No.' His hands moved restlessly in his lap.

I laughed. 'Dad didn't exactly run away with me, Emmeline. He was worried about the tuber-culosis contact. That's why I was born at Wraith Cottage, wasn't it?' I looked from one to the other of them. 'I expect you saw me before Mother and Dad left?'

Emmeline shook her head.

'Really? What about Aunt Lillian?'

'She didn't see you, no. She heard you. That's all.'

'Heard me? Was she in the cottage then, when I was born?'

'Yes.' Emmeline was staring at Dad.

'Dad? Lillian was there and you didn't let her see me? That was a bit harsh, wasn't it?' There followed another long silence. There was obviously a lot more bitterness surrounding my birth than I'd realised. Had my father really not allowed his sister and sister-in-law to see me before we left? How mean was that?

Emmeline got up from her chair and stood in the middle of the room, her fists clenched. 'When are you going to tell her, Henry? If you don't, I will.'

Dad looked over at me and closed his eyes. His voice seemed to burst out of him as if he no longer had the power to stop it.

'Lillian was there. She gave birth to you. Lillian was your mother.' He started to whimper.

I looked around, dazed. I wanted Chas, where was he? I didn't understand what these two mad people were saying. I needed Chas to come and take control. I got up and opened the door. He was just coming in with the tea.

'Nice timing,' he grinned and then stopped, looking at our faces.

Chas was here. It was all right. I could speak again now. 'Dad,' I said. 'You're confused.' I looked across at Emmeline for confirmation. 'He's getting muddled up, isn't he?' I asked her. She slowly shook her head. I took hold of Chas's hand.

'They're saying that Lillian was my mother, Chas, but she never saw me.' My voice sounded strange, high-pitched as if I was a little girl. 'Is this some sort of riddle?' Dad sat with his eyes closed, Emmeline continued to shake her head. I laughed. 'Lillian was my mother and she never saw me. So someone took me away from her when I was born, is that what you're saying?' Emmeline nodded.

'You, Dad? You and my mother – Victoria – you took me from Lillian at birth?' Chas put an arm around me but I shook it off. 'Was this some sort of arrangement, Dad? Is that what Lillian wanted?' I put my hands to my head. 'For God's sake say something!'

Dad was shaking violently now. 'No, no, no. It wasn't what she wanted. I took you against Lillian's wishes.'

I walked towards him on trembling legs; I could feel Chas's hand holding onto my arm restraining me. 'Does that mean you're not my father?' My voice had sunk low now, menacing.

'No, no, Jane. I am your real father, I swear.'

'You had a relationship with Lillian – Mum's sister? I don't understand. Why did you take me from her?'

'Because I wanted you, you were my daughter. I couldn't leave you with those two unnatural women.'

Emmeline made a noise like a muffled scream. 'How dare you, Henry? After all these years. It's you that's unnatural. Tell Jane about your so-called relationship with Lillian.'

Dad put his head in his hands. 'I forced myself upon her. It was a mistake, I was drunk. I thought she wanted me to.'

'Liar,' yelled Emmeline. 'Tell her, Henry. Tell her!'

'I raped her, Jane. I'm sorry, I'm sorry.'

'No!' I said firmly as if I was refusing a drink. 'No!' I backed towards the door, opened it and fled.

I threw myself on the bed and fell immediately into a deep dark sleep. It was as if I could only absorb the truth by letting go of my conscious mind which simply wanted to close the door tight shut and pretend that none of this had happened. Down, down I went into the mysterious depths which seemed to be nurturing me and choking me simultaneously. The fluid was warm and comforting but gradually becoming blood-tinged and suffocating. But it was all I knew and I wasn't ready to let go. Slippery tentacles seemed to be coiling themselves around my throat like an octopus. I thrashed about to try and break free which only seemed to tighten their grip. Something was groping for me, breaking through the surface where the light glowed dimly. I felt pressure on my head. I didn't want to leave but I couldn't stay now. I was being pulled and strangled, I had no choice but to submit. I felt as if I was being rent in two but my need to gasp for air overcame my desire to stay. The light closed my eyes and I breathed, great gulps of grief.

★　　★　　★

When I woke it was getting dark. I must have been asleep for hours. I felt calm, as if I had come to the surface and wouldn't have to submerge myself again. I gradually became aware that Chas was sitting in the room over by the window. He got up and came and sat beside me on the bed.

'Janey?' he said. His voice sounded tender and slightly hoarse.

I reached for his hand. 'Where are they?'

'I took Emmeline home and Henry is lying down.'

'Are they all right?'

Chas smiled ruefully. 'No. But they're still alive.'

'I'm not sure whether I'm pleased about that. What happened after I left?'

'Nothing much. Emmeline sat and glared like Medusa and poor old Henry writhed around until I thought he was going to have a convulsion. In the end I wheeled him off to bed and frog-marched Emmeline to the car. When I got back Henry was asleep.'

'Thanks, Chas.'

'What for?'

'Sorting it out. Don't know how I would have coped without you.'

'Oh, I expect they would both still be sitting there tormenting each other.'

I smiled, feeling my mouth trembling. 'I think they've been a torment for each other all their lives, don't you?'

Chas nodded. 'Looks like it. But it seems that

you've been drawn into it all now, Jane. That's what worries me.'

I sighed. I could feel a big lump rising up from my chest to my throat at his concern. 'I don't know what to do with all this, Chas.' My voice came out like a strangled squeak. 'It's not every day that you get to hear that your father is a rapist and child abductor is it? And . . . and your mother was never your mother after all – just an aunt and a conspirator in a plot.'

Chas lay down on the bed beside me and gathered me up in his arms. I started to cry then and thought that I would never stop. Every time I sat up and blew my nose and took a few deep breaths I thought of my lost mother, how I had been deprived of her for all those years and now it was too late. The deception seemed to me atrocious, that she had been living so near – just a few hours away – and I had never known. And then I felt angry with Lillian. Why hadn't she come after me? Why hadn't she got me back?

Chas comforted me as I wept and ranted and threw unanswerable questions at him. He made tea and drank most of it himself. Eventually I got myself into the bathroom and stuck my head under the cold tap.

'I need to talk to him, Chas.'

'What, now?' he glanced at his watch. 'He might be still asleep and he hasn't had any dinner.'

'Chas, I don't care if I have to pull him out of bed or if he starves to death. I want him to tell me

394

the truth. I want to hear the story from him from beginning to end. I have to try and piece it together.'

Dad refused to get up and said he wasn't hungry. Chas went off to get himself some fish and chips and I walked into Dad's room, pulled up a chair and sat beside him. He stared straight ahead as if he had indeed been turned to stone by Emmeline.

'Dad, I'm not leaving here until you tell me exactly what happened. I will stay here all night if I have to. I want the truth.' I didn't care if I sounded like an inquisitor. I didn't care at that moment if I was hastening his death. He sat still for a while longer and then sighed and nodded.

'It's as I said, Jane. Lillian was your mother. But I am your father and I felt I had a right to bring you up decently.'

'Hold on, slow down. I want to go back to the beginning. Where and how did all this start – your relationship with Lillian?'

'I knew her since she was born – dear little thing – fair and sweet. Her mother died you know, in childbirth.' He fumbled for his handkerchief tucked under the pillow and blew his nose. 'Too young for me. Victoria and I – our families assumed we would marry. I always carried a torch for Lillian though. I thought she liked me too. She was always with Emmeline, playing. Emmeline was evil, like our mother – tormented me – hated boys. Her fault you know,' he turned his rheumy eyes towards me, 'all this.'

I fought hard to keep my anger back. I had to

let him get his story out. I knew if I interrupted he would clam up again. I nodded encouragingly.

'My marriage – Victoria – not happy. Not loving, no children.' He reached a trembling hand for a glass of water. I didn't help him. 'That night – New Year – Victoria went home after a party. I wanted to see Lillian. Didn't mean her any harm. But she was there – Emmeline – I shoved her and she passed out, unconscious, been drinking. I wanted Lillian – she seemed scared, but I thought she wanted me. I forced her. Shouldn't have done, realise that now.' He paused for a while and I tried to concentrate on breathing. Marguerite's calm face kept floating into my mind. I could hear Chas moving about in the sitting-room next door.

'Victoria found out Lillian was pregnant – accidentally – she went there to tell them she was going away to get over all this, and overheard something. A plan came into my head then to pretend Victoria was pregnant. I thought I could talk Lillian into giving up her child and passing it off as ours.'

'And Victoria?' I needed to ask this now, 'Victoria agreed to all this?'

He shook his head. 'She didn't know.'

'You just presented her with me and she agreed to go along with it?'

'I had a signed letter from Lillian giving up all rights to her child and saying she wanted no further contact.'

'Lillian wanted that?'

'No. I wrote the letters and made her sign them – I told her they were legal papers to do with the hotel.'

'And Lillian, she never tried to contact Victoria?'

'I told Lillian that Victoria wanted nothing more to do with her.' He blew his nose again.

I wanted to leap out of my chair and throttle him. I got up and walked to the door and asked Chas if he would come and sit in for a while. I didn't want to be alone with this man. I wished that he would come up with a further revelation and tell me that I wasn't really his daughter at all – I was Neptune's or Woody's or some unknown drunk's – but not his. Chas came in quietly, bringing me a little glass of brandy. He smelled of fish and chips. I longed to be walking carefree along a holiday beach somewhere, anywhere with him, bare feet in the fringes of the waves. Chas sat over by the window. I returned to my chair beside the bed. I sipped the brandy, feeling the fire hit my empty stomach. Dad must be feeling hungry too. Good. Why didn't I just walk out of here and lock the door and return in a few days?

'Lillian had no idea obviously, what you were plotting?'

He shook his head. 'She wanted nothing to do with me. She said Woody was going to say he was the father.'

'Woody?'

'Yes. I wanted her to register you in my name – not that queer fellow. Said you deserved that.'

'So you saw her then, when she was pregnant?'

'I tried to persuade her to see a doctor. I gave her medicine and books.'

'I can't believe she wanted you anywhere near her.'

'She didn't. I turned up – said I was trying to get through to Victoria – reconciliation – she wanted that.'

'Poor Lillian. She must have loved her sister.'

'She did. But I loved Lillian. I wanted her. I tried to persuade her to come away with me and marry me.'

'You did? You would have divorced Victoria?'

He nodded. 'But Lillian wouldn't have me.'

'So, you decided you would have her child anyway. Great.'

I got up and started pacing up and down. I was finding it difficult to keep still now. Chas watched me anxiously.

'But you can't just plan to abduct a child. How did you know when she would go into labour? How did you know she would be on her own?'

'I planned to take you after the birth. I had her signed agreement. It was just luck. I called in the day of Woody's funeral because I knew she would be on her own and I found her in labour. I helped her through it and then left with you.'

'She didn't protest?'

'I . . . gave her some chloroform.'

'And you took me to the mainland, just like that?'

'No, I had help – a junior doctor – he wanted my assistance to get him a position at the hospital. He agreed to watch Lillian in the last weeks. I gave her some medicine to hurry things along a bit – and then he was to take you for a few days until I got you established and registered.'

'You left me with a total stranger – to be fed and everything?'

'It was difficult – you cried a lot.'

'I bet I did! I should have been with my mother and those who wanted me and loved me.'

'I did want you and love you, Jane. You were my daughter too.'

'But you didn't want me, Dad, you wanted to prove something to the world. You didn't want me, neither did Mother. You sent me away to school as soon as it was possible. When I was at home you were never there – just a succession of house-keepers. You never loved me.'

'That's not true. Victoria couldn't cope. She was always on the verge of a nervous breakdown. She'd had to be a mother to Lillian and then resented having Lillian's child thrust upon her. I didn't realise.'

'You didn't realise! The offspring of her rapist husband and her own sister. What planet did you live on, Father? I wonder she didn't drown me.'

'She wanted a child.'

'Not under those circumstances – the worst sort.'

'She wanted me to take you back to Lillian.'

'Of course you should have done. Why didn't you?'

'I told Victoria I tried but Lillian wouldn't have you back. She and Emmeline wanted to live alone.'

I put my head in my hands and thought of all the times when I'd been puzzled and saddened by my parents' disinterest. I thought about the lack of warmth and cuddling. All the guilt I felt about not being a good enough daughter for them, a disappointment. I thought it had been my fault. I thought about Victoria, how I'd saved my pocket money to buy her little glass ornaments to try and get her to smile at me. I felt tears running down my face and I started to laugh.

'And I even managed to look like Victoria, didn't I? What would you have done if I'd been blonde and blue-eyed like Lillian – a constant reminder to you of your guilt? How lucky for you.'

I realised in that moment that I was shedding years of guilt of not loving my mother enough. I often thought she was more like an aunt than a mother – a rather prudish, straight-laced aunt. And it turned out that's exactly what she was – just an aunt who didn't love me. A person who had dried herself up with resentment and bitterness and crumpled away to dust like one of her desiccated leaves. Aunt Victoria. I felt Chas's arms around my shoulders easing me up out of my chair. I felt stiff and exhausted. He led me back into our bedroom, peeled off my clothes and stood me under the shower.

★　　★　　★

I lay in bed in the crook of Chas's arm, unable to sleep, mulling it all over, occasionally making Chas jerk as I roused him with another question that had just sprung into my mind. It was difficult to piece everything together.

'What part does Marguerite play in all this then?' I asked suddenly.

Chas jumped. 'Marguerite, yes. I met her briefly when I took Emmeline back.' He yawned. 'She seems nice and I liked Wraith Cottage. I didn't go in – just saw Emmeline to the gate.'

'But Emmeline told me that Marguerite was Lillian's child by a rapist. That couldn't have happened to her twice surely.'

'I wouldn't rule out any possibility with your lot.'

'Someone's still lying. Perhaps Lillian had an affair . . . perhaps she was bisexual . . . perhaps Marguerite was Woody's daughter. Oh, I don't know Chas. Perhaps they all slept together and nobody knows who belongs to whom. Perhaps I'll turn out to be an abandoned child washed up by the tide in a lobster pot.'

I drifted off to sleep knowing that I wouldn't be troubled by my drowning dreams ever again. I had seen the person who had reached in for me and wrenched my life from its source. It was my father.

But I did wake. I felt the weight of grief sitting on my chest like a fat grey gremlin and wondered if my infant self had known she had all that separation to endure. I got up and watched the runway of moonlight on the sea and Mars pulsing red in the sky. I saw my faint reflection, silvery, in the glass and for a moment I thought it was Marguerite.

Emmeline had been shocked when she saw Henry. She didn't recognise his old man's face, but his presence triggered memories in her. Memories of the quarrels that went on at mealtimes in the physician's house. Their mother would often start it off with one of her lectures on how women ran the workplace during the war. Or that Emmeline should train to be a doctor like her father and grandfather.

'I'm the one who is going to be a doctor,' Henry would shout. 'You're just a stupid girl.'

'I don't want to be a doctor,' Emmeline yelled back. 'I don't like blood and sick. I want to be a scientist. I want to travel the world.'

'Everyone knows that girls can't be scientists,' Henry scoffed.

Father would join in from behind his paper. 'I expect you'll end up getting married and having children, like most women.'

'I will not!'

'No one will marry you. You're ugly,' Henry muttered, pinching her arm.

'Henry! Don't be cruel,' said Mother. 'Emmeline can be whatever she chooses.'

Henry would glower at her, his face full of rage.

But now, he was an old man. Where had he gone

– that arrogant, black-haired boy? She felt no fear of him now. But she still felt her hate and anger rise within her. How would she ever let it go? She paced restlessly up and down the garden, feeling Neptune and Marguerite's eyes following her. She went inside, upstairs, forced herself to lie down on her bed.

'It's time to finish the story now, Lilly, before Henry gets here tomorrow. Soon it will be all over . . .'

'What if he comes back, Emm?' I realise I am getting myself into a permanent state of agitation. I can't sleep and I am feeling hot and uncomfortable. And I am worried about Marguerite. She is still sleeping all the time and won't suck. Emm has been helping me to express the colostrum from my breasts and they are beginning to feel congested as my milk starts to gather. We are drip-feeding Marguerite from a sterilised medicine dropper. But the milky substance oozes out of her mouth and I am scared she might choke.

'She must have it, Lilly,' Emm says. 'She needs it for her resistance.' I am putting the drops into Marguerite's mouth and Emm is stroking her throat, trying to get her to swallow. We are also giving her drops of boiled water. She doesn't seem interested in either. 'It's because she's a bit premature and I expect she's small because she's a twin. Virginia might have been the bigger of the two and taken more nourishment from you in the womb.'

I am only half listening. Panic is rising steadily inside me. I am feeling agonisingly sore every time I move. My breasts start to throb and I burst into tears. Emm sighs and kisses Marguerite and lays her down in her drawer. She takes me in her arms as if I was a baby too.

'Supposing he comes back, Emm,' I say again, my voice wobbling.

'He's got what he wanted, Lilly. I doubt he'll show his face again.'

'But what if he knew I was going to have twins. He might come back and try to get Marguerite.' I feel her grow still for a while, thinking.

'He couldn't have known.'

'He's a doctor, Emm. He saw how big I was getting –' I realise then what I've said. I feel Emm freeze. She holds me away from her.

'What do you mean. How could he have seen?'

I pull myself away from her and curl up on the bed crying. Emm takes me by the shoulder and turns me over roughly. 'Don't tell me he's been here before.'

I nod miserably. She stares at me open-mouthed with disbelief.

'He's been here to see you and you didn't tell me?'

I nod again. I need to tell her now. Whatever happens I want to be honest with her.

'How could you do that, Lilly? How could you be so deceitful after all we've been through?'

I break down completely then and tell her about

Henry's visits, his pretence that he was trying to reconcile Victoria and me, that he was concerned about my health. I even tell her that he'd given me money and medicine.

She jumps up, shaking. 'Medicine! My God, Lilly. You are such a fool. Where is it? Show me!'

'I didn't take anything, Emm, honestly. I threw it all away and I burnt the books and the money.' I heave myself off the bed and hobble over to the kitchen and fumble in the bucket under the sink for the empty bottles. I can hardly stand. Emm doesn't try to help me. She sits on the edge of the bed looking at me sternly. I give her the bottles and she inspects them.

'And you swear you didn't take any of this? Not even one tablet?'

I shake my head.

'Did you ever let him touch you, examine you?'

'No! I didn't let him anywhere near me. All I wanted from him was Victoria's address. I thought he would just give me that and I would never see him again. I knew Woody or Neptune would go after him if I told you. When he came back again I realised I should have told you the first time and then it all seemed too late. I'm sorry, Emm, I'm so sorry.'

'So, he was keeping an eye on you, your progress, trying to get some idea when the birth was imminent.'

'But he wasn't interested in the baby –'

'Of course he was. He pretended not to be to

fool you. That's why he tried to get round you – pretending concern and support, even love – just to get his hands on a child that he had fathered. A bit more power coming his way.'

'But why? With his own wife pregnant.'

'Maybe that wasn't enough for him. Perhaps he saw a way of getting two children of his own. Or maybe Victoria lost her baby. How would we know?'

'Victoria must have planned this with him then.'

'I wouldn't put it past her. She would think you unsuitable to be a mother. She probably thinks she's doing you a favour.'

'But how would he know that the baby was coming? How did he just manage to be here when I was in labour?'

'Maybe he sensed it was imminent and planned to watch you closely for a few days.'

'But you are usually here. How did he know?'

'I don't know. Maybe he just struck lucky. Or perhaps there was something in that medicine that induces labour within a certain number of days.'

'But I didn't take it.'

Emm throws up her hands. 'I just don't know, Lilly. I haven't got the answers to everything.' She gets up and begins pacing up and down. 'But maybe you're right. Perhaps he did suspect that you were giving birth to twins but he didn't dare hang around any longer. We need to be prepared in case he comes back.'

★   ★   ★

406

Neptune arrives during the morning. I sit dripping water into Marguerite's reluctant mouth while Emm tells him about my deception with Henry. I feel wretched and guilty. They have been so good to me and I've let them down, betrayed them.

'Right,' Neptune says. 'First of all we need to get Lillian and Marguerite upstairs into the bedroom. I'll put a bolt on the inside of the door. We must keep the front door locked and I'll put another bolt on the outhouse as well. He glances over at me. 'I'll fetch Woody's gun over later. Then if he comes I'll shoot his bloody head off before he gets anywhere near Marguerite.'

Emm gets up from the table. 'I'm going after him, Nep. I'm going to get Virginia back.'

I feel my panic rising so strongly that I think I am going to be sick. I lay Marguerite down in her bed and stagger over to the table. 'Please Emm, don't leave me,' I whimper. 'I'm scared that Marguerite will die. I need your help.'

Emm's eyes search my face as if she is trying to connect with the Lillian that she knew and loved. I sense just how deeply I have hurt her.

'Lillian's right,' Neptune says. 'You must stay with her. Marguerite needs you both at the moment. If anyone goes looking for Henry it'll be me.'

'He'll have you arrested,' Emm says.

'Not if I'm careful. Look, the hospital staff know me. I go up there at least once at week with the fish. I could ask if Doctor Rampling is in the

407

hospital or at his house. I'll say I've got an order of lobsters for him. At least we'll know whether he's still there. Then we'll decide what to do next. That way there'll be no immediate danger to any of us.'

Emm looks at me and then nods. 'You must take care, Nep. Don't lose your temper and go after him.'

'There'd be no point, would there? Much as I'd like to gun him down.' He gets up and goes to gaze at Marguerite. 'Come on, let's get this little 'un safely upstairs.'

Neptune doesn't leave us until he has barricaded our doors and then he goes off to get new bolts and Woody's gun. He leaves Booty with us even though the poor little dog whines at the door as he leaves. I feel safer upstairs in our bedroom and I put Marguerite in her new wooden cradle. I look down at her, thinking how much Woody would have loved to see her tucked up in it.

I open the window and lean on the sill, looking out at the sea. How much longer is this fear and anxiety going to last? I wonder about Virginia. I have hardly dared let myself dwell on her. Who is looking after her, holding her, feeding her? My sister? Was it possible that my own sister could plan to take my child from me?

'Virginia,' I whisper, 'you belong here. I'm so sorry I let him take you from me.' I hear Marguerite give a tiny squeak in her cradle and I feel my heavy breasts surge with milk. I have to try and feed my other daughter. She needs my sustenance. Wearily I straighten up and fetch her.

It is evening before Neptune has fixed all the bolts and fitted a wooden bar across the inside of the outhouse door, which drops into two brackets. He has shown us how to use Woody's gun which now lies on a shelf in the kitchen.

'I'm staying,' he tells us. 'I'm staying around until we know Henry's whereabouts.'

Emm makes us a fish and salad supper. We are so tired we can hardly speak. I don't feel like eating. My whole body seems to be throbbing. I can see Emm glancing at me from time to time.

'You should really be in bed, Lilly,' she says, the kindness in her voice making me want to weep again. 'It's too early for you to be walking around so much. Go upstairs and see to Marguerite and I'll bring you some tea.'

I look at them both, their concerned faces. 'I'm so sorry,' I say. 'I'm so very sorry.' I stumble away, crawling on my hands and knees up the narrow stairs to the bedroom.

Emm and I take it in turns to coax a few drops of my expressed milk into Marguerite's mouth and stroke her throat, encouraging her to swallow. We do this every half hour. But I can't even doze in between feeds. I am growing more and more anxious. In the early hours, I unwrap her and take off her nappy. It is dry. My anxiety is more than I can bear.

'Emm,' I whisper, shaking her shoulder. 'Emm.'

She opens her eyes looking dazed. She raises herself on one elbow.

'What is it?'

'It's Marguerite,' I sob. 'I think she's going to die.'

Emm shoots out of bed and looks at Marguerite lying in her cradle, unwrapped. 'For goodness sake, Lilly. She'll catch cold.'

'No, Emm. It's very warm in here. Look at her.' Her skin looks papery. Her eyes tightly closed. Her breathing barely perceptible. Emm goes over to the chest of drawers where she has laid out Marguerite's things and some of her remedies. She comes back with a bottle of oil. She rubs some on her hands and starts to massage Marguerite's tiny chest and limbs. Marguerite lies unresponsive. Emm stands back, watching her. I lift each of her little limbs in turn. They flop back onto the mattress. We have already noticed that her left arm and leg are weaker than her right but at this moment she seems floppy all over. I look at Emm, but she has turned away to consult her remedies again. I wrap Marguerite in her blanket and carry her over to the window where the moonlight shines in. I let the light play on her face, dappled by a breeze swaying the rambling roses hanging down outside.

'Marguerite,' I whisper, close to her face. 'Marguerite, we love you, stay with us.' Her eyes are moving underneath her closed lids. I stroke her eyelids gently with my finger and kiss her soft cheeks. Her eyes open then and she keeps them open and looks at me. We look into the depths of each other for a long time. And then I feel her pain. I feel her terrible loss and grief for the soul that she had been entwined with for the last few months. I see visions of them floating and tumbling together, arms and legs wrapping and unwrapping as they play and sleep. I can see that her sister is much bigger, enfolding her often. Virginia has a different kind of energy, eager to explore and experience the world. Marguerite wants to feel and observe. I feel the anguish of Virginia as she is pulled, half-strangled, from my body, not ready to be parted from her sister.

I feel myself weeping deeply as I look into Marguerite's dark depths. She is still gazing at me and then her chest heaves and she opens her mouth. She lets out a faint cry and her body gives a few convulsive sobs. I take all her clothes off and undo my nightdress and hold her naked body against my breasts. I feel as if she relaxes and tentatively I offer her my breast. She searches around for a while with her mouth and then she seems to find her way and I feel the movement of her lips and tongue as if she is trying it out. And then she grips on to me with a small trembling sucking motion and she is taking her first few gulps of milk from me, her mother. I feel a surge of joy and look up to see Emm watching me, her hand to her mouth as if she hardly dare breathe. I know then that Marguerite is safe. I feel her let go of my nipple and I look down at her. Her eyes are closed and I can see my white milk around her lips. I hold her against me and rock her for a while and then close up my nightdress with her inside, still firmly against my breasts. I get into bed with Emm's help and we all sleep for two hours until I feel Marguerite stir and start to hunt around for my breast. I let out a sob of laughter.

'Guess what, Emm? This messy little girl has done a wee inside my nightie.'

I keep Marguerite snuggled against my chest all night and all the next day. We place strips of napkin between her legs to keep us both dry. I can feel her tiny limbs scrabbling against me, just as I had felt them inside me before she was born. She is moving her head, emitting little yells when she feels hungry. I feel so much better. I love the feel of her moving against my skin; it is a constant reassurance. I keep having to bend my neck to kiss her downy head. She is feeding quite often, just a few sucks at a time as if that is all she could manage. I can see that Emm is relieved too. She keeps sighing deeply as if releasing some of her tension. Towards evening I hear her downstairs filling the tub in front of the range and having a soak. She then fills it up for me.

'The books say you can have a bath after the first few days, Lilly. It will do you both good.'

Stepping into the warm water and lowering myself down with Emm's help is both excruciating and relieving. I still have Marguerite clasped to my chest and I lie back while Emm soaps us both and rinses us off. She takes Marguerite then and pats her dry and powders the stump of her cord. She then lays her across her knees on a warm towel and massages her with aromatic oil. Marguerite's hair is clean now, free from the last traces of blood. It glows like a fine down of palest gold.

'She's got your hair, Lilly,' Emm says proudly. I think she must be feeling glad that Marguerite does seem to look like me and not Henry. 'She looks much better already,' Emm continues. 'Her skin feels more elastic. I think we should do some exercises on her left arm and leg every day so that they strengthen up.' She wraps Marguerite in a towel and puts her on the armchair while I get out of the bath and dry myself. I look at my flabby belly.

'Oh, Emm, look at this,' I say in dismay.

'Goodness me, you've grown two babies in there, what do you expect?' She stops and puts her hand to her mouth. 'Oh, Lilly. I'm so sorry. What a thoughtless thing to say.' She puts her arms around me and we hug. She kisses me gently on the mouth. 'We'll get through. We always do, don't we?'

I pick up Marguerite. I unwrap her and fasten on her tiny nappy and clasp her to my chest again. She makes small grunting sounds and nestles against me. 'I'll hold her like this until she heals,' I say.

★   ★   ★

Just as it is getting dark, we know someone is approaching. Booty suddenly gets up and goes over to the door and starts whining.

'Go upstairs and lock yourself in,' Emm says sternly and I obey meekly, my heart thumping. Marguerite stirs against my chest. It goes quiet downstairs whilst Emm silences Booty. I wonder if she has picked up the gun. Then I hear Neptune's voice calling from the garden and Booty starts yapping joyously. I let go a sigh of relief and unlock the door and go back downstairs.

Neptune kisses my cheek and the top of Marguerite's head. I love it when he comes in bringing the smell of the sea with him. I long to be outside, roaming the beach. He heaves his bag on the table and unpacks bread and cheese and milk and eggs.

'Chickens still laying?' Emm asks.

Neptune nods. 'I sold a few dozen eggs in the market today.'

Emm puts mugs of tea on the table for us. I sit down gingerly. She is cooking one of her big stews and I am feeling hungry.

'Well,' says Neptune after he's taken a few swigs. 'I'm afraid I haven't got any good news to report.' But I'd already known that. I could tell from his face as soon as he came in. Emm had too, I was sure. 'I went to the hospital to deliver the fish, like I said,' he continues. 'Afterwards, I went round to the main entrance and asked for Doctor Rampling. They looked quite surprised and said he'd left a

414

while ago to take up a new position in a big hospital in Scotland.'

'How long ago?' Emm asks.

'At least a month.'

'A month? But he was only here a few days ago,' I say.

'Well, he obviously came back to the island for something,' Neptune said.

'Or never left,' says Emm. 'Did they say which hospital?'

Neptune shakes his head. 'I even went to the physician's house in the grounds, but there was a new family in there. A woman told me Doctor and Mrs Rampling's things had all been packed into a lorry and driven away a few weeks ago.' He looks down at his red, callused hands. 'I went back to the entrance desk and asked if they knew which hospital he'd gone to in Scotland but they didn't. He holds up his hands and then lets them fall onto his knees. 'I didn't know what else to do. I've been out checking the pots, thinking about it. I could try and get a list of the hospitals in Scotland and we could phone them all up and ask if Doctor Henry Rampling works there.'

'There'll be hundreds,' Emm says, resting her chin on her hands. 'And he won't be listed in the telephone directory.'

'He might have led everyone up the garden path anyway,' says Neptune. 'If Henry let it be known he was taking up a post in Scotland, chances are that he's anywhere but Scotland.'

'You're right,' says Emm. 'He could even have gone abroad.'

'Oh, no,' I say, 'and taken Virginia with him?' My hopes are beginning to fade fast. How are we ever going to get her back? I look around at them desperately. 'But, even if we did trace him, what can we do? He's not going to admit that he stole Virginia. He's probably had her registered in his and Victoria's name, maybe with his own child. Perhaps he's claimed that Victoria had twins.' My mind was diving into all sorts of possibilities now. 'Could he do that, Emm?' She looks at me for a while, frowning.

'Lilly, I know this is difficult, but can you remember anything about those papers that he got you to sign?'

I shake my head. 'They looked like solicitor's papers, I think. Like the papers Victoria gave me before. I just thought . . . oh, I'm such a fool. Victoria told me she'd already dealt with it all. I should never have signed them. What could they have been?'

Neptune pats my hand. 'You weren't in a position to sit down and read them. Maybe he had some sort of legal document drawn up giving him custody.'

'How could he do that without my permission?'

'Henry is a powerful man, Lillian, you know that. If he can't bully people into doing what he wants there are always those willing to be paid.'

'But Victoria . . . my sister . . .' My voice trails

away miserably. It seems that whatever way I look it is hopeless. Marguerite gives a few little squeaks. I get up to go upstairs to change her nappy. Half way up I stop. I can hear Emm and Neptune talking quietly.

'What do you think, Emmeline?'

'I'll be honest with you, Nep. I think he may have killed her. It doesn't add up. Why would he want Lilly's child so badly as well as Victoria's?'

'It's what I've been worrying over too. I can only think that he wanted to put an end to it all. If he could get rid of the child then all evidence against him would be finished once and for all. If Lillian ever went to the authorities it would be easy for him to report that she was of unsound mind and probably drowned her own illegitimate child.'

'And the documents she signed?'

'Don't know. Unless they were genuinely to do with the hotel and cottage.'

'Nep, I don't want Lilly to suspect this, but will you keep an eye open – around the shoreline for a while – see what the tides wash in? I won't let Lilly go down there.'

'I've already been doing that.'

I feel a cold wave of fear wash over me and Marguerite. I stand still on the stairs, waiting for my legs to stop trembling and my heart to settle. I shift Marguerite's position so that I can see her face in the shadow of the stairwell. I look into her eyes and shake my head. It isn't true. I know that Virginia is still alive. I can feel her energy connected with ours. She is grieving intensely, but she is alive.

The following afternoon I go outside for the first time. I sit in the garden with Marguerite cuddled inside my smock and a woollen shawl wrapped round us both. I know for sure that Henry has left the island. The fear of him has gone. I am left instead with a deep, gnawing grief, that I know only Marguerite can fully share. I have seen it in her eyes, felt it soul to soul with her.

I know that our connection with Virginia will never be broken and that we will foster it day by day until these twin daughters of mine can be reunited. I know that this might only be brought about by Henry's death – or my own – but I can't think about that yet. I have to get on with raising Marguerite with the help of my beloved Emm and dear Neptune.

I look around me at beautiful Wraith Cove and know that this is the place that will nurture Marguerite and heal our souls. But I also know that the old Lillian has gone. The daughter who unwittingly killed her mother. Daddy's pet. The sister who burdened her older sister. The girl who fell in love with Emmeline and danced a Highland fling on the beach with generous hearted friends. The young woman who tasted freedom so briefly. Gone.

I sigh and kiss the top of my daughter's head. I open the notebook in front of me and start to write:

My Darling Virginia, this was the name I chose for you after a woman who sensed deeply the beauty and power of words. But I doubt that even she could truly express how I feel at this moment . . . my soul weeps and so does that of your beautiful twin sister Marguerite . . .

Emmeline felt tears squeezing out of the corners of her closed eyes. 'Thank you, my darling, thank you for being so brave,' she whispered and then slept, her arms spread out over Lilly's scattered notebooks.

CHAPTER 20

Chas told me that Emmeline had hardly spoken as he drove her home and helped her across the field to Wraith Cottage. Marguerite had been waiting at the gate. Emmeline had reassured Chas that she was all right and just needed to rest. She leant on Marguerite and he'd watched them shuffle away. Emmeline had called back over her shoulder to him.

'Bring Henry here tomorrow, Chas. We're not finished yet.'

I didn't tell my father we were going to Wraith Cottage until after breakfast. Chas had helped him to wash and shave and get dressed. I thought back to my original idea of having Dad to live with us and realised what a narrow escape I'd had. The thought of taking him home to Birdsong with us now and having to see to his personal needs had become abhorrent to me. It was difficult to say how I felt about him at this moment. All this had taken place fifty years ago for him but for me it had happened yesterday. He had a choice in this. I had no choice. I felt I'd been used like a trophy to

420

enhance someone else's ego. It hadn't worked for them and I had been left to pay the price with the best part of my life. I knew it was going to take me a long time to come to terms with it all.

I looked at my father as he pecked away at his toast, dropping crumbs on the white tablecloth. I wanted him to know what he had done. I wanted him to realise all the implications. I wanted to hurt him. But how was it possible to hurt an elderly dying man for something he'd done in his dim and distant past? That made it even more unfair – I had no recourse to retaliation. I couldn't hit him or even shout at him without seeing his frailty.

'We're going over to Wraith Cottage this morning,' I said abruptly, hoping to scare him. Maybe he would choke to death on a piece of toast. But then there was bound to be some bright spark in the hotel that could do an expert Heimlich Manoeuvre. He nodded without looking at me. I had no idea how we were going to get him across to the cottage in his wheelchair but Chas didn't seem worried so I thought I would leave that to him.

In fact it was quite easy, apart from having to heave a few protesting gates further back than they'd been for years. The wheelchair managed steps in the hotel gardens and scythed a path through the long grass. If it hadn't been for the circumstances I would have enjoyed pointing out to Chas all the things I had discovered about Wraith Cove Hotel. I wanted to ask Dad things too – about how he remembered it as a boy – but I couldn't bring myself to show that much interest in his past.

Neptune was at the cottage. I introduced him to Chas and they shook hands warmly. Neptune nodded at Dad. What a contrast between these two old men, I thought. Neptune looked weather-beaten and wiry and made Dad look even more waxy and frail. But then Dad would be at least ten years older and had been very ill. I was hoping we would be able to sit outside and have some fresh air blowing around, diffusing the tension. But it was chilly and we had to consider the health problems of the old ones.

Chas helped Dad out of his wheelchair and supported him to an armchair. Poor Chas, he seemed to be the only one who felt able to touch him. I watched my father. He held his head down, occasionally taking a quick glance around as if he couldn't resist taking in the sight of Wraith Cottage after all these years. Marguerite was making tea. She'd given me a hug when I arrived and I wondered if she knew that she and I had been promoted from cousins to half-sisters – if it was true that we shared the same mother. At least that was one good thing that had emerged from all this sordid mess. I liked the idea of having a half-sister – and one as special as Marguerite. I hoped she felt the same. I meant to try and get a few private words with Emmeline if I could, to find out about Marguerite and the male side of her parentage.

Emmeline was subdued, padding around serving tea. Chas was the only one behaving normally, chatting to Neptune about the cottage and fishing and boats. I looked at Chas, his face seemed to portray his openness and support of whatever was coming our way in this strange situation. It was just how I needed him to be. My heart lurched with love for him. When all this was over I was going to spoil him rotten!

Finally we all had mugs of tea and plates of biscuits. I was sure nobody wanted them but it seemed like a way in. Dad was in an armchair, the rest of us at the table. Neptune was the only one who couldn't seem to sit – he stood leaning against the wall, staring at Dad.

'Well?' said Emmeline. She looked from Dad to me and back again. 'I hope you've told Jane the full story.' Dad nodded. 'So, now it's my turn. I want some questions answered, Henry.' She glanced round. 'And so does Neptune.'

I wondered what part Neptune had played in all this other than being a friend and support to Lillian and Emmeline and Marguerite all these years. It seemed it wasn't the right time to ask questions. Emmeline had him to herself now. She went about it like a professional interrogator. I could see her in one of those dark CID rooms with the tape recorder on the table, the lawyer and the criminal sitting opposite her, heads wreathed in cigarette smoke.

'I want to know everything,' she said. 'There's

no use in hiding anything any more – not at this stage of our lives. We both haven't got long and I don't want to go with unanswered questions.'

Dad nodded meekly as if he'd given in. Emmeline started to ask questions then, as if her sharp mind had them lined up for years. I knew the answers to a lot of them now after my inquisition of him last night. She began with the night of Lillian's rape, asking him if he realised just how violent he had been and how much damage he had done.

'I hope you told Jane the truth. I hope you didn't tell her it was just a bit of a mistake.' She turned to me. 'Did he tell you that he knocked my teeth out and split my lip and blacked my eyes?' She pointed to the scar on her top lip. 'Did he tell you that I was left naked on the freezing floor for hours, unconscious? He could have killed us both. Did he tell you that Lillian was covered with scratches and bruises and bled for days? And he threatened us. We were left terrorised and help-less. We knew if we went to the police they would laugh at us – two silly women who'd had too much to drink. And Doctor Henry Rampling, well, as if he would lie. If he'd given them a bit of a thrashing they probably deserved it – knock some sense into them, show them what a man can do.' She sat for a while trying to control her agitation as she relived that night.

I felt the blood draining from my face with shock and horror as I listened. I think this was more devastating to me than finding out that Lillian was my mother. I was the result of all this. I was the child of not just mistaken signals about who wanted sex or not, but a premeditated, violent rape by a man who had just savagely attacked his sister. I felt sick. Marguerite was watching me, wide-eyed, she fetched me a glass of water. I think we were all shocked, even Neptune who must have known all this. Dad sat still, his head bowed.

'Did . . . did Victoria know about this?' It was Chas that spoke next. His voice sounded incredulous.

Emmeline nodded. 'I told her eventually. Someone had to knock her out of her prim little moral cocoon. She signed over the cottage and hotel and fled.' She glared at Dad again. 'So what happened to her, Henry? Did she lose her child and help you cook up the conspiracy to kidnap Lillian's?'

Dad heaved a great sigh then and held up a hand. 'Please, Emmeline. I don't want Victoria blamed.' He suddenly became quite articulate as if he really needed to absolve her. Victoria had never been pregnant, he confessed. She had gone to Scotland to escape from the situation of Lillian's pregnancy. During that time he had purchased Winter Wood in Malvern, applied to set up in general practice and generally let it be known that he would be bringing his wife and child to live there.

'Are you saying that Victoria knew nothing? You simply presented her with her sister's child?' Emmeline's voice was faint.

'She was my child too. And Victoria wanted a child. But I soon realised I had made a mistake.'

'Why didn't you bring her back? We tried to track you down, tried to find you.' She looked for Neptune. 'Didn't we?' Her eyes were brimming with tears. 'Why didn't Victoria make you bring her back?'

Dad rubbed his eyes and told her how he'd managed to convince both the sisters that neither of them wanted any further contact. He possessed signed papers from Lillian to prove it. Victoria had been resentful at first and then resigned to it.

'Those poor, poor sisters. How could you have done that to them, Henry? Lillian hoped every day that she would look up and find Victoria standing there with her daughter. She told me she gave you letters to give to her. I needn't ask what you did with them. You used her sorrow over Victoria to worm your way back here while she was pregnant so you could keep an eye on her. You even gave her medicine and money.' He nodded. 'Well, I'm happy to say that she burned your money, and she had the good sense not to take any of your poisons.'

'It wasn't poison. Vitamins, and stuff to ease the birth. I was worried, had a colleague keep an eye out for her.'

'Oh, yes. She said she thought she was being watched. Is that how you knew she was in labour?'

'That was sheer luck.' He went on to tell Emmeline how he had called in the day of Woody's funeral knowing Lillian would be alone and found her in labour.

At the mention of Woody, Neptune walked over to Dad and stood in front of him. His hands were down by his side but his fists were clenched. I wondered if he was going to hit him. I felt Chas tense by my side. Neptune's jaw shook as he spoke.

'Did you kill Woody?' he said, sounding as if he'd waited for years to ask that question. 'You might as well tell the truth now, Henry.'

Dad looked up at him. 'No,' he said.

'You had no part in his death?' Neptune spat the words at him.

'No.'

'I don't believe you.' Neptune looked around at us, scanning our faces. 'Swear it!' he demanded. 'Swear it on Jane's life.'

Ha! I thought, that won't mean much to him. Dad dropped his gaze and raised a trembling hand to his brow as if thinking.

'My colleague – the one who had kept an eye on Lillian for me – he followed Woody home that night.'

Neptune took a step nearer to Dad; his whole body seemed to be shaking now. 'I want the truth or I'll throttle it out of you.'

Dad pushed himself back in his chair. Chas had half-risen from his.

'I . . . asked him to threaten Woody – that's all. I wanted to warn him off from putting his name down as the father of Lillian's child. There was no harm intended.'

'No harm!' Neptune yelled at him. 'So what happened? I know Woody, and he wouldn't have fallen from that cliff any more than I would fall out of a boat! So tell me!'

'It was an accident. I swear. Woody was drunk, my colleague threatened him and Woody stepped back and fell. He didn't touch him.'

'You're lying, Henry. I know you are.'

'I swear. I swear on Jane's life.'

Neptune looked down on him, breathing heavily. 'I blame you. You caused his death. You might just as well have pushed him yourself.' He strode over to the kitchen. I thought he was going to go out of the door but he reached up to a shelf and picked up something heavy.

He turned back to Dad brandishing a gun. Chas was out of his seat now.

'Neptune,' he said firmly, 'put that down.'

But Neptune was waving the gun in Dad's ashen face. 'See this? This is Woody's pistol. We should have shot you the day after you raped Lillian and attacked Emmeline. But they begged us not to go after you. But that wasn't enough for you was it? You stalked Lillian, murdered Woody – who had more compassion in his little finger than you have ever had in your whole miserable life. You alienated sisters from each other. You stole Lillian's child and ran off leaving her in the middle of childbirth. You call yourself a doctor! She could have died. Do you hear me? She could easily have died.'

He pressed the pistol against Dad's forehead. Dad

428

let out a pitiful moan. Chas was inching his way slowly towards them. Neptune took the pistol away from his head and waved it in front of his face again. 'And then I had to bring this gun here. I had to help Emmeline and Lillian protect themselves. Two innocent women brutalised and terrified by you. They had to barricade themselves in because their nightmare wasn't over. They thought you were going to come back for Marguerite.'

'Marguerite?' whispered Dad. 'Who is Marguerite?'

Marguerite got up and walked over to Neptune. She put her hand over the gun and gently lowered his arm to the floor. Chas was behind him and held his arm while Marguerite prised his fingers from the gun and took it from him. Dad stared up at her with a look of amazement on his face as if he had seen her for the first time.

'Lillian?' he said, 'Lillian?' he started to cry then, strange croaking sobs as if they were ancient griefs forcing their way up from the depths of him. Marguerite handed the gun to Chas without taking her eyes from Dad's. Neptune seemed to droop and stumbled to the open doorway to gasp for air. Emmeline sat alert in her chair, watching.

'Emmeline,' I said, after what seemed like minutes of silence had passed. 'You told me that Marguerite was the child conceived when Lillian was raped.' She nodded. 'Did you lie to me?' I asked.

'I have never lied to you, Jane.'

'Was Lillian raped again?'

'No. Lillian was raped once by your father and Marguerite's father. Marguerite is your twin sister.'

I stood up slowly, my knees gave way and I sat down again. Chas was looking at me, his jaw dropping with surprise. I stood up again leaning on the table for support. I looked at my father.

'You took me and not Marguerite?' My voice sounded rasping as if it was struggling to get out. 'But why?' Dad was still staring dumbstruck at Marguerite as if he'd truly seen a ghost.

'Yes,' barked Emmeline. 'Why did you leave Lillian in that state? As Neptune said, she could easily have died.'

'I didn't know,' he whispered, dazed. 'I didn't know there were twins.'

'Hmmph,' said Emmeline, 'some doctor you were.'

'Not an obstetrician,' mumbled Dad. 'I didn't know.'

'Just as well. We didn't want you to know. We didn't want you to come back for her.'

'Did you . . . tell her?' He indicated Marguerite who had gone to stand by Neptune in the doorway.

'Marguerite's always known everything. You're fortunate, Henry. Lillian understood you and so does Marguerite. I don't and I never will. I can never forgive you for what you did to me and to the people I love most in life.'

She pointed to me. 'Jane should have been with us – with her rightful mother and her sister. Woody might still be here. You deceived Victoria and Lillian and changed their lives forever. You even ruined our business – not to mention my face.' She indicated her scarred lip. 'Have you no idea of the damage you did?'

Dad put his head in his hands.

Emmeline leaned forward. 'Why, Henry, why?'

'I wanted what everybody else had – respect, success, a family.'

'So, you stole someone else's. Did it make you happy?'

'No. I wanted Lillian. I wanted love.'

Before I could stop myself I was on my knees in front of my father, tears pouring down my face. 'Did you never love me, Dad? You or Mother?'

He looked at me through his own tears and for the first time I connected with a little beam of tenderness emanating from him. He lifted his hand as if he was going to touch me, then let it drop again. 'Jane . . . of course we did. But neither of us could look at you without feeling remorse.'

'Why didn't you bring me back?' I sobbed. 'You could have just dumped me on the doorstep.'

He nodded. 'We should have done. I see that now. It was all too late.'

I felt arms go around me and Marguerite's cool cheek pressed against mine. Emmeline was beside me too, pushing my hair back from my face, wiping my tears with her hand. 'You're here now, you're here now,' she said.

★   ★   ★

431

Emmeline watched the sisters walk out of the door, hand in hand. At last, they knew. No more lies, no more secrets. Henry had confessed and her job was almost done. She didn't yet feel the relief that she hoped would wash through her. She wondered if that was because of Henry's presence in Wraith Cottage, or the fact that Marguerite's future was still uncertain.

She glanced at Henry, resenting the fact that he was sitting in the old armchair where Lilly used to sit. The last time he'd been in this cottage was when he'd stolen Virginia – Jane, and left Lilly to her fate. Years of anger welled up in her. She knew she could pick up Woody's gun and shoot Henry without any hesitation. What a pity it wasn't loaded. What could she do to him that would make any difference at this time of their lives? How could she know that he truly felt the impact of his actions? She realised then that she would never know. Nausea surged up from the depths of her and she staggered into the bathroom and vomited.

Marguerite knew just what I needed. We clambered down the cliff path holding hands and kicked off our shoes and stood at the edge of the sea. The waves were running slow and shallow, the sea a pale turquoise in the bright September sun. Neptune's yellow boat bobbed out in the bay tethered to its mooring. A seagull perched on the bow, waiting for the fisherman. We stood still, feeling into the rhythm of the sea. My body still shook with the occasional sob. Marguerite put her arm around my waist and my arm responded as if it knew exactly where to go. We laughed and cried. I could feel our bodies touching all the way down. She was much thinner than me and a little shorter. She moved her foot in the sand so that it touched mine. We laughed again, looking down at our feet – hers long and thin, mine shorter with red nail varnish, but both brown from the long hot summer.

'These feet have been apart far too long,' I said. I turned and held her at arm's length, scrutinising her, drinking in every inch of her as if I had never looked at her properly before. Her eyes were the palest blue and so wide. She didn't blink often, even in this bright sunlight.

'When I was little,' I said, 'I had a doll called Daisy. She had blue eyes and blonde hair. I used to wrap her in my baby shawl and cuddle her every night. I couldn't go to sleep without her. Did you know that a Marguerite is a daisy?'

Marguerite bit her lip, her eyes shining with tears. She took hold of my hand and led me to the cave in the cliff. She drew back the screen and pulled out a soft bundle and passed it to me. I held it up and shook it out. Pink rose petals showered around us, blowing on the breeze. It was a shawl, yellowed and worn but identical to my own. I looked at Marguerite in astonishment.

'Did Lillian – our mother – did she knit these for us?' She nodded. I held the shawl to my face, invoking the comfort mine had provided for me

433

as a small lonely girl. 'I must have been wrapped in mine when my – our – father took me away.'

I wondered again why Victoria had kept mine wrapped in tissue in the bottom drawer of her dressing table. Was it her connection with her sister? Did she feel Lillian's presence woven into it? Perhaps she grieved for her lost sister too.

We wandered back down to the sea, each holding a corner of the shawl. We put our arms around each other again and stood in the surf swaying. Pink petals swirled around our feet. I could feel our connection so deeply. No wonder I hadn't wanted to be pulled from our mother's womb. And Dad said that I'd cried a lot. I wished I'd screamed the place down – perhaps he would have dumped me and fled.

I stroked Marguerite's long silver hair. 'We're sisters,' I whispered, 'twin sisters.' She nodded. 'I suppose you've always known that too.' She nodded again, smiling shyly. 'Well, my sister. We will have to make sure that we stick together from now on, won't we?'

She took my hands and held them to her heart. 'I suppose we'd better go back and make sure Neptune or Aunt Emmeline haven't hung our father from the beams.'

We needn't have worried. Dad was sleeping, exhausted, in the armchair. Emmeline was sitting outside dozing, wrapped in a blanket. Chas and Neptune were wandering around the garden deep in conversation. They looked up as we came in through the gate. I could see Chas's anxious eyes scrutinising my face, relaxing when he realised I looked all right. Neptune was doing the same with Marguerite.

'I'll make some more tea,' Neptune said. He came over to me. 'I wouldn't have shot him, Jane. The gun wasn't loaded. I just needed him to feel a little of the terror that he made others feel.'

'Neptune,' I said. 'I wouldn't have blamed you if you'd blown his head off.'

He looked relieved. 'What frustrates me most is knowing that there was someone – his accomplice – living nearby, who knew exactly what happened. He could have been working at the hospital for years, Jane, and we never knew. How could a doctor – two doctors – plan such cruelty?'

Chas clamped his large hand on Neptune's shoulder. 'If there's one thing I've learned about human nature, Neptune, it's that people will sell their souls for power or wealth.'

We went inside and stood looking at Henry sleeping in the armchair.

'Do you think we ought to wake him up and get going before blood and guts are shed?' Chas asked.

'Let him sleep while we have some tea, Chas. I want to have a word with Emmeline.' I went outside and sat down beside her. I put my hand on her arm and she opened her eyes. 'Why didn't you tell me that Marguerite was my twin sister?'

'Because I wanted to find out what Henry knew

and I wanted him to be the one to tell you the truth. It was his task. And also, it seemed important that you got to know Marguerite first – before you found out the truth – so that you could see her in an unbiased way. Without any strings attached.'

'Well, I can see that makes sense.' I sighed. 'I haven't fully taken all this in yet, Emmeline. It will take me a long time – all the implications. But I do know that I felt an affinity with Marguerite as soon as I set eyes on her. It was as if – I don't know – as if she's connected to me in a very physical but invisible way.'

'You are the other side of each other.'

'Do you mean we have shared souls or something?'

'No, no. Nobody shares a soul. But because you were so close you express different aspects of each other. If you had been allowed to grow up together you would have learned from each other. Marguerite needs you to learn how to express her outer self and you can learn about your inner self from her.'

'Like I'm the extrovert and she's the introvert, is that what you mean?'

'In a simplistic sort of way, yes. But it's deeper than that, dear; I'm not just talking about your personalities. You've learned defences, how to make up a world to suit you. Marguerite has no defences, no shell, no outer coverings. She didn't need them. She is as natural as all this.' She gestured to the sea and sand and cliffs, the great expanse of blue sky. 'She is a gift, entrusted to you. You mustn't violate that gift. You mustn't try to change her or educate her to your ways. But she needs to feel your strength and know that she has that too. In return she can help you find that place in you which yearns for fulfilment. That place you told me about that you have touched from time to time.'

'Where did all this come from, Emmeline? Was it from my mother? Was Lillian a deeply spiritual person?'

'Indeed she was. But not religious or learned from a book. It was as natural with her as it is with Marguerite. Your mother never prayed, she communed. She wouldn't be able to tell you what with. She simply did what she did without question.'

Her eyes filled with tears. 'Your mother was born with an extraordinary capacity to see beyond the obvious. She always went straight for the big picture, as if she could see the whole jigsaw while I fiddled around with different pieces.' She sighed. 'The trouble is, Jane, these truly spiritual people are vulnerable. Lilly would have found it very difficult to live in a world away from here. That's why I worry so much about Marguerite.' She let out a small sob. 'How will she live away from here without losing her purity and innocence?' She grabbed my hands. 'You must teach her, Jane. You are her protection. I've seen her strengthen up when you are here.'

437

'Oh, Emmeline. That sounds such a huge responsibility.' But I thought then of when I had lost Marguerite in Ventnor and found her in the foetal position at the bottom of the bandstand. As soon as I'd put my arms around her she had recovered and dealt with all kinds of new experiences, including chips and skate-boarders.

'You are the only one that can do it, Jane. Don't you see? Because you are the perfect balance for each other.'

'Emmeline, why have I never felt all these things before? Why has all this happened since Lillian – my mother – died?'

'Lilly protected you. She couldn't find you, but she felt your grief as an infant just as she felt Marguerite's. She spent time every day weaving lights around you – that's how she expressed it. So that you wouldn't feel the pain and could get on with your life.' She looked down at her hands.

'I have to confess to you that I always doubted that you had survived. You see, I thought Henry had stolen you in order to get rid of you. But Lilly never doubted you were alive. She said she could feel your energy, and she knew that Victoria always wrapped you in the shawl that she'd knitted with such love for you – that helped to strengthen the connection.

'And then as Marguerite grew she started drawing pictures of you – she'll show you when she's ready. Even then I wondered if Marguerite wasn't just picking up her mother's need to believe

438

you were still alive. It wasn't until your books started to appear that I was fully able to accept your existence.'

She smiled. 'We were so proud of you as a writer. Lilly said that Virginia was the right name for you. That's what we always called you.'

'So are you saying that when Lillian died, I no longer had her protection and that's when I began to feel the pain and it all started to come to the surface?'

'Yes, the web of connection was tugged rather hard I think.' She smiled. 'Don't dismiss any of this as hocus pocus, Jane. Not until you've had time to experience how it all works. Believe me, I was the world's greatest sceptic. I haven't got an ounce of intuition or sensitivity in me. I just look up everything in books.'

She laughed. 'But living with Lilly and then Marguerite changed my world view. And science has a little to do with it as well.' She patted my hand. 'Your mother knew you would be a great writer.'

I laughed. 'She got that wrong then.'

Emmeline smiled. 'You haven't started yet,' she said.

Neptune called out that tea was ready and I helped Emmeline out of her chair. She leaned on me heavily as we went in and I realised she was growing weaker by the day. She didn't appear to be in too much pain. I suspected that was to do with

Marguerite's healing hands. We sat at the table. Neptune and Chas and Marguerite had made sandwiches. Dad stirred and Chas asked if he wanted some food. He didn't want to eat and just had tea. He stayed where he was to drink it.

We sat at the table making small talk. It seemed strange now that all the revelations were over. I felt I was putting everything on hold until I had time to start digesting it all. Neptune told us that the coastal management team had said that Wraith Cottage and also Puck's Cottage would probably hang on for another few years providing there were no more drastic weather conditions before the coastal defences were in place. They said the risk in living here was up to the owners. Chas asked questions about the hotel and what it was like in its hey-day.

Dad rattled his cup as he put it down on the little table beside him and started to get to his feet. Chas got up to help him but he waved him away.

'Thank you, Charles. I can manage,' he said, showing a vestige of his old pride. I wondered what he was going to do, whether he needed the toilet, Chas hovered. Dad shuffled unsteadily over to the table. We all sat looking at him in anticipation. He cleared his throat and leaned on the back of a chair, his knobbly knuckles showing white.

'I'm going now,' he said, 'but I want to say something first.' He searched our faces, stopping with

Emmeline. 'I know that it doesn't count for much, Emmeline, but I want to say that I'm sorry and hope you will forgive me for the past. Can't undo it now.' He started to move away as if that was that, as if he wasn't going to wait for a reply.

'Wait!' Emmeline commanded, stopping him in his tracks. 'I can't forgive you, Henry. There's just too much to forgive. I'm not like Lilly. The most I can do is try to understand. Lilly said she could see the pain in you that you suffered as a boy. I know you felt our parents were neglectful of you and maybe our mother drew me into her games. But I don't remember that. If I hurt you, then I'm sorry for that. But, I didn't deserve this, Henry.'

'It was Lillian I wronged, not you.' His voice sounded harsh, the old animosity still there.

'How dare you say that! You attacked me brutally. You affected my entire life. Lilly was never the same again. You stole her lightness and altered our relationship. You deprived us of Virginia – Jane – and took our dear Woody from us. If you want to make amends, start by thinking of what you can do for your two beautiful daughters. Get them to forgive you.' Her eyes blazed now, his animosity had reignited hers.

Dad looked at Neptune.

'Sorry, Henry. I'm with Emmeline all the way. I've lived here for fifty years. You turned your back. If you could have seen the suffering you inflicted on all of us you would never ask for forgiveness.' He turned and went outside.

My father looked at me then. 'Jane?' he croaked.

I started to cry again as I looked at him. 'You deprived me of my mother, Dad, I never even knew of her existence. You didn't give me a chance to even find her.' My eyes searched for Marguerite's. 'I have my sister now but I could have had her for almost fifty years.'

'I didn't know about your sister.'

'Would it have made a difference?'

He hung his head. 'I tried to give you everything. I –'

'No, Dad. You didn't give me love. You deprived me of love. I got love from others – never from you and Mother. I survived because of who I am and whom I've always been connected to. And because of Chas.' I blew my nose noisily. 'It's too early to talk about forgiveness. I need time to get used to all this.'

Dad glanced at Marguerite then. I wondered how much he'd taken on board that she was my twin, his second daughter. Did he realise that she didn't speak? Her eyes held his with her innocent gaze, it seemed to me full of compassion. Tears started to trickle down his cheeks and his eyes flickered and moved away from hers. His knees buckled and Chas caught him under his arms.

'I think we'd better get Henry back to the hotel, Janey. I'm sure Emmeline needs to rest too.' He glanced around. 'You all look pretty shattered actually.' He grinned his good-natured slow smile. 'I know I am.' He helped Dad outside and settled

442

him into his wheelchair where he sat crumpled and dejected. I hugged my sister and my aunt and my good friend Neptune and followed.

Chas dealt once again with Dad's needs and then we both had hot scented baths and went to bed early, trying to relax and empty our heads.

Chas yawned one of his huge noisy yawns which sometimes irritated me but tonight I found normal and comforting.

'It really is a lot to take on board isn't it?' he mused. 'Hard to believe.'

'Uh, uh. My father a rapist, a brute, a child abductor. And such deception, Chas. How could he play with other people's lives like that? All that awful manipulation of Lillian and Victoria. And it does look suspicious about Woody's death doesn't it?'

'Afraid it does.'

'But at least I know now. And there are some good things.' I turned towards him and put my arm across his paunch. 'If Dad hadn't stolen me I might never have met you.'

'Then I would have travelled to the Isle of Wight to steal you myself.'

I squeezed him. 'And then there's Aunt Emmeline – for a little while longer at least. I've learnt a lot from her and her crazy wisdom. And Neptune – what a loyal soul he's been. But most of all there's Marguerite – my very own twin sister. She's quite something, isn't she?'

'She is indeed. Quite extraordinary.'

'I don't know how all this is going to work out, Chas. I can't just walk away now, can I?'

'No,' he said carefully. 'I can see that.'

'I want to care for Marguerite.'

'I can see that too.'

'But how? That's the question.'

'We'll work it out somehow, Janey. We always do.' He yawned. 'Anyway, Henry can put his hand in his pocket for once. Emmeline was right. He ought to start thinking about what he might do for his daughters. He owes you that at least.'

I started to feel drowsy. Chas turned out the light. Mr Micawber, I thought, smiling to myself in the dark. Perhaps Chas would discover one day that his real father was Wilkins Micawber.

CHAPTER 21

Emmeline leant on her bedroom window sill, looking out over the sea. 'Did you see them, Lilly? Did you see your two daughters, walking hand in hand, knowing the truth?'

'I did, Emm. You know I did. And I am so happy.'

Emmeline reached outside and picked a rose. She twirled it in her fingers, absorbing its fragrance.

'And you, Emm, are you happy now?'

Emmeline sat on her bed, staring into the rose. Was she happy? Had she achieved retribution? She knew in her heart she couldn't forgive Henry, she couldn't lie about that. But she felt a certain peace growing within her. It was as if she'd cleared something out of the way and now she could look back on her life with Lilly. They had lived a quiet happiness. Maybe not the life they had expected. But they had known love – each other's and Marguerite's. And of course, Woody's and Neptune's.

'I have done all I can,' she said. 'Yes, Lilly. I am happy now.'

I slept well, untroubled by dreams of any kind. But I woke with a feeling of unease. I lay listening to Chas's throaty breathing, watching the little flashes of sunlight sneaking in as the curtains moved in the breeze. I could just hear the soft sigh of the sea. A feeling of apprehension crawled around my stomach. Not surprising, I thought, taking some deep breaths. I suspected part of me was deeply shocked by all that had happened and the aftermath was going to take days and weeks, months even, to come to the surface. I'd probably wake up one morning to find I had a crop of boils to rival the bubonic plague.

I got up, switched on the kettle and poked around in the selection of Isle of Wight souvenir pots for coffee bags. I wondered if I should make one for Dad and take it in to him but I didn't feel ready to face him on my own. I could just about tolerate him with Chas beside me diluting the atmosphere.

I decided not to wake Chas just yet, he looked so peaceful lying there with his mouth ajar. I drew the curtains back and opened the window wider and sat sipping coffee, watching the sea. I wondered how Emmeline and Neptune were feeling this morning now that they had confronted their devil. I hoped they were experiencing some relief, some sense of resolution, otherwise would it all have been worth it? Supposing it had just stirred their anguish up again and they still felt that Henry had got away with everything? No, surely not. They must have seen what a miserable life he had led as the result of his actions. And they had experienced happiness in spite of everything. I thought of Emmeline,

Lillian, Marguerite and Neptune living all those years together, grieving for Woody and for me. But they had love and the joy of each other too. All in all they had lived a better life than my father and poor Victoria.

I got up to make more coffee and my head started to spin. For a few moments I had no idea whether I was standing or falling. I grabbed for a chair and my coffee cup crashed to the floor. Everything seemed to go black for a while and then I realised I was on the floor and Chas was kneeling beside me.

'Jane, what on earth is the matter?'

He helped me up and I lay on the bed while he cleared up the debris. I got up carefully. 'Perhaps it's just a bit of delayed reaction after all the turmoil.' I went into the bathroom and sluiced myself with cold water and got dressed.

'We didn't have much to eat at all yesterday, you know,' Chas said. 'Maybe we just need a nice big breakfast.' He looked at his profile in the mirror. 'I must have lost a few pounds. Look at that,' he said, patting his paunch. He pulled on his shirt. 'I suppose I'd better go and see if the old chap needs some help with his ablutions and then we'll go and eat.' He came over to me and studied my face. 'Are you sure you're all right now?'

I tidied the room a bit in case the chambermaid thought I was a slut. Chas came back into our room looking anxious.

'Jane, Henry's gone out.'

I laughed. 'What do you mean, gone out?'

'The receptionist said he rang very early and asked if someone could help him into his wheelchair and take him outside, said he wanted some fresh air.'

'Good heavens. Do I detect a spark of independence creeping back in? Was he dressed and everything?'

'I suppose so. He can manage up to a point. I daresay he had his buttons undone.'

'Well, as long as he hasn't been arrested. I suppose we'd better go and fetch him in for breakfast.'

We went outside. There was a definite nip in the air as if the weather had finally remembered it was September. We walked around the gardens, there was dew on the grass and spiders' webs hung off every projection.

'Where's he got to?' said Chas. 'I'm surprised he managed to wheel himself very far. He finds it awfully difficult.' We walked round to the front of the hotel and there was his empty wheelchair outside the main entrance.

'He must have got someone to help him back in again. Stay here, I'll have a look in the dining-room. He's probably tucking into a round of toast.'

Chas reappeared a few minutes later. 'He's not in the dining-room or his bedroom. Nobody's seen him.'

I started to feel my stomach churning again. 'Well, he can't be far away. He can't go any distance without his wheelchair. He must be sitting on a bench somewhere. Look, I'll go one way; you go the other and I'll see you back here.'

I walked round the grounds, peering in the shrubbery, opening the summerhouse, spying out all the seats and benches. I met up with Chas again feeling sure he would have tracked him down. Chas shrugged.

'No sign. He must have gone back in and got lost inside.' We enlisted one of the staff to search the place with us, but there was no sign of him. Nobody had seen him apart from one of the cleaners who said he was sitting out on the lawn watching the sea and he'd ask her to push him back onto the drive as his wheels were getting stuck. 'Perhaps he's been kidnapped,' Chas joked, but he wasn't smiling.

'Hopefully!' I added, but I was feeling concerned now. 'If he's not in the hotel or the gardens, he must have gone out of the front gates. There's no other way out. There's a wall right round the perimeter. God, Chas, suppose he's stumbled out onto the road. He'll get run over.'

'We'd have heard,' said Chas. 'Let's go.'

We hurried down to the hotel gates. There was a few yards of narrow pavement leading to the entrance to the Botanic Gardens. 'Perhaps he's gone there,' I said. 'I'm sure he wouldn't have ventured in the other direction, to Ventnor. I suppose he thought he could manage.' I was suddenly aware of a lump in my throat and realised

I could still feel involuntary sympathy for him. I thought of him hobbling painfully on his old stick along this road, being scared by the cars. What had come over him? Perhaps he was feeling confused as to his whereabouts or perhaps he simply wanted to get away from us and what he might feel was persecution. 'Hurry, Chas,' I said, almost running now.

We were faced with the same dilemma in the Botanic Gardens – which way to go. There were a few acres of ground to cover.

'He can't have gone far,' I panted. 'He wouldn't have enough strength. He would have stayed on the flat too.'

Chas popped into the visitors' centre but it was too early and it wasn't open yet. There was nobody about. I heard a few sounds from the plant sales area at the end of the car park and we headed for that. I knew then we were going in the right direction. This was the place that held his roots. The pull of it had given him enough energy to manage this journey. He was born here, grew up here and worked here. He had lived here with my mother – well, Victoria – until he had left the island for good. But he had come home now. This is where he'd be, shuffling around, intuitively feeling for some connection.

There was a young woman in the potting sheds. She said she'd seen an elderly gentleman earlier, sitting on a bench near the temperate house. He'd smiled at her and said good morning. She told us it wasn't unusual. It was difficult to tell whether they were real people or ghosts, there had been thousands of deaths here.

'The fitter patients used to work in the gardens, you see,' she said, matter-of-factly. She pointed out the bench, empty now. 'See what I mean?'

Chas looked bemused but refrained from telling her she should seek help. I think he was beginning to accept that there was an aspect to life that didn't quite add up.

'I think he might have gone to the site of his old home,' I said.

'I'd be surprised, Janey. I'm sure he couldn't walk this far.'

'You know Dad, when he sets his stubborn old mind on something.' We walked past the children's playground and over to the grassy area where Dad had pointed out the site of the old physician's house. The sun was getting hot now, the sky an unbroken blue, the air clear and fresh. A perfect day.

I walked slowly to the edge of the grass. And then I felt my skin begin to creep and my hair prickled as I came out in goose bumps. I didn't want to think any more. I didn't want to let it in. I held my breath until my head started to spin and I had the sensation of falling again. I reached out a hand to steady myself but there was nothing to hold on to. It seemed ages that I poised on the brink; a cold blank void seemed to fill my head and chest. And then I felt myself being grabbed from behind and yanked backwards.

'Jane!' Chas held me tight. I could feel his heart pounding. 'Oh, God. I thought you were going to fall!'

His grip forced the breath out of my lungs and I knew I had to carry on dealing with my life.

'Oh, Chas,' my voice came out like a sorry little wail. He stared at me, his eyes wide. 'I know where he is.'

'Where, Jane, where?'

I pointed down. Chas held onto me as we peered over the edge. The cliff was steep here. It took me a while to spot him. The land had tumbled, littering the rocky shoreline with boulders. Dad was wearing grey trousers and jacket but the coat was open, revealing his striped pyjama top beneath. I could see it shining in the sun. It shone on his bald head too which gleamed like a little round rock amongst a million others. I was reminded of Emmeline scrambling over the stones in Wraith Cove. I gulped down a noise which was a mixture of a sob and a chuckle. Chas couldn't spot him for ages. I think he thought I was imagining things. But then he saw him.

'I'll go back and get help,' he shouted, already running.

I stood watching, knowing that my father was dead. I knew it was pointless calling all the emergency services. One helicopter or one rescue party would be enough.

They hauled him up the cliff face in a cradle, the team avoiding my eyes. Chas stood with his arm around my shoulders. Onlookers were held back. Somebody handed me Dad's stick. I felt it growing warm in the palm of my hand. I could almost feel his energy seeped into the wood which he had held onto for so many years. My father's hands – they had done so much damage and yet they had probably comforted people too, healed them, soothed them. I saw his wizened hands lying on his notes on his desk at Winter Wood. He hadn't died there after all – he had come home.

Emmeline thought that for once in his life Henry had done the right thing. In a way I agreed with her, I think we all did. It would have been very difficult for him to go on living, dependent on us for his welfare, now that the truth was out. He wouldn't have been able endure that. But I felt guilt too, that my actions had brought him to this. I could have let him be, not persisted in what seemed to me now like relentless grilling. But most of all, I was sad that he'd died alone. I could hardly bear to let myself imagine how he must have been feeling that morning when he hobbled across the site of his home and poised trembling on the edge of the cliff. What was it like for him, that moment between life and death? Did he see ghosts? Was there anybody there who comforted him on his journey? Did a repentant mother hover over him, an understanding father? Would Lillian have spread forgiving wings to cushion his fall?

Dad's death was deemed accidental, there were

no suspicious circumstances, no injuries discovered at the post-mortem not consistent with his fall. We were questioned briefly by the police and we decided to spare him the stigma of suicide by simply saying that he had wandered off early, unnoticed. Chas wondered if he had indeed fallen accidentally, perhaps he'd been trying to walk to Wraith Cottage to talk to Emmeline again. I wondered if it was the same spot where Woody had fallen from, or been pushed – a sort of penance on Dad's behalf. But just like with Woody's death, we would never know for sure.

We had his body cremated. There was only Chas, Marguerite and me to attend his ceremony. I wondered what Marguerite would make of it, but sandwiched between Chas and me she seemed to cope. We talked about the best place to scatter his ashes. The choice seemed to be between Victoria's grave in Malvern or his parents' graves in Ventnor. Marguerite shook her head at both of these and indicated the cliff where he died. Of course, I thought. That's where he chose himself. He must have had some happy times there when he was little. I imagined him playing in a garden with that glorious view, romping with his little sister, perhaps a dog, before the rot set in. I sighed, I knew I was just trying to make things better for myself.

But we had a small ritual. The three of us went out there on a fine evening and watched the sunset. We lit candles and placed them where he fell and each of us threw a flower over the edge. Then

Marguerite and I lifted the urn together and emptied our father's ashes over the cliff. There didn't seem very much left of the strapping man my father had been in his younger days and I wondered where all his substance had gone. Marguerite and I looked at each other and smiled and I realised that some of it was in us and maybe we could redeem it in our own way. We stayed until the sky blazed with stars and our candles had burned down. And still we sat, listening to the crickets singing, which was better than any hymn I'd ever heard.

So, that is the ending, Emmeline thought. She felt no joy in Henry's death but no grief either. Maybe it was the only way it could have ended truthfully.

She was waiting for Jane to speak. She had watched her and Marguerite together and knew they were going to be all right. She felt a soothing calmness growing inside her. She had no burden to carry with her into her next phase of existence, no overlap of lies and loose ends. Others had to live with it now and make of it what they could.

She felt Lilly's quiet presence, waiting for the time when they could be together again. She was content to lie in her chair outside, enjoying the September smells of Wraith Cottage garden and the rhythms of the sea.

CHAPTER 22

C has went back to bridsong for a few days to attend the final meetings to wind up the firm. He didn't seem to have any regrets. Once he'd made the decision to go it alone he seemed like his old self – still totting up life in neat columns but without the anxiety that had plagued him for the last two years. There also seemed to be a new depth to him as if he'd been deeply touched by all that had happened since January, starting with the seemingly innocuous letter informing me that an Aunt Lillian had bequeathed me Wraith Cottage on the Isle of Wight. We joked with each other that the envelope should have had a health warning stamped on it.

While he was gone I moved into Wraith Cottage to help Marguerite and Neptune look after Emmeline. The September weather was kindly and we sat outside a great deal with Emmeline, alternately reminiscing and resting. I dozed and daydreamed a lot myself, as if my psyche needed some respite, after its stormy ride. Each day we'd spot Neptune sailing out to check his pots and he'd sail round from Puck's Bay to spend time with us and potter about the cottage and garden with Loot at his heels.

One day he took me sailing with him and we stopped at a deserted bay and walked up the beach to a tiny cemetery where he showed me Woody's grave and nearby was Lillian's – my mother's. I fell on my knees beside it to read the inscription on the simple headstone. Lillian Walding 1933–2003 Beloved by us all.

'I wish I'd brought some flowers, Neptune,' I whispered. He placed a hand on my shoulder.

'We'll be back here soon with Emmeline,' he said gruffly. 'You can bring some then.' He walked away, sensing that I needed to be alone. I sat on the grass beside her grave thinking about her, picturing her, like the photograph of pregnant Beatrice who must have died in 1933 giving birth to her. The image became confused then with that of Marguerite and all three of them became entangled in my mind, fragile and fair. I shared that lineage and yet my genes had shot off in the other direction and I'd ended up in the Victoria mould – presumably taking after Grandfather Walding – Old Father William the hotelier. I remembered Emmeline's descriptions of him and hoped I wouldn't end up with a purple bulbous nose and a beer belly. At least he seemed a jovial sort.

I sighed and started to thread a daisy-chain to hang on my mother's gravestone. Why hadn't she tried harder to find me? She and Emmeline. There were ways of tracking people. But I wasn't being fair. They were a different generation of women, for all Emmeline's sharp intelligence. They wouldn't know the ways of the world, how things worked. And they had Marguerite to protect. They must have been terrified of the authorities getting involved and possibly having Marguerite taken from them. I imagined that if Henry had died first then Lillian would have tried to contact me. But would it have worked if they had found me earlier? Would I have been receptive to all this? Maybe I would have resented the intrusion into my life. Perhaps things had worked out as they should in the end.

I hung my daisy-chain on Lillian's grave. But it would have been nice to have known you, I thought. I would have liked to hear your voice, feel your arms around me, know your thoughts. Neptune was standing looking down at me.

'Ready to go?' he asked.

That evening Emmeline's glasses broke yet again and I plonked myself on the sofa to rewind the wire which held them together. There was an almighty crack and the base of the sofa split in two. Surfer shot across the room as if a thunder-bolt had struck. I was so surprised, I just sat there gaping while the others laughed at me.

'That's it,' gasped Emmeline, holding her middle. 'It will have to go now, Nep.'

Marguerite helped me up and I sat gingerly in one of the armchairs. 'I didn't think I was that heavy,' I said, apologetically.

'We were talking about it the other day,' said Emmeline. 'If that settee could speak we would have to gag it.' We all sat looking at the sofa as if we expected it to start dishing up the gossip. I realised then what she meant. I suspected that this was the place where she and my mother had sometimes loved each other, where Lillian had been raped maybe, perhaps where my sister and I had been born and then Lillian may have died here too. I didn't want to ask questions. The possibilities were enough.

'Maybe we should burn it,' I said.

Marguerite jumped up and began gesticulating wildly at Emmeline who understood her immediately.

'A bonfire on the beach? Good idea. Let's do that. We could drag it to the edge and let it tumble down.'

Marguerite unpinned the calendar from the wall and came over to me. She pointed at the date.

'Good heavens. It's my fiftieth birthday in three days' time.' I had completely forgotten about it in the middle of all this drama. And then I realised; I looked at Marguerite's excited face. 'It's *our* fiftieth birthday!' I said. 'We could have a party down on the beach.'

'Lobsters!' said Neptune.

The next day Neptune, Marguerite and I shoved and heaved the old sofa-bed over the cliff and I stayed with Emmeline while the others went down on the beach to collect driftwood for the bonfire.

'I'm glad we're on our own for a little while, Jane,' Emmeline said. 'I want to talk to you.' I nodded; I'd been expecting this. 'I won't be here for many more days –'

'Please don't, Emmeline. Not yet –'

'Jane. I can't hold on much longer.' She took hold of my hands.

'I can't bear to lose you as well,' I started to cry. I cried so easily these days.

'Ssh,' she said gently. 'Look, Jane. I want to go. I need to be with my Lilly – to make sure she's all right. I'm not scared, and you mustn't be either. There's really no such thing as death, just a change of focus, that's all.'

'That's all very well in theory. But it won't change how much I'll miss you,' I sobbed. I cried then for all my losses in one big messy puddle. Emmeline didn't try to stop me, just waited patiently for me to calm down and blow my nose. 'I'm sorry,' I sniffed.

'Nothing to be sorry for my dear,' she said kindly. 'Jane, I need to know, before I go, if you have been able to make any decisions about your sister.'

I nodded. 'Chas and I were going to talk to you together –'

'If you'd rather wait for him to come back, I understand.'

'No, Emmeline, he won't mind. You need to know now, just in case. The most important thing is that we both want to look after Marguerite.' I heard her let out a great sigh. 'I love her and I need her too. It isn't a one-way thing, you know.'

460

'I do know,' she said.

'But, this is the difficult bit. We don't want to live here all the time because we love our home – Birdsong. It's quiet there, set in beautiful countryside. No sea, but a winding river down in the valley. Marguerite would like it there. She can have a room of her own. She could paint it herself in her own colours. And Chas needs to set up his business from there.'

Emmeline didn't say anything, but I noticed she was listening intently. 'But we do love it here too. We want to keep both places going. It isn't that far after all. We'll spend time in each and Marguerite will come back and forth with us. It will help her to get used to the bigger world.' I held up my hands clasped together like a prayer.

'I promise you, Emmeline, we won't try to change her. We'll learn her language, and hopefully her wisdom, whilst helping to strengthen her with gradual exposure to new experiences which she might enjoy. It's something we can all work at together, just like you said. I've spoken to her about all this. It's difficult to get it all across but we're learning that too. I think when we actually start it will be easier than trying to explain.'

Emmeline put her hands over mine. I could see the relief and gratitude in her eyes. 'We have quite a lot of money put by for her,' she said. 'Lilly wanted you to have the cottage and land and we've always lived frugally. But we put our capital in trust for Marguerite in case it didn't work out and she had to go into care. We wanted to be able to afford the best possible place for her.'

'Oh, Emmeline, that must have been so awful for you having to contemplate that. I can see now why you and Lillian wanted me to come back here.'

'But it was for you too,' she said. 'How could we not have given you the chance to be with her?'

'I realise that now. I can't bear to think that I might have lived the rest of my life without knowing her. And there's something else I need to tell you. I know Lillian burnt Henry's money, but he left a trust fund for her that will come to me, and when I sell his house there will be even more. I want to spend money on Marguerite's welfare and I think it will be a way to heal Henry's soul too. Chas and I have talked about rebuilding the hotel and gardens. It could be beautiful. He's got loads of nephews and nieces who would love to come here to help out – maybe working holidays while they're at university, to earn money. I'm sure Marguerite would enjoy it. It would be something she can be involved in. And there's Neptune. We won't desert him. I can't imagine him ever wanting to move away from here or hang up his fishing net. But he can come and stay at Birdsong, if he wants to.'

'You won't get him away from here. He'll have the animals for company when you're away. Nep always says he wants to die in Puck's Bay and he will.' She smiled sadly. 'He'll outlive me that's for sure – the old bugger!'

★   ★   ★

Chas returned the day before our birthday looking very relaxed and casual in jeans and a polo shirt. He was going to book us back in the hotel but Emmeline was so weak I didn't want to leave her. Neptune unearthed a camp bed and we squeezed it in beside my little bed on the landing. The cottage seemed very full with Chas in it but strangely empty without the old sofa.

'So you've been smashing up the place while I've been away,' he said.

We stayed up later than Marguerite and Emmeline so that we could talk downstairs without disturbing them.

'It's done,' Chas said, making washing movements with his hands. 'The firm is no longer.'

'No regrets?'

'None. Just relief.' We held hands while he went through the details and I told him that Emmeline and Marguerite seemed happy with the tentative plans we had made for the future. 'Seems to be gradually falling into place doesn't it?'

I nodded. 'And everything seemed impossible a few weeks ago. I suppose it helps that Dad is no longer around and I don't feel pulled in two.'

'At least he did something right, poor old Henry.'

'What, dying?' I laughed. 'Yes, he did do that rather spectacularly.'

Chas kissed me and I felt my old passion for him stirring. He held me at arm's length, inspecting my face.

'You are looking better, Janey, quite beautiful in fact. Did you decide on the HRT after all?'

'No, Chas. I discovered something far more effective.'

'Did that Emmeline concoct something for you?'

I giggled. 'You could say that.'

The weather held for our birthday and Chas and I took Marguerite into Newport for the first time. I could really see now how composed she was when she was near enough to be able to touch me and how her agitation increased with every step I took away from her. I knew that we could work with that in time. We chose dresses for our party. Blue for her and red for me. I understood now why Emmeline had made her dresses that simply slipped over her head. She was unable to cope with small fastenings, her left hand fingers having that slight curl and she couldn't bend her arm up backwards easily either. We bought glittery sandals – silver for her and gold for me. It seemed we liked the same styles but different colours.

I had no wish to influence her choice or deck her up like a Christmas tree. It was tempting to go overboard and try to lavish all sorts of goodies on her as if she had been deprived. But I knew that was the last thing she had been. I asked her if she would like to buy something for Emmeline and Neptune and she chose a soft rainbow striped scarf and hat for Emmeline and for Neptune a box of liquorice allsorts.

'Does he like those, Marguerite?' Chas asked. She nodded and rubbed her stomach. 'Well, he's a man after my own heart,' he said, sticking another box in the trolley. We brought some champagne and fancy ice cream for the party, and smoked salmon and salads to go with the lobster.

'Is Emmeline all right?' I kept asking Marguerite and she would go still, her eyes unfocused and then she would nod. It was great having her around. She was like a walking mobile phone.

In the late afternoon, Chas went down to the shore with Neptune to start the fire while Marguerite and I prepared the food. Later, the men carried Emmeline down to the beach, where she sat, like an elf, cushioned on Lillian's flat stone wearing her new rainbow hat and scarf. We took the food and drink down in baskets and sat sipping champagne, watching Neptune crack open the lobsters. We passed the food around. Marguerite tasted everything with interest, Emmeline ate hardly anything. Neptune had even lugged down the old wind-up gramophone and played a few Scottish reels. I think we were all feeling a mixture of joy and sorrow, watching Emmeline fading, memories hovering before our eyes like the wraiths that Marguerite drew and that danced over the sea at night. The old sofa-bed groaned and sank down into the fire, taking its pains and pleasures with it.

Neptune sat on a rock playing quietly on his concertina, tears glinting in his eyes. It was full

465

moon and the night was mystical. The beam of silver across the sea looked like a magic carpet that Emmeline might at any moment walk across. Mars still gleamed low in the sky. Lights twinkled above us and out to sea. We all seemed mesmerised, entranced. Even Loot ceased scuffling around for food and dropped to the sand. Neptune's music grew quieter and quieter as if we all needed peace.

Eventually, Chas poured out the last of the champagne and toasted Marguerite and me on our fiftieth birthday. Emmeline's head was drooping. We needed to get her into her bed. Chas picked her up and carried her slowly up the cliff path with Neptune close behind for support. She didn't want to be taken upstairs so we lit the fire and brought down the camp bed and made her comfortable. Surfer purred at her feet as we sat around her.

Chas gave Marguerite and me a little velvet box each. Inside were identical gold lockets with our initials entwined and our birth date engraved on the back. We put them on. Emmeline was smiling. She signalled to Marguerite, who took me by the hand and led me to the wooden chest under the window. She gestured for me to open it. It was full of exercise books, the sort children used at school. They were tied in bundles. I picked one up; they had dates written on the front in a neat childish hand. Marguerite took out one of the bundles and pointed to the date – 15th September 1953 – five days after our birth.

'Are these for me?' I asked. Marguerite nodded. I looked at Emmeline.

'Your mother wrote them for you,' she whispered. 'And Marguerite kept a record of her feelings about you.'

I flicked through one – they were densely written. In between the pages Marguerite's drawings were placed. I turned some over, the events and dates were written on the back by my mother – my first day at school, my teeth falling out, my fall from a horse. My hands were shaking. This was the record of my life that my sister had drawn for me and of my mother's life, from when I was born, that she had written for me. I felt I was going to know her at last. I opened the first page of the first book.

My Darling Virginia, this was the name I chose for you after a woman who sensed deeply the beauty and power of words. But I doubt that even she could truly express how I feel at this moment . . . my soul weeps and so does that of your beautiful twin sister Marguerite . . .

I closed the book and held it tightly to my chest. 'What an amazing gift,' I whispered. I kissed Marguerite and bent to kiss Emmeline. She sighed and closed her eyes.

We buried Emmeline beside Lillian and Woody in the little graveyard where the sea sang and the wind bent the thorn trees towards the east. We scattered the graves with roses and camomile, lavender and herbs. I crept away from the others and stood looking out to sea and found myself shedding tears for them all.

I thought of poor Victoria, my reluctant surrogate mother, and wished she were buried here too. I would take flowers to her grave in Malvern when I returned to Birdsong – violets, she loved violets. And I would bring some of her wild pictures to Wraith Cottage and hang them on the walls. I thought of my father's small transmission of tenderness when he had tried to convince me that he loved me and my heart made a little lurch in response.

I straightened up and took a deep breath. It was over now. I looked back at my loved ones standing talking by the graves; Marguerite stooped to arrange the flowers, Chas placed a hand on Neptune's shoulder. We were left to heal each other and all that had happened. It was up to us. We carried it now in our souls.

I suddenly realised my fingers were tingling. I remembered that feeling. I needed to write. Energy flooded through me. I had my mother's story to read. I could write about her and her sister and their deprivation. I could write about my father and his sister and their rejection, and I could write about myself and my sister – our separation and the joy of our reunion.

Such sisters, such sorrow, such joy.